1-2798

Eve'

Eve's Mountain

Marian Coe

Manufactured in the United States of America
Library of Congress Catalog Card Number: 97-68272
ISBN: 0-9633341-5-8
Cover by Cimarron Design
Interior design and typography by Publishing Professionals

SL
SouthLore Press

For Carol and David

With special thanks to those who believed in this story during its progress, including leading Appalachian writers at Hindman (KY), also at Wildacres (NC) workshops. In Florida: friends at the Florida Suncoast Conferences, and the Pinowor Writers of Pinellas County. Personal appreciation goes to my daughter, Carol Coe, Ph.D. of Cambridge, England, and son David Coe, a southwest writer; and Paul Zipperlin, my supportive artist husband. Appreciation also goes to my editor, Sylvia Hemmerly of Publishing Professionals; the North Carolina Tourism Dept. for film of their mountain views; my advisor re stroke victim care, Joan N. Cronin, R.N.; and for his insight and information as a North Carolinian and environmental writer, Jim Ryan; also, advice from a revered spokesman for the southern Appalachians, the late Jim Wayne Miller, who gave me permission to use lines from his voice of the Briar, *The Mountains Have Come Closer.*

"From Virginia's Shenandoah. . . down into the Great Smoky Mountains in North Carolina and Tennessee, the Blue Ridge Parkway curves and crests 469 miles along the high spine of the ancient Appalachians. Come share this once-remote sanctuary of high places. . ."

FROM A NATIONAL PARKS FOLDER

"This is no ordinary place . . .
    Come fall in love, here closer to heaven,
    The perfect escape
    for a week, a month, or a lifetime. . ."

AD MARKETING THE BLUE RIDGE MOUNTAINS

"The appeal is ancient, but clothed in language for our time. . . . Serenity, luxury, exclusivity and fun—life as it should be lived. . . . Remoteness is no longer a disadvantage, it is an asset. . . The word 'escape' is key. . . ."

FROM THE APPALACHIAN JOURNAL
SPRING, '86

Mountain High
Magazine

May 1986

Off The Beaten Track column

Here's one for stressed-out souls wanting to step out of the twentieth century for a breath of serenity: a true hideaway hamlet — if a resident ghost hovering around doesn't spook you. (Her name is Eve.)

We found High Haven in the Blue Ridge Mountains of North Carolina, a curious old summer colony perched on its own secluded ridge, an hour's drive north of Asheville, adding 45 minutes of switch-back drive up to Crest Road.

Before highways brought change into the Appalachians, hamlets like this, with its summer hotel, were a presence in these southern highlands. No more. For curious reasons (some say the ghost), High Haven remains a place-out-of-time, an Appalachian Brigadoon. No marquees and motels on this ridge.

The venerable Ridgeway Inn sits against slopes (yes, called Eve's Mountain) like a proud old lady ignoring the outside world. "Amenities" here are the antique beds upstairs, rocking chairs on the verandah, and a music box chiming you in to dinner. From a rocker you get an open view of rolling, smoky blue ranges stretching to infinity, the air bracing as a breeze off a mountain stream even on an August evening.

There is a catch.

Most of the rooms stay filled by innkeeper Edmund P. Dilworth II's season regulars. Still game for the getaway? You'll find cabins for rent, hidden around on these wooded slopes.

Along Crest Road you'll also find: A "Country Sundries" with a marble soda fountain, hot soup served. "Previously Read" where a dedicated book browser could stay happily lost within narrow aisles of loaded shelves. Next door, crammed with an amazing collection, true to its name, is "Maggie Hardy's Old Timey Things."

Mornings, the small U. S. Post Office (hung with stuffed bears) draws summer people from around. They pick up the mail and their *Wall Street Journals,* swap news of the heat in Florida, and congratulate one another for being "up here, not down there."

Shop owner Maggie Hardy may invite you in, put on the tea kettle, get down some of her china cups and point you to a high-backed rocker. But don't ask about the reported ghost. Curiously enough, we found the Eve mystery a touchy subject among Havenites when we checked out the hamlet this past summer. However, the story gets retold at mountain folk fairs. Story tellers of old mountain lore add the Eve mystery to prove "strange things can still happen in these ancient southern highlands"— once you get away from the highways and fairways and reconstituted Main Streets.

Okay, the story goes like this:

On an August night, some forty years ago, before good roads cut into the Blue Ridge, Eve Kingston—a city girl who loved the mountains—

put her infant son to bed upstairs at the inn, walked out into the night (tearful, old reports say) and disappeared. No trace, no clues ever found. The following year, the successful young husband returned, bought up most of the ridge, promising disgruntled mountain natives he would not develop, nor strip the old growth timber, but would keep the mountain in its natural state, "in loving memory of his lost Eve."

The romantic version about this Appalachian Brigadoon goes like this: Eve's ghost is protecting the place from change. The other version calls it an unsolved murder and asks if ghost sightings on the back side of Eve's Mountain mean she's hovering around, (time being no object?), "waiting to do vengeance on whoever did her in."

Maggie Hardy shakes her head and tells you firmly, "High Haven is the last unspoiled place in these mountains because everybody *wants* it to stay that way." Everybody means year-rounders like herself, summer regulars, and mountain families in the hollow below Eve's Mountain.

What about the major landowner? Alexander Kingston, husband of the lost Eve, a wealthy fellow who cleared off the top of the mountain for his big summer place, Capstone, with helicopter landing strip.

"We don't mind. Mister Kingston has kept his promise not to sell off any of this ridge. That means no bulldozers and billboards can come in here to ruin the peace and beauty."

So, is High Haven closed to all but its season regulars?

"Lordy, no. We get curious tourists rolling through here, spring through fall. Some who rent a cabin are lover-couples, you can tell. Then there's always a few new faces who show up alone, trouble behind their eyes. I figure they need to be here. Hideaways, I call them. We just have to hope they don't spoil what they come for, you know, and that's a kind of sanctuary."

Your Off the Beaten Tracker

April, 1986

At **Perloin Productions**' Atlanta bureau

From his cold spring week on the Appalachian Trail, Russ Bern showed up for the Monday morning news desk meeting, still on an adrenaline high. *Perloin's* new tabloid show needed mysteries to uncover and murders to expose. Russ walked in pitching a story he had found and checked out.

To six assembled crew members, glum-faced over their coffee mugs, Russ promised, "Here's one the coast will okay. It's got everything—great visuals in a mountain hideaway you wouldn't believe, where a so-called romantic ghost tale has been serving as cover-up for the major landholder who murdered his wife."

Yes, a hot name was involved—Alexander Zackary Kingston Sr., CEO of Kingston Industries. "We can blow him out of the water with no libel problems if we go in this summer, shoot their ghost reports—which shoots down the legend. We leave the guy to his fate. A cliff-hanger show. . ."

Part One

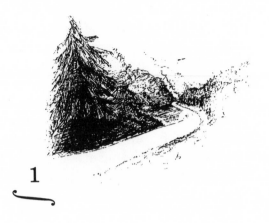

January 1, 1986

Minutes before midnight, the party clamor built toward its expected crescendo. Waiters moved through the penthouse with trays of goblets. Champagne corks began to pop. In the hum and clatter of voices, more than one arrival asked, "The silver hair and tan over there, don't tell me we have Sean Connery?" And the hostess replied, "Don't we wish, darling. You mean old handsome exuding charm and testosterone? That's Alexander. You know: Alexander Zackary Kingston. Carpets, textiles? You should see Kingston, Junior, but Zack doesn't party with big daddy."

The noise level rose, greeting the new year, 1986. Moments after, sleek women moved from the embrace of partners to saunter through the seething party toward Kingston, their flushed, up-turned faces inviting a bear hug from the most charismatic man in the room.

Alexander Kingston stroked the closest ivory cheek and bestowed smiles, aware of a mounting distraction. On impulse, he put down the champagne goblet and turned away from the party din. An unaccountable need to be alone drew him out to the cold terrace, where he stood looking into the night, puzzled at this sudden mood. For some inexplicable reason, he found himself thinking of Eve, even imagining her voice calling out to him. The black sky crackled, then exploded with arcs of spinning silver and crimson. With no warning, a thought burst into his senses, consuming as the momentary fireworks. *His life was about to change.*

He stayed rooted in the dark, his broad back turned to the party inside. For focused moments he reasoned away the enigmatic thought, until it faded like the fireworks' trail of smoke in the dark sky. At some other mental level he refused to acknowledge, the waiting began, like a subtle ticking in his pulse.

Three months later, on a March morning in Mexico, Alexander Kingston played two fast sets of tennis in a hot Acapulco sun with his Mexican host. Hours later, he turned off the furious shower, rubbed down his vibrating body and listened with impatience to the beginning beat of a Mariachi band on the patio below. He had accepted this weekend invitation as an escape from the new restlessness that plagued him. His EKG had checked out okay, but his pulse continued too fast with a nameless sense of warning, subtle as a doctor's forefinger thumping on a desk.

He decided, with grim amusement, the whole problem was this damn birthday coming up. Sixty-eight. Heading for seventy. That and the fact he was actually selling Kingston Industries. Wanted to, didn't he? It was his own decision to unload the firm and continue with his imports, a reason to travel. First, he'd drive up to Capstone to calm down. Nothing could be done about a birthday except ignore it. For one more weekend.

Kingston tossed aside the towel and faced the angled wardrobe mirror, assessing. Good shoulder muscles still. Flat belly. Could pass for a well-conditioned fifty, right? All the equipment. A thick thatch of hair. Women didn't mind the silver. They ran fingers through it. No one had to know about the restlessness ticking behind the suntanned face and confident grin. He peered in close to examine the smile. Good cap job. He'd never let down, nor slowed up, never. From the patio below, the Mariachi band sent up its feverish beat. Dressing now, he felt better. So, what the hell, enjoy the weekend. The birthday would come, regardless. Why not celebrate tonight?

Kingston went downstairs into the colorful, noisy crowd, exuding the bravado that was expected from the big, silver-haired American in the white suit, the man known as the "southern carpet king." He downed successive glasses of salty-sweet Marguerites, opened his mouth for the dripping bits of lobster pushed toward him by the host's jet-eyed sister-in-law—and enjoyed both. Spanish voices and strident music took over his senses, stirring the food in his gut. Once, he closed his eyes against the beat of it and checked. Was it gone? No, it was still there, ticking away. He reached for a drink from a passing tray.

Hours later, Kingston nodded apologies to his host and headed toward his room. He wanted only a bottle of seltzer and oblivion, not the sister-in-law's arm around his waist, chattering, leading him there. He stumbled toward the bed, knowing he looked like any drunken fool. At the edge he slipped and kept falling, falling, a descent into a dark hell.

It was dawn when he awoke, stretched on the bed, in his shorts. Across the room, rocking in a chair, a petite dark-haired girl in white. *"Eve?"* The sound came from his own dry throat, from the unconscious level where that name lived. The girl stood and walked to the bed. The white dress was a uniform. She was a household maid, ordered to watch him. In awkward English she explained that the doctor had been there during the night, had checked him, had given him a shot, and said, yes, he could fly home today if he wished. But once home, he should call on his own doctor. Kingston managed to say, "Thanks, honey, going to do just that. Tell the folks downstairs to call me a cab." He watched her walk out. *Had he actually called her Eve?*

He dressed and packed, stopping only to drink quantities of seltzer water. He was going home to have a sober birthday. A rapid heartbeat was to be expected, stepping down from a company and the image he had created. Thirty-five hard driving years of it. Zack should stay with the firm. Had to, didn't he, to support that bimbo wife? Zack had to be there—part of the deal once he sat

3

down to sign the final papers with the solemn-eyed contingency of Japanese who were buying the firm. He would leave Zack to close up the offices with the help of good old Harpy. The woman could have been a CEO herself, not an office manager, if she'd been a man. But Harpy probably knew that. He wouldn't stay around to see the dismantling of Kingston Industries. He would drive up to the mountain for a rest, to clear his head of this thing bugging him, this notion of a threat hanging over his head.

In the Charlotte, North Carolina, headquarters of Kingston Industries, Zack Kingston, Jr. cussed under his breath as he continued to clear the big oak desk of six years of his life. Under the clutter of papers and journals, the phone buzzed again. Zack ignored it. He knew it would be Tom Hill, intent on dragging him to the closing today. Good old Tommy, persistent as his lawyer and frustrated as a good friend, doing duty on both counts, trying to get him over there to the table where his father was now, sitting with the Japanese, expecting him to show up and convince the buyers they should keep a Kingston in the firm.

"I want out," he'd already told them. He wanted only to fly up to Capstone and chill out. Climb. Be alone. Get his head straight.

Damn phone. Close up an office and all hell breaks loose. He dumped more papers into the bin by his desk. Harpy could handle the calls. This morning a TV reporter had called wanting to shoot some footage up at Capstone, to do a story on A. Z. The fellow had mentioned Eve's Mountain, so he must have heard those damn ghost stories; probably the old gossip, too. Sounded like that kind of a reporter. Zack had brushed him off and hung up to dump more industry journals he'd never read. More tenderly, he pulled from the drawer Sierra Club and flight magazines he had read. At the bottom was an old '76 *Playboy*, the one with Lisa as the centerfold. He dropped the lot into the trash.

The phone again. Groaning, Zack picked it up. "Harpy, if that TV fellow calls again remind him we aren't in show business. If it's real business, tell them to wait until the Japanese land here and I'm hang-gliding off Grandfather Mountain. If it's Tom Hill tell him *no*."

He hung up quickly and leaned back in the swivel chair, polished loafers anchored on the desk, the top littered now with stray cards. Handsome, engraved cards that claimed *A. Zackary Kingston, Jr.* was a vice president around here. Bending one into a fine little arrow, Zack sent it spinning across the space of mauve Kingston carpet. Target: the large photo of father and son, the two of them in their Armani suits, posed against a paneled background rich and dark as an old master painting.

The original photo had run ten years ago for a *Forbes* story profiling his father as "both charismatic and forceful." Enlarged in the burnished gold frame, Alexander Zackary Kingston, Sr. could have been a virile and handsome actor, suited up for a role as a CEO character. The dark mane of hair was already beginning to turn silver. The heavy, darker brows marked a hearty, open face that hid more shrewd confidence than people realized at first encounter. They soon found out A. Z. was a formidable player.

The look meant something else to women. The old satyr could charm a woman into his bed. Some female had once chided, "Zack, why do you disapprove of your father? You're like him you know." Shrugging, he had replied that his father's board of directors didn't see the similarity. He had evaded the implication he was a womanizer, same as his old man. As for the other issues between himself and his father—he had to keep those questions pushed down out of his own sight. He didn't want to remember the old talk heard as a child, spending his summers up there in the mountains: *That rich city fellow did away with that girl, then came back and bought up the mountain to cover up his sins.*

Again, the phone. *Forget it, Tommy.* Zack sailed another card toward the image of himself. In that photo he looked like a Goddamned yuppie playing the role with grit and determination and no joy. True. So now was the time to get out. Helen Harper walked in, looking patiently weary and not her usual unflappable self. She picked up the phone from the still-littered desk, looking at Zack.

"Yes, he's here, A. Z. Calm down. We'll push him. They can be over there in minutes." She hung up as Tom Hill huffed in, his round sincere face flushed, muttering they were late and must get going. "Try to shake some sense into his head," Harpy said. "I have work to do out there." She shook a fist at Zack and walked out.

Zack sank back into the swivel chair. "Good old Harpy. She saved my young ass when I came into the firm. She should know I want to get the hell out now."

"And I'm trying to save your financial ass." Tom Hill shook his balding head. "Not taking my advice during the divorce settlement is one thing. But this is crucial, man. You need to get yourself over to that closing and stake your claim. A. Z. is over there now, blowing up as we speak. He's holding up the meeting until you get there. You need to, Zack."

"On the level, Tom, I've already told my father I would *not* be there. I want out, period. Out of Charlotte. As soon as these offices are kaput, I intend to get up to Capstone. Climb mountains. Be alone with the flora and fauna."

"The big escape, huh? That's a dream. You can't afford to retire, remember? Not after Lisa." As usual, Tom's attorney-at-law tones were heated with the chagrin of a friend. "Must I remind you, she got the house and the beach place plus that settlement. You still don't realize you've been too damn generous. Any other client but you, I would have dumped. You're left with practically a flat folio, one Range Rover and one helicopter, at the ripe age of thirty-eight."

"I know, old pal. But I'm bailing out. I need some time alone up there before A. Z. goes up and starts playing host. You know how it is when he's at Capstone. A drove of friends and sweet things show up."

The phone buzzed again.

"The place is crazy today," Zack mused as Tom paced. "Some television guy wants to shoot a story about Eve's Mountain. Ever hear of a Perloin Productions? I'd like to know what they're up to."

Helen Harper stood in the doorway looking stricken.

"He's collapsed . . ."

They both stared at Harpy. She repeated with dismay, "A. Z. just collapsed . . . at the meeting. They're rushing him to the hospital now."

Two days later, Alexander Kingston surfaced from the weird dreams that had held him. He became aware, slowly, of lying supine, trapped in a leaden body, on a hard bed not his own. Where and why? He remembered vaguely, shouting at an impatient lawyer, the fury becoming pain, then disorientation, then blackout. How long ago? He closed his eyes, sinking back into a dark floating place where scenes flashed from his own life.

So this is the way it happens? No bright lights, no ethereal welcomes . . . instead, this, the mind projected into a different orbit, watching yourself die? This was the past he was seeing, waiting out there, waiting all this time, existing in the dark space of memory . . . flashing now on the screen of his mind in blips and scenes like a film out of sequence.

Scenes and faces appeared and faded like meteors in a dark night. He recognized moments from bedrooms and boardrooms and places long forgotten. *A girl's dark eyes meeting his across the aisle in a train compartment, an amber Spanish landscape rumbling by . . . the bleak look on a man's face before the man's bald head thuds against the polished conference table . . . a crash of porcelain thrown by a woman, against a tapestry wall, as London street sounds hum below.*

Out of the dark void now, another moment, another time emerged. Even as it began, he knew it was the old Ridgeway Inn, that summer. *The smell of leather and an empty bourbon bottle against his face . . . waking to the feel of dawn, waking to panic . . . crawling out of the car to look for Eve . . . hearing the name echo in stillness. . . .* The image faded as he sank back in the blackness of heavy sedation.

Again, Kingston surfaced back to consciousness, enough to be aware of the tube in his arm, and the burn of a catheter. He tried to focus on the strange room. Hospital? No, he recognized the suite in the Convalescent Center, the one endowed ten years ago by Kingston Industries. He'd never pictured himself ever using the place. Hadn't planned to be ill. Or die. *What fools we mortals be*, he thought, aware he was alive enough to be capable of irony.

A tall woman, her expensive suit ill-fitting on her angular body, came in with an arrangement of flowers which she sat on the Broyhill chest. The sight of Helen Harper's back, bent to the flowers, cheered him with a surprising surge of emotion. He wasn't dead or out of his mind. There was good old Harpy. He still couldn't move, but his eyes were wet. *Did a stroke turn you into a weepy old man?* He quenched the thought, and found his voice. "You didn't look to see if I'm alive." It came out a halting whisper.

She finished adjusting the flower arrangement and pulled a chair closer to his bed. Her sturdy face studied him with unreadable scrutiny. "I've talked with your doctors, and head nurses, A. Z. You're sleeping this off under sedation until your blood pressure comes down. You could have a real stroke next time, not a serious warning."

Harpy's no-nonsense voice went on, reminding him he never wavered or looked back on a contract or decision. Kingston Industries was sold, only a few papers yet to be signed because he had collapsed before that last meeting was consummated. Two days ago. He remembered that now, with a strange lack of interest. Harpy continued in her matter-of-fact tones, assuring him that, after some necessary physical therapy, he could return to Capstone to regain his strength. Hadn't he been promising himself to take it easier? She stopped there, clicking blunt nails on the chair arms and looking around. "They've made this room more pleasant than a hospital." He knew she was letting him ask the questions that needed to be asked.

"What about Zack?" Again his words came out too slowly. He felt panic, but let it go. He was going to be all right. Harpy said so. "Is Zack . . . staying?"

"Is that what gave you the stroke, A. Z? What he does has to be his decision, you know that." Her face always softened when

8

she spoke of Zack. "You're not going to threaten him by standing at the edge of your grave, are you?" Harpy settled back and waited. In her office-manager voice, she said, "Get well first. That's all you have to do."

"Zack—a damn fool not to stay. Tell him that. He'll like the job better . . . when I'm out." He closed his eyes, listening to the pulse beat in his ears to see if anger and frustration made it irregular. "The divorce . . . I'm not against that decision."

"It's done."

The vision of the luscious Lisa floated behind his eyes a moment as Harpy talked. That blonde Barbie Doll had come on to him once at the beach house. Zack was a fool when it came to picking out women. "Harpy, I'm glad. . . ." His voice sounded as leaden as he felt. "I'm not accustomed to . . . feeling so stupid . . . helpless." Highlight of the day here would be broiled chicken and a male physical therapist. "It's hell to get old."

"A bummer, yes," Harpy said calmly. She stood up. "I'm going to beat it by taking my new RV—thanks again, A. Z.—on the open road. Maybe highways all look alike now, but the advice is a change of pace. I've stayed put too long. Too many years in your front office. While you, 'southern king of the carpet world'—don't growl, it's given you good press—you A. Z, have never slowed down. After therapy, you can go back to your mountain like a bear to his cave."

"Crawling back, wounded." Yet it was what he wanted. In that solitude, yes, he would get well, with no one else in the house but two old mountain women cooking food and looking after him like doting old hens. Cheered at the thought, he forced out the slow words, asking Harpy to crank him up. "I'm lying here . . . like a dead slab of meat. I want . . . to get up to Capstone." He sank back, trying not to hear what Harpy was telling him now.

"No, listen to me, A. Z. I had to call Victoria when this happened. Don't frown like that, anger is not good for you. Victoria is your daughter and one does let children know when the old man has a stroke. All right, a slight stroke. I also left word at Loren's school. Loren called back. He cares about you no matter how

9

private the boy is with his thoughts. Your whole brood might show up at the mountain this summer. Zack too. Definitely Zack. So expect it."

Kingston groaned. "No. I want to be alone up there." At Capstone, he would get well and these crazy images in his head would go away.

Before going into the Convalescent Center, Zack stopped Helen Harper as she came out. They stood in the May sunlight by her car, exchanging reports on the patient inside. "How is he today? Warn me before I go in."

"His speech is still slowed. Embarrassing for him. Be patient. Don't argue about anything. They're trying to get his blood pressure down."

"Don't worry, Harpy. I've promised to hang around here a few weeks to sign those papers. I'm looking for a nurse to go up with him as soon as the doctor lets him out. He needs an ex-lady-sergeant type to keep him in line. I'll fly up in the Bird and bring down one of the Gurney boys to drive him to High Haven."

"Before you go, Zack—Tom Hill has been trying to reach you."

Good old persistent Tommy. "I'm not changing my mind."

"It's about the TV company. You asked him to check. He left the message."

"Oh, that." Tom's firm had a former partner, now in LA, doing media things. Tom offered to check on this Russ Bern who had called from Perloin Productions. "So what's the message? You're still looking serious."

"It's a fairly new production company doing this new tabloid format. Tom says the Eve story has come across the desk and they are definitely interested."

"We don't want their interest, Harpy."

"I know."

They were both quiet a moment. "Tom Hill asked if A. Z. has any enemies in the TV business."

Zack frowned. "Who knows how many old lovers or enemies the man has garnered." Zack looked at this woman who had worked with his father for thirty years. Loyal Harpy. She knew the old gossip about the death of his mother. They'd never talked about it. But they stood in the parking lot glare now, troubled that anyone would dig into the old story. Finally Zack said, "Let's forget it. Let them forget it."

Harpy nodded. "Also, you had a call from Washington."

"The FBI or IRS, I hope. Don't tell me it was Tory."

Harpy nodded. "Your sister Victoria, yes."

"Half sister," Zack said automatically.

"I let her know about the stroke last week when it happened. I assured her he was doing well. Today she was on the phone again, insisting on knowing more. Anyway, be warned. Your sister is leaving Washington. She's going to Capstone to look after A. Z."

"Tory?" Zack winced. Last summer Tory had stormed out of Capstone vowing never to set foot in the house again. His own relationship with A. Z. was peaceful compared to "Little Brat" as he used to call her. "Did you tell her we're taking care of every-thing? Sending him up with a nurse?"

"I did. But she intends to go. Apparently as soon as he gets up there. She hung up before I could tell her you're not staying in Charlotte and you're going up, too."

"Too bad. Might have kept her from coming. Harpy, you know the Kingston brood. What's the matter with us? Why don't we get along? Come up to the old summer kingdom and keep us in line. Don't abandon ship."

"No thanks. Retirements should be peaceful." She gave him a rueful smile. "Loren called from school. He'll be up later, too. With the three of you in that big house, you'll have to learn to live together or kill each other. What will it be?"

"I don't know, Harpy, I have my own reasons for heading for the mountains. A. Z has his. I can't imagine what Tory wants."

On a morning in mid May, Alexander Kingston, dressed and unsteady on his feet but as happy as a man being let out of jail, consented to ride the wheel chair out the door, four nurses and Zack following along like a parade to the car waiting at the

11

entrance. Young Jeb Gurney sat behind the wheel, grinning as if he owned the gleaming black Lincoln. "Yes sir, " Jeb promised Zack as Kingston settled heavily into the back seat, "your daddy's going to get a real easy ride. Aunt Sudie and Mama are waiting. They've been cleaning and cooking up there more'n a week."

Five driving hours later, Kingston roused from restless sleep as Jeb headed the big car up the steep road to High Haven. "Trees budding out real fast since last week," Jeb sang out to his passenger. "Had snow one morning just a couple weeks ago. You aw'right back there Mister Kingston?"

"Good, Jeb. Glad to get back up here." Along Crest Road, the cluster of little shops made him smile. "Country Sundries," and "Previously Read Books" and "Maggie Hardy's Old Timey Things" plus old Caleb Potts' real estate cubby hole. Those people made him feel like King of the Mountain and he knew why. He was their non-interfering landlord. Coming out of her shop now to wave was Maggie, a sturdy little woman stuffed into jeans and big sweater, her gray hair pulled back tight in a pony tail.

Standing in Maggie's doorway as they passed was an interesting looking young woman Kingston had never seen. "Who's the lady?" he asked Jeb.

"She showed up at the Inn a couple of weeks ago," Jeb answered as they climbed the curving drive that led on up toward Capstone. "She walked up to your place one day and Mama came out and talked to her. Mama says she acts kind of quiet and spooky. Her name is Selena something and she was about the first one to show up at the Inn. Well, here we are, Mister Kingston. I gotcha home aw'right, didn't I?"

As Jeb turned in through the column of tall firs that made an entrance to Capstone grounds, Kingston sighed.

"You've already got a nurse moved in," Jeb said as the car purred toward the big stone house. "She's a bossy, red-faced woman. And I meant to tell you about that old oak over by the headstone. It got struck by lightning back in April. Uncle Dolan had to take the whole thing down." Jeb pulled around the house to the back terrace. "Zack says you shouldn't climb the stairs. I got cousin Tag waiting to help me take you up to your room. You gonna get well now?"

"I have to, Jeb, I have to," Kingston murmured, suddenly exhausted, thinking of the headstone he'd planted there for Eve, exposed now at the edge of the open knoll.

2

One week after the nightmarish dawn, she drove toward Stapleton International with a single desire. *Refuge*, away from Denver. But where? How did one disappear?

Until now, she had never run from anything. Until now, she had been Dr. Selena Hempton, the poised, empathetic listener in the plush privacy of her own consultation room. How many times had she leaned forward to some troubled woman client to ask so gently, *"But would walking out be a solution or only a postponement? If you run from a painful situation, left unsolved, won't you carry the pain with you?"*

How innocently arrogant, that professional dictum. Even in this numbed state she knew now, yes, flight, as well as fight, was a reflex for survival.

They think I killed my child. And she couldn't talk to them, couldn't explain, until she knew herself what had happened, and she couldn't know until she could think clearly. Until she could sleep. Now, to close her eyes meant seeing Roby down there on the rocks below the terrace, curled and still, looking like a six-year-old asleep, looking normal.

She drove like a robot, knowing only headlights and tail lights and, now, Stapleton ahead. She parked the Mercedes, took the small bag packed in such a hurry, and emerged into the glare and crowds of the terminal, into the flow of late hour strangers along the concourse. The smell of food made her ill.

Again and again she wheeled around, expecting to see her husband's neat figure and cold disapproving face.

Where, where to go? She wanted mountains, seclusion, but not anywhere Drew would look. At a newsstand she chilled at the sight of the tabloid, the one that had shown her picture with the caption "mother of the dead child." They had taken it from a professional conference folder, a head shot of a poised woman, looking so coolly capable, pale blonde hair swirled back in a chignon.

Now the tabloid cover showed a movie star's face and new scandals. A *Guide to National Parks* offered the reminder there were other mountains than the ones she knew. Southern ones. The ancient Appalachians. A map showed the Blue Ridge Parkway curling down from Virginia, miles of it, promising exits where one could find "a patchwork of small towns, valleys and farms."

Finally, a flight east, through the limbo of an endless black night. An infant's frequent cry jabbed at the scream still trapped in her body, laboring her breath. *"Control yourself,"* Drew had demanded when the emergency crew's flashlights found Roby. His order had frozen the scream. Sleep deprivation and Valium had since held it down. Silent, she had appeared composed. False composure, but a place to hide.

In the plane's humming darkness, she closed her eyes. The day played itself back in chaotic bits. Drew, this morning, holding the *Denver Post,* had cursed under his breath, "The first story wasn't enough for them? Now this."

"Yes," she had answered because he expected a response. "Yes, I saw it." Story and photo of the terrace, one taken from the layout done seven years earlier on the home of "famed surgeon Dr. Drew Hempton and his wife, Dr. Selena Hempton, therapist." Once, that terrace and its mountain view had been her place of needed peace. Now, it meant revulsion.

An investigation would be made, the story said. Hospital policy called for a report to the Denver police on any fatal accident.

In elaborately denying these two prominent professionals were considered guilty of child neglect—or worse—the newspaper implied that they might be. She saw the quiet rage behind Drew's tight features. She knew why: the indignity of an investigation, and the fact the story said the Hempton child was autistic. A former nursemaid, one of the many who had come and gone during Roby's six years, was quoted as saying, "That little fellow was a real problem to deal with. They kept him in one wing of that big house, not in the fine part."

The investigator arrived. A tall woman in a dark suit, short clipped hair, and inscrutable impersonal smile asked to see the child's room, the hall, and the terrace from where he fell. Drew handled the interview with icy charm just short of impatience, the manner he used in dealing with complaints from patients or interns. Selena murmured brief answers from behind the false composure.

Finally, the woman investigator closed her black notebook. They followed her to the foyer where she gave them an impersonal good-bye. They waited there in silence, in that white marble perfection, listening to the sound of the car going out the front drive, heading back to the city.

"So much for that," Drew said stiffly. Impatient to leave for his hospital board meeting, he waited at the door, brow furrowed under the crisp pepper-salt hair. "This was procedure. Under the circumstances, I'm sure the interview was uncomfortable for the woman herself."

Considering who you are, of course.

". . . and your performance out there did nothing to end this thing, Selena. You must stop this psychotic silence, this catatonic look of yours, or people will believe . . . believe what these stories imply."

She looked away from him, from his accusation, pulling back from something she was too tired to confront. He was telling her again, "You must return to your practice or you'll invite questions."

"No, I'm not ready."

". . . and you must stop going into the child's room."

The child? Your son, she thought but had no breath to say it. She watched him open the heavy door to the chilled Denver air. He turned back to say, "I have told Mrs. Creighton to start booking for you. I believe she has two scheduled for Monday. Your clients seem loyal; however, Mrs. Creighton has to deal with their curiosity."

Creighton, you sadistic witch, you're protecting him, not me. The anger for the office manager always flared but faded as quickly. The poor old thing worshipped Drew. *But didn't I, once? What have I done, trying to please him?* Like electric shock, and a momentary release the thought surfaced: *How long have I hated you, Drew? How long have I loathed this house?* She didn't believe in hate, so hadn't recognized it. She had coped with it.

Drew's MG swept out of the drive. Facing the closed door, she imagined a whole corridor of closed doors she had slammed shut, so as not to see what was behind them. Still wasn't ready to look behind them. She needed a door open to sunshine. One that led somewhere else. Where? Anywhere else.

In her bedroom, the one she had taken a year ago to be near Roby, she packed a small carry-on bag, then found what cash she had from every purse. In the airport she would use a credit card for money then destroy the card. In Drew's study, she sat down to write a note. *Drew, I must get some rest and must do it away from here. I'll go to Vancouver for awhile. The Mercedes will be at the airport.*

The message had been false but necessary. She meant to go in the opposite direction. It would take longer for him to find her that way.

Selena opened her eyes to the humming darkness. She was still flying east. Had she screamed? No, only cried out. An attendant stood there. "Are you all right, Miss? Can I help you? We're approaching Atlanta now."

Selena shook her head.

Morning. Another terminal. Walking dazed and still sleepless, she searched a news stand and found a *Mountain High* magazine. The cover promised places "Off The Beaten Track." The page showed an old mountain hotel, the Ridgeway Inn, sitting on its own knoll, slopes rising just behind. It looked utterly peaceful.

Hours later, face against the jet's cold window, Selena watched the plane bank and shudder, preparing for the landing at Asheville, North Carolina.

"Always bumpy over these mountains," offered the man next to her. Since Atlanta, he had attempted conversation, saying she looked a lot like that good actress Meryl Streep. She managed a nod and turned back to the window.

Unlike the Rockies, these contoured mountains undulated across the landscape, wave after wave, beginning to be furred now with spring green. Down there, somewhere, she meant to find anonymity, a space of time to think clearly, to understand what happened.

In front of the terminal, in May sunlight, cars moved away, filled with satisfied faces. Finally, the cab came. She told the driver, "The closest motel near a car lot, please," and leaned back, unable to answer his friendly drawl. It was enough to know she appeared to be one more travel-weary woman in tailored wool slacks and suede jacket, bare fingers gripping the carry-on bag. The rings were deep in the bag.

In the Spartan motel room, the TV turned to noise level, she stood under the pounding shower, daring the scream to release, and whatever remorse, guilt or disbelief that would come with it. The water poured, icy then hot. Nothing broke free. Only nausea churned.

She left the shower, drained of any feeling except an engulfing lassitude in the bland silence of the Asheville motel room. She would sleep now. Regardless. But until exhaustion took over, she sat down and emptied her wallet of green bills, identifications, and gold charge cards she had used for the last time. Save the driver license, yes, and hope not to have to show it. All of Hempton credentials—proof of years of study, hopes, accomplishments and the charge cards—went into a glass ash tray. She struck a match and watched, even smiled, thinking, *Burning bridges.*

In the mirror above the chest, she saw a weary smile, saw strands of champagne blonde hair spilling loose from the tight coil. She had always worn her hair pulled back into a shining chignon to show clients a serene brow, a fully listening self. And, yes, she had given them that. She'd helped women accept their own power, yet with Drew she had none of her own. The fingernail scissors took time, but clipping and whacking accomplished the purpose. Looking back at her now was a pale face, tired looking blue gray eyes, framed by a short, uneven, butcher boy cut. The remainder of that professional persona went into a paper bag into the trash basket.

She put back the license, the cash, and the rings she'd sell, and looked at the two pictures unearthed from the deep recesses of that wallet. Here was Selena Hart, RN, Chicago, 1967, clear-eyed, innocent and determined. The young Selena, before Denver Hospital, before Dr. Drew Hempton, the mentor, took over her career, her life, briefly as the lover, then the controlling husband. She would be Selena Hart again. Tears of recognition rose then sank again into the gray fatigue.

The second small picture was the only one she had of Roby, when he was four. It showed her crouched behind him, trying to smile, her arms holding his little body, rigid and protesting in her embrace. She stuffed the snapshot back, deep into the wallet, leaving only the Selena RN face showing under clear plastic. From the carry-on bag she drew out the magazine bought in Atlanta. She opened the pages of *Mountain High* again to the *Off The Beaten Track* column.

With foggy eyes, Selena read about High Haven, a hideaway hamlet in the Blue Ridge Mountains . . . a place out of time because the major property owner Alexander Kingston has refused to allow commercial interests to come in.

"No marquees or motels . . . but the Ridgeway Inn sits like a proud old lady ignoring the world. . . . If you're really game for this venture, you'll find cabins to rent . . . hidden away. . . ."

3

As Alexander Kingston's black Lincoln rolled past her shop, Maggie Hardy paused in her window polishing to wave at her landlord. "Did you see that, Selena?"

Selena Hart nodded. Waiting to talk to this cheerful little woman, she watched the car crawl leisurely along Crest Road, a curving corridor of sun and shade banked by summer green now that the trees had leafed out. The very air seemed different here, cool as spring water for a parched tongue. Denver, a lifetime away. Yet what she had brought was still with her, unreleased, buried like a stone in her chest.

Walking helped. Every day she had walked, rain or wind or sun, down this curving Crest road, and into every woods path she had found. Walking to exhaustion. At sunset she would trudge back to the Inn, in time for the Ridgeway's supper chimes, grateful for the reality of the fragrant, bustling dining room but having to turn conversations back on themselves, when other guests, older women, wanted to know, "Now what is a pretty young woman like you doing here all alone?" Upstairs in the small dormered room, she could sink into the small deep tub and later, in the deep bed, fall asleep from earned fatigued.

Three weeks of that, but now her cash was running out. To stay, she had to find a job. Who could she ask but Maggie, who kept her shop door propped open and knew everything about the ridge. Behind the granny glasses, the lively blue eyes, round cheeks and southern voice invited confidence.

"That was Alexander Kingston in the back seat, the one I told you about. Owns most of this whole ridge except the Inn," Maggie said, as they watched the Lincoln disappear up the drive past the Inn, to the private road that led up to Capstone, the Kingstons' summer place.

"The young fellow driving, grinning to beat the band? That was young Jeb Gurney," Maggie said, looking pleased. "Glad he has the job. His mama and aunt are housekeepers at Capstone."

"I heard he's ill . . . Kingston," Selena said.

"They say he had a stroke in Charlotte, but he looked like himself to me just now, waving from the back seat." Maggie gave a final swipe to her front windows. "Now you come on back in the shop and have some tea."

Selena followed her in to the colorful chaos of "Old Timey Things." Tables held quilts, crockery and lamps. Baskets hung from wall and low ceilings. China filled various breakfronts. One glass case held odd watches, clocks and jewelry. A vintage, upright Victrola sat by the open door.

"Now you sit down and visit," Maggie invited. "I keep these two rockers right here in front, ready for company. These old things comfort the body. Won't take long for the tea. Do you take sugar? I have an electric kettle back behind the cash register. You been walking again today? My, but you must have tried every trail we have around here. I see you starting out of a morning."

Selena sank into the rocker, looking around, murmuring, "Where did you find all this?"

"Everything here is a piece of somebody's life. Some of the best pieces are from folks around in the valley who don't value grandma's old things any more. They've learned to like K-Mart stuff."

"The weavings . . . they're quite nice."

"New crafters are doing what the old used to do. These I have are from Addie McRae, from the hollow down by Ruby Creek. Her weavings and baskets are the real thing, let me tell you. Quilts are mine. I quilt all winter. Then I get lots of throwaways from summer people who have houses on some of the other ridges around here. They like to claim High Haven as their own village, because they come here to the PO—that's what we call the post office."

Maggie brought out the two china cups of tea on a tray and set it on a needlepoint foot stool. "You have the nicest voice, Selena. Makes me think of someone in an important office. I guess you needed a vacation from that?"

Evading the question, Selena nodded and sipped the fragrant brew. "Do many people show up in High Haven during the summer? Other than guests at the Inn?"

"Some. I call them roll-through tourists. They may have heard about Dilly's big dinners at the Ridgeway. Or maybe just cruising around. I'm afraid we get a lot of folks who drive out of their way to get here because they've read about us in one of those tourist papers."

"The ghost story," Selena murmured. "I've heard about it, at the Inn."

Maggie rocked back and sighed. "People come up here asking about that with little crooked smiles, though I think they'd like to believe strange things can still happen in these mountains. We don't like the story repeated. It gives folks the idea we're a tourist spot promising some kind of gimmicky attraction. Lord help us, no!"

Selena looked up from the delicate china cup, waiting to ask her own question.

"If they stand there jiggling their car keys," Maggie went on, "if they look at me and ask, *"Is this all there is?"*—as if they couldn't look around and appreciate a view of infinity without a billboard in the way—then I send them on to gift shop places, like Gatlinburg or Pigeon Forge."

"Maggie, I love High Haven for the reasons you do. Mr. Dilworth, I'm afraid, is wondering how long I might stay. He notices I am running out of cash."

"Oh! Don't think Dilly is rude. He's an old worry wort. I have to explain Edmund P. Dilworth the Second to outsiders. He owns the Inn. Runs it like a sacred charge handed down by his mother, Mrs. Cora Dilworth. The same guests come in every summer, the Regulars he calls them, mostly widows and old couples. Once or twice he's had a young woman like yourself, checking in alone, then her husband shows up and makes a scene. Upsets Dilly more than it does his guests."

Selena smiled, still holding her question. "You know everything about this place, don't you?"

"Been here twenty years. Which reminds me, when you run into Ethel Pickett next door, you know, sitting behind her TV and cash register over there, don't worry if she asks too many questions. I'm always reminding Ethel, as well as Dilly, outsiders have a right to come here, same as I did. I was a forty-three year old Alabama widow, restless as a mama cat who had lost her brood, when I came to stay and bought this shop. I believe in trusting people until they prove otherwise."

Selena managed a smile. "Dilly, as you call him, is not the only one worried I'm running out of cash. That's why I wanted to ask you about a job. Oh, not here, I know you don't need anyone. I'm a nurse, a good one, really. I need a home duty case. I've worked with stroke patients. I heard at the Inn your Mister Kingston was coming up here to recover from a stroke. I would be so right for the case. I hoped you would speak for me since you must know them up there."

"Oh, Honey, I'm afraid that job is taken. Zack, that's the son, has sent up a nurse from Charlotte to live in. And at the PO this morning, Sudie Gurney told me the daughter is coming, too, to look after her daddy. Sudie doesn't complain about much, that job is her life, keeping that house and kitchen. But Sudie looked real down in the mouth this morning telling me that daughter is planning to show up."

Selena rocked in silent disappointment.

"I can't blame Sudie," Maggie went on. "Tory Kingston is such an uppity young woman. She'll stand right by you at the mailboxes in the PO and never give you the time of day. Had an actress mother, A. Z. Kingston's second wife. Mostly you hear about his first wife. That's why they call the slopes back of the Inn, Eve's Mountain."

Selena rocked silently as Maggie talked on about the Kingston family. She knew how to hide feeling, anguish or anger and how to make silence appear as poise. Necessary living with Drew, and dealing with her tormented child. Thinking of Roby, the hidden scream churned deep inside her, like a small ugly trapped animal. For control, she looked around at stacked china and lamps.

Maggie took away their cups and came back. "Now wait, don't look so sad. Doc Bradley has a clinic down the mountain at Mica. He might find you somebody down there. And I can suggest some summer people on the next ridge who have children who might need looking after."

"Oh, no. No children." Selena jumped up, forced her thanks and said goodbye. Outside, leaden with disappointment, she dropped to the bench in front of the shop and tried to concentrate on the moment, not next month when she'd be out of cash. She pulled in a deep breath of air smelling of spring woods. Across the road, two huge maples already shaded the little post office. Petunia beds bloomed along its walk.

A car pulled in. Selena watched the couple and their two children troop into Old Timey Things. From inside came giggles and the thin sound of Caruso's tenor from the Victrola. The family left, and drove away. Still, she couldn't move.

A Mica County sheriff's white cruiser pulled up. The stocky young man in khaki and gear stalked in, glancing at her from behind his sunglasses and handlebar mustache. "Bo Hilrey! Come right in," Maggie called from inside.

Selena sat there, a numb eavesdropper, listening to Maggie and the sheriff.

Maggie's voice: "Mister A. Z. got in just awhile ago, did you know? Well I guess you do, with Jeb driving him up. Your Aunt Sudie is probably up there now putting out a big mountain supper."

"I reckon," said the gruff younger voice. "Came to ask you something, Maggie. Have you seen any fellow around asking questions, claiming he's with some television show? Told me on the phone he'd been up here."

"Nooo—unless it was the one who stopped by my place awhile back. Late March I think it was. I was in the yard, chopping wood. He got out of his car, smiling like a salesman. Talking like a reporter. He'd heard the ghost story in Asheville. Lord, I wish they'd quit telling it. Why you ask, Bo?"

"Well this fellow on the phone said he worked in the Atlanta office for Perloin Productions on the coast. I guess he meant California. He wanted to know what the county records say about the Kingston woman's death way back there."

"Did you tell him the sheriff then was your daddy?"

"Told him just as little as I could."

"Bo, we both know Sheriff Will Hilrey was a good man. He must have handled things proper back there. That old talk should have died down a long time ago. You going to start worrying about that again?"

"I don't want it to start again," Bo grumbled.

"Don't blame you. Why would they want to know about something that happened up here almost forty years ago?"

"He wanted to know if Alexander Zackary Kingston still owns all this mountain and wasn't that like some *feudal lord?* I told them there's no feuding up here. It's a little unincorporated community. A peaceful little place."

Silence from inside.

So, everyone had secrets, Selena thought, still on her bench, waiting for strength to start toward the Inn.

Inside, Maggie's voice again: "Maybe this TV fellow was curious, like a nosy tourist. Maybe it doesn't mean anything."

"Naw, Maggie, this character on the phone was talking about sending up some kind of a crew to take pictures. Acted like he was doing me a favor, wanting to know if I'd like to be on camera, looking at the grave on top of Eve's Mountain, and saying we didn't know what really happened to her. I said, 'Sir, you're talking about going on private property. I don't think Mister Kingston would like that.'"

"What did he say?"

"Asked if I worked for the county, or was I a paid employee of Kingston."

"Bo, there's nothing wrong with your family working for Kingston even if you are sheriff. That's no easy job they have, looking after that place. Sudie, and Lottie keeping that big house nice and cooking for a house full of guests. Your Uncle Hogan opening and closing the place anytime of year Mister Kingston wants to come up with a bunch of people. And you are conscientious as the day is long. I'll tell anybody."

Bo Hilrey stood in the open door, his solid face set. He turned back to Maggie inside the shop, "You know how to answer folks, Maggie. If some smart-assy TV people show up asking questions. . ."

"I'll tell them we don't claim any ghost and don't want any. And if anyone figures on sticking a camera in the face of folks around here, or down in the hollow, well, those in the hollow anyway, they would be as welcome as a naked rock band at the Mica Baptist Church."

When Bo Hilrey walked out, got into his cruiser and drove away, Selena rose, crossed the empty road and started up the driveway to the Inn. The porch was emptying as the music box inside chimed its call to dinner. At the steps, she paused and looked back. Beyond the Inn's sloping grounds, with its old oaks and rhododendron lined drive, the horizon of layered mountain was darkening with sunset. How timeless this place seemed. How comforting the thought. The old music box's melody floated out, a weird blend of sadness and joy. And hope? She went on in, knowing, *I must find a way to stay here.*

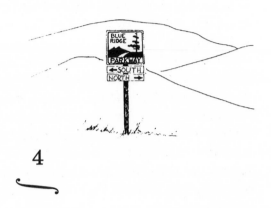

4

In her Georgetown apartment, Tory Kingston paced with her glass of brandy. A hell of a way to spend one's twenty-eighth birthday, alone with a bottle, but she had a problem to think out. She was tired of Washington. Bored with showing over-priced real estate to new wives who came in acting like frightened old house cats or newly-elected queens. She'd had enough of D.C., the men too, a breed as alike as their attaché cases. It was time to move on. But where? She needed a plan.

Since Helen Harper's call from Charlotte, the idea of going to Capstone and seeing A. Z. had nagged at her mind like a perverse notion. Hadn't she sworn never to go back up there? The fact he hadn't allowed her a place in Kingston Industries was a moot point now that he was selling. But the old frustrations simmered at the thought of her father. Had he actually collapsed at the closing? This bigger-than-life A. Z. Kingston? The image of him being felled by anything was a curious thought. When Harper called, the old gal had said it was a light stroke. It meant he would need therapy in Charlotte and a nurse to go with him up to Capstone.

Tory poured more brandy and sipped it absently, looking down on the restless traffic. She thought of calling Marja. It took some doing to find her mother's more current phone number. Marja's last husband, Kenton, in New York, had supplied that. "Still in D.C., Little Bit?" Kenton was okay at a distance.

She dialed the California number. Half amused and also annoyed, she listened to her mother's voice on the recorded message. Marja sounded more Bette Midler than the image she tried to portray, something closer to sexy Cher with curves. Tory left her own message and went back to the window, nerves as tight as coiled wire, in spite of the brandy. Half way through the bottle, curled on the bed, the muted TV flashing with police cruisers racing through the D.C. night, Tory picked up the phone to hear her mother's exuberant, "Darling! Baby! I've just come from the most exciting party. . ."

"Listen. I'm thinking I might come out there."

Marja crooned dismay. "Darling, I'd *love* to see you but I'm very close—*very close*—to something important out here . . . all right then, *someone* close to the action. So, it is not the right time to show off a twenty-five-year-old daughter. Oh, *twenty-eight*? Impossible! Come out next year, truly. I'm pumped at the thought!"

Her mother's ebullience simmered down to purring curiosity. "What's that rich old daddy of yours doing, Baby?" Marja listened a moment before declaring, in more deadened tones, "That proves a point. Don't get old. Be a smart girl. You had better start looking after yourself in that regard. You don't want him to bow out and leave you a few bucks and the portrait of Eve. Go hold his hand, darling."

Behind the wheel of the silver Porsche, Tory Kingston sped along the curving ribbon of the Blue Ridge Parkway, ignoring cautions and the posted forty-five mile limit.

The high road could mean tourists straggling along ogling the changing view. But this was May, so it shouldn't be a problem. Besides, before showing up at little old High Haven, she needed this time alone to think out what she meant to do.

Zipping up the suede jacket, Tory punched down the window. Wind sharp and crystalline whipped her short hair and stung her face. Open valleys swept past to the left, then around the next curve to her right. She drove, chin lifted to the wind, taking pleasure in the sense of control and power by the mere pressure of her toe in the size five boot.

On the phone from Charlotte, her father had said a reluctant, "Yes . . . I'm going up . . . yes if you insist, Victoria . . . come up if you wish." No warmth, same old civility barely covering disapproval. Yet, hearing the slowed diction had tightened her throat.

Shivering, she closed the window. *So, Father old dear, you still stir up a mix of feelings in daughter here.* What do you do when you hate and love someone with equal intensity? No therapist had given her any answer on that one. I only wanted some response from you, some approval, she might have told him but why didn't he know that? At least that, for God's sake.

Craggy rocks rising first on one side then another made her think of her father's face. Rough-hewn, but a strong kind of handsome, a face to go with a solid, muscular chest and broad shoulders, carried with assurance above the leaner flanks. Even in the moments she literally hated A. Z., she had to admit, "Now that's the way a man should look to turn me on."

Forget that. This was now. She didn't need Marja to remind her she should deal with her father if she wanted to come out with more than the tacky trust fund. Last year she'd vowed never to go back up there but here she was, heading for Eve's Mountain.

Eve's mountain, hell! How she despised the sound of that long dead woman's name. The romantic tale her father pitched to magazine writers long ago had reaped good PR for him. He'd played along with that.

Her father had made the image of Eve more important than his own family. At the thought, the old anger flared and she took the next curve too fast. For adrenaline-fired seconds she gripped the wheel, aware of a foggy valley yawning below. With cold nerve, she brought the car and herself back under control and clicked on the radio.

Languid dulcimer music trickled out. She punched again, but silenced the disk jockey's yak as quickly, preferring the hum of the car. A couple stood next to a motorcycle, pointing a camera at some wildflower along the grassy road edge. She swept past giving them a smirky smile. All right for you, lovers. These mountains meant nothing but loneliness for me. Reason enough to act the brat, wasn't it? That's what Zack had called her. Had any of them known what an unhappy kid she was? No, it was more like, had anyone cared?

Daddy-O, Daddy-O, I don't even know what happened to dear dead Eve but in playing that role to the hilt, do you realize how you screwed up all of us? Even Zack, Eve's own son. Zack, the charming procrastinator, the passive aggressive, who never lets anyone get to him. And Loren. That kid had hidden his feelings from the beginning. *Where did you get the youngest Kingston, dear old dad?* He had never bothered to explain why he showed up one spring with an infant and a horse-faced nurse, but no wife.

She had been nine that year but she remembered. Zack, back at Capstone from his first year in prep school, dealt with that surprise with a righteous indignation of a 19-year-old and had left as quickly. Went off to California or somewhere. Had her father ever explained Loren to any of them? Even to Loren? *Not to me, your own daughter, dumped on Capstone every summer like a legal liability.*

Marja had done the dumping, of course. But she didn't hate her mother or even think of her with the same intensity. Who could blame Marja for going on back to her soap opera roles in New York? Leaving her those childhood and teenage summers at Capstone where she had watched her father charm women, watched him play the big host to assorted guests and sycophants, and the bountiful landlord to that minuscule village. He had played those roles so well, too. Alexander Kingston should have been in acting, not carpets. People loved him. He pretended to love back. Yet he had not even pretended to love her, his only daughter. Every visit ended in some kind of confrontation. Last summer, she had stormed out after being there three days. And here she was, going back. But with a plan. Not worked out yet, but a plan. It was too late to be a part of Kingston Industries but she wasn't about to let the mountain property slip out of her hands forever.

She drove fast again, glancing occasionally at yawning valleys, thinking how High Haven was two hours away from any bright lights and dark humming lounges. Never mind. She would handle it. This time things would be different. She hadn't asked Harpy about Zack, but he should have his hands full back in Charlotte with the new owners, and that wife of his. Or did she hear he was getting a divorce? Nevertheless, Zack wouldn't be a problem. He'd fly up in the Bird and be gone again. There would not be a house full of guests this time. She knew A. Z. well enough to know he wouldn't want to be a sick man in front of his cronies or ladies. So no one would be there but the two old Gurney women who ran the kitchen and looked after the big house. This time they'd know daughter was calling the shots. The nurse too, if she were still around.

With cool-headed anticipation, Tory wheeled off the Parkway, exiting onto a rural road. At a country filling station, she looked into a cracked mirror and applied coral color to thin lips that kept shaping into a taut private smile. The real and private mission here was more than the issue of property. She intended to make her father *look* at her for a change, to realize his daughter could be as shrewd as he. *Father old dear, you're going to see what I can do.* Another thought made Tory want to laugh outright. Once it was no longer *Eve's Mountain* but hers, she would have killed off dear little Eve for good.

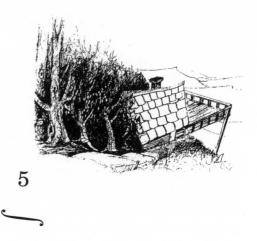

5

Following a long, overgrown driveway into the woods, Selena found the chalet that faced an open view. She stood looking down on the angled roof, for the first time in months feeling a pleasurable shiver of desire. *This is what I need, this is where I can feel safe.* From what? Colorado authorities? Or safely alone to deal with what she still held inside—fear of her own guilt, entangled with anger. More often, it made itself known as a dull, heavy sadness, carried like a pathology in her cells.

The house was small, some city person's idea of a chalet, apparently long closed, perched on the edge of the steep slope. She followed the weedy gravel path down to the side door, locked of course, but the glass panel revealed a tiny kitchen inside. A low railing circled the open deck. Selena climbed over and walked out on the creaking wood, past a dry and rusting Jacuzzi. *Yes, oh yes!* The expanse of cloudless June sky and horizon ringed with hazy blue ranges seemed accepting as open arms.

Deep below, hidden in trees, would be Ruby Creek Hollow. The cone-shaped mountain closer, heavily wooded with hardwoods and spruce, was Kingston's private mountain, the one called Eve's Mountain. The flat green strip on top must be where Zack Kingston landed his helicopter.

Maggie had told her, "It's noisy but I don't complain because I like that boy. Zack comes in here now and then, treats me like I'm a favorite aunt."

A breeze moved through leaves like a contented sigh. Then silence. Now birdcalls. Selena went to the crusted sliding glass doors and peered in. A large paneled room waited there, with couches and fireplace and a round table out from the shadowed alcove kitchen. An open loft level must be a bedroom.

Turning back to the wooden bench that shaped the deck, Selena sat there drinking in the view. She could scream here and no one would know. Let out the guilt, the anger, the sadness whatever it was. Nothing happened. She wondered, would the dream follow her here? The persistent dream of searching for Roby, going to his room, finding only the scuffy toy bear staring up at her from the floor of his room. If it held a message, she wasn't ready to accept it.

She climbed off the deck and back up the path, stopping once more to look down on the steep roof. Again, her skin prickled with discovery and hope. She needed this place. But she needed a job first. Tonight she would ask the feisty little innkeeper again if he had called the doctor that Maggie had mentioned.

Dr. Gordy Bradley hung up from Dilworth's call, knowing this Selena Hart could be the answer to his quandary about the situation at Capstone. But if she wasn't right she could be one hell of a new problem for himself.

On the phone, the innkeeper had sounded testy about this young woman, but then that was Dilly for you. The man kept the Ridgeway Inn running like a well oiled antique clock, the kind no one made anymore. "I promised the lady I'd call and tell you that she is a nurse and needs a job," Dilly announced. "But understand, I don't know the first thing about her. She's probably on her way to see you right now. That VW bug of hers is gone. First time she's moved the thing since she showed up here three weeks ago."

Doc leaned back in his creaking swivel chair, finger tips together, pondering. Beyond the glass window that said *Mica*

County Clinic, Gordon Bradley, MD, he could see the feed store across the county road doing a lively springtime business. The local pick-up trucks lined the front, sharing parking space with the vans and sedans, Florida licenses. Spring gardening, he mused, the common denominator there. Why didn't he close up this practice and go home and tie flies and go fishing? Hell, home was too quiet and he went fishing enough; besides he had to do some good around here, to live with himself. Sometimes that meant looking after a kid's broken arm or a diabetic grandma, and now and then handling an emergency case—a sawmill worker's hand cut half off or some summer retiree with a heart attack—then seeing them flown to the hospital in Asheville. A patient like Alexander Kingston was more worrisome.

A few weeks ago he had accepted that responsibility with pleasure. Now and then in the past, Doc had gone fishing with A. Z. Kingston, a robust, hearty fellow who was so rich he didn't have to be a bore and brag about it. With Kingston back on his mountain, after a stroke, Doc had promised Zack Jr. he'd look in on his father regularly to keep check on his medications. Zack was sending along a live-in nurse. Charlotte doctors had said the stroke was mild, a small clot in the anterior cerebral artery, leaving the man with a little damage but nothing a strong fellow like Kingston couldn't get over with the right therapy and attitude.

No problem, Doc had thought at the time. Kingston was an independent cuss, more to the good, and wanted to recuperate at Capstone, a place the man loved even if he had been everywhere in the world. Came back up to the mountains whenever he could, and seemed to be unaware of any old talk about him. At least he never mentioned it to Doc those occasions they'd shared a beer on a creek bank. Doc liked the fellow. He had looked forward to his weekly visits to that upstairs room at Capstone.

It wasn't working out that way. Kingston had fired the nurse right away. On every visit, he'd been a pain in the ass, spent the whole time cussing the Gate Belt on his waist and the walker and the weakness in his left leg. Then there was the daughter, the one who had taken over.

Doc Bradley rubbed his bristly goatee and wondered how such a little bit of a woman as Victoria Kingston could be so officious. She'd cross examined him about the medication. She had brought in young Jeb Gurney to help out mornings with the bath and dressing, but Kingston needed therapy too. Where could he find a good nurse here who could handle both the man and the daughter? Doc told Dilly on the phone, "Sure, I'll talk to this Selena. I'm ready to close up but I'll wait."

Not fifteen minutes later, an old green VW pulled up out front. From behind his desk, Doc Bradley watched the young woman who stepped out. This one was no old retired RN on vacation, for sure. Slim hipped in tailored pants, boots, a red knit cap over short blonde hair, she made him think of a rich tourist, the skiing type. She was studying his window with a determined, troubled look.

He opened the door of his front office to the small empty waiting room and went back behind his desk. She found him there and extended her hand in a strong shake.

"Dr. Bradley? I'm Selena Hart. Mr. Dilworth at the Inn may have called? Good." She sat on the edge of the chair facing him across the desk. "I'm a nurse. In the past I've worked in a rehab center. I'm looking for a private duty case here. A convalescent case, perhaps. I believe you have a patient at Capstone."

At his nod, she talked quickly, pleasantly about her experience. Certainly she was a professional, her conversation and answers proved it. She opened a wallet and handed him a single piece of identification, a card showing Selena Hart, RN, dated fifteen years ago in a Chicago hospital.

"This is all I have with me," she said, her lovely, modulated voice showing a quiver of nervousness.

Doc asked more questions but not yet the main one. Lord, she did sound like what he needed up there. "Kingston's daughter doesn't want any more live-in nurses. She expects me to find somebody to come up for an hour each morning."

Selena Hart sat straighter. "I wouldn't need to live in. I plan to rent a place close by." She gave him a tense smile. "Your patient needs both therapy and counseling and I can provide both."

Doc leaned back in the swivel chair, fingers together, parrying for time.

"Most of my patients are locals. Families whose folks have lived back in these hills before roads cut through, and long before some of these mountain highways started sprouting gift shops. I'm from Raleigh originally. I came to the mountains after my wife Hattie died and a big hospital didn't interest me anymore."

He saw her looking patient, saw her fingernails digging into her palms.

"Oh, I reckon I do some good," he went on. "You get the same problems here as anywhere. Older hill folks likely end up using old time remedies instead of my advice and the drug store prescriptions. But they're good neighbors. Good people. Stubborn and independent and Baptist, like their folks before them. The young ones are something else. I have one from Ruby Creek hollow who comes in here for her birth control pills. I could use somebody like you part time to take that kind of counseling off my mind." The thought occurred to him with welcomed relief.

"I know stroke patients," she persisted softly. "I could start immediately. I think you need me up there."

Doc Bradley sat up, feet flat on the floor. "And you're right, I need somebody as good as you sound. But I have to be honest, Miss Hart. I think I'm looking at a woman who has been more than a nurse the past ten years. Maybe a doctor who ran into trouble, like a malpractice claim or drugs? The daughter of his would find out and my tail would be in a ringer. I'm too old for that kind of trouble. Miss Hart, I'm leveling with you. I need you to do the same with me. I can't send you up there without knowing why you're here, and what you're running from."

She let out a long breath. "Doctor Bradley, I'll answer that, but only under these circumstances. I will tell you exactly why I'm here if you agree what I say will be held in professional confidence. Listen until I finish and if you don't believe me, then

I'll walk out and find some other place to go. But you say nothing to anyone else. And if you do believe me, you can protect my information and send me up there to care for Kingston." She sat back, and said more softly, "I can only afford to stay if I have the job. And I want very much to stay."

"I'm listening, Selena Hart. Professional confidence."

"I'm an RN, yes, with a doctorate in therapy. I've had earlier experience in a rehab center. In March I left a counseling practice as Dr. Hempton. I shared an office suite with my husband, a surgeon of some fame in Colorado. I left after the death of our child. Roby was six. He needed special attention, he was autistic." She was silent a moment before going on, her voice a monotone. "Roby fell to his death from our terrace. There was an investigation, about child neglect. A tabloid hinted at ugly untruths because the gate on the terrace was somehow unlocked—and I was there, alone, asleep when it happened."

"Were you or your husband accused of anything?"

"Not officially. But the news stories hurt. And the tabloid story was cruel." She looked away for a moment. Then continued crisply, "My husband didn't help. Drew is an exacting man, intolerant of any error, even innocent negligence. I had to get away from him and from where it happened."

"So you left. And you're using your maiden name."

"Yes. As a therapist, I understand psychic block and the desire to get away, and I know it doesn't save one from anguish and memories, but that's my private problem. It has nothing to do with my skill and training. I need the work to be busy. I need the job to stay here."

The front door slammed shut. A coltish young girl burst in, stopped short with quick grin of apology. "Doc, I lost that little book of pills wherever I hid them. Honest."

"Ariel McRae, this is a nurse, Selena Hart." Bradley wagged his head in dismay. "What am I going to do with you, Ariel?" He gave Selena a helpless look. "Miss Hart, let me call you at the Inn on my answer to our conversation. Right now, you can do me and Ariel a big favor. I'm going in the back to get what she needs and to lock up. I'll leave you two for a woman-to-woman talk. About birth control pills and everything else she ought to know. Thank you, Miss Hart. Yes, M'am, I heard every word you said. You'll hear from me, one way or another."

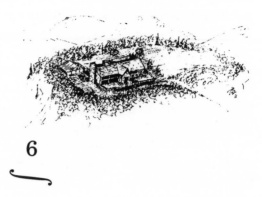

6

At the Charlotte airport, Zack Kingston waited at the controls of his helicopter. The pale, turbulent sky looked as uncertain as his immediate future but he was ready, leather jacket zipped, earphones humming, waiting for departure control.

For a man leaving everything behind, he felt damn good. Not dumb and happy about chucking a career, and handing over so much loot to Lisa and her lawyers, but finally getting away. The thought brought a good charge of adrenaline, the kind that came with a free fall parachute jump into the unknown; the big leap, no backward glance, and not knowing if it meant catching a good current or making a hard landing.

In forty minutes he would set the Bird down at Capstone, welcomed or not. On the phone Tory had sounded icy about his impending arrival, but what else would he expect from her? The Brat, or Lil Bit, he used to call her. A. Z.'s response was surprising—a mumble of acknowledgment, not the expected explosion about his bail-out of Kingston Industries. Had Tory subdued him that much? At the Convalescent Center, A. Z had been his old adamant self, joking and protesting as those admiring nurses wheeled him out to the Lincoln where young Jeb Gurney waited. Was his father worse, not better after three weeks at Capstone?

Surely not. The earphones vibrated with "north, northwest cleared." Zack dismissed the worry, let the helicopter rise, and with it his spirits.

Good old Bird. Skiing had its visceral satisfactions. Running sent his mind traveling ahead on its own. Climbing to exhaustion and beyond did it for him, too. But being aloft in the Bird was the peak, next to getting laid. Between departure and landing he was suspended in time, focused in the present, no past to worry about, no future to figure out. All alone up there, dealing with the demanding moment. He liked that. What had that woman said to him in Aspen that time? "Zack Kingston, for all your gregarious charm, I suspect a different, private guy looks in the mirror."

The Bird turned west. Below, highways funneled traffic back toward town. Tommy Hill would be speeding along in that flow, still shaking his head. All the way out to the airport, Tommy had groused, "What do you expect to do up there? Find yourself a Daisy Mae?"

"I'm headed for the hills, Tommy, but not to screw in the daisies."

"Wanna bet? Seriously, pal, you're going to regret cutting out—and for some fool notion about going home to the scene of kid summers? Must I remind you again, it's A. Z.'s mountain. The way things stand now, you won't get an acre if he does what he claims, leave it to the state. How are you three Kingstons—no, four with Loren—going to get along up there?"

The Piedmont fell behind. Flying northwest, Zack leaned back, dismissing the unanswered question. God, but he loved it up here even with the skies blustery. Fog could come later, but today, clear as an angel's conscience. Below, the land seemed to move in rolling waves, becoming Blue Ridge foothills. He'd made this hop often enough, commuting for a weekend. This trip had an edge to it, going back, life in limbo.

Mountains now. Soft furry shapes that wouldn't be yielding or forgiving if you plowed into the granite outcroppings. The Blue Ridge Parkway threaded along a ridge. Moving under him were shadowed valleys and dark green slopes of spruce and hemlock.

A different world from the six-laned interstate he'd passed over minutes earlier. Hardwoods had budded out now. Maybe he'd come alive too, rather than faking it.

He looked now for High Haven. You had to know the place was there to spot the Ridgeway Inn's green roof. Rising behind the Inn and Crest Road were the forested slopes of his father's mountain. Now the stony shape of Capstone came into view and the green stretch of landing strip behind the house. But he wasn't ready to take the Bird down yet.

So I'm a procrastinator, he admitted, and angled back low over the knoll. Late sun bronzed Capstone's amber stone and flashed light back from its broad glass windows. It waited down there like a lodestone in his heart; that and the man inside, ready to challenge him. Below, someone ran out to wave at the noisy helicopter. Not Tory, but someone aproned, good old Sudie Gurney, no doubt. At least the two women in the kitchen would be glad to see him. First, another turn. Sudie ran back in.

Had he hated or loved the place all those summers spent here? From earliest memory he'd heard the stories about his mother, how he'd been kicking the slats in his cradle at the Inn when she disappeared in these mountains. Summer nights, as a lonely kid, camping out down there, he'd imagined seeing her at a distance, looking delicate and beautiful, a fantasy he kept to himself. He cherished the notion, like other discoveries he'd made, kid ventures while prowling the woods. He was back from California, back at Duke, when he heard about the ghost story. When he learned the damn tale had been written up as fact in some collection of mountain tales, he had been furious, as if some intimate, personal experience, embarrassing as it was, a child's fantasy, had been stolen from him and exposed.

The Bird angled around the steep side of the mountain, above the county road where people claimed at times they saw something ghostly. Quickly, he banked in a wide arc to fly over his father's two mountains and lake between. During those early summers he had learned every amazing rock, every secret path and hiding place. Friendly hiding places. Ah yes. He looked down, remembering the girl from the Inn. A kid really, sixteen wasn't she? Followed him like a puppy that summer. Finally, she hadn't been a child to him but a woman giving comfort, engulfing him in a release he had never forgotten. He couldn't even remember her name, only the pleasure and residual guilt. *So much for young love in the bushes.*

The sun was low now. Time to land and deal with the present. He wouldn't let Tory ruin it for him, he'd simply avoid her as much as possible. Loren, too, when that solemn and solitary kid showed up from whatever school junket he was on. With A. Z. ill, he wouldn't butt heads with the man. Now of all times he couldn't ask his father questions that lay like a snake deep in the back of his mind. Okay, why had he come back? As the Bird hovered over the landing strip, Zack knew. He meant to climb these mountains to exhaustion, sit somewhere high and alone, a thirty-eight year-old man needing to ask himself: *Where did I screw up in the satisfaction department?*

"I'll do the honors," Tory said, letting the two Gurney women know they should tend to their cooking and watch Zack's arrival from the kitchen. She didn't want him here, but she would deal with it. She walked through the dining room and out to the back terrace that faced the knoll. The red and white helicopter hovered, then settled down neatly. Zack hopped out, looked toward her, saluted and went about tying the thing down. In the sudden quiet, the wind was no more than a sigh.

He started toward the house, a sinewy amble, swinging a small satchel, his tan deepened by the sun. Tory had to admit, *You're a good looking devil, big brother*. He wasn't bigger than life like A. Z., but he was tall, with good shoulders, and the leaner features and deep set eyes could light up with the old Kingston charm. They hadn't seen a lot of each other these years, but Tory figured she knew men. Zack's disarming nonchalance hid whatever was really bugging him. Men could be so dense about themselves, she thought.

42

She strolled on out from the terrace, studying his white toothed grin. She was almost glad to see him. "Well, if it isn't Junior. I thought that flying machine didn't want to land."

He whipped off the sunglasses and pretended surprise. "If it isn't Little Bit, the Brat. Grown up beautiful but still Little Bit." He dropped the bag and wrapped her in a quick, brotherly hug.

She pulled away from the smell of leather and something undeniably male that stirred frustration and made her angry because of it. Already he was looking past her to the house. He's older, she saw. Fine lines around the eyes. The thick Kingston hair, once auburn, now looked bronzed, the brows still dark. Deep set searching eyes denied the easy grin. She said teasingly, "So Lisa took the money and ran. Yet I hear you passed up any chance to stay in that big fancy office in Charlotte."

"And I heard my little half-sister had it made with some press secretary in our nation's capital. But here you are in the mountains."

Tory shrugged and smiled sweetly. "The Gurney girls are all adither in the kitchen. Big prodigal homecoming."

"You're the prodigal. I've been around, in shouting distance of A. Z. for years." He picked up his bag, the quizzical grin gone. "How is he, Tory? Clue me in. What's going on? Why did he get rid of the nurse I sent?"

Zack started toward the back terrace so quickly she had to walk fast to match his pace. "He's asleep now and will be off and on until morning. He'll be angry if you wake him up. Wait until tomorrow to talk to him. Don't look like that. When Jeb comes in early to bathe him, you'll think he's his old self."

Zack stopped at the back terrace. "What are you telling me, Tory?"

"He's getting—strange." She gave him a weary look. "It's a good thing I came."

"Then why in the devil did you let him fire the nurse? Gordon Bradley called me. Or did you get rid of her? Don't tell me you came to play nurse?"

43

She didn't hide her annoyance. "He hated the woman. She was only too happy to leave. Remember, Zack, he is *my* father, too. I have a right to be here. Don't think it's been easy." She gave him a hurt, reproachful look.

"Of course. But we'll have to get somebody else. Bradley says he might have a replacement but he didn't sound very sure."

Tory kept her voice soft, knowing the two women from the kitchen waited on the terrace to embrace him, "Zack, Father is not doing well. I've had Bradley up here to check his medication. I make sure he takes it or he wouldn't, you know that. And Jeb sees to it that he is up and bathed and dressed each morning. Not that he appreciates anything I do." Her voice broke. It wasn't a pose.

"I'll look in. Talk some sense into him."

"In the morning," she repeated. "There's a big dinner waiting and Sudie has put you in one of the guest bedrooms downstairs with the big tub. There's still a bar in the living room."

She stood there, watching Zack stride toward the open terrace where the two Gurney women waited, Lottie grinning and Sudie with arms open. Why in the devil did he have to show up, to be an interference? Zack had his own problems with dear old dad, but always this begrudging loyalty, too. He would try to oversee her business unless she kept him out of her way. That shouldn't be too difficult. Regardless, she wouldn't let Zack or these doting old women get in the way of her plans.

From his morning duties with Kingston, Jeb Gurney bounced into the kitchen, announcing, "Your daddy's roaring around up there this morning. Something's set him off."

"Don't worry." Tory picked up the breakfast tray, ignoring Lottie Gurney's silent disapproval. "Just show up tomorrow. He likes you, Jeb. And I need you." She saw the boy's face flush and avoid his mother's tight-lipped stare. As Jeb swaggered out, the spare old woman said peevishly, "Mister Azzie would like some eggs straight up and grits a whole heap better than what you've got on there."

"For lunch, Lottie, maybe some of Sudie's baked chicken. Good Lord, not the dumplings. Or soup beans. Don't expect him to handle those big meals as before."

Tory walked out with the tray, ignoring the woman's thin, pressed lips. Almost nine now and no sign of Zack yet. Fine. He had stayed out most of the night going God knows where. She'd put him downstairs, out of her way in a guest room. Her own room was upstairs next to the library near her father's suite. The library was a good place to work, with the big desk there and now the private phone line. The library would be her domain as long as she ignored the damned portrait on the wall.

Balancing the light tray, Tory climbed the stairs, shivering in a cashmere sweater and wool slacks. Coming back to Capstone had proved more upsetting than expected. Too many childhood memories here. Her father had played host to a parade of people: the freeloading titled English couple, the arty pair from Manhattan, the old cronies from Atlanta and Charlotte, the young business partners with their still younger deb wives. And after Marja left, single women. She wouldn't have hated it so much if her father had ever pulled her onto his lap, against his chest, if he had ever said with pride to the others, "This is my daughter, Victoria."

This morning she found him seated in the wing chair by the wall of windows, dressed in slacks and shirt, bare feet stuck in leather sandals. She set down the tray, stood back with her arms crossed, her chest tight, waiting. He continued to stare out at trees and sky. *I'm waiting, Father. I've waited all my life for some proper notice from you!* She poured the tea into the cup and forced a casual tone. "Hey you—wake up."

Kingston rubbed his face with his right hand, the left one shaky in his lap. "Where . . . is he? Zack . . . is here but where?" His words were quiet but the jaw muscles twitched with anger.

"Asleep. He'll be up soon enough. After all, he's moving in on us."

She watched her father lean back and look again toward the window view. Under the heavy unruly brows, his deep set eyes flickered from whatever thoughts were going on inside. "Damned fatigue," he finally muttered. "Can't sleep at night. Sleep all day. Have Sudie send me up a real breakfast, Tory. And coffee. Not this tea and toast crap."

"Your blood pressure is on red alert," she said crisply. She hated his slowed speech, knew it was energized only by anger. "The last thing you need is to get into it with Zack. He hated the business and you know it. I would have been good in that spot— but that's past, isn't it?" She kept the old anger out of her own voice. "This is now. Here, take your capsule. Your vitamin."

"What is it you want, Tory?" he asked wearily. "You're not here . . . to put up with this nursing business."

"I'm here to look after you. And Capstone, because you've paid no attention to it for some time." At his deepened frown, "I know you don't want to talk about it but we must, when you're in a better mood." She punched on the stereo before going out, not looking back to see if the old *South Pacific* tape calmed the savage breast. In the hall outside, she stopped, as Zack bounded up the stairs, his face flushed, combing his hair with his fingers. She caught his arm. "Keep it light, Junior. He's beginning to imagine things and shouldn't be argued with. You don't want to give him another stroke do you?"

She waited a moment when he went in, wondering if she should follow to monitor that meeting. No need, she decided. Zack didn't relish arguments. He avoided them. She'd give him enough to make him glad to stay out of the house, out of her way.

Downstairs, the Gurney women looked up from their dust cloths and furniture wax. "You had a call on the library phone. Might have been them Perloin folks," Lottie said. "I told them you weren't accepting any calls, like you said, and hung up." But Sudie announced, "I picked up down here on the last one. It wasn't those folks. I do think it was your mama asking for you. I won't ever forget that voice."

Marja? She had been avoiding the phone, letting the women answer. "If she calls again on that line, ring the dinner bell and I'll answer." If her mother called back, she wanted to say, yes, I'm here, but for my own reasons.

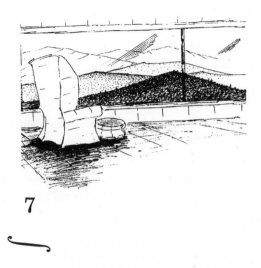

7

In the dark of the four poster bed in his suite, Alexander Kingston opened his heavy eyelids. Across the room, the wall of windows still showed black. In dead stillness, with no wind outside, the wall clock ticked like his pulse.

The craziness was about to happen again, as it had back in the convalescent center. He knew the precursors. First the humming in his pulse and his skull. Any moment the images could start. Pictures, flashing behind his eyes, on the screen of his mind, while his still-drugged body held him against the bed, helpless witness to what chose to be shown.

Was he losing his mind? Or was some judgment being dealt out by an invisible tribunal? He wanted to cry out to this unknown thing, or his own brain, whatever was in control here. *Damit, I'm not ready to die.* He had living to do. Loose ends to wrap up with Zack and Loren.

It always started as blips and grids, then became faces and scenes, out of sync, but recognized as moments of the past. He was being prepared for something. For seeing Eve again? That had to be the meaning. One of those scenes yet to flash would show him the night he had last seen her, a memory buried too deep to recall by choice.

Since he had returned to Capstone, she had been present in his senses. The first day, before allowing Jeb and the other boy to get him up to his room, he had sat in the library and looked at her portrait. Mistake. Her face had stayed with him. Any night now she would come to him, behind his eyes or to stand before him.

Kingston gulped in the cool night air to clear his head. Maybe the blasted medication was causing this craziness. What they called a bad trip. He wanted off the stuff now, the drugs and the other capsules Tory forced on him. She claimed they helped him sleep. He needed the vitamins, she said. Without telling Tory why, he threatened to flush the whole handout down the toilet. She threatened back, "You'll die of a heart attack." So he swallowed what she poked at him, hoping the sedative would work, give him some peace.

Nothing had. He kept waking up like this, before dawn, the images happening, faces flashing, scenes zooming in close for a millisecond before fading. Some of those flashes left him curious for more. Some stung him with remorse and fear. Each moment showed him more than he had understood when it happened.

The grandfather clock bonged. Only one o'clock. He tried concentrating on the present, the daytime frustrations, those damn realities. Zack, for one. He was angry at Zack for walking in like party time and walking out as quickly, claiming he had some job or another.

Another gripe was the food he was getting. What was the matter with Sudie Gurney, sending up those piss-ass trays? Only once had the old gal come upstairs herself, hands deep in apron pockets, telling him she had to fix what Tory ordered, then ducking out.

Tory. He had too much of Tory. She with her pretense of love but using it to control. He hated women like that. She was like Marja. No, she was worse than her mother. Marja was a woman who could be anyone on stage, enchantress or witch, but offstage, restless without the spotlight and not content to share his. The chase had been exhilarating, a challenge, played out in their mutual spotlights. But the marriage was a losing gamble, an impossible merger from the start. Wouldn't have lasted three months if Marja hadn't become pregnant. So, they had Victoria. How did two hot-blooded individuals, different though they were, produce such a cool, calculating little bitch?

Sharp mind, true. Maybe he should have brought her into the company. He wasn't against women with brains but there was something furtive and manipulative about Tory. He had preached and practiced team spirit attitudes at Kingston Industries and Tory would have been nothing but trouble. Now she had moved into this house, taking over Capstone. Playing nurse but with solicitude devoid of warmth. If a woman wanted anything of him, she had to have warmth, whether she was heavy on brains or boobs.

Thinking about the present daytime frustrations didn't help. He tried to think of the office as it was, as he was himself, only three months ago. Harpy, good old Harpy, reading off a list of appointments including his next plane flight. No. The feel of it wouldn't come. The memory seemed like so much baggage left back on another planet, called the past. He was stuck here in unreal space, this state of drugged half-sleep that had opened doors he couldn't close. He sank back into troubled sleep.

The clock struck one. Kingston roused, aware of the strong vibration in his skull. *So let it happen.* On the screen of his mind, a young man's face, eager, smiling, showed itself. Jim, an early partner, long dead now. Boating accident. He wanted to say, *Jim, I've lived and you didn't have the chance, did you? But whose fault? Wasn't it fate, whatever that is?* Yet, the remembered young face left dregs of sadness as it faded.

Other images flashed and disappeared as quickly. An instant on a street in Stockholm. Now a fetid hot night in Bangkok, around food, with three shrewd men, tiny brittle Oriental men amused at his bulk. Now yet another time and place. The flushed face of that woman, mother of the girl, righteous with her angry tears, making her demands, as a Catholic nun put the baby in his arms. Loren. The scene was there, real again, before it dissolved to blackness behind his eyes.

49

The grandfather clock bonged the half hour. Now it came . . . the image he feared yet waited for. Eve's face, a pale oval looking up at him that summer night, wind blowing her dark hair and white dress. He was standing again in the back garden of the Inn, his body roaring with a young man's anger, righteous male rage demanding control of what he loved, what he thought he possessed. His hand raised—had he struck her? The image faded. He tried to remember but could not. He was seeing the old Lincoln, his first. He saw himself sprawled inside, his face against the leather seats. He smelled the drained bottle of bourbon.

The clock ticked on. Now he heard a sound faint as a chime in the wind, a high whisper of leaves. A woman's voice. Inside his head? Or beyond those glass windows? Had he heard Eve's voice?

He pushed his weak left leg off with his right and sat with his feet flat on the floor. He rocked there, inhaling cool air for strength. The metal walker gleamed dully within reach. He braced his right arm on the thing and pushed himself up. The floor might have been a magnet pulling him down but he forced his arms to grip the walker, willed his legs to move, to carry him across the dark room.

At the window wall, he braced with the walker and listened. A faint light of dawn edged the distant ranges. The mountains sat out there, a quiet solidarity that fed his own strength. All those hectic paced years, he had returned here to refuel his own powers. *Eve, I learned to love these mountains too.* Of the stories people had written about him and this place, that part was true.

Beyond the window was only hazy dark. Then the faint sound again. Was it a wish or a fear that he heard it, from within his head or outside?

He balanced himself with fingers against the cold glass. Below, beyond the stone terrace where the dark bluff gradually gave way to the steep slope of mountain, something white moved. With his sight or his mind, he saw her down there, felt her looking up into the dry, lonely cavern of his soul. He closed his eyes to answer. *Eve, I did love you . . . you were the fuse of all my ambition.*

Kingston opened his eyes, straining to see the dark bluff below. Nothing. He sank heavily in the chair, knowing with certainty, beyond logic and beyond doubt, that what happened between them that August night years ago still existed out there and within himself, buried in memory. And Eve would come to confront him and make him remember.

In the dark parking lot of the roadside bar, Zack Kingston stomped the accelerator of the old Chevy, trying one last time to make the motor turn over. If the thing was still dead, he had the girl on his hands. She stood watching, outlined by the dim neon, her arms folded over the ample area of red T-shirt with the Benny's Bar lettering. Zack climbed out, groaning silently. "You have a very dead battery, among other problems."

She rocked on her heels in a display of fatigue. "I'm purely kilt. Gotta get to the house."

"Come on. I'll take you home." Zack led the way to his Range Rover and opened the door. The girl hopped in, saying "Thank *yeuuu*," in her high nasal way. Behind the wheel, Zack looked at her. "Well?"

"Ten minutes down the road, then you turn right, then . . ." She sighed. "Go on, I'll show you."

Zack wheeled out of the gravel driveway, onto the highway, looking straight ahead, not at what he had there, wiggling beside him in the dim light of the dashboard. Had he started this back there in the bar? His full intentions were to get in early tonight. Find Tory in the library. Do the confrontation he'd been avoiding all week. Now this. Okay, he'd drop this girl off and be gone.

"My name's Pat," she offered. "Turn here."

Off the highway, a knoll rose to the left of the road, littered with hard shapes. In the cloudy night, he could see it was another dump of junked cars, looking as if they'd been spilled from the sky, to tumble down and rust where they landed. As always, coming upon such sights in an otherwise pastoral setting, Zack mentally played angry God, vacuuming up the whole mess, sucking it up into a black hole of space. If he could do that, would the

hillside heal? And if green growth did come back, wouldn't somebody from the outside come along eventually and build time-share
condos? So what the hell? It hadn't happened here yet, but in time
it would.

Beyond the dump, along the narrow country road, the girl
said, "See that turn off? I live down the end."

It was more of a dirt path than road. Zack slowed past the four
rooted mobile homes. When she said, "Whoa, this last one's mine,"
he stopped, foot on the brake, glad to see those plump jeans wiggle
out. But she leaned back in to tug at his arm. "You come in with
me? I just hate to go in there in the dark. There's no key to this
old place."

She ran ahead and Zack followed, wondering how a girl like
this got along. Apparently she did, out of necessity. Some of his
best friends would be laughing at him now, about being a sucker
for trying to save struggling women who take you for a short ride.

"Come on in." She pushed open the door. He couldn't turn heel
and go. This Pat of Benny's Bar was a true survivor, the girl
deserved some courtesy.

In the minutes it took for her to find a light switch that
worked, Zack stood patiently in the dark, grinning in spite of
himself, remembering how irked Tommy Hill's wife had been with
him last month as they stood in a symphony night intermission
crowd. "She's my friend, Zack Kingston, a really sharp lawyer and
you don't want to meet her? Do you know it's chauvinist to act the
pal to bright women and spend your libido on the cuddly ones?"

In the trailer's sudden yellow light, Zack saw the girl's bleak
look and the low ceilinged room. *Some survival,* he thought,
touched by the sight. She was bustling around sweeping the couch
free of papers and stray popcorn and a kid's plastic truck. "Sit
down," she trilled.

Zack didn't want to sit down. He wanted to walk out.

She faced him, hands on the hard jeans that molded her
chunky lower body into rigid shape. "You're the son of that rich
guy lives up in that stone house above Ridgeway Inn, aren't you?
Well, that's not why I let you come on to me." She shook her head,

a shaggy mop of dull blonde hair. "You're the one who flies around in that whirly-bird like a traffic cop? Well—I'd sure like a ride in that thing." Her shiny round face beamed at him like a hopeful kid.

Zack picked up the truck and turned it over in his hands. "Where's the driver?" He waved the toy and set it down.

"Naw. He's staying with Momma. You wait here. I been in these things ten hours." She yanked at the red Benny's Bar T-shirt and left him there.

The sound of a shower pounded from the other side of the wall. Restless, Zack looked over the musty room, with its sagging chair and couch, its scattered toys and magazines. He got up and paced, enjoying his disgust like a self punishment. Not disgust for the girl. But himself. He should get home and have it out with Tory. Find out what a guy named Mitch Mason wanted on the phone early this morning. Half awake when he picked up the phone in his room, hearing a man's voice and not interested in any lover in Tory's life, he had hung up quickly. But falling back half asleep, he'd realized the tone was strictly business, the subject property. Eve's Mountain. What was little sister up to? He had been avoiding Tory but now he would have to confront her. And he had to find A. Z. a new nurse.

The shower still rattled beyond the wall. He couldn't walk out on this girl. Trapped, he sank down on the couch. The shower slowed. He could hear her humming. Zack leaned back into the creaky couch. He could use pounding hot water on his own back, but not here. For awhile, there in Benny's Bar he'd felt pretty good. Now he ached again from good hard labor of the past week. He'd taken the job hoping physical work would clear his mind, put Charlotte well behind. Only then could he start looking for something to care about.

So far he had been too busy getting up at five, riding forty miles in a truck with two tireless, rawboned hill boys to wooded slopes of a new resort to handle stone all day. The three of them had built a fine solid flagstone stairway up an impossible slope for a pink-faced Miami banker who would probably never use it.

Zack knew the type. The Miami guy, a new retiree from lofty levels of finance, probably intended to sit contentedly on top of his own world now. More likely, when the guy wasn't at the clubhouse or on the fairways, he'd be stirring another Scotch and watching stock reports on TV, not the fine view from his fifty-foot long deck.

The Miami fellow came out often enough to give a CEO frown to their stone work, but only once offered cold beers. Zack had kept his own mouth shut and watched the two locals, craftsmen both, nod and mumble inaudible thanks. There was no humble posturing in that reticence. More like polite forbearance, Zack knew. The two fellows, native as the stone they placed, didn't offer opinions to outsiders. When the older of the two allowed to Zack as how, "Some outsiders are nicest folks you ever wanna know. Then there's the *other kind,*" Zack figured he had been accepted into the exclusive group of outsiders who were the good folk. He was sure of it when they asked him to stop in at Benny's Bar on the way home, like a reasonable fellow who understood how the world worked. The Benny's stop, one wet county away from dry county Mica, had become habit.

On the other side of the thin wall, the girl sang to herself, eager and tuneless. Groaning with indecision, Zack paced again, catching his foot in a tangle of cord on the floor. He grabbed up the phone, dialed operator, read off the number from the dial and asked for a ring-back service check.

With a "Ta-daa!" Pat burst into the room, in a moist warm cloud of heavy gardenia perfume, posing for him in a black lace teddy with pink ribbons, the lipstick a pink purple. "Ordered it from a catalog. You like it? Hey, did I hear you on the phone?" The dark blonde eyebrows arched, uncertain.

"My father." Zack sighed with his frown. "He's ill you know. I left a message."

The phone rang and Zack grabbed it. "Yes. Sure. I'll come as soon as I can." He clicked down on the operator's sputter and faced the girl's flushed face, frozen with disappointment. "Don't worry about that ride in the Bird, Pat. We'll try it sometime. Soon. For sure."

With ambivalent relief he escaped into the cool May night, slid into the Range Rover and crunched out along the rutted dirt road. By the time the car hit asphalt, his own pulse humming like the motor, Zack felt better. He sped down the dark empty highway, alone and in control, a peaceful feeling he liked. He felt like an actor might feel escaping the stage. Smart women guessed that about him. Maybe that's why he kept those at arm's length.

Fog began setting in as Zack headed for Capstone. Reaching Crest Road, he passed the cluster of little shops and turned up the drive, past the Ridgeway Inn then past Maggie Hardy's log house, on up toward Capstone. He drove the steep, private drive, yellow fog lights on, watching for Hoke McRae or his blue pick-up truck. That last visit to the county jail probably hadn't yet convinced McRae to stop snooping around the Kingston property. *Are you out here tonight having your kicks with the shotgun, you crazy devil?* Just try it, Zack thought, I'd like to talk to you with my foot on your chest. Tell you to cut the crap about your claim to any Kingston land. Hoke had been muttering that since the two of them had shared the same fourth grade classroom one winter. *Shape up, Hoke McRae. I don't want my father disturbed.*

In the fog, Capstone loomed like something out of Scotland. Zack pulled up to the garage, walked out to the open landing strip to make sure the Bird was still tied down. The two Dobermans followed him back to the dark and silent house. It was too late to wake Tory and start a scene tonight. But on impulse Zack climbed the amber lit stairs to his father's suite. He looked in. The four-poster was empty.

"Dad?"

Worried, Zack walked in.

His father's pajama clad figure sat slumped in the wing chair by the window wall. In the pale light, the mane of hair was a tousled mass of silver, the face shadowed. Dead? Asleep? Zack knelt down, grabbed A. Z.'s big hand, limp in his own. The contact triggered a tenderness in his chest like a wrenching pain. At this moment, he didn't give a shit about unresolved animosities. He wanted his father to talk to him.

"Dad, it's Zack. Come out of it and look at me. Are you going to die on me, without us ever leveling with each other?"

The heavy gray eyebrows raised. The cool hand pulled back. "Zack? I have seen Eve. I saw your mother down there."

Good Lord, the man was hallucinating. Zack stayed crouched, seeking his father's shadowed face. "You're dreaming. It's the medication."

"You don't give a damn."

"For God's sake, what do you want me to do?"

Kingston leaned back in the chair, his words halting, coming from deep in his big chest. "I'm not ready to die, Zack. I've got to get well. Before she comes back. I must get everything settled. This place, all of you, everything. Too tired to explain now. Tory mustn't know. But I've felt Eve. Tonight . . . saw her. Tory wouldn't understand."

Zack stood. "Let me help you back to bed. It's almost three." Ignoring the muttered protests, he helped pull the man to his feet. Bracing his father's heavier body, Zack led him across the floor, the burden of it washing him with compassion tinged with bitterness. Alexander Zachary Kingston, the Senior, the hard driver, helpless here in sagging pajamas. *There have been times when I would have gloated. Not now.*

At the bed, he allowed his father to sit first before helping him lean back onto the rumpled sheets. Zack lifted the heavy legs, swung them into position on the bed. He stood there gazing down at this still powerful looking man. But the silver hair looked helpless against the pillow. A great deal was happening behind the closed eyes, shadowed by frowning brows. "We haven't talked enough, have we, Zack?"

"No, we haven't, A. Z." And now it was too late. This hallucination business. Bad sign.

"Are you going to help me—or are you in this with Tory? She comes in at night and talks. I try not to listen. Are you with me, Zack? You always do your own thing. You aren't around."

"I'm here, Dad. What do you want me to do?"

"Get me off this medication. Talk to Doc Bradley. He's no fool, tell him to send me some help. I need more than Jeb. And Tory." He paused, chest working hard with obvious distress. "Find me some therapists who know what they're doing. And you, Zack. Quit running away, damn you. And get the boy here. Get Loren. That has to be settled too. I can't afford to die anytime soon, Zack. I want to get things right. Before Eve stands in front of me again."

8

"**Y**ou had a phone call, Miss Hart." In the hall, Innkeeper Dilly, in red bow tie and plaid vest, continued to crank the old Reginaphone's brass plates, chiming his guests to dinner.

Selena stopped short. Had Drew found her? The quick panic surprised her. Panic or anger? No, it could be Gordon Bradley finally calling back with his answer. Both hope and dread at the thought. She seized on the hope and waited there as guests streamed past, chattering and content, drawn from their rooms and front porch rockers toward the aroma of country ham.

Finally, Dilly straightened up, the music box sounds fading, his round pink face studying her. "It was young Kingston. Said he would call again." Dilly looked mollified as she thanked him. "I did call Doc Bradley for you. He must have talked to the son." He trotted on toward his bustling dining room.

The phone booth sat there in the hall, an oak antique, the black phone inside, still silent. Holding on to hope, Selena paced the hall, waiting. Then back to the now empty lobby. The hand-carved Black Forest cuckoo clock ticked along peacefully. Beyond the open archway to the main parlor, mellowed chintz couches dispensed a glow of comfort. From an ornate frame in the lobby Mrs. Cora Dilworth peered down, an imperious presence with stern mouth and lace collar.

Tense as she was at the moment, Selena had to smile back at the old lady. The portrait seemed to monitor the front oak desk where son Dilly carried on her charge to keep this place a peaceful refuge. For that cause, Selena had already chosen to forgive the man's fussy caution.

She walked back to wait by the still-silent phone booth.

From the dining room came the high hum of voices, the tinkle of iced tea glasses and from the stereo, hidden in an old breakfront, strains of Frank Sinatra's plaintive *September Song*.

Memory flooded in. Another room like this. The boarding house off campus those sophomore and senior years in Colorado. She had arrived there, insulated within herself but energized by innocent self-confidence, the eager, dedicated student. The sense of belonging found in that boarding house was a new experience, a pleasure she'd never known growing up with older parents, two resolute, pragmatic people already subtracted from her life by age sixteen. Their deaths meant funds for college and in turn, their continued, silent demand for achievement. Yet it was a demand she seized upon. Studies had been her life, always had, except for the fifteen months with Jerry.

Alone in the Ridgeway hall, she was surprised at the heat of the memory engulfing her. *Jerry.* When had she allowed herself to think of him? Jerry, the only free-spirited, irrepressible, passionate man she'd ever experienced, before or since. Exuberant but patient, he had coaxed her out of the narrow self-image of lone student. He had taught her to play, to imagine, to experience. He had unlocked her capacity for passion. Trusting him, loving him, yes, she had learned more about relating to others than degrees in clinical psychology could ever impart.

Jerry hadn't failed her. But his teachings had. Dear Jerry, believer in making one's own fate, had died in the crash caused by a student pilot. The self that had come alive with him closed down. That self receded like a memory of a person once known. She leaned against the wall, eyes closed, putting it away again.

From the dining room now came poignant strains of an early Sinatra, *I'll Never Smile Again*. She thought ruefully, *But you do. You go on one way or another.* After Jerry, she had gone back to the safe challenges, dealing with the demanding hours at the hospital with what appeared to be unflappable confidence and drive. When this attracted the hospital's famous surgeon, Dr. Drew Hempton, known as genius in the operating room, she had assumed it must be a reward of a kind and one to accept, first the strong-willed mentor, then, inevitably Drew as husband, one who expected her own counseling practice to be a useful adjunct to his own, a bulwark between himself and patients.

Was he ever a lover? A user, not a lover. A man who demanded perfection from anyone around him and she had given him an imperfect child. Yet she stayed all those six tense years, behind a facade of calm, dealing with Drew, her practice and Roby's problems . . . until the nightmare happened.

Don't think of Denver. Later but not yet. Not now.

Inside the oak booth, the phone jangled. Selena slipped inside, answering in a rush, "Ridgeway Inn."

At the other end, a man laughed, a rich, easy baritone. "You don't sound like Dilworth the Second to me. This is Zack Kingston calling for Selena Hart."

Introductions were made, the invitation given. He would pick her up at the Inn in the morning for a visit with his father. "We'll see if this will work out for you and the old cuss. You'll want to check him out before you decide to take him on as patient."

More calmly than she felt, "Don't worry. I've handled post-stroke therapy before. I understand a patient's emotional problems as well as the physical." How formal she sounded, in spite of a racing pulse.

"We'll see. The senior Kingston can charm your socks off or be a hard case, Miss Hart. Ahh, something else. We'll have to convince my sister too. But two votes out of three ought to make the case, right? See you at ten in the a.m."

L ike a patient given a new lease on life, Selena walked into the dining room. Already the peach cobbler was coming out of the kitchen and the table conversations hummed like a comfortable family reunion. Maggie Hardy waved Selena over, patted the seat next to her and brought the ham platter closer. "I've been saving this place for you. I called that widow in Miami about the chalet like I promised. She'll rent it to you, if you're willing to clean it up. Been closed three years, you know."

Gratefully, pulse humming with silent elation, Selena sat down, listening to the details as Maggie drew bowls of squash and candied yams toward her plate. They were alone at one end of the long table.

"How wonderful, Maggie, thank you. It's exactly what I hoped for. I'll love cleaning it up. Because I just learned I may have the job at Capstone. Zack Kingston is going to pick me up in the morning to meet his father."

Maggie beamed like a doting aunt. "I'm so glad. Sudie up there is worried about that man. He came home looking like his old self but he's not doing so good. You know how a sick man can be, grouchy. He ran away his last nurse."

"But not me." It felt good to smile, to look around, to have purpose.

"He'd be an old fool if he did and Kingston has never been accused of that. He's an important man, you know. I mean besides owning most of this ridge. And he's up here to get well."

Maggie finished the last bite of her cobbler. They had the table to themselves by now. "Since you're going to be staying around, it's time you got to know the people here. Especially some you're going to be dealing with." She nodded to a table across the room. "See those two fellows getting up over there? The one in the sweater who looks like a college boy? He's from Florida. And the older one with the gray beard? He's a professor, a social anthropologist from Chapel Hill. They're both here planning on seeing Kingston. For an interview or something. And from what Sudie tells me, that daughter of his isn't letting anyone come calling on her daddy."

At Selena's nod, "Now, don't think I'm a busy-body like Ethel Pickett. I'm a people-watcher and I always know what's going on, not that I'd tell what I know to just anybody."

In her dormered room upstairs, impatient for Saturday morning and unable to sleep, Selena sat in the window seat, open to the cool shadowy night, remembering the dining room conversation. Without saying so, Maggie had been suggesting she look beyond her own private problems to know the people here she'd be dealing with.

Ethel Pickett. A warning had been there under Maggie's funny descriptions of her neighbor from Country Sundries. Ethel was the skinny woman with the frizzy red hair who sat behind the cash register, watching her portable TV without missing anything going on outside. "Now husband Ray is a real sweet man, even if he is the most solemn fellow you'll ever find. But Ethel is an old gossip. Don't let her imagination bother you. Why she already thinks she's seen your picture in a tabloid of all things. Ethel watches too many talk shows and soap operas."

Then, the two men who wanted to see Kingston.

"That's David Tyler coming over now," Maggie said, turning a bright face at his approach. "He's going to rent one of Caleb Potts' old cabins. That boy's here alone but he's not single. Says his wife's in Europe for the summer—why David, there you are. Found yourself a place? You know Selena Hart here?"

Lanky David Tyler looked down, a smile playing behind the brown eyes, "Our hiker here? I wave but she doesn't wave back."

"I thought you were some kid who had escaped in the family van. You look that happy when you pass," Selena replied.

"You're about right. I'm escaping school for the entire wonderful summer." With a mock groan, "I'm a high school English lit teacher back in Jacksonville. Sarah, my wife, is off doing Europe, first class, with her very rich mother. With my blessings."

The smile broke free, an impish grin. "I'm here to hole up in a cabin and get down to work, find out what kind of a writer I am, besides a reporter. First, I have to turn out a story on Alexander

Kingston, then—it's me and the Mac and the muse. We'll see." He rocked there like a restless runner, waiting to spring.

"Make sure you get it right," Maggie said with feeling. "We've had too many reporters coming through here for a day and writing us up to look like fools, or cause folks to show up later, expecting some kind of tourist show."

David smiled. "Don't you worry, Maggie. I'm not into ghost tales. I string for the *Wall Street Journal*. This Kingston story is for a legitimate environmental journal on the man's promise he'll never develop his thousand-plus acres of mountain and old growth forests. He's wealthy of course. Doesn't need to sell. But since when has that fact stopped a corporate type from going after a few more millions? I've done some homework, but have to talk to the man to write the story. So does the Professor." He told Selena, "He's a social anthropologist from the state university at Chapel Hill."

Professor Edwin Enholm had joined them, a courtly man, fingering his pipe in the tweed pocket, obviously ready to get out to the porch. "Yes, here for the summer."

Selena recognized melancholy behind the man's Abraham Lincoln cheekbones, the dark rimmed glasses and neatly clipped beard. A bachelor in his late fifties, or early sixties, she guessed, the dedicated academician. She liked his serious but mellow voice, speaking briefly of his work, ". . . because the past shapes the present. . . ."

"For a place or a person," she replied, winning his solemn nod.

"This summer colony is an anachronism, as you must know," Enholm said. "It presents a rare opportunity for the study I wish to do, regarding outsiders settling in an area long exclusive to natives. Those who have relocated here in this county came in before these southern highlands began to be actively marketed to outsiders as the good life—in their terms, perfect golf fairways and resort amenities and privacy from behind landscaped entrances, all this in a perfect mountain setting."

"Our summer people aren't the resorty types," Maggie told them, obviously proud of that fact. "They've had houses hidden around in these woods for umpteen years. They call High Haven the 'village' and claim it as their own, even if they drive aways to the PO, or lots further to Boone or Asheville if they want a city. We've got some old hippies around, from everywhere, mostly they're potters and crafters and artists now. They came to get away from any city."

The two men had moved on, the dining room almost empty, the kitchen girls scurrying around, when Selena and Maggie got up to leave.

"That couple over in the corner," Selena asked. "Why are they here?" The sandy haired, ruddy faced man bringing metal crutches from the corner back to the table now. Always so distracted, yet solicious to his wife, a bone thin girl, her pale face looking sullen from out of the limp dark hair.

"She hates the leg brace she's hiding under her long skirts," Selena told Maggie. "That girl is so unhappy, I wish I could speak with her, help her." *It's coming back, the desire to work with someone else's pain,* she realized. It helped to sublimate her own.

"That's Mitch Mason from Atlanta," Maggie told her. "His wife there, name's Lucie, poor little thing, was in a car accident a year ago and just won't get well. He hopes she'll do better being up here. He's bought some throws from me and he's been rewiring the stone cottage up there behind Capstone on Eve's Mountain. It was a guest cottage but the Kingstons had it shut up for years. Well! That means this Mason fellow got to Mister Kingston when nobody else has. Sudie didn't know about it. Zack didn't mention those folks when he came in other day to see me."

Back in the lobby, as they were saying goodnight, they watched a new arrival, a trim young woman with copper colored hair, smartly suited as if expecting a Hyatt-Regency. She strode in on clicking heels and with a weary look tapped the brass bell on Dilly's front desk.

"Just between you and me," Maggie had murmured, "there's someone who didn't come to rock on Dilly's front porch. Well, we'll find out, we always do. My, I sound as suspicious as Ethel Pickett Good night, Selena, and good luck up at Capstone in the morning."

9

Saturday dawned blustery and cool. In her room, Selena looked over the meager contents of her closet: the light wool slacks and sweaters and suede jacket packed in haste before her flight. Good clothes, but now well worn, loose on her hips from these weeks of relentless walking. The bureau mirror showed her someone else than the Selena Hart-Hempton of beige silk suits and shining chignon. A relief, at that. But she needed things, boots for one. Even make-up. She'd brought along a single pale lipstick in her purse. It didn't matter. Being away from Denver mattered. Having a job here mattered.

Zack Kingston was due at ten. An hour and half to wait. In the dining room, she sat next to the bald headed fellow known as Colonel. He liked to talk and only required a listener, not someone else's story.

"Morning Selena," he greeted her over his plate, still steaming with grits, sausage, scrambled eggs and hot biscuits. "We've got another pretty lady in here now, our newcomer over there. Came in last night. Pretty as that actress, what's her name, Ann-Margret."

The newcomer with the copper colored hair was wearing designer jeans and shirt this morning, flashing her smile in answer to older guests from up and down her table. You're being friendly, Selena thought, but you're here with secrets too, for whatever reason.

At their elbow, with a pot of coffee, the kitchen girl Sally told them, "Her name's Paula Crossing. All the way from California. She came in wanting to know if the Kingstons are still around. Well, of course. Mister Dilworth gets real huffy when folks think the Ridgeway is just a place to answer questions about those people up at Capstone."

Minutes before ten, waiting alone on the windy porch, Selena rocked with fingers tightly laced. Zack Kingston could have been here by now. Had the sister interfered? A BMW rolled up, stopped in front. Getting out now was a tailored, compact man of about forty-five. His dark glasses reflected back from a slim, olive skinned face. Zack? No. She watched, warily, a habit now, checking out strangers who might be someone sent by Drew. Why this fear? *Don't think about it.*

The man standing by the BMW looked up at the white banistered verandah with annoyance, as though he'd stepped off an elevator expecting a suite of offices and, instead, found himself in a 1930 time warp. He walked briskly up the steps, crossed the empty porch and claimed the chair next to hers with only a glance her way.

Pulling out a flat silver cigarette holder, he lit one and exhaled with obvious impatience, muttering about mountain roads. "They can give it all back to the Hatfields and McCoys. Or should it be Indians?"

His voice was precise and curt. "Why would anyone come to a place like this when there are resorts, ships, cities? What do they expect to find here?"

"Peace, maybe."

"Piece of the action, that I could understand. Not here, however. I don't see this place as a prospect. I left the main highway one hour ago." He studied her for the first time. "What, may I ask, brought you here?"

"I came for a walk." She leaned back, satisfied this man was no detective. He was an arrogant male, a professional out of his element who would probably have his first heart attack on some racquet court in a year or so.

A second sports car swung in alongside the BMW. A silver Porsche this time. Sliding out was a small-boned young woman in brown leather pants and pale yellow sweater. Large sunglasses almost hid her perky, confident face, framed by close cropped brown hair. With a sassy grin she called up to the man on the porch. "Harkin Johns, I finally lured you to the mountains."

"First and last time," he said. Leaning over the banister, he flicked his cigarette into the pink impatiens below. "Victoria, love, if we're going to meet like this again, let's make it Gstaad next time. Mountains with class."

So this was Tory Kingston, the daughter from Capstone. Tory waited by her car, coral lips in a tight little smile as Harkin Johns sauntered toward her, sliding his arm around her waist, face close to her ear. Selena saw the girl stiffen, pull back, the coral smile set, with thinly veiled annoyance.

"And if you're as good an attorney as I think you are—but lunch first. An hour from here, I can show you a clubroom with pandering waiters and a view of civilized fairways. Then, back to Capstone to see the man."

Harkin Johns glanced around in a wary perusal of the spring morning. "I am not fond of your mountains, Victoria, but okay, if you'll drive these damn roads."

Selena watched them wheel away in the Porsche. So, the daughter did not know about any conference with her father this morning. Or had she stopped it? Eyes closed, Selena rocked and waited in limbo.

At the crunch of gravel below, she looked up to see a dusty Range Rover whip to a quick stop. A man jumped out, waving both arms. His thick unruly hair looked chestnut in the sun. He might have been a Kingston's grounds keeper in his faded plaid shirt and jeans. With kinetic energy, Zack Kingston bounded up the porch steps and toward her, expressing exuberant remorse for being late. She guessed he had waited until his sister was out of the house.

Yes, she was ready. She let him play gallant, hand cupped under her elbow, and a running monologue of funny excuses, leading her to the car. He stopped short to glower at the BMW. "Did you see the character driving that puppy? Never mind. Let's go. Ready to enter the lion's den?"

"*Lion's den?*" Selena Hart asked as they started off.

"That's the image I had of my father when I was a kid—larger than life, appearing lovable but growling often. Well, up the hill to Capstone we go."

Zack Kingston settled Selena Hart in the Rover, thinking, *Pretty woman, looks intelligent, self-contained. That's fine.* Not his type but what he needed now for A. Z. On the phone, Doc Bradley had said as much, concern in his voice, "Zack, she will know what your daddy needs, but it's up to you to put her on the case or not."

Zack handed over his father's medical records from the Charlotte doctors. He drove slowly out the Ridgeway driveway, turned up the private road that led to Capstone, keeping his mouth shut. Glancing at Selena Hart's clean profile studying the folder, he asked, "So what can you tell me? It was a mild stroke, right?"

She looked up from the papers. "Yes. A blood clot in the anterior cerebral artery, the center of the brain which causes damage to a small area on the right side of the brain. He had a semi-paralyzed left arm at the beginning. Re-hab at the hospital has helped that, but he needs continued physiotherapy."

He took the curves slowly, listening to her warm positive voice answer his questions and asking his own. "Don't worry about the spastic leg," she said. "That's a plus, promising recovery. Given his previous good health, I'd say with proper therapy and positive attitude on his part, it's possible your father could be back to normal or near normal, in say, three months. Right now, he must be having some dizziness and confusion."

"Confusion is right," Zack said grimly.

"The medication schedule here looks right. He needs to continue this of course. But stroke patients also require a great deal of family patience and attention."

"Ah, patience. We could all use some patience. New experience for A. Z." He hoped fervently this meeting would work out. Besides knowing her business, this Selena Hart was pretty enough to please, and calm enough to handle the man, if A. Z. wasn't in one of his exasperated moods this morning.

Selena closed the folder. "I saw your sister Tory a few minutes ago. She was taking a guest somewhere for lunch."

"Yeah. Harkin Johns, from the law firm that once represented Kingston Carpets." Zack bit down on the urge to say more. What in the devil was Johns doing here? His father didn't use the firm anymore. "Harkin is not my favorite individual, though I gather he's a guest for the night."

"Your sister didn't seem to know about my visit this morning."

Zack drove in past the high stand of sentinel firs that made the entrance. "Don't worry about it, Selena. My sister likes to run things her way. I'll deal with her later. What's important is for my father to have the right care and a clear head. We need a good nurse. She has to agree to that."

He led her upstairs, glad she wasn't a chatterer, but attentive enough to murmur her appreciation of the house. They walked in to find his father slumped in his wing chair by the window. "Here she is, A. Z. Meet Selena Hart. Doc Bradley says she's a good therapist, knows her business."

He watched his father wanting to stand, angry because he couldn't, watched Selena Hart quickly pull a chair close before extending her hand, facing him like an admiring guest. "I am most pleased to meet Alexander Kingston."

Standing back, Zack thought, *Now that was the warmest, most comforting voice I've ever heard,* an inspired nurse's voice, not the reserved woman he had picked up at the Inn.

"Leave us, Zack. I haven't entertained a young lady alone for awhile," his father said finally. Zack walked out, hoping Selena Hart could handle this.

Selena looked around the room, then back at this big shaggy haired man, unaccustomed to being the invalid but once a power behind polished conference tables—and probably in bed with women. Both until recently, she guessed. Illness was rough on a man like this. What he had thought was an indestructible body had now turned enemy. She waited, letting him study her with troubled dark eyes looking out from under heavy gray brows. The thick silvery hair spilled over his solid forehead but didn't hide the deep frown. He was embarrassed to be a patient in front of her.

"What a beautiful room," she said softly. "What an excellent place to become well again." And it was. A spacious, oak-paneled, richly carpeted, handsome, masculine suite. The wide expanse of window wall and balcony provided a cat bird's view of wooded slopes and panorama of distant blue mountain ranges.

"So you're a nurse? Real one? I fired the last. . . . You look a hell of a lot better . . . but hand it to me straight . . . don't spoon it out . . . what can you do for me?"

"Just how willing are you to work?" Color rose in his face, but she kept her voice unhurried. "It will require working together. Also patience and trust on your part in what we have to do. I can imagine you've handled challenges before. This one is much more personal. Agreed?"

She held out her hand and hid her relief when he grabbed and held it, searching her face. This man needed her as much as she needed this case. "A pact," she said. "Now, you can tell me exactly how that body is working. For example, the spasm in the left leg? Painful probably. But actually, Mr. Kingston, that is an encouraging sign of recovery."

He looked gratified, his gaze hinting of tears. "Call me Alexander, no, Alex. My first wife—a long time ago—called me Alex."

Twenty minutes later, Kingston leaned back, looking pensive. "If this was last year, Selena Hart . . . we could have flown to Spain or any fool place . . . to talk about it there." As if the energy for satire exhausted him, as if he feared he might actually cry, he covered his face with his right hand, the left in his lap.

"But this is now, isn't it?" she told him gently. "If you're willing to give one hundred percent, I am too. I have worked in a rehab center before. But right now I want only to stay here in High Haven. I'm renting a place very close." She breathed with silent relief.

Not sure how the meeting would go, but hoping, Zack had left Selena Hart with his father to wait downstairs in the kitchen, talking with Sudie Gurney. "You'll like this one, Sudie. Don't worry. We'll get him going again."

Sudie's long honest face showed her worry. "I sure pray so, Zack. I thank the Lord you came home to see about him."

When Zack walked back into his father's room, he saw what he'd hoped for. His father had color in his face, pride in his voice. "Get this woman back here by Monday. To hell with medicine." Selena's blue gray eyes glistened with her own satisfaction.

Zack got them out as quickly as possible. He wanted to be gone before Tory and Harkin Johns showed up. Once out of the room, "Let's talk in the car."

Back in the Range Rover, he looked at her with relief, guessed at her own silent pleasure. "I see you made a total conquest." He started the car. "I'm sure you noticed the man likes women, even when they're explaining therapy and asking about bodily functions. I had better warn you, Kingston, the Senior, still considers himself a lover. He's probably already in love with you. Are you going to be able to deal with that?"

"Don't worry." She smiled. "A man either hates his nurse or romances her, by way of maintaining his male dignity. We'll do fine."

Zack felt comfortable with her. "Now Kingston, the Junior here, has put the lover role on hold for the present." Good God, he thought, chagrined. Did that come across as an egotistical pitch, letting her know I'm not available?

But she was saying, "I know what you mean. There are times when one must be available for oneself only." She looked away as they followed the drive out of the grounds.

As they reached the Inn, he thought to ask, "Interested in a ride down the hill to do some shopping? I have to pick up a tire down on the highway. There's a bunch of new cheapo stores but they're the closest ones around."

"Oh, yes, I would. I need walking shoes. And jeans."

"A hiker, huh? Know about our mountain weather yet? These woods can be a rain forest at times." He glanced at her profile: nice bone structure, fine grain skin, no makeup, light blue-gray eyes, a pensive look about her. Her hands in her lap were capable nurse hands with blunt, unpainted nails. No Lisa of the perky voice and spiky red feline nails. And no Pat of Benny's Bar, with the chewed fingernails and big boobs. He should have known better than to go back to see Pat.

"I'm learning. About your mountains."

Zack shook Pat out of his head. "I've climbed around here since I was a kid. In town, I run. The preference is to fly. Maybe you've heard the Bird." They were rolling along Crest Road now, both of them waving at Maggie Hardy and Ethel Pickett, sitting in front of their shops under the wooden overhang. "Watch out for Ethel, she's a gossip. But Maggie is a fine old gal."

"I know."

"Level with me, Selena. What's my father's condition? He perked up with you just now but since I've been here, he seems more out of it than the medical jargon from Charlotte indicates."

"I'm sure you know he's angry at the helplessness. He needs a great deal of emotional support. It's imperative he gets daily therapy to extend the range of motion. He spends too much time in bed, I gather. Weakened muscles can atrophy." She explained a daily regime of active and passive exercise.

"I'll need his cooperation—and your sister's. I understand she's administering all the meds since the other nurse left. Does Tory keep a careful record of the schedule for each drug—time and dose, and his blood pressure? For example, he's taking a blood thinner which is necessary but dangerous if given too much. The nurse on duty should be keeping that record."

"We'll deliver that news to Tory later." He didn't want to worry about that now. "You'd think she should be glad to be relieved of the responsibility."

"I can handle his meds and therapy and questions, but a stroke patient needs family support. You must expect him to be impulsive with a short attention span at first. He doesn't need distractions."

Zack blurted out, "Something else I'm worried about."

"Tell me."

"Afternoons when I go in, he seems his old stubborn self. But late at night if I check in, he can sound bonkers. I believe he's been waking up at dawn—with some kind of hallucinations."

Selena nodded. "Medication plus emotional trauma can be causing that. I'll have to work with him to know. Just remember he needs patience."

"The Kingstons aren't a patient lot. He gets more attention than he wants from Tory."

They rode in silence for a time as if studying the kudzu beginning to cover trees on one side of the road. Finally Selena said, "About your sister Tory—if she's such a strong factor in the household, will she override your decision to bring me in?"

Zack didn't hide his groan. "Is that a polite way of saying Tory is the one with balls—I mean clout?"

"I'm sorry. It's just that I need to know if I have family approval for the case. I don't want to start, then be hampered or asked to leave."

"Don't worry, Lady Selena. I will handle little sister Tory." He got his sense of humor going again. "Maybe I make her a problem by the fact I do ignore her as often as possible. That does make a woman angry, doesn't it?"

She studied him. "You don't seem to be the type of man who resents a strong women."

A straight question. He didn't detect any barbs in the voice. "Lordy, ma'am, I like 'em all. I am my father's son. Strong women may be the most useful creatures on earth. I believe it. Honest. Strong ones, I mean, who don't need to attack like a

73

she-devil to make a point. But that sounds like I bleed secretly, doesn't it?"

He was talking himself into a trap with this quiet woman. He tried to redeem himself. "I can relax and enjoy a strong, unbitchy woman. They know how to be a friend." Did that sound condescending, a put-down? She was studying him with a faint smile.

He tried for pure confessional honesty. "Let's just say, I manage to get myself entangled, involved, or married to women other than the calmly capable ones." Like you, he thought. Now he really wished he'd kept his mouth shut. He'd probably have to hear her professional analysis of him or her own story of some unfeeling husband she'd left behind. No? Selena looked away, at passing valleys, apparently lost in whatever her own story was. Thankfully, she didn't intend to explain it to him.

Cheered immensely by that, Zack said, "Okay! Monday you start. This Harkin Johns will be gone. I will have talked with Tory. She has to realize A. Z. needs therapy and even with all her smarts she can't do that. Besides it would free her up. Tory likes to take off for Asheville most Mondays."

He stayed on safer grounds. "Monday I'll give you a grand tour of the house. You'll meet the Gurney sisters. That pair turns out better country fixings than Dilly's crew in the dining room. Only trouble, no one stays around in the house to eat it. So they'll love you being there. You can come up after Jeb Gurney gets him bathed and dressed, then stay and have lunch with him in his room. Stay for supper whenever you like, though we won't be demanding all of your time. I'm glad you'll be close, though. Tory didn't want a live-in nurse." He glanced over, saw her brown lashes close down on some strong feeling. She must have really wanted this job.

They were on the highway now, the new lineup of stores just ahead. Zack pulled in to the expanse of parking lot fronting a supermarket, discount department store and a string of little shops, all backed up to a gouged out red bank of earth. "For this, we lose a mountainside."

"But they must sell shoes. Where do we meet?"

"The drug store, in an hour. On the way home I'll give you the saga of Eve's Mountain so you can check it out with other versions, okay?" He stopped the car, sensing suddenly this woman must be short of money.

"First, I might as well pay you a week in advance, to show how happy I am you're going to be with A. Z." He thrust the previously agreed amount in her hand. Her quiet thanks sounded like well disguised relief.

Zack watched Selena Hart walk toward the shops before he drove on to the garage. He was pleased with the morning. Surely he could handle Tory. He could tell this Selena had her secrets but he thought, *Who isn't running away from something?*

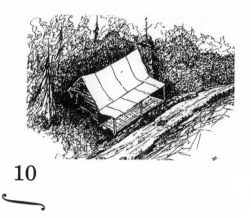

10

Sunday morning Selena stood on the Inn's front porch, studying the threatening sky. She should be relieved today, willing
to wait for tomorrow and Capstone, not restless as the wind
blown clouds. She needed to walk, regardless. Zipping up the new
plastic jacket, she started down the rhododendron lined drive as
Maggie Hardy came trudging up.

"I came for breakfast," Maggie greeted her. "You out already?
I wanted to tell you to come by the shop next week when you get
to cleaning the chalet. You'll need brooms and mouse traps. I have
plenty. Oh, you're real welcome."

Selena had the urge to hug the woman's solid shoulders but
instead stood nodding to Maggie's admonitions. "Don't go hiking
up to the chalet on a day like this with the clouds so full of rain
and wind. You ever tried the old logging road along Ruby creek?
That's awful pretty and closer."

"Thanks, Maggie. That's what I'll do."

Further down Crest Road, Selena turned into the wooded path
that followed the creek and divided Ruby hollow and the steepest
Kingston slopes. The fast-running stream, almost hidden by oaks
and maples, opened occasionally to a patchwork of meadows, like
postcard scenes of rural tranquility, complete with old, weathered
barns—vine covered pieces of the past. The reality of the present

showed too, with a trailer home here and there, plastic tricycles out front, a rusting car buried in high grass.

On this overcast morning the creek flowed with a melancholy rhythm. Or was she listening to her own pulse? Why this feeling of threat, from outside or within herself? Proof of her own advice to other women: *Running away from a problem is a postponement not a solution. You hide with your own anguish.* She walked on but stopped again to study the old house on the other side of the creek bank.

Flat stones led across the stream to the house. The tin roof sagged over what seemed a back porch facing the creek. It was surrounded by a thicket of trees. The old place might have been an artist's subject, painted in dark green oils. It must be the one Caleb Potts warned her about. "If you're poking about closed-up places on your walks, Miss, don't you go nosing around that old house on the creek. It ain't closed. Spooky old woman lives there. Addie McRae. Doesn't take to company. Killed a man once in that house. Now Ariel, her wild hellion of a daughter, that Ariel gets around, yessirree bob. You don't want to meet up with Hoke McRae either. Claims to be a logger, but probably grows mara-wanna when he's not eating off the county in the Mica jail."

Selena walked on, smiling at the memory of her encounter with Ariel bursting into Bradley's office for birth control pills. She'd found Ariel to be an intelligent and spirited wild fawn of a girl, with remarkable clear green eyes. Quick on defense but candid, Ariel had declared, "Sure, I'm careful. I got some of those things when I was going with this old boy who's a trucker. But I'm no dummy. I have plans for myself. What are you doing in this old place, somebody like you? I'm outa here soon as I get some contacts, let me tell you. You know anybody in the music business in Nashville?"

Thinking of Ariel and trying to ignore the cheap new shoes rubbing at her heels, Selena walked faster, head down to the mountain wind. She stopped abruptly, disappointed to discover she had run out of woods. The dirt path ended at the edge of the gray ribbon of county highway, a silent strip of rural road caught in Sunday morning inertia. Damp wind rattled signs on the closed-up gas station. On a slight hill above the road, a dozen cars flanked the small white church. Its steeple rose against dark scudding clouds.

Rain started with a soft patter then a roar. As quickly, the new plastic jacket clung wet and cold against her shoulders. The cheap shoes hurt. Now came torrents of rain, and anger at herself for believing she could be safe here from what churned now inside. Across the road, hymn singing drifted from the church. The sound stirred ambivalent feelings from childhood but she ran across the road up the gravel drive. Even a hard pew out of the rain would be welcomed.

Unzipping the limp jacket, Selena walked into the open door and sat down on the back bench, occupied only by a heavy overalled man. A mistake, she realized five minutes later.

The piano player ended with a flourish. Heads swiveled, scrutinizing her arrival, before slowly turning back to what was happening on the low front platform. A young man paced up there, shoulders lost in the black suit, tie loosened at his Adam's apple, his bouncy announcements of the morning sliding now into a rhythm, a cadence, mournful in its low tones, exuberant as his voice rose.

". . . because we know, ohh, yes . . . we know . . . there's no place to hide from the eyes of the Lord. Oh, yes!"

No, don't tell me that. She sat rigid, chilled with outrage, with pain. To her right, the huge man slumped in sleep, snoring softly. Rustling in to her left now was a young woman in a flowered dress, balancing a baby on one arm, the other hand pushing forward a boy about five who crawled onto the bench and stared up at Selena.

". . . no escape from the sins in our hearts!"

The wooden bench shook with the boy's short legs thumping, thumping to the preacher's rhythm. The mother's hand touched the child and he stilled and leaned his head against the girl's shoulder looking up at Selena with a shy smile.

78

Don't look at him, Selena told herself. But the chubby legs, the scuffed brown shoes drew her gaze, held her. *Don't think of Roby.* But she saw the stick thin legs of her own child, whose nervous system had been so wired he could never be still, trapped in a feverishly kinetic body.

Sobs rent the preacher's relentless cadence. "Not one of us, no one of us is *worthy* of His forgiveness. Yet if we come . . ."

No, you're teaching guilt. You make healing impossible. She sat rigid between the sleeping man and the wiggling child. Beyond a window, a tree bent to the lashing wind.

The preacher's exhortations went on with relentless cadence. "Ohh, yes, no place to hide from His Eyes. Go to the ends of the earth—or wrap yourself in goods of this world—ohh, yes—you won't escape until you confess the sins of the heart."

Panic stirred. The scream, held down so long . . . the scream laced with self-loathing or self pity or guilt . . . stirred now like nausea. It must not happen here. She had to get out.

The young mother leaned over, whispering, "Kindly hold my boy and don't let him follow? I got a leaky diaper here and that bathroom's no bigger'n a minute." She struggled up with the baby and left the boy.

Selena looked into the child's inquisitive eyes, the firm full cheeks, a pink wet curve of mouth, grinning at her now. A normal child, curious, open, willing to be held. She and Drew had made a child, sperm and egg, but without love. Their fault. No, her own body's fault. She had not been able to do what this bland-faced girl had done so naturally, this girl who had produced two healthy babies who would grow as young creatures should once they had emerged from a mother's body.

The preacher's voice trembled. "Later, there will be only wailing and gnashing of teeth for the sinner who hasn't repented. Let the burdened heart cry out now! Before sin keeps you in its grasp. . . ."

The scream rose to her chest, held by her tight throat. She settled the boy on the seat and stood, fighting for control to get out of there. Faces turned. The preacher watched her, his hands uplifted, waiting. The piano began. Bodies shuffled to stand. They began singing, *"Just as I am, without one plea . . . Oh Lamb of God I come, I come . . ."* The young mother plopped back in her seat, baby in her lap. Selena stumbled past them and toward the open door, feeling their eyes on her back. She ran outside into the pounding sheath of rain and down the gravel path, and across the empty highway.

Once in the woods again, Selena ran blindly ahead on the rough path, propelled by the churning revulsion, the scream, rising like a wildness in her throat, in her pulse. At the creek bank, she threw herself on wet grass as the scream broke free, a high, animal cry, searing her throat. Finally, she pushed herself up, sobbing confessions, not to the preacher's idea of a vindictive God, but to her child. *I'm sorry, Roby. Forgive me Roby. I meant to save you but I failed you.*

Hugging her knees, she rocked there on the creek bank, hair matted with rain, jacket soaked. The nightmarish dawn that had been too painful to remember surfaced now with all its questions.

She had awakened, feeling drugged, surprised to find herself still in slacks and sweater. Why? The night before as he left for the hospital, Drew had handed her a Valium. Had the usual five milligrams done this? Never before. Somewhere in the house, the sound of muffled voices. Standing in the doorway was Drew, a man who was always in control of a situation and angry when he wasn't. Now something was out of control. She could see that even in the shadowy room with her body and eyelids so heavy. Behind Drew stood a young man in the white fatigues of an emergency crew. Her first panicky thought: if they wake Roby, he will scream.

But Drew was telling her Roby was not in his room and the terrace door was open. He was saying she had failed to lock it last night.

"Ma'am, we looked all over the house before we woke you," the other man said.

The waking nightmare had just started. She walked past them. Yes, the doors were open to the terrace. Men were out there

80

with sweeping flashlights, the sun only beginning to outline the Rockies. Someone below the wall shouted, "Here." At the wall, her fingernails dug into the stone. Down there on flat rocks below, a man crouched over Roby.

That's when the scream began to rise from the depths of her body. But had stopped. Why? Drew's hand snapping down on her arm like a vise, demanding that she control herself. Telling her to go inside and let him handle this. The aborted scream stayed in her body and became guilt, accepted guilt without reasoning the extent or shape of it. She had known only one true thing, *Roby is dead . . . somehow it's because of me.*

On the wet creek bank, trees shuddering overhead and spilling rain, Selena sat stilled and emptied, open to knowing the truth.

Yes, she *had* gotten Roby to bed the night before, had given him Bear, the only thing he loved. Had checked the doors as always. Especially the terrace. *Yes, all locked before I fell into bed myself.*

What was her guilt? She knew now it was as simple and tragic as this: she had stayed too long in that house. She should have taken Roby and left the practice, the sham of a marriage and the house at least three years earlier. But she had allowed herself to be trapped by Drew's threats. Had told herself she was protecting Roby to keep him there, with paid caretakers and her own care at night. She had slept in a room next to his, kept him away from the rest of the expansive, open house with its sterile perfection. *Some regrettable damage will happen to the house or the boy if you insist on keeping him here.* Yes, Drew had said that more than once.

And it had. He must have allowed it to happen. But not to kill his child, surely. No, she couldn't believe that. What he had done was to give her a stronger sedation, leave for the hospital that night, then return before dawn to open the locked terrace doors near Roby's room. Then what? Did he go into his study and take a belt of Scotch? Must have. She had smelled that on his breath when he faced her that terrible dawn, ashen faced, accusing her. She had believed him because actual shock showed in his face as well as the accusation.

The rest of it emerged with a chilling awareness. By now, Drew should know she realized what happened. If the investigation was continuing in Denver, if they came to him with further questions, he would actually accuse her. Had to, to protect what meant most to him: his image, his fame. Already he had implied her guilt to those men and the woman investigator.

She knew now what she had instinctively known when she ran away. Drew must not find her. She was in danger from him.

The rain had ceased, like her own inner tumult, the trees continuing their sad, dripping sounds. She rocked here on the creek bank.

On the wet path now, soft footsteps. Slim legs and sandaled feet stood near. The girl stooped down, smiling in her face. "Hi. You been walking in all that rain? Well I'm glad to see you don't always look so calm and collected like at Doc's office."

Selena got to her feet unsteadily. The glinting wet trees, the rushing stream took on a magic unreality. She managed to say, "Ariel."

"That's our house over there. I'll fix you some of Mama's special herb tea. You look like you need it."

Shivering in the wet jacket, Selena felt like someone who had been ill for months, freed of the toxins but not out of danger. This woods sprite named Ariel was repeating her invitation.

Her own voice sounded strange. "Your mother—I thought she didn't like company."

"She doesn't. But you're a nurse and Mama needs looking after now and then. You couldn't get her into Doc's clinic on your life. If I take you in now, she might like you and let you come back sometime. Follow me across, it's easy."

Light headed, Selena obeyed, her steps unsteady across the stones. For the moment she could only be grateful for hot tea with this spirited mountain girl and her mother.

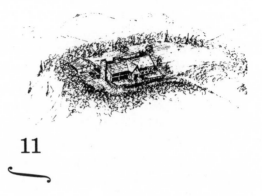

11

From the window wall in her father's room, Tory Kingston watched Caleb Potts climb out of a polished old Buick and swagger toward the house, his Stetson hat bobbing. The old guy was showing up as requested, on the dot of five. Fine. Everything was going as planned. Zack was still out, thankfully. And for the past hour, Harkin Johns had cooled his hyper manner down to the mode of caring attorney, skillfully convincing her father the papers they presented would relieve him of concern about needed repairs.

Now to let Potts witness the A. Z. Kingston signature. Once the document was signed before the old notary, she would hustle Potts out. Only one more problem remained for the immediate present. She had to endure the rest of the evening with Harkin Johns and keep his arrogant hands off her body. Thankfully, he had to leave early the next morning.

"Here's Potts now," she said cheerily.

"Potts? What's he doing here?" Kingston sat dressed in slacks and sweater, slumped in his chair by the window wall, distress carved in his heavy face.

"I told you he was coming, remember?" Tory ignored her father's frown. She faced Harkin's faint smile with a false one of her own.

Damn your soul. "Potts is the only notary around and he gets a charge out of thinking he's one of Father's friends."

"Tory, Tory." Kingston rubbed his face. "I'm tired of hearing about water line problems. Both of you get out. I don't sign anything without a clear head."

"I have a clear head for you. Precisely why I need to have the power of attorney to do what has to be done here. We have gone over this. You've agreed you don't want to be bothered with the details." She said it carefully, and brightly, as if any doubt had been settled. "Now, you two talk carpet business and old cronies, while I run down and collect the fellow."

She hurried downstairs, remembering another annoyance. Zack had brought some woman therapist up here this morning. When she and Harkin Johns returned from lunch, she'd found A. Z. positively happy about this Selena Hart. "Without talking to me—you hired a nurse?" she had demanded. "But you have Jeb."

"Sure. Need the boy mornings. But Selena is just what I need." Under the shaggy brows, the brown eyes showed their old Kingston gleam. *Control*, she reminded herself. Right now there were the papers to sign. The capsule to get him to take. She had thrust it toward him and in his good mood, he swallowed it down without complaint. She'd make no issue of the nurse now. Later.

Welcome smile in place, Tory opened the front door. Caleb Potts rocked on his boot heels, Stetson pushed back from the bald dome. "Howdy, Miss Victoria, I was glad to hear from you. Been wanting to see that daddy of yours." He tromped behind her upstairs, head swiveling, admiring everything in a cigar-roughened voice. Tory smiled. The self-important old geezer was thrilled with this call on his services.

Potts marched into the room, placed the Stetson on the smooth spread of the four-poster and ambled over to the two men waiting by the window. "Well sir, A. Z." He blinked at Harkin, the stranger, before easing into the chair facing the two men. "Don't tell me Alexander Kingston's going to sell this land. I'd be happy to represent any parcels, look after you real good."

84

Kingston seemed to rise from the chair but sank back, breathing hard. "Where the devil did you get that idea, Potts?"

"My father," Tory interrupted, sweetly firm, "has decided to let me assume some of the responsibility of keeping up this property. Old Mr. Hogan has not kept it up. I had to let him go. Our attorney here, Mr. Harkin Johns of Charlotte, has prepared the papers so I can go ahead with necessary improvements. The entire drive needs resurfacing. The water system promises extensive problems. We wanted your signature as witness to our family arrangement. You go ahead. I'll get the Bailey's Irish Cream for a little toast." Across the room, her hands shook pouring the liqueur.

Thirty minutes later, in the downstairs hall, Tory pressed the bottle of Bailey's into Potts' hands. "That was a quick visit, I know, but he does like to nap before dinner. So . . ." She smiled a dismissal until Potts tipped his Stetson and headed toward his car, bottle under his arm.

Tory stood a moment, biting her lip, listening to Potts leave, and hoping to hear Zack drive in. He'd want to know what Harkin was doing here and that would lead to another argument. But a necessary distraction. At the kitchen door, she looked in on Sudie Gurney, moving a sweet smelling ham from the oven to the marble counter. Did they expect Zack for dinner? Sudie reckoned she didn't know. "He lit out after bringing that nurse in to visit."

"Hold dinner an hour. He might show up." A couple of drinks on the back terrace might keep Harkin entertained until dinner and she'd make sure he had brandy after. He must be fifty now. He was surely a heavy drinker. With enough under his belt, and with any debate from Zack, he should be willing to go to his room early and be gone after breakfast. She went back upstairs to finish pacifying her father and cajoling him back to bed.

Later, as she and Harkin descended the stairs, Tory said, "You'll want to settle in before dinner. Then how about a drink on the back terrace?" He followed behind her, silent, as she said, airily, "I have two mountain women in the kitchen preparing a dinner you won't forget. They've readied one of the ground floor guest rooms. If you can take rosebud sheets." She was talking evasive nonsense now, hoping for the sound of Zack's Range Rover in the drive.

At the foot of the stairs, Harkin Johns stopped her with a steel grasp on her arm. "Rosebuds? You can do better than that, Tory Kingston."

Late sun and stained glass panels colored the foyer and darkened his face and thin mocking smile. Behind his gold rimmed glasses, slitted eyes studied her. She thought, *This must be how you look psyching out a jury, you cold son of a bitch,* but held on to the cheery hostess smile, ignoring his remark. "Bring in your bags and I'll show you your room."

"Let's start with a drink. A real one. I brought my Cutty Sark. Get some ice." He went outside to the BMW for his bag.

Ice. Not from the kitchen. She didn't want the Gurneys to hear anything Harkin might say. Shivering, she turned toward the cavernous living room with its polished stone floor, heavy Oriental rugs and massive stone hearth. The bar was a carved wood thing her father had bought from some old hotel. All those parties had been in this room, when she had been the small, ignored child, furtively, watching. Behind the bar, a seldom used portable refrigerator hummed away and yielded ice. She filled a glass, found some brandy for herself, poured a snifter full and took two fiery swallows. She heard Harkin reenter, felt him watching her from the foyer. He waited there, this shrewd little man who had just played along with her plans. "Well, hostess?"

She poured more brandy in her own glass, took another swallow and walked toward him. *You arrogant son-of-a-bitch, I'll handle you.* She was paying him his legal fees, wasn't she? Arrogance didn't turn her on. Too bad. She had not been with a man since D.C. No, she'd forgotten that sales rep she'd met in the lounge at Asheville.

God, at this moment she should be happy celebrating a successful step in her plan. Here she was miserable, having to be chatty with a man whose touch made her recoil. "Your ice," she said. *Oh hell, Zack, where are you?*

"Bring it. You were going to show me?" He smoked his cigarette in quick nervous draws.

"Your room, yes." She led the way down a hall beyond the foyer, past Zack's room. *Zack, show up, have a scene, anything.* Along this hall, more than once, she had crouched as a child, listening to sounds some woman was making behind closed doors, the woman's voice curling around her father's own, or his moan. How she'd hated them both.

The door was open. She stood just inside, waving her brandy snifter at the pleasant room that was sweet with sachet and inviting with a bowl of wild flame azalea. "You're supposed to say they don't make houses like this anymore. Dinner will be ready as soon as we finish a drink on the terrace. Six-thirty is the time around here. You're in the mountains."

"I know where I am. You asked me here, Victoria. Hospitality time."

She had walked to a window to act casual and stay beyond his grasp. Bad move. Now Harkin pushed the door shut, set his bag on a polished tabletop, got out his bottle. She'd look like a fool if she tried to run out. *I can handle you, buster.* She eased past the trim shoulders, the sleek brown, almost silver head bent to the precise task of filling the tumbler of ice with his Scotch.

He turned and caught her arm, clinked his glass to hers. She drained the last swallow of brandy, thinking, *You are like so many men in D. C.* Underneath the public armor, underneath all that male superiority, actually they were insecure creatures. In bed, demanding, but seldom satisfying.

Ignoring his hand on her arm, she watched him empty his glass. He turned to pour another, still holding her. She looked at quilted chintz on the handsome old bed, mellowed by fading light. An erotic need, ignored for weeks, flushed up her body. *But no.* She looked into Harkin's moist dark face. Too bad she despised him.

His grip loosened with the second drink. Maybe she was home free. She said lightly, "I'll leave you to this slightly faded country elegance."

Again his hand closed on her arm and held her there as he looked around. "I remember this room," he said dryly. "My wife and I stayed here. I remember you were a spoiled brat."

He sat the empty glass down and pulled her against him. She wasn't surprised that his hands on her back were like ice.

"Now you're a clever little bitch, aren't you, Victoria Kingston? Not that I blame you for whatever you're doing." The narrowed eyes behind the glasses studied her. "When I got you out of the marriage sack with that hillbilly, you were still a spoiled brat. But a cunning female—now that intrigues me."

His fingers fumbled at the back of her bra, through the sweater and gave up. "Damn it, take the thing off." He placed his glasses on the table next to his drink and cigarette tray. Without them, his eyes had a bare, vulnerable look.

She stepped away and forced a smile. "But Harkin, you just said you are not dealing with a stupid, spoiled brat this time, remember? I'm going out now to ring a dinner bell . . ."

She was backing away toward the door but he stopped her, his jacket yanked off now, the tailored shirt coming off. He drew her back from the door, and jerked her against him, his moist face nervous but threatening. She stood caught in his grasp, too angry to struggle, staring at his bare chest with distaste. To turn her on, a man had to have solid shoulders, a real chest, and he had to have electric, knowing fingers. Not these insensitive hands, not this wiry man pulling her close to his concave rib cage. "Stop it, Harkin," she hissed in his face. "I'm not your dumb brat . . ."

"Then stop acting like one. You expected and got cooperation from me. It works both ways." He yanked her sweater up, pulled it over her head and fumbled again at the lace bra.

Revulsion bubbled up as a shaky laugh. *That's not the way to go about it, you dumb jerk.* His grip was strong but it was the distracted intensity in his eyes and his labored breathing that numbed her protest. She realized why. He pressed against her but hadn't unbuckled his belt. The man was not ready. Desperate and unready.

88

Shit. The last thing she wanted, a wired-up man on her hands, frantic for a hard-on and expecting her to make it happen. All that male superiority afraid it was going to show up as inadequacy. The situation would be amusing if the vulnerable male ego didn't make it dangerous.

Tory felt herself being pushed back onto the chintz spread. Her throat tightened. Sorry-for-herself tears blurred the ceiling above her. Another part of her knew nothing but anger, as if watching this stupid scene happen to two different selves, one trapped, the other needing this, but by a real man, not this clumsy fingered bastard with his arrogant assumption of a pay-off. She heard his labored breathing as he kicked off the pants, felt him fall next to her on the bed, rasping demands. Without looking over, she knew he still wasn't ready and was getting more wired because he wasn't ready. She had on her hands a drowning man, ready to pull her under with him if she didn't get him across the chasm to the other side. Drowning men were dangerous. Besides he would tear up those papers.

No choice but the obvious. Save the repulsion for later. She couldn't have this creep leaving here angry. She might need attorney Johns again.

12

When Tory Kingston hung up on him with a flip dismissal, David Tyler marched out to his van, determined to face the daughter keeping guard on big daddy up there at Capstone. Selena Hart was starting up there today as therapist so why couldn't he call on the man, at least to introduce himself?

The five-year-old van, accustomed to sea-level, sputtered in protest on the steep curves. *Come on, old baby.* David pushed it along, exhilarated. The damp spring woods smelled like freedom and he had a good story waiting.

After the first curve, a genuine log cabin sat back from the road, front flower beds beginning to bloom. Maggie Hardy's house. People came into Maggie's shop asking about the log house and wanting to buy it on the spot. Telling him that, Maggie's round face had beamed. "Of course they can't. Mister Kingston is my landlord and he doesn't sell." From the next curve, Ridgeway Inn's green gabled roof showed through green foliage. A few minutes later, the drive turned into a high corridor of firs, entrance to the summit that was Capstone grounds.

David cruised along the front drive. The open grassy knoll was fringed by deep woods. The house sat forward on the bluff which David figured must be about six hundred feet above the Inn and Crest Road. The man did have himself a modern castle up here.

No turrets, but the stone and glass place was impressive. What a view those windows must have.

Beyond the front terrace, a circular drive accommodated a four-car garage that looked like a low stable set back from the house. He could see a couple of vintage cars, a polished Lincoln Continental, a gleaming red Austin Healey and a dusty Range Rover. He glimpsed Selena's old green VW parked in back. David turned around and stopped at the front terrace and got out. Two black dogs, lean Dobermans, flashed from the back of the big house, barking their fool heads off. They barreled toward him, unconvinced by his own loud, "Hey, you guys, I'm a friend."

It was the daughter who saved him.

The dogs growled at his feet as a silver Porsche whipped around from the back drive. The driver called to the Dobermans. A young woman hopped out. In the tight pants and pale silk blouse she strode toward him like a sassy teenager, her pert face about as friendly as the dogs still pacing around him. "And who are you?" she demanded impatiently.

A breeze whipped short dark hair around the gamin face as she confronted him, arms folded over high round breasts. No teenager, David realized. This neat package of formidable woman had to be the daughter who guarded her father.

"Well?" Amber eyes flicked over him as if deciding whether to listen or tell the Dobermans to go for it. The dogs hunkered down to wait. "Are you the creep from the *National Inquirer*?" The voice was acidly precise.

David gave her his best sanguine smile. "No, I'm the patient guy who's been calling you. David Tyler. You're Victoria Kingston?"

"Tory Kingston," she corrected. "What do you want here, David Tyler?"

"I'm with the *Wall Street Journal*." Time enough later to explain he wasn't staff, but stringer, though the story he was after could easily make a *Journal* front page feature in addition to the environmental piece already okayed. "The sale of Kingston Industries is worth more than the original brief mention, don't you agree?"

Decisions shifted behind her steady gaze. "My father is recuperating from a stroke. I won't allow him to be disturbed." Impatiently, "A nurse is with him now. I'm going to Asheville and you're holding me up."

"I'm staying here in High Haven. I want to meet the man, let him know who I am, and come back for a visit." David assumed a friendly looking slouch. "We thought the Kingston founder would like to comment on his career." And why not? The man was famous for colorful statements and grandstand plays for feature writers. David watched her eyes narrow again. Light amber eyes capable of darting out silent warnings. Damned if he was going to let her brush him off. He smiled. "Maybe I need to talk with you first?"

Her little chin lifted. "I'll talk to you. Follow me."

She led him around the side of the house to the covered back terrace that looked out on the open green, probably the landing strip. Dilly had complained about the younger Kingston's noisy helicopter. They entered a sunny country kitchen where a spare, aproned woman looked up without speaking from the fragrant soup she was stirring. They passed through a sunlit formal dining room, then into a living room with a high-beamed ceiling and a massive fireplace. Except for the rich oriental carpets about the stone floor, it might have been the fine hunting lodge he'd seen once in Canada.

A second woman, as reticent as the first, looked up from her basket of wax bottles and rags.

"Go ahead, Lottie. We're going to the library," Tory said quickly. As they mounted the polished wood stairway that rose from the foyer, she turned and gave him a twist of a smile over her trim shoulder. "No, those carpets down there aren't Kingstons. My father happened to love his imports better than his own."

"Fine house," he said, following her neat jeaned figure.

"I hate it."

The second landing was windowed toward the view. The carpeted corridor led to any number of rooms and David wondered if he'd get a glimpse of Kingston. Sensing his curiosity, she snapped, "As I told you, my father has his own suite and can't be disturbed. Here's the library."

They entered a richly paneled room that reminded David of English movies filmed in fine baronial houses. This one was more American and eclectic, however, showing the owner must have gotten drunk in a lot of places—Africa, Morocco, France, the Orient—and brought back whatever he'd fancied. Bronze and lacquer and marble made the room a showcase, yet it was the bookcase of rich leather spines that made David sigh. What a library. You could stay lost in this room for a month, if you could look away from the panoramic view of blue gray mountains.

Tory Kingston went directly to a breakfront bar and uncorked a crystal decanter. "Bourbon? Scotch? I'm a brandy person myself. That's legit in the morning." She was already pouring her own.

"No, thanks." Was she an early drinker or nervous under that cool demeanor? His sweeping assessment of the room stopped at the dark paneled wall opposite the window view. An oil painting hung there. Within the frame, a delicate-boned, dark-haired young woman sat in deep grass, a small book forgotten in the lap of her full skirt. She leaned forward on one hand, haunted and as wistful as a Wyeth figure. Her gaze seemed to pierce the muted light of the library, dragging the viewer's own attention to follow hers into the timeless presence of mountains that lay beyond the windows. David stayed rooted, looking into the portrait face, like a man falling in love.

Tory Kingston bristled with impatience. "My father had it copied by a fine artist from a snapshot. And if you are here to repeat that stupid long-suffering story about poor dear Eve, I will throw you out this instant."

He pulled his gaze away, back to Tory at the bar with her brandy snifter, under the beige silk, the round breasts rising and falling with agitation. "I said—if you're here to write about a dead woman, I will yawn with terminal boredom and kick you out of here."

Lady, you look angry, not bored. "No, I don't rewrite other people's romantic tales. But I am enough of a romantic to say too bad to kill a legend."

"It's past time. I'm twenty-eight. I've wanted to kill her off, oh, since I was five. Tried to shoot the eyes out of this painting when I was seven. They caught me with Zack's BB gun. I asked if you wanted a drink."

"No thanks." He eased into a leather couch, the color of dark green shade. "Why? She's the reason your father owns the mountain, am I right?"

He saw the question was a mistake. Cold reproach in those light brown eyes told him this daughter had a real problem with Eve.

"My mother was a second Kingston wife," Tory snapped, but she came over and sat down in a wing chair opposite him. "She was an actress. Still is. But I had to hear all about Eve. We all did."

David leaned back, satisfied. He had her talking.

In the thicket of woods beyond the open knoll and landing strip, Hoke McRae sat crouched on a low stump with his 12-gauge shotgun, waiting. He wanted the Kingston girl to come out, or the whirley bird to come back, either one. Or better yet, he'd like to see old Kingston himself walk out of that big old house, though folks said the man had come back sick this time and had took to his bed.

Hoke raised the gun and squinted at the bead. A van was parked in front along with the little gal's fancy silver sportscar. So, she was having herself some company. His trigger finger itched to pepper the shine off her fancy car. He wasn't of any mind to be scared off, no matter what Sheriff Bo Hilrey said. *I have a right to be here. I have a born right because this oughta be McRae land.*

Maybe if that little Kingston gal didn't come out, he would ping some dents in that other car when it went back down. Hoke lowered the gun and stretched his aching back. Bent over so long, his muscles burned like he'd been branded. Hurt so damned much he wasn't in no mood to jack off, like he'd done last time he sat in these woods, watching the Kingston gal priss around up there back of the house, on the bald, with those dogs.

She must have gotten rit of old Hogan's hounds and brought in these black devils instead. They'd be sniffing him out now only they were hanging around the car. Next time, Hoke thought, I'll bring them a good hunk of meat. There wasn't no dog, fancy kind, bear dog or mutt, he couldn't train good.

He squatted in the thick brush, looking out at the green knoll bright with midday sun. Place used to be knee-deep grass when he followed Will up here, bird hunting, when he was seven or eight. After Addie shot his own daddy Roy dead, Will acted like his own daddy, even if he was too slow and easy for a man and let smart city lawyers talk him into selling his side of the mountain to Kingston.

But it wasn't right. With both Will and Roy long gone, Hoke figured he had rights to this land. He was no dummy. He'd been around, trucking and logging. Always came back to look at this land that rose just above the hollow. Came up here and looked at that big house with its fancy cars. Junior Kingston still played here, only now it wasn't a motorcycle, now his toy was a helicopter.

Hoke peered at the sky, waiting for that flapping thing to show up.

The creek house down below was his because it was the McRae place. Addie and Ariel had to let him move back in ever' time he got out of jail or from a job. They knew they couldn't get rit of him. Nighttime in his back room, he could listen to the creek sounds, same as when he was a kid and Nonnie was in the kitchen. Addie never talked much but she cooked as good as his old granny. One reason he came back. Not that Addie's cornbread swayed what he thought of her and her wildcat daughter.

It rankled Hoke to his bones that here he was, a forty-two year old man, living with a weird acting woman and a girl he couldn't touch with Addie around.

Hoke squinted up toward the house again. Not a sign of anybody yet. His back jaw tooth kicked into hurting again, like a reminder not to sit and wait on things. A low whirring sound broke the quiet. He jumped to his feet, itching to spray buckshot soon as the thing landed. *Look at that, Junior up there, acting like he owned the sky too.* Gawd, but he hated that glass buzzard even if it sure was a pretty sight. Hoke raised the shotgun, following its path.

Branches crackled behind him. He wheeled around, gun pointed, until he saw the gleam of her dark hair pushing through the tangled branches. *Chit.* He lowered the gun. "Aw, Ariel." She tromped toward him, the dark hair roped on the top of her head, showing off that little white neck and nothing under that blue top but pointy breasts. She crashed on up, glaring and cussing through those pearly little teeth.

"I knew it, you bastard. Saw you headed up here. What you think you're doing?"

"Aw, Sugar, why you bird-dogging me?" The glass buzzard was hovering now. He turned away from her, shotgun raised.

Ariel squealed, "You dumb billygoat!" and crashed on toward him, her foot striking square in his rear. He landed face down, rolled over, spitting bark. Laughing riled her more than anything. He was laughing so hard, she shoved him flat again, staring down at him as mad as a ferile mama cat protecting kittens.

Hoke sat up, grabbed her arm and sat her down hard next to him. "Aw, Ariel, no use trying to protect Junior. No Kingston is going do you any favors. Wiggle that little ass of yours in his direction ever' chance you get, won't do no good, 'cept make your mama mad if she knows. You can get some truck driver to take you to Nashville sooner than he'll give you time of day."

Ariel sat back, eyes glinting like shiny green glass. "You stop laying out for these folks up here or I'll make you sorry, Hoke McRae. When the sheriff comes around looking for you, Mama has to shut the door in his face. That makes her sick." She sat back on her heels, like a hissing cat. "Another thing, if you figure to come back to the house to stay this time, you gotta act re-spectful to Mama, and keep clear away from me."

He grabbed her a minute, so close, he got the sweet smell of her, like damp woods and woman mixed, before she pulled loose like the wildcat she was and spit just past him.

"I mean it, Hoke McRae. You try anything to make Mama feel bad and I'll fix you good. I'll brew some of her herbs that'll turn you into an old woman. And you won't know how or when, I promise."

Hoke sat where he was, watching her slip through the brush easy as a rabbit, her skinny girl legs flashing under the short blue thing she wore. He grinned. Once Ariel simmered down, he knew she'd start prissy-footing down the road, singing, pretending to be a Grand Ole Opry star on TV.

David Tyler pulled his gaze from the Eve portrait as Tory came back to her chair, swirling a refill of brandy. He kept his voice casual. "So this long dead woman has been a problem? Because of the ghost story?"

Tory shrugged. "That stupid story, too." She looked into the brandy glass for a moment before saying with icy disdain, "Every time my father refused to sell this land, every time someone wrote about the colorful Kingston, his ownership of this mountain property was mentioned, and the business about Eve was repeated. All that soft soap about my father's undying love for the first little bride. So he kept it up too. " She looked away for a moment. "That damned story screwed up our lives. Zack's too. And the youngest Kingston, Loren. So you see why I don't want to hear any more about it and don't want it repeated."

"Some feature writers can get carried away," David offered. "But those stories have been favorable to, and for, your father."

"He's not adverse to a good press." She regarded him coolly over her drink. "What's your interest? I've been blocking his calls, yes, because I am here to look after him. Zack tells me he's had a call in Charlotte from some damn TV show of all things. What could they possibly want here but to intrude on our privacy? He's no movie star. Though he might have been." She almost smiled. "So you can understand I must protect my father while he is recuperating. Most of the time Zack is off climbing Grandfather Mountain, or doing some fool job . . . or in the sack somewhere . . . or playing around in the Bird . . . so much for *his* responsibility. That's all I have to tell you." She drained the glass and sat upright, her hard gaze telling him he could go now.

Angry lady. And worried? For a moment David felt some sympathy. But she'd made him curious. What was this business about TV? He ignored her cue of dismissal. "Miss Kingston—okay, Tory—I pride myself on accurate reporting. Sounds like that's what you need, a legit reporter. I don't blame you for being annoyed at those who take liberties with the truth. I'm interested in writing about a land owner who has promised to protect an old growth forest. Also, people like to read about others who have managed that basic dream, to have one's own personal island or, in this case, a private mountain."

"And to report the lost joys of privacy you would disturb my father's privacy."

"You're a very protective daughter."

"*And why not?*"

"You're protecting his health. And his good name?"

Icily, "*So?*"

If he brought up the old original gossip—the uncertainty of how that first wife died and the lack of investigation—this daughter might leap up and shoot him with worse than a BB gun. He'd read those old reports in doing his homework on Kingston. Hell. His environmental story was going down the drain. Served him right for approaching a story with preconceived notions of a closet idealist rather than a hard-nosed reporter. But a story was here. The woman was hiding Daddy for a reason. Why?

David hid his disappointment and kept his casual tone. "Maybe it's time to get the right story out. I could help by writing a decent retirement story. Is your father leaving Eve's Mountain to the state as the earlier stories say?"

He saw he'd really hit a nerve. He knew to lean back and wait. Tory had dropped into the opposite chair. Giving her time, he looked back at the portrait of Eve and her soulful gaze.

Women came in such varieties, he mused. Lovely, exasperating, unknowable varieties. This petite woman sitting here clicking coral nails against the brandy snifter was as tough-minded as they came. His own wife caused no stress, he always reminded himself, because Sarah was insulated and self-satisfied. If such placidity had a deadening effect on his libido, that was his own problem. He repeated his subtle pitch. "An accurate story about your father and this mountain could put an end to the false ones."

Tory sat the brandy glass down. To his surprise, she smiled. A minxish smile. "You are quite right. Maybe I do need you." The sharp little chin lifted. "I may have some news for you later but it is premature at the moment."

"But you know it now." He could sense he had triggered something she cared about. "Trust me."

She took the bait. "Let's say there's going to be a new Kingston corporation. Kingston-Haven properties. To take care of the real future of this mountain. How do you like the name Havencrest?"

He sat back, surprised at sudden warmth in her voice and the sharpness of his own regret. She was talking about development. Marketing Eve's Mountain as Havencrest or some such pipe dream of the good life. He kept disillusionment out of his voice.

"Miss Kingston—Tory—any plans to develop pristine forested land in the heart of the Blue Ridge is worth, say, four inches of copy, and only when the plans are firm, not speculation. However, anything more than a mention calls for A. Z. Kingston's comments on the decision." *When did that bastard change his mind? Had he been reaping the good press all these years, waiting until this property increased in value?* " So, I'll still need to speak with him."

The answering gaze held venom. "You're looking at the person who can speak for Kingston-Haven. Unless you have something against women?"

"I'm sure you can handle it. As I say, any announcement still calls for your father's comments."

"Which would be premature at this time, as I said." She seemed flustered, sorry she had spoken. "So we have nothing more to talk about at present, now, have we? I'll see you out." She stood.

"I'm here for the summer to do some personal writing." He stood too, taking one last long look at Eve Kingston's poignant face in the portrait.

"Stop staring at that damn painting." Only the whirring noise above the house stopped her burst of disgust. "That's the Bird now." Her quick glance was an order. "If you meet Zack, you are not to say a word of what I've told you. He can add nothing because any plans are between father and myself at this point."

David followed her downstairs and out to the grounds in back of the house. From the grass, they stared up to the helicopter hovering at fifty feet. It dipped, and a man waved from the glass bulb.

"Zack at play," she said with a smirky smile. A shot crackled in the air from the woods beyond the knoll. The helicopter lifted and headed away, gleaming in the sunlight.

"What in the devil was that all about?" David asked. The Dobermans pranced around, barking.

"You just heard Hoke McRae, local character and pain-in-the-ass, expressing himself. He lurks in our woods sometimes. Gets his kicks by annoying us. He's not your comic moonshiner. He is a local son-of-a-bitch." She flashed a sardonic smile, turned and started back toward the house.

David waited but the helicopter disappeared into the pale sky. In the silence, he thought again of the woman in the portrait. In that painting she had the look of reaching out to something that she'd found and knew she would lose. He felt the same right now. So much for the gullible belief in Kingston's promise to leave this mountain unspoiled. What was going on here? He meant to find out and write the truth of the Eve legend and Kingston to set the record straight. But to know the truth, he still had to talk to the man himself. He didn't trust this daughter.

David pulled out of the drive. This was his summer for freedom and good writing. He wasn't going to let anything take the shine off that. Next step was to find his cabin in these hills, get set up there. To hell with the Kingstons until he could dig into the story more. Professor Enholm should be a help. And Maggie

Hardy. And surely, Selena Hart. A few minutes later, down the road, David had to wonder if he should be worrying about the McRaes as well as Tory Kingston.

Beyond the entrance to Capstone grounds, a man burst out of the woods in front of the van. David jammed on his brakes not to hit the damn fool. The gangling figure gestured in front of the car like an animated scarecrow, one long arm swinging a shotgun. David sat there, foot on the brake, more angry than frightened. The fellow stalked toward him, shaggy head of hair, high cheekbones, cuffed brown mustache hanging over his grinning mouth. "Skeered you, didn't I?"

"A nice fellow like you?" David hoped sarcasm wouldn't offend the goon. "Hoke McRae?"

Hoke stepped back, looked over the car, shotgun still cradled in the crook of his arm. "Wouldn't do me any good to shoot up this old thing. Hellava finish. You Floridy fellows are supposed to drive Caddies."

"You're looking at a teacher who can't afford a new paint job." He thought of saying, my wife owns the good car. He stayed patient while the man looked at him from deep set eyes, dark and dancing.

"You come up here looking to buy some purty mountain land?"

"Visiting."

"For buying, it ain't the Kingstons you wanna do business with. It's me."

"I'm not here to buy. Anything I can do for you, before I move on?"

Hoke put his face in close again. No smile this time. "Yeah. Next time you go visiting old man Kingston and that daughter up there, you tell them they're sitting on Hoke McRae's land. You help impress them with that fact."

The man stood back, swung the gun over his shoulder and ambled on down toward the battered blue pickup, parked off the road, hidden in roadside foliage. David waited until the truck backed out and barreled on down the drive toward Crest Road.

He took his cramped foot off the brake and started down, slowly. Around the next curve, a girl in a shapeless blue T-shirt of a dress walked at a swinging rhythm, buoyant as a dancer. *Look at that.* These private woods were full of surprises. This one looked like some wood nymph child.

David idled the van as he rolled alongside, meaning to get a good look at this happy creature without scaring her, making her scream and run home to mama. Or maybe cruising rapists weren't a problem here. Wasn't sweet little old High Haven a safe summer Mecca for urban escapees? The girl kept walking alongside the van, turning a big smile his way, asking, "Drop me off at the shops?" A country voice, as David expected, but with a lilt and a purr.

At his nod, she danced around the front of the car, threw open the passenger side door and slipped in. No child, right, maybe a teenager, maybe seventeen? Her face was that of an innocent but not those green eyes. His mind spun with poems not yet written, women not yet known.

David pulled his gaze away from the girl and drove. She wiggled around on the seat beside him, vital and sweet smelling, a dusty, still blooming wildflower he'd yanked out of the woods without thinking. What was she doing? Tucking her tanned legs under her small bottom, she leaned in to investigate the radio dial. "You summer people?" she asked. "Haven't seen you before. I'm Ariel McRae."

"I'm a teacher from Florida, looking for a cabin for the summer. Have some work to do here." It sounded as stodgy as he felt.

She jabbed orange fingernails at the radio buttons, going past his NPR station. A country singer's wail filled the car. She leaned back now, stretching out slim legs in barefoot leather sandals, pumping her knees to the beat. The kid was making him grin as if the smart ass young females he taught weren't the bane of his life. This was one of the mountain variety.

He turned on his patient teacher's smile to look at her again. The clear green eyes were assessing him, the voice more earnest than coy. "Do you think a girl can make it as a country singer if she don't have 'em big as Dolly?"

"If she doesn't have what?"

"Boobs like Dolly Parton." She yanked the cotton knit tight over her chest, showing him the two peaked nipples. "Or red hair like Reba's?" She whipped her long dark hair up from her moist neck and sighed. "I love Reba McEntire to pieces."

"The voice should have something to do with it."

"Then I'll make it." She leaned back and began singing along with the radio lyrics, her thin vital body moving with the beat. Her voice ran through him like crystal water on a parched tongue. Reaching Crest Road, he swung into the angled parking in front of the shops. She jumped out but stuck her head back in. "I'm Ariel McRae. You remember that because I'm gonna be famous."

After her quick skinny legs took her into Country Sundries, David sat for minutes behind the wheel, dismissing a confusing sense of pleasure he tried to label as amusement.

13

From her first day with Alexander Kingston, Selena came into the Inn's dining room late, agreeably exhausted, even hungry, and relieved to see she was no longer the only curiosity among the older guests. Now it was Paula Crossing from California. Selena watched Paula sweep out, waving like a departing model, leaving the older guests nodding over their rhubarb pie and commenting. "Says she's a photographer," the balding Colonel let Selena know.

She sat down and helped herself to baked chicken and dressing, waving away the biscuits but asking for the cut glass bowl of cranberries. She wanted only to enjoy her dinner, get upstairs to soak in the small, deep tub, then get into bed and read until oblivion the ten-year-old *Ladies Home Journal,* found under the night stand. Tomorrow afternoon she would move into the chalet if the power had been turned on, then spend evenings cleaning it.

She looked around for David Tyler, expecting him to seek her out to compare notes. He must have gotten to talk with Tory Kingston today before she drove off to Asheville. David wasn't in the dining room. But Professor Enholm paused at her table with his slow, melancholy smile. "How did you find your patient, my dear?"

"He looks well, considering. With everything else, the man is emotionally distressed with his condition. He needs a great deal of help."

Since Enholm waited patiently, she added ruefully, "I understand you want to see him, but the daughter is running things up there, and she is all too adamant about no visitors. I don't think I could have gotten inside the place this morning if Zack Kingston hadn't been there, paving the way, before he took off. Flew away, literally, in his helicopter."

At the professor's solemn nod, Selena added, "You might ask David Tyler about Tory Kingston. I believe she brought him into the house before she left for Asheville."

Later, heading for her room, Selena spotted Paula Crossing in the hall booth, holding the phone, eyes tight and biting her lip. With a sting of compassion, Selena thought, *You have your own problems, don't you?* She hurried on upstairs, thinking ahead to tomorrow, the troubled man waiting for her. Thankfully, she had this first week alone with Alexander, with Tory in Asheville for a week.

In the hall phone booth, determined to prevent any quiver in her voice, Paula Crossing inhaled deeply, letting it out slowly, as she listened to the phone ring in the San Diego office. Finally, "Clive, please. Tell him it's Paula."

A voice she didn't recognize told her to hold, then came back to announce he was tied up in a meeting. As a reprimand for her absence? Paula kept the doubt out of her chilled response. "Tell Clive that Paula called from North Carolina. Tell him this family business will take longer than I expected and I'll need time here . . . maybe two months."

At the other end of the line, the new voice started to protest. "Don't worry about it," Paula snapped. "Just give him the message. I have the time coming. He knows. Tell him I'll be in touch."

The time she had coming was to be used with Clive when he went to Europe in September.

Paula hung up quickly and leaned against the booth. For the first time in years, she felt unsure of direction. Already the Europe jaunt seemed vague. Only her purpose here felt real. She would stay here at the Inn until she saw Alexander Kingston and found out what she had to find out. She had to *know* before going on with her life.

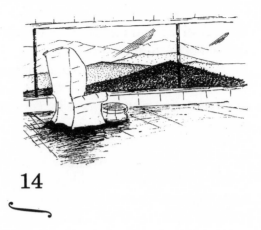

14

Selena Hart came out of Alexander Kingston's suite to find Tory waiting outside the library, arms crossed, face set like an accusing child. No, with the arch impatience of a chief-of-staff questioning a new nurse on the floor, demanding, "Are you here to give my father physical therapy or to sit in there all day allowing him to play host?"

"Tory, a stroke patient must deal with depression, even when he's a strong personality like your father." Selena kept her voice calm, even bland, the way she had handled Drew's knife sharp criticisms. "He has to be listened to patiently. He needs counseling as well as the therapy, and neither can be rushed."

"You don't have to explain my father to me," Tory snapped. "I think you're being taken in by him—or he by you. I intend to speak to Zack about this arrangement."

"You do that. Zack should be in on this. I thought he was. Also, you might speak to your father. We're talking about his interest, aren't we?" *You're angry or fearful about your control here, aren't you?* She tried a softer tone. "Look, Tory, I know he asked you to stay out of the room when we work together and he might have been abrupt with that request. But understand his concern. It's embarrassing for the man to be wearing the Gate-Belt and walking with a therapist, or to be heard confessing his worries.

It's easier for him to do this alone with a nurse. You must be patient with him at this stage."

Selena walked away from Tory, and headed down the stairs, aware that Tory's icy stare followed her like a chill between her shoulders. So, if this was to be routine with daughter, *I'm the one who will need the patience.*

The first week with Kingston had progressed so well, with Tory in Asheville. Alexander had responded like the confident, determined man he must have been before the stroke; enough, in fact, to begin playing the host rather than patient. She had handled that, made a friend of him, reminded him of their pact, then set up the immediate goals for regaining his balance and vigor. He seemed to relax somewhat, trusting her enough to confide his frustrations, moving from agitation to self-deprecating humor. "Keep these visits human even if you do lead me around with that damn leather belt," he had ordered.

So what had happened since? Now, she might walk in to find her patient confused, mumbling about his hellish nights, clumsy in his movements, angry. Then this morning, another cross examination by daughter, waiting there in the hall. The cold shiver from Tory's stare didn't leave Selena's shoulders until she reached the sun-filled kitchen.

Sudie Gurney put down the potato she was peeling. "Lawd, but you look plumb wore out. Is she still bossing you about your nursing?" As usual, Sudie avoided using Tory's name. "Set yourself down. I'll fix you some sweet tea."

Selena sank into the kitchen chair, grateful for the warmth of the room and the woman's honest solicitude. "A nurse has to work with the family, Sudie. But it is difficult when a daughter insists on having all the authority."

Sudie brought the glass to the table and sat down opposite. "I'm making potato soup. *She* claims he ain't hungry and shouldn't take on big meals." The thin country voice hushed to a whisper. "It worries me no end how he ain't eating. But when I ask to take up the tray myself, *she* has a fit, like I was going to

108

hide a pork chop in my apron pocket." Sudie bent closer, pale blue eyes shiny with concern. "How's Azzie doing?"

"I'm not sure. I'm puzzled, Sudie. I must get Doc Bradley back up here. We need to look over his medications. And I must talk with Zack." Their short conversations on the driveway as she arrived and Zack drove out left her baffled and annoyed. "We should be discussing this. Why haven't I seen him around in days?"

"That boy cares about his Daddy, he's just keeping outa the way of *her*. Got himself a job at Grandfather Mountain, hacking out more paths for hikers. Has to be flying back to Charlotte, too, to see Azzie's lawyers and the folks buying his business." Sudie's face softened. "He comes in late. I leave him a big ham or beef sandwich and some cobbler. Sometimes I leave him a note hidden under a sandwich. *She'd* get riled up if she knew I was complaining. She comes down here at night, after I'm gone, to fix Azzie his hot milk to go with his last pill."

"Then leave a note for me. Tell Zack we must talk and not here, not even on the phone." She knew Tory had a private line in the library but could listen in on other calls to the house. "Ask him to stop by my place. He knows where. It's the old chalet on Hawk Ridge."

Sudie followed to the back terrace door. "Don't let that woman run you off, Se'lene. I reckon Azzie needs more curing than what my cooking can do."

Behind the wheel of the Volkswagen, chugging out of Capstone grounds, Selena thought fervently, Sudie, I've got to stay, for my patient's sake and my own survival here. And after that? In three months, fall. Then winter. Deadline to leave. *No, don't think of that now.* She drove slowly, again going over questions that plagued her.

Alexander wasn't improving. Was it the meds or the other thing he confessed today? She pushed that problem away for the moment. The medications were right for this case—if they were being given correctly. Stridently efficient Tory handled the

109

late afternoon blood thinner and night capsules for anxiety. Did she take his blood pressure accurately, were her records correct? The girl would explode if challenged. *But as nurse on the case, I should have that responsibility.* Zack should know. Let him demand some agreement from Tory. I can arrive earlier and return later, she'd tell him. Let Tory give her father the late night Xanax.

She drove slowly away from Capstone, wondering. Didn't Zack realize the situation? Did he only go in to see his father after Jeb left Alexander showered, shaved and dressed; on mornings the man was impatient for his workout, full of disparaging wit? Didn't he go in mornings when Alexander sat withdrawn, mumbling about a hellish night, off balance when he finally got to his feet?

As she had found her patient today. It took cajoling to get him to use the belt, allow her to check his balance. Finally, they had walked the big room, moving close as troubled lovers. On the balcony, they rested, still silent except for Alexander's heavy breathing. The air was cool from rain-washed trees, the slopes canopied now with full green foliage.

He stood there, hands gripping the balcony railing, his private anguish showing behind his ruggedly handsome face, the heavy brows tight. He gazed down toward Crest Road then turned to look back toward his other mountain, his Hawk's Ridge.

"She's out there somewhere," he muttered. "I want to see her . . . and I don't. She tries to come to me during the night. Yeah, I'm drugged with the damn pills but I know what I'm talking about." He shook his head. "Never thought I could be afraid of anything. Until now. I feel so Goddamn helpless, Selena. I want to strike out at something but don't have the strength."

Back in the room, he sank in his chair by the window. "Gotta rest. Enough old man calisthenics for the day." He hid his face in his good hand, big shoulders shaking. Selena pulled up the stool and sat close, massaging the hand on his knee. "Alexander, don't be ashamed of tears. It happens after a stroke. From confusion and desperation." At his silence, she went on. "Daily physiotherapy works on your physical coordination. But for the body to heal, emotions must be dealt with too. Even erratic fears."

He rocked his head against the back of the chair, eyes tight, the frown deep. She waited, resisting the urge to smooth the tousled silver hair. On impulse, she picked up his idle hand, pressed it to her face, knowing as she did so, *I'm becoming too emotionally involved here.* Pressing his hand back on his knee, she was rewarded with a sleepy grin and the old seductive gaze.

"You're my kind of woman, Selena. Tough but with feeling. I need that more than any bossy nurse—or shrink."

"You need both a therapist and a friend, and you're looking at one and the same. I keep reminding you that medication and isolation, even here in this fine suite of rooms,—plus the inactivity, is all new to you. This is allowing—"

"Forcing," he muttered.

"Forcing you to get to know yourself, and that includes reviewing the past. A stroke can affect parts of the brain that control memory and thought. Whatever comes up in the mind, be it real or imagined, can be highly disturbing. But it doesn't help to hold it inside. If it feels like guilt, go ahead, you can talk to me about it. Hidden guilt inside—imagined or real—festers and grows like a malignancy. I know that's true from experience, believe me."

She met his gaze, and held it. "Alexander, I've heard you mumble about Eve. Do you want to talk about her?"

He shook his head but the answer escaped his clenched jaws. "The hellish dreams . . . half awake dreams . . . make me wonder. Those old mountain boys back there believed . . . *God, I don't know.* All I know is that I was drunk and jealous and angry as a young bull because Eve wasn't ready to come back with me. I had shown up a month early to take them home. I swear, that's all I remember." The deep eyes were brown bullets for an instant, testing her reaction. She nodded for him to go on.

He sat shaking his head. "I went on with the house, getting it built up here. And I worked hard as a man swimming for his life to a different shore, a different reality. Now this damn stroke and crazy nightmares."

She sat silent, the realizations unwanted. Had this man actually killed his wife, and blocked the memory with denial? It happens, she thought. Angry, passionate men have murdered the women they claimed to love. For a still, hollow moment she watched his silent torment and dealt with her own. Why didn't she recoil now? Because she didn't want to believe he had caused Eve's death? And having this job to see him well again meant her own safety, her own sanity? At his heavy, labored breathing, she jumped up. "Blood pressure time." She rolled the machine to him. His heavy muscled arm stayed limp and obedient.

"Hear me, Alexander. Fear of our guilts is the most insidious kind. Push it down into the subconscious and it still works against you and your body. Believe me, I do know. Since coming here, I had to face certain fears of my own. I'm getting better for having done that." She didn't add, I'm still in danger but it is a literal one, outside of me, not from within.

"Tell me about Selena Hart," he asked in a hoarse whisper. "What are you doing in these mountains? I want to know."

"I needed a place like this. Away from Colorado." She took the blood pressure equipment away and came back to the stool in front of his chair. "Now, about you. About Eve."

"I don't remember what happened. That's the hell of it. I was drunk."

"Will you allow me to help you, Alexander?" She saw the lassitude taking over.

"Don't know how you can help. Have to get back to bed now. Day is the only time I can sleep. Tell Sudie to wake me up for some real food in a couple of hours. The old girl doesn't come up any more. "

She had left him in bed and went outside to find Tory waiting for her.

Driving now back to her own place, Selena knew what she must do. Talk to Zack about taking over the med schedule from Tory. Let no one visit her patient while he was in this state. And third, find out herself what did happen when Eve Kingston disappeared thirty-eight years ago.

She had read old yellowed clippings she'd found in a scrapbook at the chalet. Who could she talk to, in confidence? Even Maggie Hardy, friendly soul that she was, loving to expound about High Haven, even Maggie closed up at any mention of the Eve mystery. Why, Selena asked herself now. *Because Maggie knew the truth?* Then she would go to Maggie.

Leaving her car on the drive above the chalet, Selena walked down the sloping path to the side kitchen door. Something white caught her eye on the weedy gravel. A half-smoked cigarette. A fresh one, tossed there a few hours ago.

At the stoop by the kitchen entrance she looked around, carefully now. Yes, one more stub was caught in the bushes by the door. Someone had been here, had tried the door. Someone curious about the place, just as she had been? Or looking for her? The key was still hidden under the flower pot by the door. She had not bothered to lock the door, since the place was so peacefully secluded.

She went in. Stood unmoving in the tiny kitchen. Had the smoker been inside? Only the smell of old wood and Maggie's cinnamon broom greeted her. Yet her skin prickled with warning. What would anyone want here?

Nothing but her identity. Who could want that? Only Drew, rather the person he would send. Or the Denver police.

She climbed the narrow stairs to peer into the low-ceilinged open balcony, her bedroom. Then back down to the main room to stand still, listening to the thud of her own pulse. The closer green slopes looked back, assuring and peaceful, even as they darkened now in the slanted rays of late sun. If someone had been here searching for Dr. Selena Hempton, they had found nothing. Only the Colorado driver's license hidden in the VW would show that. Nothing was disturbed here but her privacy, her sense of safety. She would not go out tonight to call on Maggie Hardy. She wanted only to lock the door and try to sleep until morning.

15

" **W**hy, you come right in," Maggie Hardy said, surprised to see Selena Hart at the front door, the green VW parked out front. "I've been hoping you'd stop by the shop because I have some lamps and pillows you can use."

Maggie drew Selena inside, knowing something was on the girl's mind besides a visit. Selena stood looking around with a deep sigh, then a shimmery smile. "This is what magazine photos try to show when they're talking about country charm. Yours is the real thing, Maggie. And look, a marvelous cat in the window seat."

"Well, you sit right down and I'll tell you about it." As her guest sank onto the couch admiring the crazy quilt that covered it, Maggie took the rocking chair opposite. "I'm lucky about this place. Real logs you can tell. But snug as you want on a cold windy day. It was built as a guest cabin for Capstone but it was too far away from the big house so I've been here all these years. Your patient up there is a real good landlord. That crazy quilt you're admiring? It must be eighty years old, made by the old lady who first owned the shop. The throws on the chairs and table are some of Addie McRae's weavings."

Now what was on Selena's mind? Here she was intense again, holding something back. Since going to work up there at Capstone, Selena had been real friendly, without that tight look behind her eyes. Asking now, "Am I interrupting your dinner?" But not worried about that, Maggie knew.

"Stay for supper. That's spice cake you smell. And curry in the pea soup on the stove. It has to simmer thirty more minutes. How is the chalet kitchen working? That place has been closed an awful long time."

"It works. Besides, Sudie sends me home with more food than I need. Oh, that cat. What a picture of relaxation."

"Hemmie is my sweet old tom. He used to be with me in the shop. Now he likes to stay home and sleep on the window seat, or in winter in front of the hearth. That's where I spent my cold nights too."

"I wish the summer could last, " Selena said, suddenly wistful. "How do you handle winters up here by yourself?"

"Summer people ask me that. They say I ought to rent a little place in Florida for the cold months. And I say, why? To sit around with other lonely widows and play bingo? I'll admit, winter can try your soul at times. But you live by the seasons up here and each has its reasons and its lessons. Spring makes you come alive no matter how many winters you've lived through."

Maggie leaned back in her rocker, watching her guest, glad her pretty skin showed color these days. "Come spring, I get spunky again. Can't wait to sweep out the shop, ready for the regulars to come back and the tourists to roll through."

Because Selena sat there really listening, Maggie confided, "I don't try to explain to just anybody, but . . . on cold, clear days, when the slopes are winter bare and shadowed purple, they look back at you like wise old beings."

At Selena's nod, "The wind can still on days like that, the air clear as polished crystal and alive inside your lungs. The mind gets still too, and so clear. That kind of day is a gift to body and soul."

Maggie looked past the window seat, out to the drive that led up to Capstone, amber in the fading sunlight. "Sometimes your mind gets too clear, and you think back to the past, wondering if you did the right thing or not back there in your life."

"That happens. Don't you get lonely?"

"There's wood to chop, and once a week I go down to a couple of stores in the hollow. I quilt in front of the fire. Nights I read,— old paperback mysteries sometimes, but mostly I reread the Psalms and Walt Whitman and Ralph Waldo Emerson and Annie Dillard. Now there's a woman who knows being alone in the woods is not really being alone . . . A TV? Oh yes, I have a little one over there on the kitchen counter, but I watch just enough to check if the world is still going on the way it does out there. Most of the shows you can't tell from the crime news. You going to stay and have supper with me?"

Selena shook her head. "But thanks, Maggie, you're very kind. That's why I'm counting on you to help me now. Hear me out. I know you don't like the subject but I need to talk to you about the Eve story."

Lordy. Maggie didn't hide her sigh. She rocked hard. "Haven't I told you? That story stays alive because outsiders want to believe these old mountains can still spawn mysteries. I'm a Christian woman and believe the soul goes somewhere but I'm not supposed to believe in ghosts. Well, that's the past. How is your patient up there at Capstone? We've all been wanting to know. Sudie Gurney tells me he stays in his big room upstairs and the daughter wants him left alone."

"Maggie, that's what I came to talk to you about."

Selena leaned forward, appeal in her steady gaze. "Confidentially, my patient is not doing as well as he should be. Stress is blocking his physical recovery. Somehow Alexander has been reminded of the old gossip implying his guilt. Maggie, I must get him to talk it out. But first, I need to know more about the facts of Eve Kingston's disappearance from the Inn. I know the romantic versions, and the old gossip. I've read the old clippings that say Eve could have been running away, or kidnapped by someone who worked at the Inn. Weren't two bodies found later in the wrecked car?"

116

Maggie rocked harder. *Lord, this girl is persistent, soft voice and all.*

"So I need to know as much of the truth as possible, Maggie . . . please. I need to know what happened between Alexander and Eve the night she disappeared. I feel you know more than most."

Maggie let out a sigh. "I came to stay twenty years ago. I was a forty-three-year-old widow from Alabama at the time, think I told you, restless as a mama cat who'd lost her brood. Well, I had lost a baby, then a husband. I bought the shop from an old lady quilt-maker. Oh, Selena, it's no good to bring up the past."

"But your landlord and my patient's past is being brought up. These people wanting to see Alexander for whatever reasons. In his present state of mind, the man couldn't protect himself if they got into the Eve subject. And they will."

Maggie nodded and sighed. She liked David Tyler and the nice Professor who came visiting every morning, but she was worried about both being so determined to see Kingston. Now this Paula Crossing from California had shown up asking Dilly about the Kingstons. And did Selena know about the TV people? She told her now about the calls to Bo Hilrey from a TV company wanting to come up and ask people about High Haven's ghost. "If that's the only thing they do, they'll still make us all look like fools up here for believing in ghosts or trying to claim one."

"You see, Maggie? Before any of these people get to Alexander, he must be well enough to handle it. You're loyal to the man. I'm trying to help him. But to do that, I need to know as much as possible. Trust me."

Maggie looked out to the darkening drive. *Lord, how much should I tell?* "Developers have been wanting to buy this ridge for years. If anything bad happens to the man, he would have to sell out. They'd come in with bulldozers and motels and this ridge would look like everyplace else. Or a private club place with a gate keeper.

"I'm not saying we're the only peaceful hamlet left in these mountains, the kind of place outsiders need, you know, to feel they got away from the rest of the world until they're ready to go back.

The mountains have little places like Lake Lure and Chimney Rock and Cashiers and Valle Crucis and Little Switzerland. I'd say Blowing Rock and Highlands but they're getting to be big and stylish. High Haven is special because it hasn't changed and we want it to stay the way it is. You ought to understand, Selena. You came to find a peaceful place. And I've never asked why."

"I know, I know. But if Kingston is in jeopardy, the place is too. So help me help him. To work with him, I need to know more than he remembers. You may not have been here when Eve Kingston disappeared, but you must know . . . must have heard . . ."

Maggie stopped rocking. "Selena, honey, I was here when it happened. You look surprised."

"Surprised, but grateful. Oh, Maggie, I felt you *did* know the truth."

Maggie stood, aching in every bone in her body. Maybe that's what reluctance did to you. How much should she tell? "Wait until I turn down the soup and turn on a lamp."

Maggie came back from the kitchen to sink again into her rocker. "I'd have to start at the beginning."

"Good." On the crazy quilt couch, Selena leaned back, stroking Hemmie who purred at her side.

"When I was a chunky twenty-five, and single," Maggie began, "I spent the summer at the Ridgeway Inn looking after a cranky old aunt. She was a chore, but I was happy as a lark being there. High Haven was more remote than it is today, but the Ridgeway was a famous mountain hotel, the kind you could find back then in these highlands. Most have since burned down, or become bed and breakfast places. Back then, people came to stay the summer, older couples, wives and children mostly, their husbands back in the sultry towns, had to come visiting. I loved High Haven, enough to come back years later when I needed peace for soul and body."

Maggie spread her hands over her denim skirt, seeing in her mind that summer she didn't talk about to anyone.

"After supper, everybody would rock on the verandah—front porch we call it now—listening to the player piano in the parlor. It's still there today. When Dilly puts on Chopin, I shiver, remembering."

Maggie closed her eyes, seeing it even better. "Alexander Kingston brought Eve and the three-month-old baby up in June. That was Zack. I look at that boy today and think back, *oh my*. Those two young people—Eve was twenty and Alexander twenty-nine I guess—gave the old couples and widows something to watch. She had long, dark hair, piled high in back from a face like on a Victorian valentine. She was that delicate, because she'd had a difficult birth with the baby. Alexander was this big handsome outgoing fellow who would come up from Charlotte most weekends to visit. He'd walk in there bringing a fresh gust of energy for the whole place."

"I can imagine that," Selena said. "Go on, Maggie."

"He would drive up in a shiny Lincoln, a black one like he drives today, and bounce up on the verandah calling out, *Where's my doll?* He treated Eve like his prized possession."

"And Eve? How were they together?"

"She wouldn't be on the porch with the rest of us. She'd be out in the back garden, the baby upstairs with the hired girl, but always she'd have a book. Poetry is what she read. I saw her trying to get well with her books and by looking out at the mountains. The older wives said she behaved more like a dreaming school girl than a wife and mother. They didn't approve of her admirers either."

"And who were the admirers?"

"There was a young fellow, bookish type, who came up from Duke now and then to visit his aunt, but he spent most of his time reading to Eve on the far end of the porch like some lovesick boy. He was too shy to be friendly to anyone else."

Maggie went on. "Then there was the red-headed rascal who worked in the kitchen. A real scalawag, that one, with poor mountain girls always showing up at the back kitchen door looking for him. The fellow hung around Eve Kingston whenever he found her alone in the garden. During the afternoon, when most everyone else was taking a nap, you could look down on the back garden and see him down there with her, prancing around, making that solemn girl laugh, whittling her a walking stick. Did I tell you who the hired girl was, looking after the baby? That was Sudie Gurney."

Selena nodded. "I know how loyal she is to Alexander. Did anyone see any trouble between Eve and Alexander?"

"Only that once. He had shown up to take Eve and the baby home a month earlier than she'd expected. They were to leave the next morning and everyone knew that girl sure didn't want to go."

Maggie kept rocking, recalling what happened: How Eve had run upstairs and stayed there all day, her husband following her up. They didn't come down until dinner. Everyone saw Eve had been crying though she sat there straight-backed and real stoic, like a punished child in a pretty white voile dress.

"And Alexander?"

"Usually he would be all over the dining room being friendly to everyone. That night he sat there looking grim, eating his dinner. Eve went upstairs to see the baby put to bed. And to pack, everyone figured. The older wives were saying they could understand the girl's disappointment having to leave, but she had yet to learn what they could have told her—a man had to be humored, and his decisions accepted, even with a fine young husband like Alexander.

"I didn't much like that advice myself then," Maggie said as Hemmie leaped into her lap and settled down. "I can imagine how it sounds to young women today."

"Men have had to learn, too," Selena said. "Some still haven't learned about a balance in power. Maggie, don't skip anything. Tell me everything you remember."

"Lord, I'd put all this behind me. But now you're bringing it back. No, I'm all right. I can tell you about that night . . . Lord, I've never told this to anyone else."

Maggie rocked slowly, seeing that night. "After dinner everyone had gone out to the verandah as usual. It was a sweet-smelling, cool August evening, clouds racing with the wind picking up. Eve came out alone and stood on the top step looking out into the dark. We all watched because amber light from the front parlor kind of haloed her there, standing as still as an ivory statue, wind blowing her dark hair and that white voile dress against her legs. Thin, girl legs. White slippers, we all remembered later.

"Finally, she stepped down into the yard. Yellow light by the steps made it a shadowy yard, but beyond the Inn it was a totally dark night. We thought Eve was going to look for her husband, sulking in his car. Somebody had seen him go out there with a bottle. But no. Eve turned the opposite way. We watched her take the path around the end of the porch. Watched her disappear toward the back garden. Where, it seemed, *that girl disappeared forever.*" Maggie opened her eyes and looked at Selena.

"You didn't know then? Did anyone look for her?"

"Not until the next morning. The wind had picked up with a bite of fall. Everyone stirred and went on up to their rooms. Mrs. Dilworth had feather beds in those days. No, there was no reason to wonder about her. There was no place for anyone to go from the garden but back in by the kitchen door, or around to the front porch door. Doors didn't have to be locked. No strangers were ever around there."

"The garden was in back where the apple trees are now? Was the brick wall there against the slopes that go on up to Eve's Mountain?"

"No wall then. Just the prettiest flower garden, shady with a couple of low trees and seats. Little paths led up here and there but nobody tried to go very far. Those woods were dense with big boulders. You can see the rocks now. Besides, back then we knew bears and foxes and I don't know what all were up there. Foxes show up at night, still today."

"What about Crest Road back then?"

"An empty mountain road, no tourists rolling through like today. Nobody from the hollow ever bothered coming up in their old trucks. This was 1948, you know, right after the war. Only a few cars sat at the Inn. Mostly guests were delivered in spring and picked up before fall. The kitchen fellow had an old Ford. The boy from Duke had a car. "

"What happened the next morning?"

"An awful cry woke up everybody, about dawn. We stuck our heads out of windows and came on down to find out. Alexander Kingston was standing out there, shouting *Eve . . . Eve . . .* I'll never forget how that name echoed again and again in that quiet pink morning. No answer came back."

"What then, what else?"

"An early smoker told everybody he had seen the husband stumbling out of his car where he must have spent the night. Saw a bourbon bottle fall out with him. Saw him storm upstairs, looking for Eve, and right back down to shout to the mountains."

Taking in a new breath, Maggie told about the search party tracking down the road and up into the slopes, through dense rhododendron thickets. "Sudie rocked on the porch, crying, holding baby Zack in her arms. We all knew if that delicate girl had gone beyond the garden to shed private tears of goodby to the place, she couldn't have gone far on her own. But not a slipper was found."

"And Alexander?"

"Came tromping back with the sheriff's search party with a face like thunder. In the parlor, he was calling on the phone and then talking to the sheriff. That was Bo Hilrey's daddy but don't go expecting Bo to tell you anything the way I'm doing here. Oh, it was a strange time there at the Inn. A reporter came from the *Charlotte Observer.* Alexander Kingston was already making a name for himself in the textile business."

"Tell me, how did Alexander look and act?"

"M'mm. I guess he looked ready to explode with grief or maybe anger. But Selena, not a soul there at the Inn wondered if that man was guilty of anything. Everyone liked him better than they liked Eve. All summer the women had called her stand-offish. Second day, he roared off in his car saying someone had stolen his Eve and he meant to find them. I think he was sort of crazy at the time, not wanting to believe she was lost and eaten by a bear or something." Maggie studied Selena. "So what do you make of all that?"

"He remembers going into the garden to look for Eve. And remembers waking up in his car at dawn, with an empty bottle. Whatever happened in between is buried in him. And it's trying to come up now. What about the version that says two bodies were found in the burned out car months later? I've read all the old clippings. Why didn't that end the mystery at the time?"

Maggie rocked thoughtfully.

"The kitchen fellow had this old Ford. Yes, it was found crashed down off some mountain dirt road, in a ravine a county away, with burned bones in it. A man and a woman's. Anyway, Kingston buried the bones on top of the mountain after he came up here and bought all that property. He has a marker up there now."

"Why didn't that stop the talk, Maggie? You don't seem sure about the story."

"They didn't test bones in those days like they do now. Besides, those old mountain boys at the saw mills and mica mines were spitting angry. They'd used this mountain all their lives for hunting and fishing. A group in Charlotte had owned the ridge. A judge and some others had planned to establish a family summer retreat up here near the Inn but it never worked out.

"So the locals had the backside of this ridge and Hawk's for themselves, as well as some parcels around, family owned for generations. When they found out they'd sold to the same rich city fellow they felt like they'd been tricked. They started saying the man had done away with his wife and had gotten away with it."

"Alexander knew. What stopped the talk?"

"It quieted down. I guess the sheriff helped do that, which caused that poor man his own grief. Anyway Sheriff Hilrey, Bo's daddy, let it be known they could still hunt and fish, same as ever, except around the top where Kingston was building his summer house. After it was built, some national magazine wrote up Capstone, and about his promise to the memory of Eve."

"I saw that in the scrapbook too. But the old gossip—can you still hear it today?"

"You can if you keep your ears open down at the hardware store or feed store in the valley when Kingston's name is mentioned. Or when Zack flies in and out with that noisy helicopter. They grumble about rich outsiders getting away with murder."

"And they'd say as much to some reporter or TV crew?"

They were both quiet for minutes.

"But not any one around Capstone, close to Alexander. Not Sudie or Lottie."

"That job is Sudie's life," Maggie told her. "The only life she's had besides helping with other Gurney offspring. All these years Kingston has been coming up here, bringing a bunch of guests, she's been housekeeper and cook, herself, then with Lottie's help. Sudie has never complained. Their Uncle Hogan looked after the grounds until the daughter fired him. Lord, Selena, help that man get well."

She stood up as Selena did, surprised at that quiet girl's quick hug. "I intend to. Thanks for trusting me."

At the door, Maggie was already worrying about telling so much. "What are you thinking about . . . all that I told you?"

"I think Alexander Kingston was a domineering, possessive young man. But I've found you learn a great deal about a person when they are groping through an illness. What do I think? I don't believe he killed his Eve. But imagined guilt can kill him. And for that reason, so would any of these people here wanting to probe into the past."

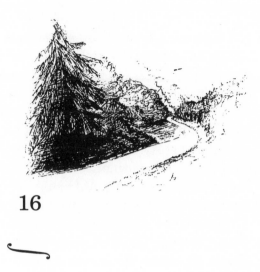

16

David Tyler figured if Tory Kingston was determined to hide big daddy from visitors, he would depend on Selena Hart to find out what was going on up there. He found Selena that afternoon in front of Maggie's shop, stashing quilts and a basket of utensils in her VW. Actually smiling at him, animated as a pretty woman should be. Good sign. "Can I buy you a Mountain Dew?" he offered. "I'm even good for a bowl of Ray's soup."

"Thanks, David, but I'm expecting the phone company at the chalet about now. They'll need to get inside."

"Hey, I'd like to see your place." At her invitation, he jumped into his van and followed the little green car up to the hidden away chalet on Hawk's Ridge. The BellSouth truck was waiting. At Selena's suggestion, David looked into the ancient refrigerator for two cold drinks. By the time she joined him, he had two chairs out on the deck.

"You have the place looking great, but I had to get out here and covet your view," he explained when Selena settled down, stretching her nice legs in the denim skirt and propping the white nurses shoes on the low guard rail. He rested his long legs there too. "Are we looking at Roan Mountain over there? Or Mitchell?"

"I haven't learned them yet. but I love every peaceful, silent shape out there. I've finally run off the spiders and encouraged the mice families to move out. How is your place working out?"

"It's one room plus. No view but it's a sanctum of privacy in the woods. It's what wannabe writers dream about. I have my Macintosh and printer set up. But I'm stumped. I never can get going on a story until I know my facts and right approach. I need to talk to your patient, Selena. I thought, sometime when Tory Kingston is out, you could bring me upstairs and introduce me to the man. Then he should be willing to invite me back."

Selena's silence felt like a stone wall. Finally, "Believe me, David, Alexander is in no condition to talk to any visitor now. About anything. Stroke patients are dealing with emotional problems as well as physical. Let him get well first."

"Sorry to hear that." Irked was more like it. "I have a deadline for this environmental piece. He should be pleased to do it. I promised the daughter I wouldn't get smaltzy with the Eve story. I'd handle it straight. But let's face it, his promise to his first wife does give the report real human interest. I promised an editor he'd have this story on his desk by the end of July."

"David, didn't you say at the Inn you were here to sample freedom from classrooms? Maybe you need leisure more than another story."

"I need both. So far I've only done the goofing off part. Have you been in the book shop next to Maggie's place? Of course you have. What a collection, once you get behind that little front door. I could spend an entire summer lost in those narrow aisles. I've been driving around, ending up at the bookstore, reading with a bowl of Ray Pickett's soup in front of the shops. Extra entertainment is listening to the tourists who pull in and ask, *Where's High Haven?*"

"So give yourself that freedom," Selena said.

"I could do it with a clearer conscience after turning out a story." He leaned back and laughed at the image that flashed in his mind. "Listen to this. As a kid from Cleveland, I thought the big outdoors was something in books. Then, when I was about ten, I bussed down and spent a month at an uncle's farm in Georgia. The first morning I looked out and saw my first green meadow. Couldn't wait until I ran out there tasting, yes, *freedom.* I ran barefoot through that thick grass, expecting to take off and fly."

Grinning with the memory, "I ran until I came down on a coil of rusty barbed wire. *Yow.* It still hurts to think of it." He glanced over at her sympathetic smile. "Maybe after that, I figured you'd better stay on the path and not trust a free run." *Also to get married at nineteen.* For the first time in days, he thought of Sarah.

"I know the feeling," Selena murmured. "I knew a stunt pilot once. Jerry. A totally uninhibited, life-loving man. He died in a crash. Forgive me, I don't prescribe morbid thoughts as wisdom. I believe we trap ourselves, we just don't realize it at the time." She asked about his wife.

"Sarah is a pragmatic little person. Give her a tennis racket and a good court and that's it. She's doing Europe this summer. Guess I told you. I have to explain to the old ladies at the Inn. Sarah doesn't care if I'm up here lost in the woods. She doesn't admit to club friends she's married to a high school teacher with only a M.A. degree. What did you leave behind in order to sample mountain seclusion?"

"Counseling. Office hours. Will you go back to your classrooms this fall?"

"Afraid so. Whatever writing I manage to do up here, teaching seems to be my fate. A foregone inevitability. When I told that to Professor Enholm he gave me the slow smile and said, 'the word fate suggests any number of unforeseen inevitabilities.' "

David got up to leave, telling himself he had to hang loose now but he would get back with Selena. "Looks like I'll have to drive down the mountain and put in some supplies. Tomorrow maybe. Bring you anything?"

"I've made that trip," she told him. "See my discount denim?"

"Selena, you'll let me know when I can talk to the man?" He had to be satisfied with her nod.

David walked into the Ridgeway dining room late. He found the tables deserted except for Mitch Mason, alone at one, his stocky sweatered shoulders hunched over his coffee. Nowhere in evidence was Lucie, the pale-faced wife with the sullen expression. David sat down next to the man. "Guess I'll have to buy myself some groceries tomorrow or move back in here. You and your wife staying the summer?"

Mitch Mason looked up, still distracted, mumbling they had come back last night for the night as he had to be away on business down at the county seat. Dilly hustled in, round face flushed above the bow tie. The innkeeper leaned close to Mason's ear to rasp, "Doc Bradley says she's all right and don't you worry. Selena Hart is going to stay with her awhile. But Doc says to wait, let them talk before you come in. Oh dear, I have to go explain to the ladies on the porch everything's all right." Dilly scurried away, panting audibly.

David kept quiet, waiting for Mason to say whatever.

"My wife must have taken too many sleeping pills last night. She can't sleep without them. When I got in this afternoon, I couldn't wake her. You can get trapped needing those things. Easy to take one too many."

David nodded politely. He filled his plate with country steak and mashed potatoes and peas as young Sally from the kitchen poured more coffee. Sally hesitated behind the two of them before blurting, "Eating always helps. When you get ready, Mister Mason, I'll have some of the hot apple pie and ice cream for you to take in to her. Maybe you can baby her into eating."

When they were alone in the silent dining room, Mason said, in a voice gruff with feeling, "I still think the summer up here will help. We are in the cottage now. The stone one behind the Kingston place."

"On Capstone grounds?" David stopped, fork in midair. "How did you get the place? I mean, when did you get past the daughter to Kingston?" *Damn.*

"I haven't met the man myself, though I need to." Mason studied his apple pie and put down the fork without touching it.

He sounded more weary than unfriendly. "I'm doing some work for Tory Kingston. Or will be."

David leaned back, looking into his coffee. He was remembering, table talk here had said this Mitch Mason was a developer out of Atlanta. So, was it true, what Tory hinted? Were daughter and father planning to slice up the mountain to make some mega bucks?

If so, he would damn well sure get out a story about a hoax and bad faith, not the story he came for. It would serve Kingston right. The man had reaped good press for years out of his promise to protect these slopes. So tough-minded daughter wasn't hiding old dad in the tower after all. Tory was acting as his shield.

He wondered if Selena knew this. Or wasn't it her concern? Selena was all integrity, all nurse, for sure. She probably didn't care about anything but helping her patient get well. Or had the man taken her in, insisting on his need for recuperation time so as to keep anyone from bothering him until he was good and ready? David turned back to Mitch Mason and asked more calmly than he felt, "You're a developer, right? So what's happening up there?"

With a grimace, "I'm here to resurface the roads. For the present. Yes, I've designed and put in the infrastructure for two other major developments. At present, you're looking at a man bankrupt in more ways than legal and monetary, not to mention a husband worried as hell."

Mason sounded like a man talking out loud to himself. "I had to get my wife out of Atlanta. I'd work for the devil, even for Miss Tory Kingston, even work as her road man, if necessary, to give Lucie a summer in a place like this. A quiet, pretty place, removed from the familiar and the heat. It hasn't started well but I'm still hoping. Don't know what else I can do. She won't talk to doctors."

David picked up his fork and again began eating slowly.

"The accident happened over a year ago," Mitch Mason continued. "I was driving the damn car. Lucie had a small dance studio in Atlanta. That's kaput of course. She hates the fucking leg brace. Nothing was working for us in Atlanta. So, here we are.

129

The only thing she pays any attention to now is her music. Don't know if that's good or self punishment. She doesn't listen to me or anyone else. Forgive the complaints but you asked." He scowled at David. "You look like a happy fellow."

"I'd be happier if I had the interview with Kingston behind me. If you're going to work up there on the roads, wouldn't you be talking to him at some point? I'd like to know just how sick he is. Or if he's saying to hell with anyone wanting to see him."

"Getting to big daddy Kingston is high on my list of problems too. Tory insists that, until he improves, he might not make any sense and would just be an interference. What can I say? I need the job."

David watched the man leave the room, broad shoulders bent and determined. So, they were all waiting to be granted audience with A. Z. Kingston, king of the hill. A stalemate, but he wasn't going to allow a little delay spoil his pleasure in being here. Tomorrow he would go down the mountain for the first time, get some food supplies and a decent desk lamp. Why had he kept putting that off?

In the empty dining room, finishing his apple pie alone, David realized why he hadn't gone down the mountain yet. He wanted to laugh out loud at the crazy notion: if he walked into an ordinary supermarket, it would dispel the satisfying sense of being in a high place, removed from the mundane realities of his life.

"Want anything from the big highway?" he asked Maggie the next day. "I'm going down this afternoon. But promise me this. Don't let anyone change this place before I get back."

At five o'clock, David headed down to the new highway, forty minutes away. When he finally shambled back into the cabin, it was a foggy midnight. Nothing had changed on the mountain but the concept of himself and the realization of his own vulnerability. He sat there in the dark, remembering the professor's remark about fate and inevitability.

17

On the broad expanse of asphalt fronting the highway stores, a flatbed truck made a stage, plastic banners flying, two amplifiers wafting country rhythms into the late afternoon air. David Tyler stashed his groceries in his van and ambled over to sample the action.

A crowd of shoppers stood in clusters, faces lifted, watching four musicians plunk away on the bass, banjo and two guitars. Next to him, a hefty father, a child riding his shoulders, offered, "That ain't no old-time fiddling. That there's the jazzy kind."

A commotion in front of the drug store drew attention from the band. A girl in ruffled red-checked gingham skirt pummeled fists against the chest of a rotund fellow in a white pharmacist smock. David recognized the girl's elfin, animated face. He strode over. "Ariel? You need help?" As quickly he realized it was the flustered man who needed intercession.

Ariel wheeled around to focus on David, her voice trembling with defiance, green eyes shiny with tears. "I'm supposed to be singing with the boys. The fiddle player *promised*. But this fellow don't like my costume and he says he hired the band and not me."

David tried to sound as casual as he did back in a classroom dealing with a kid's temper flare-up. "Maybe next time, huh? How about a Coke? I see a Hardee's over there."

He gestured for her to follow and turned away from the knot of gawkers, surprised that she complied. Fuming under her breath, Ariel caught up with him. "He *promised.*"

Once out on the open parking lot, beyond the crowd, Ariel stopped and stepped out of the ruffled skirt. "I didn't like this dumb thing anyway. I found it in a flea market. Thought it would look kinda sassy on stage." Shrugging, she balled the skirt under her arm and marched on toward Hardee's, sandals clicking, a leggy young thing in the loose red T-shirt that just covered her bottom. David followed, groaning to himself. *Jerk, who asked you to play protector to this girl? You came to get away from adolescents, remember?* This one reminded him of a kitten in the wild, ready to scratch if cornered. He knew all about hyper kids as well as the impassive ones. And from any of them, the hormone-driven recklessness that made him feel old. Right, old at twenty nine. *You're also up here to forget school teacher frustrations, remember?*

Later, with his own hamburger finished, and still amused at her flurry of exasperation about missing a chance to sing, David leaned back in the plastic seat to watch the girl devour her first sandwich and start into her second. Where was she putting all the food? His two hands could go around her waist. Her wiry body looked childlike in the shapeless red shirt, yet radiated vitality even now that she'd stopped talking to concentrate on her hamburger.

Ariel finished quickly, drew her drink closer and sighed. "Someday, when I come back here—*if* I come back—they'll build me a stage and treat me royal. You'll see, David Tyler. Just remember what I said."

"Going to be Dolly Parton, Jr.?" he teased. "Is that all you want?"

"Is that *all?* Don't you see what she's done with herself?" Ariel sucked furiously at her Pepsi, rattling the ice. He watched her lips around the straw, the upper one thin as a child's, the bottom lip full like a pout. Her mouth was the natural color of raspberry, a better color than the lipstick she'd eaten off with the sandwich.

The green eyes studied him from a serious young face. "Actually, I'm going to be Reba McEntire. I told you about her. She has this red hair. I love her to pieces."

"You don't have red hair."

"But I can sing like her." She bent again to the drink.

David looked at the finely cut profile of fair Irish skin, the curled lashes and high cheek bones, behind the sweep of dark hair. Those Scotch-Irish genes were still being handed down in these hills, weren't they? Touched by her vulnerability as well as her toughness, he told her, like the dutiful teacher he was, "It's good to have dreams. Trouble is, you kids have been force fed by TV. You think fame is the only goal." And carte blanche on morals along with the big money. "Fame and big bucks."

"You don't want any yourself? You satisfied to be a plain old teacher?" Ariel licked salt from her fingers. "Bet you have to work real hard and don't get paid nothing."

"Paid anything," he corrected. "Or let's say, paid enough. I'm talking about what you want. I'm reminding you it's not a free ride for those people you see in the spotlight."

When she widened her eyes like that, the green made him think of a clear gemstone with dangerous qualities. He looked away, but stuck to his speech. "Celebrities pay a high price for being at the top and trying to stay there, haven't you noticed?"

She pushed away the empty cup and flopped back against the seat. "When you *know* inside you can do a thing, know you were born to do it, don't you have to prove it? Not just dream about it and be too chicken to try?"

David thought about his writing, all that was still inside of him, untested. Would it be any good, or did he only hope it was?

"I'm going to try out in Nashville just as soon as I can," Ariel said softly, as if to herself. "I can't leave yet, not as long as Mama needs me. I can't leave her with Hoke around causing trouble. She can't walk good. So I have to wait."

"So you won't go until she dies?"

"That's mean!" The green eyes glittered.

"Sorry. You're quite right. I'd like very much to meet your mother by the way. She must know everything about these mountains. I need to talk to people like her for the story I'll be doing." When Ariel frowned he went on. "About going off to Nashville, you have to know the realities. Even if you are good at singing, even if you're better than famous Miss Whoever up there at the mike getting applause, there's no guarantee talent will get you there too."

He rushed on, intending to finish off his good teacher lecture and get away from this girl. Already, twilight was fading. "We'd better go. I'll walk you to your truck." He had seen her once on a mountain road in an old red pick-up.

When she followed him out, silent, he told her, "I had a friend at Florida State once, a talented fellow. Played guitar, wrote music, good lyrics, original. Cut some tapes in Nashville at twenty one. A couple promoters promised a lot because he was good. But it didn't happen. For those you call stars, there must be many more as good who never make it to that spotlight. My friend is an engineer now, and still bitter. True story. One of thousands."

Ariel squeezed his sweatered arm. The soft giggle was delight. "Then you know about going to Nashville. You must know how it can work. Or you could find out. Because you're a reporter, aren't you, not just a stuffy old teacher?"

He ignored that. "Ready? I'm heading back to High Haven. Where's your truck?"

"I came with the old fiddle player and look, they've all gone now. You can take me home. But first! Lemme show you something. It's Friday, country music night at the Fireman's Hall in Arrowhead. Don't cost to get in. You said you want to know about mountain folks, well, I'll show you."

He kept walking. She hurried alongside, the ball of red gingham under her arm. "Listen! Really, it's just fifteen minutes from here. Maybe they'll let me sing. Then you can drop me off home." Standing at his van, she blinked those green eyes. "Or else I'll have to stand at the filling station and hitch a ride with Lord knows what old boy is headed that away."

What could he do but call this a local color expedition and let her hop in his car? Later, he would try to remind himself the inevitability started here.

On the fifteen minute drive to Arrowhead, David Tyler didn't have time to worry about delivering this kid home. He had enough to do following the dark winding road, listening to the girl's candid recitation, infused with youthful angst and, he had to admit, touching enthusiasm. He interjected, "You don't expect to go in, much less try to get on stage, in that short thing?" Ariel said quickly, she'd fix the skirt. She set to ripping off tiers of ruffles and pulled the remaining short skirt back on.

The small town looked closed. No, the soulful throb of electric guitars filtered out to the gravel lot lined with cars. He parked between an old church bus and a truck. Ariel hopped out, impatient. *"C'mon!"* She led the way toward the firehall's lighted doorway, sandals crunching the gravel, legs flashing under the mini-skirt she'd devised. David followed like a reluctant guardian. The music beat sounded like rock, maybe country rock, as they approached the open door.

A string of Christmas lights shaped the low ceiling above the popcorn machine. A three-foot-high platform, bright in harsh white light, backed by a couple of flags, made the stage. Four solemn-faced men, bent to their steel and electric guitars, were shifting now into a slower, foot-patting beat. Three woman, young, middle and older, leaned into the mike to croon, *"Jes' a lettle talk with Jesus makes it all roit . . ."*

David waited inside the door, Ariel at his side scanning the situation. She leaned into him with an urgent whisper. "That's Gladys by the counter, she's the one who runs things. Go tell her you want to hear me with a band."

"Hey, I'm just your ride home, remember? Do your thing then let's get going."

She sashayed toward the pleasant faced woman who watched the stage while handing over cups of Pepsi and selling squares of home made fudge. David looked around for the best vantage point, which seemed to be the wooden church bench against the back wall. He sat down. The bench throbbed with the beat of the hefty fellow at the mike now, thumping out a Hank Williams number, lamenting, "*Never felt more like singing the blues . . .*" On the seat next to him, an old fellow munched popcorn, his long nose almost meeting his chin as he chewed. "Now me," he told David, "I like a hoe-down better, but these here boys are good, ever' one of 'em who show up these Friday nights."

Where was Ariel? Leaning over the counter talking to Gladys. David settled back against the vibrating seat and studied the crowd filling the dozen rows of metal chairs that faced the stage. Grandmothers, family clusters, wiggling kids. More just like them walking in now, already beating their palms to the wailing beat. Others stood around, glad-handing or sober-faced, waiting for their turn to go on stage. Were they any different from the people he knew? He studied the hefty and the lean in their trucker caps and work jeans. T-shirted chests that said Nashville Music City; a goateed fellow in cowboy hat and Dixie flag on his black shirt; and women who looked like they'd eaten a lot of biscuits and gravy. He stopped counting macho belt buckles, black cowboy hats, and trucker wallets bulging in jeans, chains and keys clinking with the beat.

He looked for Ariel. She was waiting at the edge of the stage, watching Gladys take over the mike to tell the crowd, "We're running a tad behind, but we got to pass the bucket now to pay for the lights and ever' thing. Miz Lil done went and crocheted this throw we gonna auction off. Twenty-five cents a chance. Ain't it purty?" Ariel hiked herself up to sit on the edge of the three-foot-high stage, beaming at Gladys busy at the mike.

"We have a real good time here," Gladys went on. "I'm proud to say we've had no trouble cause we have no drugs and no alcohol. Sometimes we poop in our messkits but so far we done all right with these country music nights giving ever' body a chance up here."

On the stage edge, Ariel hugged her knees, waiting.

"Looks like we've got Ariel McRae tonight busting to get up here. Boys, you wanna do . . . what's that you're saying? Oh sure, we gotta cake walk first. Somebody going home with a coconut cake. Billy Joe, give us some cake-walking music."

David watched Ariel having to wait, her smile frozen but holding. Half the crowd got up to circle the room, past the stage, past the drink counter, past the popcorn stand and the little kids ready to show off their clogging. A few cake-walkers looked to be tourists. A petite Vietnamese wife marched too, waving at the gray-permed mother-in-law juggling a couple of olive-skinned children and the lean and solemn husband who'd brought her home to these Blue Ridge mountains. There you have it, David deduced, there is no isolation today from the main culture. These country cowboys could be dressed this way anywhere with this music. And this brunette beauty about Ariel's age, with waist long brown curls and pink midriff showing between tight jeans and top, could be any Florida teenager hanging out in a shiny mall.

Yet something was different here. An intangible, fine difference. The local beauty was walking around the room, confident as the high school beauty queen returned to the admiring bosom of the family reunion. That was it. This scene, like the town, still knew the extended family thing. Limiting, maybe, but loving and familiar. The emotions being sung out tonight were their own, not just a product exported and exploited by the music industry. Like the quartet of motherly looking women up there now, preempting Ariel again, to sing one of their originals about stoic women and bad husbands or wayward sons, *Tears on my pillow, sweet memories of you . . .*"

David took Ariel another cold drink. "Hang in there." He went back to his bench.

"And now," Gladys said finally, "let's get Ariel McRae up here."

David watched like a sponsoring chaperone. Ariel bounced to her feet on stage and adjusted the mike like a pro, the harsh light haloing her dark hair, bare legs stiff as a child's under the short dress. With a murmur to the guitar player, she faced the audience to ask, "You-all heard Reba McEntire sing *Fancy*? She sings from her heart and that's what I like to do."

David listened . . . the whole room listened . . . to Ariel up there being a determined girl named Fancy, sent out from the shack by mama to *"be good to the gentleman Fancy,"* the words clear, the tone sweet but pure and exulting with the right touch of heartbreak. *My God, you're really good, Ariel. Go to it, give it to them.*

At the applause, she leaped off the stage, the short skirt fluttering. More applause for the acrobatic descent. David grinned. Ariel, will you always fly off stages?

He drove in silence back up the mountain toward High Haven, eyes on the dark curvy road. Beside him Ariel talked in a rush, despairing in one breath, exulting in the next, demanding to know how it went. When he admitted yes, she was good, a really pure sound, the right pathos break in the voice that seemed to go with those songs, she kicked her legs with pleasure, stretched, and quieted down to stare out at the passing night.

The car hummed and groaned up the dark road. Sighing, Ariel curled up on the seat beside him, her back to the door, hugging her knees, asking sleepily, couldn't he help find out about Nashville, since he was a reporter and all?

David drove with a tight mouth, looking straight ahead, not at her, curled up easy as a kitten, sleeping beside him, young as any of his students. He drove, trying to visualize Sarah, his work, the writing he intended to do. Couldn't focus on any of it. He had a problem here. This moment. He had to monitor the danger. He was the danger.

He took the county road around Eve's Mountain, remembering where it cut off into a narrow road that led toward her house along the creek hollow. He had to get her out of his car, see her into the house. The road turned into a path. When the car scraped a rock, and banged against another, he stopped. *Damn, had he burst a tire?* Ariel roused, looked around, murmured sleepily, "You shouldn't oughta come this way, you'll get stuck."

"Now you tell me." He peered out at the narrow dirt road and heard gurgling creek sounds. He turned off the car. Total blackness out there . . . silence. He could hear his own heart. He would have to get the flashlight and walk her home. "Ariel? Wake up." She was asleep again, her back against the door. If he went around and opened it, she'd probably fall out.

He slid from under the steering wheel closer to her. He stroked her face with an index finger. "Hi, Reba McEntire. Time to go home." His own voice came out strained, dealing with the crazy urge to gather her up.

She opened her eyes and moved closer to his face. Her arms slid around his neck. He put his hands under her armpits to push her away from him, gently, as he might lift back a child. *My God, seventeen was a child, wasn't it?* He meant to push her away but she lifted herself toward him, swung her right knee on the seat beside him, straddling his lap. She buried her face into his neck, her slight weight trembling against him.

Oh no, he couldn't let this happen. His hands went up to grasp and push her back but they found her waist, her thin hips instead, felt the muscle and bone snuggling against him. Against his ear, his neck, she smelled of sweet sweat and desire, murmuring, "Oh David, I could love you to pieces."

18

Leaving Capstone in the afternoon, Selena followed the winding road down, slowing past the second curve. Paula Crossing's leased blue convertible was still parked there, had been since noon. The car didn't have a flat so what was Paula doing inside such dense woods? Four hours was a long time to take pictures.

Around the next curve, she slowed again at the groaning tractor digging a drainage ditch. Mitch Mason in work khakis stood alongside, mopping his face with a yellow towel. He came over, sweat and sun glistening on his open, amiable face and sandy hair. He leaned in, thanking her for attention to Lucie that night at the Inn. "I wish you could stop in and see her again, at the cottage. And Selena, I've been wanting to talk to you about your patient. When can I see the man?"

"Later, Mitch." She gave him the same answer she had given David Tyler. "Here's why I stopped." She told him about Paula's car and her concern, and would he check? "You remember Paula at the Inn. She doesn't look like a mountain climber."

"More like Miss California." Mitch gave her a sly grin. "You didn't see if that Kingston kid, Loren, was anywhere around, did you? I've seen him in that blue convertible. I'd hate to flush out some illegal lovers. Hey, forgive me. You're right. We should check.

I'll go up now and take a look." He shouted to the tractor driver. "Back in a few minutes."

Selena rolled on. Farther down, a tall fellow emerged from the woods and started down the winding drive at a trot. David Tyler? She slowed alongside and told him about Paula Crossing's car. "You didn't see her anywhere in those woods did you?" At David's quick frown, Selena explained, "Mitch Mason is up there checking to see if she's all right, but since you're out hiking, you might go back up there and help him look for her."

"Sure," David said quickly. "Right now." He started up the drive in a fast lope.

Selena put the noisy VW in gear and continued on down, too tired to wonder about David Tyler or Paula Crossing or the Tory situation at Capstone. Loren Kingston had shown up, a lanky seventeen year-old with the Kingston brows, but unlike father or brother, Loren insulated himself behind a studied dignity. A protective thing, Selena reasoned. Not unusual for a boy who had a life at school and became a visitor at home. Why didn't Zack spend some time with him since his father couldn't?

No, don't worry about Zack's reluctance to be around when she needed him. At the moment, she wanted only to get home to her own privacy. Tonight she meant to throw some of Sudie's packaged offerings in a pot for soup, then settle down again with that scrapbook of clippings kept by Kingston's older sister, who had built the chalet.

Paula Crossing had not come downstairs that morning until eleven o'clock, relieved to see the dining room crowd had dispersed to the long porch, or to bridge tables in the parlor, or off for their morning strolls and bird watching. Dressed in a silk pants suit and sandals, she poured her coffee from the electric pot in the TV alcove room, and stood debating, again, what action to take.

The entire night, at least until three a.m., had been spent sleepless on the too-soft mattress upstairs. Tossing and debating. Should she leave now? Go on back to San Diego? On the phone last night, Clive had been coolly curious of her false excuses for staying here any longer. The European junket wasn't even mentioned. Here she was, gambling with the job and the man who were her stake in the future. At least eight years had been invested toward that goal.

At the end of their brief, unsatisfactory conversation, she had hung up the phone, still like the gambler who calmly watched a croupier rake back her chips. She had only a few more left to play. The month of July, at the most?

She walked slowly to her car, in the shaded lot next to the Inn. She had taken the blue convertible on an extended lease in Asheville after turning in her rental car, as if giving herself time from the beginning. Two weeks now. She still hadn't gotten up there to Capstone to confront Kingston, and find out what she came to find out. On the phone, the daughter had been curt before hanging up on her request to take pictures. Tory Kingston must have known she was lying.

Face it, Paula told herself, starting the car and rolling slowly down the drive, you've accomplished one thing. Spent time with Loren Kingston, though not enough. She had asked his help in photographing a biker's pleasure on the Blue Ridge Parkway. It worked. He had spent the morning with her. Then another.

Later, sitting in the car at an overlook, eating the sandwich she'd brought from the Inn's kitchen, Loren had talked about mountain biking. His enthusiasm for speed and movement had broken through his pose of detachment. She had savored every moment, watching the lean planes of his young face, listening to the intelligence under his studied dignity. She had to stay to see him more. She had to drive up to Capstone and demand to see Alexander Kingston, alone.

Paula drove slowly toward Capstone, jolted at every turn by memories. These mornings, standing in her dormered room at the Inn, she could remember being sixteen again. The murmur of voices below could be that other summer, her mother one of the women down there on the porch.

On the way up, a roadside indentation, a hint of a narrow foot path leading into the wooded slopes, triggered a shiver of recall.

The urge to investigate was so strong, she turned around near the tall cedars at the top and drove back down, looking again for the path.

There it was. She parked, stuffed the keys in the pocket of the silk pants and got out. The leather sandals were all wrong for tromping in tangled woods, but what the heck. Standing at the road edge, under midday sun, she remembered white tennis shoes. Remembered being a chubby adolescent with a terrible frizzy perm, and simmering passions not yet understood and never shown. On that summer, in this spot, she hadn't hesitated at this path. She had wanted only one thing, to follow the tall lean boy wherever he was going, though he waited there, annoyed she was still with him.

Even when he glowered, "Okay, go back to the Inn now. This is my private place," she hadn't left. He must have been nineteen that summer, and he had flushed at the childish admission of a secret place, proof of his own loneliness. She had seen that need, had felt older and wiser than he. "Let me go with you," she'd said. That had been the first time they had used the path.

Excitement building, Paula stepped into the woods. The sun was straight up, the woods inviting with cool breezes. The narrow forest path was overgrown but still visible, leading, she knew, to their special place, a stone ledge further in. It had to be there, still, the same as in all her dreams. High Haven might be the only place left in the world that hadn't changed. Especially here on Kingston property. She stepped over a rotting log and saw a continuing trail. Skin prickling, she followed it, regretting the sandals but not caring that branches caught at the thin pants.

Far overhead, trees whispered against clear summer sky. She moved gingerly, alone with the crunch of her steps, and the woods sighing and breathing around her. Distant birds called and others answered. A high hum must be a stream somewhere, water running over rocks.

Her entire body flushed with memories now, Paula maneuvered the narrow path, where first one side then the other sloped down with a tangle of new and old trees and thickets of rhododendron. Deeper in, she could look down on the place remembered. Enormous flat boulders, embedded in the mountainside, hidden, unless you knew they were there. As Zack had known.

One rock extended out like a flat ledge, shaded by towering trees, a place so private, it freed every cell of your body to open to the other body who had climbed to this spot with you. A place so protected, you could merge with this other who became the missing part of yourself. It could happen that way, even for a naive adolescent on a summer day, safely away from the scrutiny of a mother who had taught you to trust no one and to hate all men.

Paula tracked on, breathing hard. Oh yes, this was the path. In a moment . . .

She stopped abruptly, steadying herself with a tree branch. Voices? No, surely not in here. She moved on, stepping carefully. Pulse thudding, she pushed aside foliage. Did she imagine movement down there? Other people? *Oh no,* this was her place, revisited endless nights in her dreams. She took another step closer and stared down.

A man and a girl, down there on the flat boulder. The man sitting with his back against another stone, the girl prancing around the flat ledge as if it were a stage. The girl dancing close to the edge now, arms up, dark hair swirling as if addressing the world . . . no, singing to it . . . the sound clear as bird call.

The man shouted out, alarmed. He leaped up, yanked the girl back, pulled her into his lap, wrapped his arms around her. The girl pushed his chest, made him lie back on the stone and sat astride his long body, ripping off her blouse and rolling it into a pillow under his head. Was he laughing? The girl bent down, her long hair covering both their faces, the two of them colored by shade and sun.

No, Paula murmured, *no!* Tears distorted the view of the crazy girl down there, rolling with the man. *No, it wasn't like that. There were leaves, soft green leaves, a bower under overhanging branches where no one would see and my mother would never know . . . What happened was gentle and powerful and the only complete moments in my life.*

Paula backed away, trembling, confused, feeling the fool, cheated by these interlopers. She turned, blind with fury, or loss, pushing through the heavy brush to get away from them.

On the narrow path, she stumbled and had to jerk free a sandal caught in a gnarled root. It spun her off balance. She fell on her back at the edge of the high path. For interminable seconds, she kept falling . . . rolling and sliding . . . down through the tangle of brush and roots. Grabbing at a sapling, she stopped, clinging there, angry at her own stupidity.

Grasping branches, Paula crawled back up with scratched hands and bloody knees, one ankle already numb. Head swimming, she lay there, looking up to tree tops and blue sky beyond, wondering vaguely if to let go and cry would keep you from passing out.

Two cars crunched along the drive above the chalet. Looking out from the kitchen window, Selena saw David Tyler at the wheel of Paula's convertible and just behind, Mitch Mason's Jeep. She threw open the door and waited as the two men lifted Paula from the Jeep. A pale and disheveled Paula with muddy torn pants. They carried her riding their crossed arms, her own arms braced around their necks. Selena opened the door wide.

"Hi, came to see you." Paula sounded giddy, relief and a tinge of hysteria in the shaky laugh.

"Well, Paula Crossing. I'm very glad to see you," Selena said calmly as a receiving nurse. "Take her in the bathroom first. Then both of you find all the ice you can in the fridge. Get the basin from under the sink."

In the bathroom, freed of the torn pants, seated on the edge of the tub, Paula talked fast through chattering teeth, as Selena cleaned the deep cuts on her right leg and the scratches on her hands and arms. "Crazy to go in there, I know, don't ask me why . . . do you know how hard it is to get out of your pants to pee in the woods when you can't stand up? And how weird it feels to call for help and hear your voice echoing, nobody answering but the birds? Whoops. That burns. Can't stop shaking."

Selena took her flower-sprigged robe from the hook and pulled it over Paula's head. "There, you look like a country angel." She called out to the two men. "Let's get her in there to the ice."

Five minutes later, in the chalet's living room, Paula lay back in the recliner chair, as Selena wrapped her swollen right ankle in a thin towel, then a plastic bag of ice. "You're lucky. It doesn't seem to be broken. But we'll get you down to Doc Bradley tomorrow and let him check it. Meanwhile, you need to stay here tonight with that leg elevated."

Mitch watched. "Good thing you had us look. Right, David? You don't find a Red Riding Hood in the woods just any day." He beamed down at Paula in her cloud of robe, her face pale, voice shaky with thanks.

Selena turned to the men. "You're my first guests—the rescued and the rescuers. Stay both of you and let's celebrate. I found some dusty bottles of wine in this place. They look promising. And this afternoon I made a pot of barley soup." She wanted them to stay. She must have been more lonely than she'd realized.

"Can't pass up an offer like that," Mitch Mason said. "Besides I have to look at this place. These walls are real chestnut, how about that? A craftsman made that fireplace. David, can you stay for soup? I can drop you off later."

David Tyler stood at the sliding glass doors looking out at the salmon pink sunset. Quieter than Selena had ever seen him. Finally he turned around and looked at the three of them. With a wry smile, "This place gets to you, doesn't it? It drops you in the present. Makes you forget what you left and have to go back to."

In the kitchen, Mitch sampled the cheese as Selena heated the soup. "Remind me not to stay too long. Lucie, you know. But I'd be happy to get a fire going on the hearth once I open your wine here."

Mitch busied himself opening the wine bottle but finally said what Selena knew was on his mind. "I promise you, Selena Hart, not to ask again about seeing Kingston, but you will let me know soon as that's possible? And don't mention my request to Tory."

His grim look gave way quickly to his easy smile. "You must know what I mean. She's officious about guarding Big Daddy. You're the only one who gets the pleasure. Or, I guess it's not a pleasure from what I hear."

Selena nodded and turned the soup on to simmer. Mitch carried the tray of wine and crackers and cheese back into the room and set it on the low wooden table in front of the couch. Selena followed with two fat white candles and wine glasses.

David had found the record player on the old breakfront. Grieg's *Hall of the Mountain King* filled the chalet. The men sank into the couch near Paula's recliner, Selena in a chair, all of them voting on candlelight and firelight over lamplight.

As the sun sank behind darkening mountains, they drank wine and swapped stories about High Haven and Dilly and his regulars. "The man looks like Truman Capote in a red bow tie," David mused.

Selena sat back, watching their faces, listening with pleasure she hadn't known in a long time. She saw how David looked away from Paula's occasional studied glance and how Mitch kept turning to Paula's animated face with a look of longing he probably didn't know was showing. Mitch Mason seemed to be a man enjoying himself for a change with no desire to talk about the road work he was doing. When they turned to Paula to talk about her reason for being here, she said, "I came for a funeral, my mother, in Virginia. Wanted to see these mountains down here."

Evasion, Selena knew. Just as she did herself when they turned to her. "You've heard the old saying? *Stop the world I want to get off.* It means you need some quiet new space to clear the mind and drop the tensions. Not easy is it?" She smiled at all three of her guests. "But here we are."

"Let's drink to that," David said, looking relaxed for the first time.

Mitch put another small log on the hearth. With David Tyler's help, Selena brought out the bowls of soup and the conversation flowed again over the clink of dishes and crackle of logs.

David painfully confessed his disenchantment with teaching, but looked comforted when they all declared he *did* care. It was his private idealism that was bruised, not relinquished.

Mitch Mason's hearty southern tones slowed to pensive as he told of his contact as student with architect Pei, and his inspired plans at the time. Mitch kept his story funny, with groaning asides. "Instead, I went with a residential development firm doing suburbs because I had a first wife by then and big bills. After that was over, I met Lucie—let's end the Mason saga there. Somebody else. Paula?"

Paula complied with a funny story about her job, leasing agent for a major California mall developer. Again they turned to Selena, but she stood up. "Did I hear someone outside?"

"What I won't do to get a party thrown in my honor. Did I tell you—," Paula stopped abruptly as Selena opened the door. Zack Kingston stood there, wind blown and frowning, taking in the candle-lit party. "Didn't expect you to have company. See you another time, Selena." He had turned and walked out.

Soon as they heard his car leave, the two men shrugged, and stood for their genial goodnights. After they left, Paula nestled back in the recliner chair under the blanket, her bright voice turned to a weary whisper. "Thanks, Selena, it's been quite an afternoon and night. Need to sleep now."

In her loft bed, Selena remained sleepless replaying the evening in her mind. What happened there when Zack Kingston made his sudden appearance and departure? The two men had regarded Zack with male consternation but Paula had gone totally still.

Later, in half sleep, Selena came awake instantly. Was that a sound outside? On the gravel path or on the deck? She lay still, listening. Yes, again. She rose. Stood looking down on the living room where Paula slept. Beyond the sliding glass doors, was that a shadow moving? The deck out there with the old Jacuzzi was weather-warped, wind could make it whine. She clutched the loft railing and listened. Yes, the deck creaked. She reached for the flashlight next to the bed and swept the small spotlight back and forth across the black glass. Listened again. To silence she didn't trust.

Below, Paula sat upright. "What is it? Selena, what's going on?"

"It's nothing. I'm coming down." She thought for a reason. "I can't sleep and I want to make a cup of hot tea."

19

After the noise that woke them both, Selena lit the candle by Paula and left her sitting upright and wide-eyed in the recliner. She came back with two steaming mugs of camomile tea. Paula took the hot cup with both hands. "Thanks. Tell the truth. Didn't we hear some noise out there on your deck? I'm used to traffic, not weird sounds in the mountain night. I hope you have a bear or raccoon for a neighbor not a mountain version of a sicko peeping Tom."

Selena sat down with her own cup, meaning to sound reassuring. "Nothing should be out there but woods and below, Ruby Creek hollow. Raccoons maybe, even a fox." In the kitchen waiting for the kettle, she had shivered, trying to dismiss her own fear, grateful for company and wondering how much to confide. She studied Paula nestled down in the robe and blanket, the copper colored hair tousled, the gauze wrapped leg still extended. Without the clever makeup, her guest looked more like a fresh-faced teenager than the classy Paula, hyper businesswoman, probably her own age.

"An old place like this has to creak," Selena mused, already feeling better herself. "Can you imagine the winds it must have taken? Of course at two a.m., it's easy to imagine ghosts. You must have heard the Eve story. Old ladies at the Inn like to tell it. If you have—what do you think?"

Paula looked beyond their circle of light to the darkened room. "Memories are ghosts. They come to life and kick in without warning. That's why I fell."

So, Paula was here dealing with private ghosts. I'm not surprised, Selena thought. All the signs of inner conflict were there, the tightened eye muscles, pressed lips, the flutter of pulse at the throat, and right now she was obviously trying to decide if she wanted to talk about it. To give her time, Selena mused, "Memories are like old pictures packed away in an album, aren't they? You want to be able to bring out the good ones. But not the painful ones. They're the ghosts and can haunt you, hidden away or not."

Paula's pale pink lips softened to a pensive smile. Selena continued, "People leave ghosts of their experience in a place like this. Everyone must come to these mountains looking for something. Maggie says they don't always know what it is. But it's something different from what they have. Someone left a card on the refrigerator with lines from Emerson: "The influence of fine scenery, the presence of mountains, appeases our irritations." In this old chalet, I've found books from metaphysics and meditation to a stack of romances; the plaque over there, "Lift up mine eyes to the hills;" the package of gauze I used on you; and the wine we drank."

"What did you come looking for?" Paula murmured.

"To feel safe." At Paula's questioning look, Selena added, "I didn't mean to sound dramatic. I was waiting for you to decide if you wanted to tell about the ghosts that caused your fall."

Paula set down her cup and pulled the cover to her chin. "Safe, huh? You know, Selena, when I first watched you at the Inn, I thought what a frosty, detached dame. Then we came in here tonight, me a mess, with those two nervous guys, and you calmed us down and gave us a party. Nurses must be good as calming influences as well as first-aid for crazy women who do fool things like I did, tromping around in woods with slippery sandals. Now you sit here, looking serenely in control, when you are worried as hell about yourself. Am I right?" Paula smiled. "Makes me wonder—do you caretakers know how to take care for yourselves? I'm serious."

"You mean, can a thoracic surgeon lecture to smokers because of what he sees, then go ahead and smoke like a fiend in his BMW? Oh, yes." She had to laugh at Paula curled up under the quilt, bright-eyed again, looking at someone else's problem not her own. "Very perceptive, Paula Crossing. You are doing to me what a good therapist does, making a space, inviting me to come out with it, dump the pain on the table."

"Why, are you a therapist? Not an RN?"

"Actually, my nursing days were fifteen years ago. It so happened I needed the RN credentials for this job at Capstone. Until I found this place, I had my own practice. Rather, one connected to my husband's practice. In Colorado. I counseled his patients and troubled women—for all the reasons women are troubled these days."

"We do have our reasons. What did you tell them?"

"First, I listened. Helped them recognize their own feelings before looking at the situation. Invariably I had to remind them that ignoring a problem, or running away,—was a postponement not a solution."

Selena paused a moment, then said it quickly. "I believed that, and still do. Nevertheless, I ran away from *my* situation. My child fell to his death from a terrace. The stories in the paper implied it was my fault."

"Was it? Forgive me, Selena. Tell me about it."

"Roby was hyper kinetic, something they're beginning to call ADHD, or Attention Deficit Hyperactivity Disorder. Roby, I know, had neurological and emotional problems. A child like that is a victim of his own impulsive tantrums and refuses to be held or comforted. All of his six years, I wanted to take him away with me to find some answer, some solution, to save him. Instead . . ."

"What stopped you?" Paula asked gently.

Selena found herself telling of Drew's threat to institutionalize Roby if she left her practice, and how she had felt trapped to stay in the negative, painful climate of that beautiful, sterile house with a perfectionist husband who hated her for giving him an imperfect child. "In the office I had to be the confident professional but I fell asleep late each night with the help of one Valium, five milligrams, because I was emotionally and physically exhausted."

With her dislike for self-pity, Selena told it quickly, knowing the brevity might sound unfeeling and banal.

"Did you have help?" Paula asked.

"Yes, caretakers and housekeepers came and went in an endless succession. Each one left because of Drew's demands as well as Roby's behavior. Yes, I should have taken Roby and left. Somehow. That was, and is, my guilt. I had to come here to realize it."

Paula's attentive face invited her to go on. "You know, Paula, I sit here wondering why you would want to hear this and I'm remembering the women who sat across from me, thinking the same thing. *Why try to speak of it? Why try to explain? Why not leave it hidden inside?* But it's toxic held inside."

"I'm no counselor," Paula said. "I'm a woman, listening, at one a.m. So tell me. What happened that night?"

"I didn't try to remember the details until weeks after I was here. On a Sunday afternoon, matter of fact, on a rainy creek bank. That's when I faced the whole nightmare. When I did, I realized Drew must have given me something stronger than the five milligrams before he left for the hospital. I know now he must have come back well before dawn, to open the doors that I had locked as usual, even drugged as I was. Drew always warned something would happen to Roby or the house and I realize now he meant to show me that it could. I believe he opened Roby's door, unlocked the terrace doors and went into his study for a drink. He had Scotch on his breath when he woke me up later, at dawn, looking strange, as if something had gotten out of his control."

"You give the bastard more credit than he's due. And here you are, Selena, still hiding from him. So it's not over, is it?"

153

"No. The investigation wasn't complete when I left Denver. Ran away, unable to breathe in that house. The circumstances do suggest child abuse, or worse. When they come to Drew with questions, he will accuse me to save his reputation."

"Who is this guy?"

"A genius in the operating room. The ultimate perfectionist. Famous in Colorado. Drew had been my mentor first. He controlled my life." Selena smiled at Paula. "Ironic isn't it, to be so controlled by the man, when during office hours, I was the wise, compassionate counselor to emotionally battered women? It's possible to play two roles. Not healthy, but possible."

Paula murmured. "Co-dependence, the latest designer word for an old hang-up. Does he still have power over you? If someone shows up from Colorado, can't you tell them the truth?"

"They would believe Drew, not me. I'm the one who ran away."

"That son-of-a-bitch lets his child get killed and he blames you. Are you afraid of him? Or the police? Good Lord, you need to let this out. Go on."

Selena nodded. "Dr. Drew Hempton will not allow anything to interfere with his schedule, much less his prestigious career. By now he must realize I have figured out what happened. He implied my guilt at the initial investigation. There's no question, Drew will accuse me to assure his own protection."

"You think he's around looking for you?"

"He wouldn't use his own time. He would hire a private detective to find me. Unless he can sit back, waiting for Colorado to find me." It was a relief to hear her own voice say it calmly.

"Couldn't you return the favor—accuse *him*?" Paula asked.

"With what proof but my word? His office manager, Mrs. Creighton, would do anything to please him, like vouching for an emergency call to the hospital or the record of his time there. Their word against mine."

"There should be something you remember that would help."

Selena studied the strong candle flame. "I keep dreaming about that room, the empty bed, the toy bear on the floor. That old bear was the only thing Roby loved. He'd scream if Bear was out of his sight. When I went in his room that morning, there it was, thrown in a corner. I still dream about that."

A chill of realization moved like ice through her veins. "Paula! Roby wouldn't have willingly left that room on his own without Bear. So someone took him out of his bed, throwing Bear into the corner. And no one was in that house while I slept but Drew."

Paula nodded. "There's your proof! If they come asking, couldn't you tell them that?"

"As I said,—who would believe me?" She reached over, grasped Paula's hand a moment. "Thanks. Talking it out does help when you have a good listener. I know too well the worst psychic pain is the one you hide from yourself." She leaned back again, listening to wind sigh against the still dark windows. "It's a safe place to talk, isn't it? Now it's your turn. Before I started with this, you were about to tell me why you turned pale and went silent when Zack Kingston walked in and right back out tonight."

"Ah, Ha!, you *are* perceptive about us troubled females." Paula swung her bandaged legs out from the quilt and studied the swollen ankle. "At this moment, however, after you help me hobble to the potty, I'd like to crawl back under this cover and sleep. Give me coffee in the morning, black, and I'll tell all. I want to, because I need your help. I have to see Alexander Kingston and I hear that's not so easy. I have to talk to him face to face, alone. Can't do this on any phone."

So Paula was the fourth person trying to get to her patient. She'd have to answer Paula in the morning. "Here, let me help you. Grab an arm. Keep the your weight off that foot."

Paula stood, accepting the help. "I heard about Eve Kingston the summer I was sweet sixteen. Tell you about it in the morning, okay? I've held this in for eighteen years. It can wait one more night."

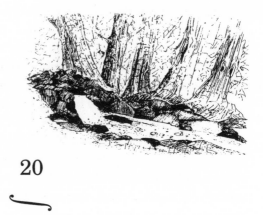

20

"Coffee coming up," Selena said, leaving Paula seated at the table by the window, leg propped on a chair, looking out at a heavy fog.

Back in the alcove kitchen she set out the cups, thinking of her guest's admissions before they went back to covers and sleep. So, Paula had been here the summer she was sixteen. Alexander would have been forty-nine or fifty then. If the man had made use of a girl as young and innocent as Paula inferred, *I will be painfully disappointed, Alexander.*

Working with her patient, she had seen him angry at his body and erratic with his agitation; but in quieter moments, she had seen the man he must have been before the stroke, forceful, with enormous drive and charisma, the kind of confident power that didn't have to be deceptive in his dealings, but up front about his motives and passions. Not anything like viciously self-centered Drew Hempton. Under Alexander's garrulous male ego, there was the capacity for caring. Passionate caring. *But I can't believe you'd strike someone you loved, with intent to murder.* Selena's hand shook pouring the hot coffee. So, admit it. She had allowed herself to become emotionally involved here, as Tory accused. Regardless, she was a good nurse and intended to help the man. The thought came unbidden: *to save his life.*

She brought out the coffee and toast. "Fog like this is one reason they call this ridge an Appalachian Brigadoon. One day clarity, the next morning you wake up, totally fogged in, with no clue to what's waiting out there. Also true of life, isn't it?"

"I'm foggy now," Paula said, coming out of her own reverie. "Ah, good old caffeine. And look at you! White turtle neck sweater. Denim skirt. Short bouncy hair, no stylist has touched. Proves a woman of style can make out from one of those cheapo stores down the hill. When are you due at the Kingston castle?"

"Ten o'clock. Stay comfortable here, there's lots to read and a radio. Keep that ankle up until we see Doc Bradley. But right now we have time to talk. What do you need to say to the man in the castle?"

"I was afraid you'd remember to ask. No, not really. I need your help."

Selena waited, watching Paula drink half of the coffee before setting the cup down, looking determined. "I want to ask him—did you meet with my mother in Virginia, at the Sacred Heart Clinic, on a day in May seventeen years ago? She would have been the delicate looking lady, very old family Virginia, very Catholic, emotional, but underneath the tears, adamant as the righteous can be. The wounded righteous."

Paula studied her reaction then looked away, her voice soft. "I need to tell him, he wouldn't have seen me. I was still dopey on hard, sterile sheets. The ceiling was white too, and a water faucet dripped. I had difficulty waking up because I was totally out of it when they took something from me. I woke feeling it had been *ripped* from me. I remember a nice bland face, white capped, bending over me. A nun. I never even heard the baby cry. I was still too doped up. So I didn't know if it was alive. Or if it was boy or girl. My mother told me nothing. After all I had made *her* suffer so much, having to hide me away for awhile."

Paula paused to let out a held breath. "How's that for old time melodrama? You had to know my mother to believe it. You said last night we women start explaining our stories with our excuses? I have a classic one. It's about being the sheltered child with a mother who loathed anything in pants, warning me since I could remember, that if your skirt got over your knees something terrible would happen. And to think, a lot of kids my age were in Haight-Ashbury not long after, kicking over all the traces."

"But this was happening to you. Go on."

"She hadn't told me anything but the warnings. When my periods started, she was really nervous and delivered this cheerful little thought. I remember her voice. Like this." Paula closed her eyes tight, doing a melodramatic whisper. *"Caroline, I'd rather bury you with my own two hands than see you get . . .'* She couldn't even tell me *what*. I knew of course it meant get pregnant before the priest said it was okay."

"You're still angry. I can understand that." Selena gave Paula time to gulp down more coffee. "I had a void of family life myself. I grew up with older parents, quiet Pennsylvanian Dutch people. Part of my so-called calm came from being alone too much. Alone, with my face in a school book. I didn't date, didn't have a lover until I was in my first year of nursing. I was twenty, but as new as sixteen. I learned a lot about myself that year from being in love with a man who challenged me to feel and live. Go ahead, I'm listening."

Paula told it quickly in a husky, tense voice. "Mother and I stayed the summer at the Ridgeway Inn. Me, the innocent frizzy-haired Caroline, three months before my seventeenth birthday. Mother found people to talk to on the porch. Her surveillance on me eased. I read books and hung around, and one day got invited to a party at Capstone. Some woman with a young daughter was visiting up there and they needed another young thing to entertain her. So I went. I remember that big house being alive with people, and I remember the host looked handsome as a movie star. Like Sean Connery today. The other girl and I didn't connect, she preferred to play with the bratty little sister, but she provided my excuse later because I wandered out back, made friends with a big Collie dog. And met Zack."

Selena nodded. *So that was it.* Paula continued. "He came hiking up from those woods, and because the Collie liked me, he sat and talked. Treated me like the kid I was then, while he was nineteen, restless to start prep school that fall. You know what's coming. Shall I say it?"

"Now's the time."

Paula dropped the bantering tone and told it slowly, with feeling. "I have never loved . . . as I loved Zack Kingston that summer. The first few days we hung around on the grounds up there, like a couple of lost children, he teasing me but talking honestly, admitting he wasn't happy with his family, meaning his father. He even told me about his mother being lost. To say we became *lovers* that summer, as we mean it today, sounds too crass. It was more than that. It was a giving and receiving. It was becoming whole and complete for a few summer days deep in those woods."

With a pensive smile, "Selena, in the years since, I've had a husband briefly and more lovers than I can remember, but it's been role-playing all the way. The only way I can have an orgasm is to fantasize that wooded place where we were alone together. The place and that boy's touch. So now you know why I did the dumb thing yesterday and went into those woods alone. I wanted to see that place."

With a wry smile, "Guess what? I wasn't alone. I saw David Tyler down there with some girl. Don't tell him I told you. They didn't see me. That's when I bolted and ran in those damn sandals and fell down the dumb slope."

Ariel, Selena thought, remembering David's face when Ariel was mentioned. "Paula, did you come back to find Zack, or speak to his father?"

"I didn't even know Zack would be here. It's been a long time. He wouldn't remember me. Last night for sure he didn't see little Caroline, of the southern tones and brown hair. No, I came to see his father to ask what he did with the baby. I can't leave until I know. Already I believe it is Loren. He's a Kingston all right. But I have to talk to the man, to know, to be sure he's my son."

159

"How did you find out?"

"After my mother's funeral in Virginia, I looked through her papers. Found letters and a poem or prayer in her feathery handwriting. About 'save the soul of this poor babe born in sin but placed in the bosom of its own kin.' And there was an address in Charlotte for Alexander Zackary Kingston. She must have called him, put the baby in his arms and threatened him with holy hell if he didn't do right by it."

"Loren Kingston is seventeen," Selena said softly. "Said to be Kingston's youngest."

"I know. I need to ask Kingston what he's told Loren. And Zack. You're shaking your head, telling me they know nothing. Selena, I still need to talk to Kingston, look him in the face."

"Paula, not yet." Again she was explaining about emotional stress and how it was interfering with his physical progress and why he couldn't handle visitors right now. "Do you have to return to California immediately?"

"I should. I have a lot at stake there. But I have to know Loren better. That's what's important. He's a strange boy, a real loner. Intelligent, but so wary. As if he's all on his own, even if Kingston does send him to expensive schools and student junkets. Selena. I can't leave yet. I haven't decided what to do beyond that."

21

In the stone guest house behind Capstone, Mitch Mason scrambled through the box of tapes, looking for one to please Lucie.

It was a relief to get her settled in here though being this close to Tory Kingston could be a problem. Tory had called twice today when he was out working. Tonight, she'd better call. She had taken the papers signed by Big Daddy to the bank in Asheville and should know by now if they were getting the initial construction loan.

On her way in from Asheville today, Tory had waved from her car with a thumb's up and impish smile. He was due more than that. The woman was frustrating as hell.

The phone rang. Mitch grabbed it up, knowing Lucie watched resentfully. On the other end of the line, Tory's saucy, "Hi. Walk over here now and we'll talk," sounded more like a summons than an invitation. Mitch said sure, and hung up quickly. "That was Daughter," he explained casually as he could.

"The witch," Lucie contradicted, in her now habitual apathetic monotone, laced with irony. She sat in the deep window seat, back against pillows, gazing out at woods and fading sunset. The ruffled cotton peignoir he'd bought at the highway stores pooled over her legs, hiding her thinness and the metal brace.

"You look like a romantic damsel on the cover of one of those romances," Mitch said, trying to ignore the mood she set for them.

"You mean a horror paperback. The hollow-eyed damsel hidden away in the Hansel and Gretel cottage."

"Do I hear some sense of humor surfacing there?" He went into the kitchen on the other side of the open bar and poured her a glass of wine, trying not to appear hurried. "No? Lucie-love, for God's sakes, I'm trying. Why don't you?" He regretted the outburst instantly.

"You run when she calls."

"Such is often the case with a boss." He handed her the wine and went back to the stereo to fill the atmosphere with something soothing.

"Boss? For a job of scraping and patching her roads?" Lucie downed the wine and left the glass on a pillow so he had to retrieve it.

"Not even that job unless Big Daddy's Daughter has gotten an okay on funds. I told you, Kingston isn't well. He's probably a pain in the ass to deal with too, and he seems to be letting Tory run this show. I am trying to put up with this because I want to stay here."

He punched the tape player. *Afternoon of a Faun* wafted through the place like audible incense. And tranquilizer, he hoped. Mitch came back to cup his wife's chin and search her thin face, her eyes dark circled. She closed her eyes, shutting him out, wracking him with a sense of tenderness and frustration. He hoped the soft melody would soothe her until he got back. Lucie demanded music constantly. As an escape? Or self-torture. Maybe she danced to it behind her eyes, then opened them to a reality she refused to accept.

Mitch forced a smile. "You've got to admit, this is one fine little place for a summer." He ran his fingers through her long lusterless hair, waiting for some answer. Before bringing her up from the Inn, he'd done a lot of labor in the place, cleaning out cobwebs, rewiring, bringing in knitted throws and lamps and such from Maggie Hardy's shop. "Even if this does turn out to be a summer labor job, we need it."

"To pay my bills to insulting, useless doctors." She drew back from his hands.

"Stop it, Lucie." Again his impatience had flared louder than the music. As usual, it quickly became remorse. The see-saw of emotion was wearing him down. "Look, Lucie-girl, Selena Hart is going to come by and see you some afternoon, not as a doctor, just to visit, woman-talk. She offered and besides she comes up every morning now, directing therapy for Kingston."

He thought grimly, at least Selena was allowed in that upper suite. Maybe she didn't want to say the man was turning senile with the illness, or was too ornery to talk to the people trying to see him. The phone rang again. Mitch grabbed it up. "Yes, I'm coming." With his wife's silent gaze chilling his back, he walked out.

Mitch headed across the landing strip toward the back terrace of Capstone. Already he felt better in the bracing air. The lilac twilight promised a full moon. The tied-down helicopter, crouched in the middle of the open knoll, reminded him of his encounter with Zack Kingston outside the post office a few days ago. Zack's greeting had been abrupt: "You the road man renting the cottage? Nothing should be done up there without A. Z.'s okay."

Without waiting for a reply, Zack Kingston had walked back to a tall kid with hair pulled back in a pony tail, waiting by a custom made mountain bike. Loren, the youngest Kingston, Mitch guessed. Tory had already told him, "Loren's showing up from school, but he won't be here long," as if dismissing the younger half-brother as a temporary annoyance. Poor kid.

In the fading light, Mitch strode toward the big house. Someone waited on the dark terrace, curled against cushions in one of the wrought iron lounges. Tory. Always at first glance, the petite figure looked young as in vulnerable and appealing, until the lady spoke, voice clipped and specific, self-possessed as a female lawyer demanding his deposition.

At his approach, Tory stirred, and settled again like a languid cat. "Sit down, I wanted to show this to you when we weren't

163

bothered with distractions." She explained quickly that Loren was finally off, backpacking on the Parkway, and Zack was going out for the night. She opened the folder in her lap and turned it toward him. "Take a look."

He glanced through the legal papers from the bank, looking for Alexander Zackary Kingston's approval. The power of attorney paper in the folder did have the big man's ragged signature. He wanted to study the loan application but Tory was taking her folder back and hugging it to her chest, smiling up at him. Still standing, Mitch asked, "Shouldn't we go inside to look this over?"

"No. This is just the first step. It means road money. Besides, Zack's still here. We just finished a brother-sister fight over this. I won." She drew up her knees and hugged her legs. "I made him admit the roads up here are in bad repair and the water lines need replacing."

"That's only the first phase. What about the whole project? And what's the problem with your brother?"

"First phase certainly, but the necessary beginning. Zack and I made a truce." She looked away toward the knoll and fringe of trees that were darkening now. "He'll stay out of my way in handling what has to be done up here. And I gave in about that woman therapist. I agreed not to throw her out. So I won't. At least not right away. Actually I need someone here. I can't be tied down completely. For Christ's sake, sit down. It's nice out here."

He complied. "I know the nurse. Selena Hart is a quiet one but seems like a caring person who must know what's she's doing. She helped Lucie one evening at the Inn just by talking to her. How is she doing with your father?"

Grudgingly, "Selena is a convenience at present. She can't do too much harm until I check her out." Tory shrugged. "I need to be out. I need to stay in touch with how it's going in Asheville. But it's best if you look after the water line permits at the county seat. I feel a resentment there against Kingstons I don't appreciate. Why has the roadwork stopped?"

Mitch told her he owed his two men, Banks and Estel, two weeks pay and didn't want to call them back until she could write those checks. "They know you fired old man Hogan. These local fellows are all related, or know each other." In the dim light of the terrace he could see she was smiling at him now, leaning back, the thin yellow sweater shaping her breasts. High round little breasts for such a petite woman. Little Bitch.

Angry at himself for noticing, he tried again. "Tory, you know damn well why I'm here. My wife's health. But I can't afford to be kept dangling about the extent of the project beyond the present. We still need your father's approval for the construction loan on the total infrastructure. When?"

"That calls for another signature from my father. It can't be pushed."

"Then you should want me to talk with him so I can answer any of his questions. He deserves to see my credentials. I could give him an idea of the phases this will take."

"Ah, what professional integrity. Laudable, okay, but also a pain in the ass. I know Mitch Mason's record, I checked on you before I asked you up. I know that Georgia lake development going sour wasn't all your fault but you haven't had a job since, right? I'm giving you a new opportunity if you stick with me. You're looking at the person in charge here, must I remind you? So let's stay in the present. One phase at a time. That's how I have to work it."

He leaned back, cracking his knuckles. "And your brother understands this? He doesn't want to be in on the planning? He glowers when he passes me on the road. At the post office the other morning, he warned me curtly his father had to be consulted on anything done up here."

Tory waved a hand in dismissal. "Zack is too self-absorbed right now to be interested in the project and would only interfere if consulted. He's having himself an early mid-life crisis or whatever."

Damn, this impervious, difficult woman meant to undertake this project at her own timing, like some kind of personal game. His endurance was already taken up with treading around Lucie's moods. This one meant to handle him with obstinate control and coy smiles. And managing it. Who would put up with that? Mitch glumly conceded the answer: No one but an out-of-work bankrupt developer. He told himself, *Stop grousing, hang in there. What else can you do?*

Mitch stood, biting down on impatience. The knoll reflected a sheen of moonlight now. He looked for a yellow gleam from the stone cottage across the way but it was still dark over there. He'd better get back over. But he waited, frustrated as hell with this woman stonewalling him about Kingston senior. He tried again. "Forget your brother then. But since we depend on approval from your father, he needs to meet me. We should talk about this."

She surprised him with a languid sigh. "That has to wait." Tory uncoiled from the chair, to face him. "My father does say he wants this place looking perfect. *For Eve.* He thinks Eve is coming back."

Mitch frowned. "You mean—?"

"Yes, losing his marbles. He's begun to hallucinate. Oh, I expect him to come out of it in time. Meanwhile, we have to go forward as carefully as possible. We have his first okay for road funds. Be satisfied with that."

Damn. His hopes for this job sank like a wrecking ball. So Daughter was protecting Father, after all. Lousy fate. Damn shame too, a dynamic tycoon like that becoming a mixed-up old man in months. The stroke must have been worse than first reported. Maybe her stubborn stance deserved some sympathy.

"I have to get back." He meant to jog across the knoll, back to the cottage but she followed him out, murmuring about her responsibilities here, and how Zack was so hyper and distracted with his own self, and how angry he was with Loren for being seen talking too often to some red-haired woman tourist twice his age. Talking, hand on his arm, Tory walked with him all the way to the anchored helicopter. Mitch stopped there to say goodnight so she'd go back.

Her face turned up to his, pert, heart-shaped in the moonlight. "Don't worry, Mitch Mason, you'll like working for me." Her hand stayed on his arm, her voice warm, almost sensual.

For an uncertain moment, Mitch met her gaze, eyes dark and liquid, her slight figure too close, the soft breasts rising and falling. He knew better than to read an invitation into the pose. Tory was independence personified and dangerous as a small, sharp-clawed cat.

She swayed there, her breath brandy-scented, her words actually wistful in the moonlight. "So I do need your help."

What the hell, maybe the gentlemanly thing to do was to give the lady a polite hug. A quick one. She surprised him by staying against him a moment before stepping back with the minxish smile, fingers tapping his chest. "Solid. Nice."

"Goodnight, Tory." He walked away toward the cottage hoping to God Lucie was not at the window just now, watching that moonlit tableau. Before going in, he looked back at the open knoll, fringed by the wooded slopes. Mitch smiled, feeling like Moses viewing the promised land that was peaceful and pristine. He almost wished it could stay that way. It was this sense of beautiful privacy they would use later to sell this project.

He looked across the silvered knoll and visualized how many prime view lots he could carve into the slopes of Eve's Mountain.

Tory Kingston watched Mitch Mason hurry back toward the dark cottage, head down, shoulders hunched, a man with problems on his mind, and stuck with being the boringly faithful husband. Too bad. He was perfect for the job she needed done. He'd do for what else she needed too, but what the hell. Her trips to Asheville would help keep her own sanity. Loan officer Virgil Means at the bank was promising on all scores.

The sound of Zack's Range Rover whipping out the front drive made her angry. Men took what they wanted for the moment, even dumb grabs like bedding down with something from Benny's Bar. She had overheard Jeb Gurney telling Zack, *You should hear that girl talk about her whirlybird ride.*

Tory walked back toward the terrace, shivering in the cool air, wishing for a cocktail lounge, an attentive male face across a narrow table, low music, drinks warming, spreading, not just another brandy in the silent upstairs where her father slept, drugged for the night in his four-poster bed. Coming back to Capstone had been rough, in spite of her reasons. And now, to find the Eve business was public fare, that ridiculous ghost story being repeated, was a new insult. Never would she admit that the dead woman seemed an amorphous presence in the house itself. She would have taken down the portrait and destroyed the thing only it would be admitting her hatred and the Gurney women would somehow report it to her father.

On sleepless nights, trying to talk to him when he seemed half awake, she had found him mumbling Eve's name. Maybe he really *was* going bonkers as she'd told Mitch. "Is she after you, Father? So, you really did push her off a mountain? That story is still around," she had said standing by his bed.

Back to the terrace, Tory stopped, too restless to go in and settle for a brandy nightcap. Moonlight and the live whispering night mocked her loneliness. She wanted to scream. *No, dammit,* she had to stay in *control.* Must remember to get her own prescription refilled next trip to Asheville. She had a purpose here, and more sure of it every day. She had to force her father to see what she could do, but only when she had it going. In the meantime she had to keep him sedated, just enough to keep him out of her way, long enough to get that second signature for the construction loan.

She stood still there on the terrace. It was hours before she had to give him his Xanax and his warm milk, flavored with bourbon and her own little addition. Tory called to the two Dobermans, stretched on the terrace, and ordered them to follow.

The front drive looked white in the moonlight and, since Zack had driven out, eerily silent. No. A noisy motor sputtered to quiet just beyond Capstone's entrance. With the dogs at her side, she walked toward the sound. Outside the firs, she stopped short. An old pick-up truck was parked there, in the shadow of trees, off the road. The battered blue hood looked familiar. Hoke McRae. The rush of adrenalin was anger as well as fear. *The nerve of that hillbilly.* She should be out here with a gun, as well as dogs.

What was the matter with the stupid dogs, running ahead, barking as if they were welcoming Zack or Jeb.

The truck door creaked open. Hoke McRae stepped out, a tall rangy mountain man who looked as natural in this place as any weather-scarred trees rooted in the rocky slopes. His shadowed face regarded her briefly before bending to the leaping, barking dogs. The fool was handing them hunks of meat, pulled from a rough shirt pocket.

She froze, watching Hoke croon to her dogs and stroke their sleek heads. He straightened, leaned back against the hood of the truck and casually lit a cigarette. In the flare of the match, she saw heavy brows, his head a curly mop of black hair. Behind his smoke now, his eyes glinted, watching her. Under the thick mustache, the smile easy as if amused.

When her surprise gave way to fury, Tory screamed at the exuberant Dobermans leaping around the man, their friend. In a hiss of rage, "Stop! Stop handling my dogs. What the devil you doing up here again, Hoke McRae? You've been warned."

The match arced away into dark foliage. He regarded her with lazy insolence. "Restless bitches, aren't they? Purty, though. I know how to handle 'em. Sooo, you're the little gal from daddy's big house." The words rumbled up from his depths, tolerant, as if she were the interloper.

"What are you doing here?"

"Admiring the moon. Your daddy don't own the moon, little Gal."

"He owns this property as you well know. You've been warned to stay away. If we have to complain one more time, we'll have some real charges." The damn fool was ignoring her, looking out at the night.

"I usta hunt up here with my own daddy," he mused. He dropped the cigarette, ground his boot heel on it, and took a step forward.

She backed away but he was stooping down to stroke the prancing dogs on their sleek black heads. "Yeah. Fine bred but that makes bitches too uptight, know what I mean?"

169

"My brother Zack . . ." she began.

"Ain't here. I know where he goes."

Hoke sprang up to his rangy height, his shadowed face so close she could smell his tobacco sweat. It made her head spin, flashed memory of Harkin's sickening cologne, and moments ago, the sweet tense warmth of Mitch Mason's neck. This creature loomed too close with his own animal smell; this crude stud of a man whose big hands could close around her body, squeeze the life out of it. And with it, all the pain and nameless hunger.

Control. She had to show him who was in control here. "Leave my dogs alone and get off my property. You know damn well my father bought this land more than thirty-five years ago. Don't pull this hillbilly feud shit with me, Hoke McRae. We have nothing of yours. Our payments for water rights have been your mother's income all these years."

"Addie ain't my mother." Cold anger in the growling response. He moved closer. "But maybe I got something you want."

She stepped back, chilled. *I will not run from him, I will turn and walk away.* "Get lost McRae."

"Law, law, for a lil' bitty thing, you got foxy nerve. I was about to say, Old Addie and me know tales on your Daddy before he got to be a rich old man. Worth more'n you pay for the water out of Ruby Creek."

"What in the devil do you mean by that?" Was he daring to blackmail her? "No, you can't pull that. Don't you think I've heard those stupid stories? Get in your truck and get out of here."

"Like I said, I reckon I know something about your daddy's first wife more'n the old talk."

"You're lying." She pulled at the collar of the nearest dog, backing away with him, stumbling backwards over the second dog, falling flat against the hard earth and wet leaves. Screeching with dismay, she saw his arms reaching down for her. "You . . . you bastard, don't touch me!" His grinning face came on closer, big hands gripping her shoulders. He set her on her feet as he might a flailing child and for an instant his hard thin body smelling of tobacco held her close.

170

"I do like a gal with spirit. Don't like the whiny kind." The rough stubble of his chin scraped her forehead as his big hand brushed away the soft dirt from her backsides. With a low growl of a laugh, he released her.

Backing away, shivering with indignation, she heard her own dismay escape like a hiss. "This minute. Get off this property." She turned, shouting at the dogs to follow, and began walking. Once inside the grounds, Tory ran, sobbing, with a frustration she refused to name.

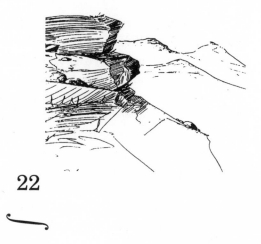

22

Eager to hear what she might learn from Professor Enholm, Selena walked down from Capstone to meet him at Ridgeway Inn's Fourth of July afternoon party. Maggie had told her, "If you're bent on knowing more than I could tell you, you need to talk to the Professor. I convinced him to go ahead."

In a new blue cotton skirt, white blouse, sun hat and new walking shoes, Selena hiked down the silent drive. Mitch's crew had begun to widen the road, but not on this holiday. She walked, immersed in the satisfaction of the last few minutes spent with Zack.

With no Tory around, he had her join him on the back terrace for cold watermelon slices offered by Sudie. Loren was nowhere to be seen. Tory was in Asheville. They sat there eating dripping melon, looking out on the sunny knoll and the anchored helicopter, and talking about the place and the patient upstairs. There were no intimate exchanges, but when Selena left, she was satisfied that Zack did have to be away so often. He was stuck with the responsibility of completing the legal negotiations back in Charlotte with the new Japanese owners.

"It leaves you with the responsibility here," Zack said. "And I know that means putting up with Tory."

The moment was so pleasant, his trust so evident, she held back what she'd have to tell him later. Unless Alexander forgot it himself. On the edge of sleep last evening, he had told her, *Someone or something is trying to kill me.*

She hurried now, nearing the Inn, hearing voices from the party. From each end of the second story balcony, a breeze-blown flag flapped and unfurled against a cloudless blue sky. On the shady side of the porch, wedges of red watermelon lined two long tables. At another, several women from the kitchen, with help from some of the guests, cranked old fashioned ice cream churns. Card tables covered with red and white checkered cloths with folding chairs waited under the sun and shade of oaks and maples.

The crowd moved around like colored confetti as a four-piece string band plunked and twanged out *Old Kentucky Home* to a peppy beat. The only car leaving down the front drive was the blue convertible, Loren Kingston driving. Next to him, Paula Crossing, hair shining in the sun.

Maggie Hardy, in her usual blue denim, gray hair tied back with a red bandanna, waved Selena over. "Professor's over there, stuck with some old bores. But he's expecting you."

Clusters of guests and summer people from neighboring ridges made up the crowd. Younger, T-shirted groups seemed to be tourists who had been passing through High Haven. With his face beaming above his usual bow tie, Dilly rang a bell for attention and introduced someone's visiting son-in-law, an Air Force captain in uniform, would lead the Pledge of Allegiance. Selena paused to share the moment, hand over her thumping heart. Murmurs followed, tinged with nostalgia.

At the edge of the crowd, Professor Enholm, in khaki and Orvis cap, greeted her with his courtly nod. "Would you like to sit under an apple tree with an old man?" She did, knowing he meant the garden. Or what had once been the back garden.

Leaving the music beat and chatter, Selena followed him to the back of the Inn and an old wooden bench. A brick wall shaped the end of the Ridgeway property. Beyond the wall, the wooded mountainside continued up, studded with old rhododendron, cedar and oaks.

"Maggie said you could help me, Professor. I suppose she told you why I need to know. She said you knew something about the burned car that was found. Why didn't that settle the mystery? I'm afraid the old gossip has gotten to my patient. It could kill the man now."

He sat silent beside her, the Orvis cap shading his thoughtful face, and polishing his glasses with a linen handkerchief. "Suspicion has a life of its own, like Kudzu vines that take over a southern roadside. It travels far from its origination and shapes what it covers. But my dear, what I know may not help your patient."

She felt a jolt of disappointment. "Tell me."

"As I have told Maggie, I am satisfied that Kingston's young wife did not die in that car that crashed and burned. A young woman did, but not Eve."

"You seem so sure. Why?"

"What I've found here. And, because the night Eve disappeared from this garden—I was there." He looked around. "I was here."

"You were, Professor?"

"I had to remind Maggie that I was an awkward sophomore from Duke visiting at the time. I vaguely remember her as the young woman looking after an aunt. I was the love sick college boy she might have told you about, the one smitten with the young Mrs. Kingston. You cannot imagine how blind a boy in love can be, and how focused, when the experience is his first, and his only previous emotional involvement has been with books. Poetry, Thomas Wolfe, Fitzgerald."

He turned to her with the self-depreciating, melancholy smile. "A woman's tears can undo a boy like that. I was in an adolescent fog of desire to comfort Eve Kingston."

She nodded, braced for more.

"There was indeed a young fellow from the kitchen, one who came and went in an old Ford. Tice was his name. He was as engrossed with Eve as I was. Yes, it was his car they found, crashed in a ravine and burned. In those days in these mountains, there was no forensic determination made about bones found in such an accident. It was assumed—but I knew better, even then. Since being here again, I have found out more."

"Tell me." Selena told herself, *Wait until you hear what he says.*

"That night, I had watched the two of them in the dining room, her silent tears, his disapproval. I knew how upset she was, having to leave the next day. Later, I had gone alone to sit on the back kitchen steps, away from others on the front porch. Tice came out, carrying a package of some kind. He had been fired, of course, so he muttered to me, 'ain't stealing, it's mine.'

"A girl was waiting for him in the shadows. The same thin mountain girl who had been showing up at the kitchen door often, looking for him, begging him to come home. At that moment, Eve came down the side path, into the dark garden. I recall the white dress she wore, how it looked in the dark. She thought she was alone. Tice's girl ran toward Eve, startling her with accusations, with her fists, striking her, putting her off balance, stunned. I ran to protect Eve. Even as Tice walked over, jerked at the girl's arm and pulled her away with him. They left. I stood there with Eve, who was trembling in dismay. I could only guess at the girl's accusations."

"You were alone with her then?"

The words seemed to come up from some deep place in his chest "I held her, trembling in my arms. The first time I had touched her. At that moment, Alexander appeared. Whether he had witnessed the other scene or not I do not know. Probably not. He was drunk and angry looking for his wife and now he found me holding her in my arms. I recall the grip of his hand jerking me away. I was suffused with guilt. I thought it was wiser for her if I walked away."

Selena felt the man's silent remorse as he said, "Through these years, I have felt responsible for what happened by having her in my arms and then leaving her there."

Disappointment leaden in her chest, Selena asked, "So you left them there, alone? "

"Yes, I walked away and down the front road, then back to the Inn and upstairs to my room. The wind was strong by then and the porch empty. That is all I can tell you, my dear. I came here to face Kingston, challenge the man perhaps, attempting some closure for my guilt. But with the man's illness, I have relinquished my desire to see Kingston. After all, it was my own guilt I must deal with not his. I sense this is not what you wished to hear. But it is what I know."

They walked back to the party. *That's only one piece of the story, I have to learn more,* Selena told herself.

The crowd had scattered, some back to the porch, others standing about the front drive. Huffing toward them now, waving her arms, was a woman in a red polka dot dress. Ethel Pickett. "It's happening this minute. A whole traffic jam over on the county road."

People paused in their conversations and turned to listen.

"Ray got caught in it and had to turn around. Folks getting out of their cars and standing in the road, ever' body craning necks! A girl is sitting up there on the outcroppings! On the edge of it, weaving around. Right up there where the ghost is supposed to show at night."

Loren drove the convertible, top down, wind whipping his curly brown hair tied back tight into a pony tail. At his side, Paula watched the strong young profile. "You must be an expert in handling anything on wheels." Loren kept his attention on the road ahead, a curving two-lane ribbon of highway that led away from Grandfather Mountain.

"Mountain bike. Motorcycle. I suppose you'll want to fly too," she said.

Loren shrugged. "Zack won't teach me yet. That's okay. I'll learn. I'm taking the Harley out tomorrow. So I won't be able to drive you."

"Then I'll give the ankle another day's rest. But another time? Tell me, how does it feel riding one of those things on these mountain roads?"

He took his time answering. "Like an eagle. Soaring. Being free. Not like highways where you have to be quick and put up with traffic. Most streets are boring. But here, it's good. On a down hill, you use your body like a skier, bank on the side hills, press down in the hollows. You use the terrain rather than the brakes."

On top of Grandfather, she had followed his lithe figure across the swinging bridge and back, snapping pictures of the bears, and the mountainous horizon, and below, green valleys and golf fairways. She shot her pictures, not giving a damn how they turned out except the ones she had managed to have Loren in the foreground. Back in the car, as they rolled past sun-flecked woods, she tried to appear relaxed, even as she studied his profile and the lean strong fingers on the wheel, remembering Zack at nineteen.

Loren surprised her with a flash of a smile. "My brother is steamed up about me riding around with a sexy looking older woman."

"What did you tell him?"

He looked back at the road and shrugged. "Told him you were okay. That you had some man and an important job waiting for you back in California. And that you'd come east for a funeral and were resting up here. Besides, Zack knows I don't let anybody get to me."

"This man in California has a son about your age. I don't know much about seventeen-year-old boys. Tell me, Loren. Are you happy? What do you want out of life?"

Oh God, dumb questions like that really shut him up. She pretended to ignore his silence and continued, sounding casual. "How is your father?"

"I'm hanging around until he's well enough to talk. Then I'll probably go biking in Virginia with some guys. He keeps telling me to stay, he has to talk, and he wants me to hang around Zack more, go with him on some of his jobs to know the place. They all act like I haven't been on my own. I think he's really sick. More than the stroke business. I would be a little crazy too, with Tory ordering me around. I hope the nurse will get him calmed down. She's okay."

"And Zack?"

Loren shrugged. He was quiet again until she got him talking about biking through the Netherlands. Nothing about his school. Nothing about friends. They were on the road now that led around the high bluff behind Eve's Mountain. Beyond a curve, Loren slowed. Cars lined both sides of the pavement. People stood in the road, looking up.

Loren stopped. "Somebody's up there. A girl's up there on one of the outcroppings." They left the car and walked toward the others, Paula forgetting to limp on the bound ankle. A man leaped out of his car carrying a Camcorder, calling over his shoulder, face excited. "She's going to fall or jump!"

Another car door slammed behind them. David Tyler ran past, toward the park ranger who stood by his white Jeep, talking into his mike. Paula thought, *he's frantic*. She hurried after him. "David?" He turned with a glazed look of relief.

"It's not Ariel," he said. "Not her. The dark hair, I thought it was Ariel." He took a breath and shook his head. "I think it's Lucie Mason. Mitch's wife."

Paula looked up, focusing on the figure on the high outcroppings as the rest of the crowd was doing. In the quiet, the green mountainside looked gold tinged in late sun. On one of the higher ledges of rock, the figure wavered, a girl in white.

"She's falling," a woman shrieked. The crowd moaned as something like a white robe billowed around the figure plummeting past rocks and trees. The crowd's sigh followed as the girl's body disappeared into the green foliage above the road.

23

"*I met a lady in the mead,*" David Tyler quoted in his best amused tenor, "*full beautiful, a fairy child, her hair was long, her foot was light and her eyes were wild . . .*"

From the top of the bookcase across the small room where she perched, Ariel McRae studied him. "Me? Aw, you just talking poetry again."

"John Keats," David said firmly as if he were in front of his English Lit class. He pushed back from the computer, determined not to turn it off, but let the screen saver colors kick in. "I do have an extra chair you know," he said, not to call her closer but to get her off his makeshift bookcase of boards and bricks. She had shown up like a gust of leaves, breezing in from the woods outside. Finding him at the computer, she had paced the small room, dug into the box of cookies on his desk then hiked herself up on the narrow shelf. Good thing her bottom was that small and her balance good.

"You look funny." She bit into a cookie and made a face. "Ugh. They're blah. Whatsa matter? Are you aw'right?"

He was all right the way a thirsty traveler is all right, discovering the taste of a mountain stream, flowing with effervescent water from a pool as clear and Irish green as her eyes. He should back away, not crawl closer. Ariel had happened to him. No undoing that experience. Since, he had reasoned he would stay teacher-advisor-friend to the girl, nothing else. Do Ariel some good.

Convince her to cool the notion for Nashville. To let it be a goal, fine, but stay in school. Sing where she had the chance but get herself into a college. Mars Hill, Appalachian State, either one, was close enough to home that she could still keep check on her mother. He meant to convince her if she didn't, even if she found some spotlight, she'd regret being out there without a framework of reference. He had told her that while lying under trees or parked at some lookout in his van, his blood roaring with the need to fall into that clear bottomless pool.

On his bookcase now, Ariel bounced her heels on the books below, kicking off her sandals, saying they were *ruint*. He told her, "If you're going to sit up there like a little monkey, get a book. Read it."

Watching her bring up a small volume, thumb idly through the pages, he agonized. Where had she been the last few days, what had she been doing? After that first night in the car, realizing this girl was no virgin, he had asked, flustered, *Do you know how to protect yourself?* The vehement answer: *"Don't you worry, I'm no coal miner's daughter, I'm not going to get caught with some old husband and kids. I got things to do first. Don't worry. Doc and Selena look after me."*

He had told her, "Ariel, no one can take care of you in that regard but yourself," adding, with painful chagrin, "Don't depend on the man, not when you turn him on." Nights now he would wake, agitated, after dreaming about Ariel hitching a ride with the first trucker she thought would deliver her to the big time. Lying awake, remembering her voice, the feel of her supple body and the sweet woody smell of her dark hair, he would throb with need, confessing to the darkness, *David Tyler you are drowning in that green pool.* Mornings brought cold rationality but no relief. He couldn't kid himself. His body was painfully alive, impatient to see her again.

He tried to sound gruff watching her now. "Where are you supposed to be? It's foggy out. And it's after seven."

"On my way home from the flea market. Well, I'm close to home. I stopped by to see you but not some mean old grouch. Maybe I'll go." She slipped down off the shelf to mince around the room, humming. She picked up a book, set it down. "You don't have any music here. Just words."

"Words have their own music. A word can pack a bunch of meanings to resonate with your own thoughts, some you didn't know you had. It's a pleasure when you find somebody's words that speak to you. Poetry can do that like music. Hand me the book you just pitched."

A mistake, David thought, even as he said it. Shouldn't give her a chance to sidle over to him. He was the one who had to keep this under control. He pretended to ignore the rolling gait, moving toward him. In some respects, she was still innocent, wasn't aware she didn't need movie starlet tricks, didn't know that the vitality she exuded was a more potent turn-on. He said sharply, "Stop acting, Ariel. Let me read you something."

He opened the Robert Burns book to lines he had read last night, thinking of her. "Here's one you could sing, like your Scottish mountain ballads. 'My love, she's but a lassie yet, we'll let her stand a year or two, She'll no be half so saucy yet' "

He glanced up, at skin texture fair and smooth as a child's, framed by the tumble of dark hair. The eyes were not a child's. Under the fringe of lashes, they invited him in. *You're a Circe*, he thought, hiding his desire to smile, to give in. *A teenage Circe I've had the misfortune or good luck to find in the Blue Ridge Mountains.*

He read one more line, ignoring her hands on his shoulders. "'Under the greenwood tree, who loves to lie with me . . .'"

"I do." She took the book away and nestled closer, pouting when he gripped her thin shoulders and held her out from him.

"What about that visit with your mother? She's somebody I need to talk with for this story I'm doing." He sounded brusque, trying to ignore the blood rush in his body. He kept holding her away, looking into the clear green eyes. "Have you asked her? You promised."

"And you promised to write to your friend about Nashville, about who to talk to and if I have to make a tape first and send it. You know."

"I wrote him," David said miserably and dropped his arms.

She sucked in her breath and rested against his chest, arms around his neck.

"You should go home Ariel. It's getting dark outside."

"Okay," she teased. She wheeled away, fell back on the bed, arms spread. Lifted one leg straight up, wiggling bare toes toward the ceiling, like a kid playing in water. Inviting him in. "Want me to go?"

If you don't, he thought, *I shall sink further and the pool is bottomless*. The computer screen kept swirling with its pattern. He turned it off.

In the hazy dark, with Ariel curled at his side, silent, David swam back up to the surface, to lie there, spent, relaxed, aware again of the piney room, the woods outside, rattling now with a soft rain. He lay supine, not caring to move, unwilling to feel guilty, at least not for the moment. Some words of Milton floated into his consciousness. "The mind is its own place and in itself can make a heaven of hell . . . a hell of heaven"

He turned, needing to understand her silence. In the dark, her face was inscrutable, eyes like dark reflecting pools but not open to him now. He should send her home. The guilt for himself, worry about her, propelled him up.

Back at his desk, he said, "Ariel? " When she stirred, not answering, he said gently. "About that visit with your mother, shouldn't I know something about your father first? So I'll know if I should speak of him or not with her? You've never told me about him."

She sat up quickly with prim dignity and looked toward the open window, dark out there now, trees dripping. "Told you. Mama don't talk to strangers." At his automatic murmured correction—

doesn't talk, Ariel—she bounced out, slamming the bathroom door behind her.

David flipped on the table lamp and shut down the computer. He was dragging his feet on the writing, yet now he had a clearer purpose. He meant to do a comprehensive story about this ridge, its past and future, with an honest in-depth profile of the people along this ridge, and how they were affected by the presence of Alexander Kingston, and what the man did with his land. That story called for opinions from real natives. The McRaes would be the logical start. They'd been mountain people forever.

Ariel sauntered back into the room to perch on the edge of the bed. "I told Mama there's a teacher here trying to get me to read stuff."

"Then she shouldn't mind teacher paying a visit."

"Told you. She don't—*doesn't* talk in front of strangers."

"Selena has been to see your mother." Selena had told him, with conviction, if Addie McRae really had shot someone in that house, it must have been a case of a woman protecting herself from domestic violence. Selena had told him about Addie McRae, how she worked at the loom, how old paperbacks lined two rough hewn shelves. He asked Ariel, "Does she read those books?"

"I bring them from the flea markets where I sell her baskets and weavings. Mama reads more than she talks." Ariel sighed. "Why you wanna see her?"

"Your mother is a native. Hasn't been too affected by the world outside her home down there on the creek, I would imagine. But if she's a reader as you say, she would appreciate an honest writer who is looking for an understanding about his subject from those who know it better than an outsider. According to Maggie Hardy, your mother knows the old Granny knowledge about herbs and healing. That's interesting lore, becoming lost, I'm sure."

"Maybe I'll take you. But why you wanna write about this place?"

Moments like this, she seemed vulnerable, a real innocent kid. He wanted to hold her thin shoulders but controlled the urge.

"Ariel, you're trying to escape from these mountains because you're young and have things to prove. Understood. You'll have to leave to realize what you've left behind. This ridge is still an *authentic* place, unlike a created mountain resort or gift shop towns or tired suburbia or sterile highways. High Haven as a summer retreat might have been typical forty, fifty years ago. Today it's a disappearing piece of the Appalachians."

"Mama ain't typical of nobody."

"*Isn't* typical, I know. Who is underneath? If you go to college, you'll try to be typically co-ed for a while, then typically anti one thing then another. After that, hopefully, you'll find out who or what Ariel McRae was meant to be. Most people hit forty before they wake up and say how did I get here? I predict you'll know who Ariel is a heck of a lot sooner."

She looked pensive. "Mama don't—doesn't— go to town ever. Some folks call her crazy for that. That would of made my Daddy mad as fire."

"Come sit at my kitchen counter and tell me about Will McRae. I'll make you a cheese sandwich. Might find a Pepsi." David dug into the little refrigerator, pleased that she followed. She perched on the stool to watch, chin cupped in her hands. "No ice but it's cold," he said setting the glass in front of her. "You remember your father, don't you?"

Ariel sipped at her drink for a moment. "Hoke says he wasn't my daddy. Says maybe Roy was. Roy was—well, he was the mean one, the one folks say Mama shot before I was born. I only remember Will. Far as I'm concerned, he's my daddy."

"You're smiling. Tell me about him."

"One day he took me fishing down on the creek, just the two of us." She told it like a dreaming child, without the protective sass. "We sat on the stone to eat our egg biscuits. I remember the sun on his beard and the way his voice sounded, like thunder rumbling far off. He told me he wasn't feeling so good and didn't know if he'd see me all grown up so he had to tell me things."

"Sounds like a good memory, Ariel. Sad but good. Go on."

She tightened her eyes, remembering. "Told me my mama was a delicate little thing like a hurt bird but that she was the finest thing that had ever happened to him in his whole life."

She looked at him and past him, saying, "He and his brother Roy had lived in the creek house with Roy's sick wife and boy. That was Hoke. Roy went off racing all the time. His wife died when Hoke was no more'n four or five. Daddy said he and Roy and Hoke went on living there by the creek but they needed the help of a woman with Hoke. So they went up to east Tennessee to ask their mother to come live with them. That was my grandmother, Nonnie.

"Well, Daddy said she wouldn't come unless she could bring this sick girl she was looking after. So Daddy brought Nonnie and this sick girl back to the creek house to live."

"And the sick girl?" David prompted.

"Yeah, that was my mother—later of course after she got better. Daddy Will told me that seeing her get well was like watching a plant perk up and start putting out blooms. He'd say, *That did pleasure me.* They got married before Nonnie died. A traveling preacher come to the house and did it. Mama didn't want to leave that house, ever."

Ariel's face lit with a sudden smile. "Daddy said Mama was like trillium that grows in the woods come spring, so pretty, but it just wouldn't survive if you picked it and took it out. But she can get mad when she has to. After Daddy died, she pointed the shotgun at Hoke more than once when he was trying to mess with me." The smile faded. "So I guess if she had to shoot somebody, she would. Maybe she did shoot Roy. I don't know. That was before I was born."

"Anything else make her angry?" David wondered if Will McRae's widow shared Hoke's anger. "How does she feel about the Kingstons?"

"Maybe she hates them. She won't say. How do I know? Well, once when I was about twelve she caught me talking to Zack Kingston. He'd come down to look at the pump house near the

185

creek. They get their water from that pump. Well! Mama came panting down toward us, grabbed my arm and pulled me toward the house faster than I knew she could walk. When she runs, she has to hobble. Her legs aren't even. Once back on the porch, she was trembling so I guess she was pretty mad. Told me to never, *never* go around that man again. I said why, and she said, because he's a Kingston."

Part Two

24

In pre-dawn dark, Zack Kingston tied on running shoes. In the silent kitchen, he downed a cup of coffee. Five-thirty a.m. The day was only a faint glow on the other side of Capstone. On the back terrace, he stood with the prancing Dobermans, breathing in sharp, cool air. A good moment, this stillness, a balm he needed. He had come here looking for peace, not the complications buzzing in his head and kicking at his gut. At least Pat was no longer one of the complications. He'd had sense enough to pull away from that situation, even before he found out the other guy who showed up there was Hoke McRae. *Spunky Pat, good-bye.* Real problems remained to be handled. Tory's bitch about Selena for one. For another, his own anger about the road work Tory had ordered. Rising up over all of it, Lucie Mason's suicide. To deal with that, he needed a good work-out.

Ordering the two dogs to stay, Zack walked out into soft darkness. Once beyond cedars, he began an easy jog. He knew how to pace himself. Let those Achilles tendons stretch now, let the cardiovascular system adapt. First, jog at pace, let the sharp air slap the face and feed the lungs. By the time he passed Maggie Hardy's place, the rough breathing had smoothed out, muscle, legs, lungs and heart working together. Pleasure in that. Sweat poured.

Now his body moved at its own rhythm, senses quickened, attuned to what he passed. Trees rooted so long in these rocky slopes, the whispering, gurgling sound of streams hidden in the low tangle of growth, all of it as alive as his own sweating body. This mountain was a living thing, belonging to itself, even if legal papers said his father owned it.

He jogged on easily, his mind traveling ahead of his freed body until the problems slammed back into his thoughts as if they had waited down the road like a specter. *Lucie*. Damn. Her white face flashed in his mind. Dark eyes begging, demanding, looking at him out of that pallor. Now Mitch Mason's florid countenance, anger fueled by shock and blaming him for visiting Lucie in the cottage, taking her up in the Bird. Mason had been in no condition to hear explanations. No chance to tell the man, yes, I visited the cottage twice. Both times looking for you, Mason. Both times got trapped by your wife, Mason. Yeah, I know, a thin pale girl in a leg brace but she made me sit down and listen. Vulnerable females in need get to me, always have. But your Lucie was no quiet little thing telling me her story. Angry, but you know that don't you? Angry about the accident, the loss of her body, herself. Saying it was your fault. Despair and rage like an aberrant passion. Begging me for a ride in the helicopter. Said she wanted to feel the freedom of being up there.

Zack ran at pace, fueled now by the memory of the girl's pleading. So yes, he had carried her out to the Bird one day and had taken her up. Only one flight. He had shown Lucie the mountains from an eagle's vantage point. Saw her face come alive, which pleased him, until she had asked, too coy, too teasing, *Does anyone ever fall out of a helicopter?*

He had answered, "Don't worry, doors won't open with air forward motion unless the craft is hovering and unless some fool tried to lean out without his seat belt on." Her smile turned cunning. He saw her thin fingers tapping the seat belt. A crazy notion, or instant reflex, made him dip, then lower, then sit the Bird down again on the knoll. He had carried Lucie back to her cottage, as she protested and cuddled in his arms. But Mason, I got out of there quick. And when I came back, days later, looking for you, I didn't go in, and I refused to take your wife up again. You didn't see but she stood in the doorway of the cottage, calling, screaming, the next time I was out there, checking the Bird.

God, in a way I am guilty. Refusing to take her up could have tipped her off. But could he tell Mason, *Look fellow, I did not knowingly mess with your wife's will to live, she almost made me an accessory to suicide.* Did you know your Lucie had a single-minded drive to make you sorry for that accident? Maybe Mitch Mason didn't know, maybe he did. Not that it helped now.

Zack slowed to a jog, stuck with the same vision that must be haunting Mason, the thought of Lucie hobbling out of the cabin, maybe going slightly mad getting herself through thirty feet of woods to that high boulder above the road. Sitting up there some interminable emotional time, then letting go, plunging down. As a crowd watched. *Christ, taking pictures.*

He took in a long deep breath and picked up his rhythm. No way could he afford to tangle with Mitch Mason now about the road job. Or tell the man, *Hey take your trouble and go, leave this job.* Only an asshole would kick the fellow out now. He wanted to stay, according to Tory. Little sister was all worked up about resurfacing the drive and replacing water lines. Her attention to that kept her out of his path, and allowed him to stay out of hers. So let Mitch Mason be her job foreman. No local road man would take orders from Tory. He would stay clear of Mason. Clear of Tory too, except he'd promised to deal with her complaints about Selena and his father. Maybe Selena was letting the old cuss fall in love with her.

Zack groaned as he ran, thinking of the other unwanted hassle. Lawyers in Charlotte. No way out but to finish up those issues for A. Z.'s sake. With the Bird, at least he could make the trips quick.

The sun was up now, orange against a pale sky. He ran along Crest Road, keeping to the soft grassy shoulder. Turned up Bear Wallow Lane, maintaining his rhythm but slowing his pace on the steep narrow road that led to the chalet. These old slopes were his favorite, his father's "other mountain" with the lake below where local fellows fished. His aunt had built the crazy chalet hanging on the edge up there. The place stayed closed more than rented as long as he could remember. Must be just right for Selena Hart. A real loner, that woman. Carefully impersonal and efficient as any head nurse in starched whites. He had been relieved to have such help for A. Z. Made his short visits upstairs bearable. But what was happening? Where was the improvement? The man who was always bull-headed, impatient, a powerhouse of ideas and negotiation skills, now seemed distracted or damned *needy*.

Tory claimed Selena was the reason A. Z. was withdrawn. Said he was getting entirely too attached to the woman. Zack had argued, *We should be damned grateful to have a good nurse.*

But after Tory's last bit of news—Selena, here under a false name?—he promised, *I'll look into it*, I'll talk to her. He didn't mention Selena wanted to talk to him. Sudie had passed along Selena's request. He had tried. Walked in that night to find her having a party no less. Miss Reserved, having a candlelight party with two men he didn't want to see, and some red-head with a bandaged leg who stared holes in him.

On the narrow drive that ended above the chalet, Zack dropped down on a smooth rock to allow his breathing to slow. Her green VW waited there. He ought to get this over. He couldn't do anything now about the sweat stained jersey. Honest sweat, he'd tell her. What the heck, this wasn't a social visit.

He stood up and stalked down the path that led to the side door, wondering if he was too early for any kind of visit. Before pulling the rusty bell, he stopped. He looked over the railing to the front deck, colored now by early morning sun. What do you know? She'd had the old Jacuzzi fixed. Steam rose from the small tub of bubbling water. At that moment Selena come out of the sliding glass doors. She stood in a loose blue robe, facing the view, her back to him. Unwilling or unable to move, he watched her touch the water with a toe, drop the robe, and stand there, arms open to misty mountains like an warm ivory figure of supplication.

He didn't move. Couldn't. Mesmerized, he studied every contour, every outline, every shadow. His gaze followed as she sank into the steaming water, into the bubbling depths. Watched her float there, supine, arms on the sides, head resting against the rim, turned away from him, unaware his eyes violated her privacy and searched her beauty.

He jerked back, afraid she could feel his eyes. Pulse roaring, he made himself turn and move soundlessly on the grassy edge of the path, back up the slope. Above the house, on the path, he sat on the stone again, dealing with the guilt of spying on a woman and surprise at what he'd found. Behind the starched facade, a Diana, of soft flesh and warm blood.

For hard breathing moments Zack sat there, angry with himself, until he could focus his exasperation back on the reason he had come here in the first place. Maybe Tory was right about Selena. Maybe she was seducing a sick man. He would go back to Capstone, shower, and catch lady nurse for a talk when she arrived, before she went upstairs. He sat there longer, in a wash of uncertainty, until his breathing slowed down. The sun was full on the trees around him when he pulled himself up and started moving back toward the road.

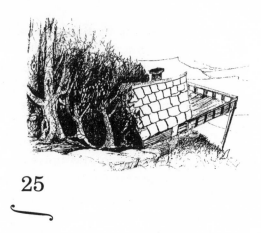

25

After the exhilaration of the hot tub, Selena dressed quickly in jeans and white cotton sweater, ran a brush through her hair and went into the kitchen for her coffee. Seeing movement on the path above, she stepped out on the stoop. Zack Kingston, walking away? She called out to him. He stopped, stood there, before turning. Finally, he stalked back toward the chalet and down the path to the side door where she waited. She meant to joke about his quick departures but stopped at the perturbed look on his flushed, sweaty face. Alarmed, she drew him in. "Is your father all right? I was dressing. Did you knock?"

"No, out jogging. Happened by here." He said he'd come back after he cleaned up. Yes, they needed to talk.

"No, please stay. I do want to talk. How do you take your coffee?" She was grateful to see him.

When he came out of her bathroom, looking somewhat refreshed, combing his curly wet hair with his fingers, Selena handed him the black coffee and watched him stand there drinking it, looking out on the deck. What was the matter with the man? Where was the easy warmth they'd shared that July morning, and other times as well, brief as the meetings were.

Zack turned back finally. "You have this old place cooking again, I see."

"Yes. I even have a phone now. Oh, the Jacuzzi? Jeb Gurney and one of his plumber friends managed to get it cleaned and working again. I was enjoying it on moonlight nights until I began to hear noises." He seemed distracted, so she waited, studying his face, a slimmer version of his father's more blunt features. The damp hair was longer now.

"Seriously, several times I thought someone was outside or had been around the place while I was gone. I keep it locked now, if you can lock an old place like this. What do you think?" She waited, annoyed at his quizzical distraction.

"Noises? You might be hearing raccoons. You are isolated here. This place seldom gets rented." Finally, "You've really made a conquest of my father."

So, that was it. Accusation in the remark echoed Tory's opinion. Disappointed, but not surprised, she drew back into her reserve, to the lonely but safer place. "It's not a matter of making a conquest. It's gaining his confidence. To work with a stroke patient you have to establish confidence."

At his silence, she insisted. "Sit down Zack. It's time we shared some concerns. Ask your questions first."

He finished his coffee and set the mug down, but stayed standing, cracking his knuckles. "My sister is—oh hell, you know she is a controlling little bitch. But she's also gung-ho on taking care of A. Z., the man as well as the place. She has Mitch Mason—God, I hate that about his wife—she has him cutting a road around the mountain, and plans to widen the beginning of the drive to forty feet, and thirty five all the way up, when it's been a seventeen foot drive all these years."

He sank down in a chair. "Lots on my mind as you see. Forget the road. Forget the Masons. It's my father we're talking about. He came up here in pretty fair shape, considering. You told me at the outset he could get back to normal in months. His doctors in Charlotte said the same. A. Z. knew he needed help so I brought you in. I thought we'd be seeing real progress by now. Instead, he's worse. Anytime I walk in, he is too lethargic to talk, or he's talking nonsense."

"I wondered if you realized that."

"I go in there and he starts in saying we've got to have a real talk soon—when his head is clearer. Acts like he's rocking on the edge, fighting something he can't see. And this man has been a force all his life, invincible behind the charm. Now his eyes look haunted. What's going on? Tory is on my back about what's going on between the two of you."

Where to start? "What is Tory afraid of, Zack? That you've hired a strange woman who is planning to talk her father into changing the will and leaving everything to her?"

He grimaced. "She's still teed off being ordered to stay out while you're with him. And angry that you question how she handles his medication schedule."

"A nurse should have that full responsibility. That's one of the issues I've needed to talk to you about. Zack, you must know Tory is jealous of anyone else taking care of her father." She didn't add, *a paranoiac jealousy, that has little to do with love.*

"It was his request that she leave us alone. You know that until I came, he had refused to wear the belt or the brace in his left shoe. I have his sense of humor going with those aids, but with anyone else watching, his macho embarrassment kicks back in." *This is not our main problem but I'll get to that.*

"Figures." Zack studied her, as if puzzled. "Tory has the idea you're here under an assumed name. Doesn't have anything to do with your nursing, does it? I have to ask."

"Where did she get that impression?" Selena kept her voice even. At his shrug, she said, "My parents named me Selena Hart all of thirty-five years ago." *Oh no, the driver's license.* Sheriff Bo Hilrey had stopped her days ago and asked to see her license. Had mumbled a reason, something about the VW's tail lights, walked to his cruiser, then back with an apologetic smile. Had Bo Hilrey done that for Tory Kingston? At her request? She felt the hot flush of anger, her privacy violated.

"Must be Tory's imagination. Forgive me, Selena." He seemed contrite, weary. "So what's the score on A. Z.?"

"First let me go over the physical problems." Again she reminded him that a stroke even a mild one, left sensory motor weakness. This was the reason for hand rails she'd requested for his bathroom. Why he needed time to handle the passive and active exercises.

"The weakness compromises his ability to judge distance, size and position. That makes a person impulsive and easily distracted as well as opens the risk of falling. A fall is dangerous for anyone taking blood thinner. Tory gets impatient with him—and me—but I hope you realize for someone like your father, the very compulsiveness that drove him to success becomes a problem."

"You have your hands full with him, I can imagine. And I'm glad he trusts you." Zack's scrutiny gave way to a weary smile. "I warned you, he likes pretty women. Sorry, Selena. I know the man. Or I did. I don't stay long in there with him because we get into it and it's not a fair fight now. I'm glad you've charmed the old bear into cooperating with you."

"It wasn't a matter of charm. Your father *can* take orders from someone if they're delivered with some honesty. And caring." *But that's not the problem now.*

"I realize Tory is jealous. Crazy isn't it? They've never gotten along. But when she's on the scene, she wants to run it. You have more to tell me. I'm listening. Lay it on me."

"It's this. He is *not* improving as fast we had reason to believe." She didn't allow Zack's frown to stop her. First, she went over again about the prescribed medication schedule, Procardia 20 milligrams three times a day to keep blood pressure down. Coumadin 5 milligrams daily to keep the blood thinned to avoid a clot. For anxiety, Xanax, three times every twenty four hours. All of that had to be carefully monitored. Too much blood thinner could cause internal hemorrhage.

"But the lassitude is worse now. We need Bradley back up here but he's in Morganton at his daughter's, going in tomorrow for a gall bladder operation." She hurried on. "I've mentioned this earlier but I find it is necessary now. I should have the responsibility of giving him the meds and keeping the schedule of blood

195

pressure readings. Not share it with Tory. And there's the other problem." Finally.

She studied his face as she told him. "You have mentioned hallucinations. Now they are reoccurring dreams and they've taken on too much reality for him. He has even said . . . someone or something is trying to kill him."

Zack frowned. "The man has never been afraid of anything, Lady Nurse."

"I can believe that. But weakened by illness—"

"Is he brain damaged, Selena? Tell me. Tory claims he's losing it."

"Don't take her assessment. But the brain controls memory and along with his medication and forced inactivity, he is susceptible to believing once he goes into a drugged sleep. Now, awake, he is becoming obsessed by what happened between himself and your mother."

Silence, then, "He's sick with guilt, huh? Finally, huh?" The flip answer was edged with bitterness.

"False memory can be perceived as real. He needs to get it out of him, into the light. I want you to know I've encouraged him to talk about it. I am trained for that. Counseling takes time and patience however. That's why I stay later than the morning visit when Tory claims I'm in his room playing host."

Zack slumped in the chair, silent, biting his bottom lip.

"Your father is dealing with suppressed memories, surfacing now, full blown into guilt, the worse kind, self-inflicted."

"So if anyone did get in to him now and asked questions, my father would blurt out his sins, I take it?" Bitterness, or was it hurt, crackled in the flip words. "The great landlord of High Haven might confess he killed my mother, by mistake or however? And played the noble land protector all these years to cover up his little mishap?"

"Oh Zack, is that what you've thought all your life?" No answer. "I can not believe your father would hurt a woman, physically. I don't believe he would cover up an accident. Don't give me that sardonic look. I've known him now for less than two months but on good days I've listened to him talk of his life, honest memories, not just boastful ones. On bad days, I've listened to his sedated ramblings. Zack, I thought this out and I can't believe your father is guilty of anything but suppressing memories from a painful loss."

He sounded subdued. "So Tory is right to keep him guarded up there, hanging up on anyone trying to get in."

"She's doing that, but I don't believe your sister realizes what's going on with Alexander. I hope she doesn't. Zack, don't tell her about his dreams." She didn't explain, *Your officious sister would shame him and make the obsession worse.* "But for that reason, I've discouraged everyone who seems to have such urgent reasons to see him. Especially reporters. Maggie Hardy says a television company will show up here in August wanting to do a story about Eve's Mountain. Did you know?"

Zack groaned. "Still? I'd forgotten them. Last thing we want, especially now, right? I told them to get lost and thought that was the end of it."

Watching him pace the room, she had to block the urge to follow, touch his stricken face, put her arms around to comfort him. She didn't move.

"So you're willing to stick with him and handle this?" he asked grimly.

"I have worked with emotional traumas as well as physical ones. If he comes through this emotional crisis he could be a calmer happier man than you've ever known."

"And if he doesn't?"

"Guilt can be a phantom that kills. I want to see him free of it."

Zack looked out toward the Jacuzzi. He sounded miserable now, not angry. "Nurse Selena, I hope you're right. Carry on. He needs you. I'll try to keep Tory out of your hair. Tell her you should have the responsibility. I have these meetings in Charlotte. I'm doing that much for him or he'd be coming out on the short end of the sale."

"I'm going to Capstone early today so let me take you," Selena said.

"Thanks. You really are into this case, aren't you? Tory says you are to be there at ten, after Jeb."

"Usually. Those are her orders. But Sudie invites me for breakfast when your sister is away. That way I can spend an extra hour—until you convince her I should be free to work with him any hour. I could come back late evenings for the meds. Let her do the Xanax at night. Have I answered your questions?"

He nodded and led the way up the path, appraising her parked VW. "The old bug with somebody's green paint. This one probably saw Woodstock. Lets see if my legs still fit in one of these things."

She drove down toward Crest Road, aware of the unsettled energy of the man sitting next to her, staring ahead with set jaw, needing a shave. They hadn't talked about his scene with Mitch Mason over Lucie's suicide. This morning wasn't the right time. She understood Zack better now, knew why the senior and junior relationship had been stormy. Zack truly cared yet all these years he had to wonder if his father had really killed his mother. Now she knew what he hid behind the throwaway charm.

They rumbled down the gravel road. To break the silence, she said, "How are the long legs doing in my green bug?"

"I adjust." With fresh anger, "My kid brother has been cruising around in a blue convertible."

"That's Paula Crossing, Zack. Believe me, she's okay. She has been shooting pictures of Loren biking the Parkway." The man had enough concerns clashing under his cover of nonchalance, she might as well ease the one about Loren. Paula would have to take it from there.

"Paula wanted to take her camera to see your father. I said no. But you should meet her, Zack. Do yourself a favor. Call her at the Inn.

"Why?"

"Tell her yourself your father is not well enough for interviews now. Speak to her. Trust me."

When he asked her to pull in to the post office, she saw why. Paula's car was parked there. He untangled his legs and hopped out. "Thanks for the lift. I'll walk up from here. And Nurse Lady, thanks for your honesty. I'll leave A. Z. to your good care." He patted her hand on the steering wheel and walked away.

Selena didn't wait for Paula to come out to her car, to watch the meeting. She drove on quickly, feeling Zack was again a friend but she was giving him away now to Paula Crossing.

26

F*rustration*. In front of his computer, David Tyler smacked at a spider crawling up his arm. The thing could be crawling his whole nervous system for the way he felt. Had felt all afternoon, listening for Ariel's light steps on the path outside the cabin, trying to convince himself he was relieved she hadn't shown up. Again, he deleted the lines on the screen. The story wasn't working. He couldn't fake it. Didn't want to fake it.

He shut down the Mac, finally, walked out into the cool August dark and leaned against his van. A sliver of moon rode high over the thicket of trees. What an eerie quality of timelessness this place had, opposite of the banal reality of a cluttered Florida landscape. So why couldn't he relax and take it in? Proved he was still the outsider, looking on. The thought slammed his attention back to his story. He couldn't write it as an outsider. He should have gleaned more insight from Professor Enholm. The man knew these mountains as a native as well as an anthropologist. Why hadn't he spent time with the man? Too caught up in Ariel, of course. And now for a week, too worried about her absence. *Ariel, you should stay away*, he groaned silently. *But stay out of my mind, too.*

At the Ridgeway Inn, David bounded up the front steps, hoping Enholm wasn't inside with the bridge players. He spotted the man's lean frame, settled in a rocker at the far end of the verandah, smoking his pipe.

From inside the front parlor, murmurs and exclamations from the bingo players drifted out to the dark porch. David pulled the rocker closer.

"Professor, I need your help. I'm in trouble with this environmental piece I'm doing. My deadline has been extended to September, but the concept is broader now so I'm coming up with questions and I don't have the answers. As an outsider looking in, I don't know enough at this point."

Enholm drew on his aromatic pipe for a moment before replying. "That is your first good judgment, to require integrity of yourself." The man's deep tones, sounded languid in the dark. "If you detect a sweet scent to my tobacco, it is peach. The extent of my decadent pleasures."

"I need help," David said. He felt like a freshman confessing to the department head. "I'm caught in a quandary."

"Because Kingston remains unavailable?" Professor Enholm placed the pipe in his jacket pocket and settled back in the rocker.

"That's part of it. Until I talk with him, I don't know if he is the benign landlord, a legitimate conservationist who is really too sick to talk, or if the man is a self-serving rich fellow who has been sitting on this outpost of privacy, waiting until he's good and ready to cut it up and sell off. From my meeting with the daughter, I'm guessing it's the latter, though she's cagey and I can't go on anything that woman tells me. At any rate, I don't have a story until I know more."

"I gather there is more to your quandary than Kingston."

"Right. You saw me when I came here two months ago hot with the notion of enjoying a respite from the twentieth century. I wanted a Brigadoon."

David nodded toward the sound of bingo players. "They must come here for the same reason every summer. I imagine the Floridians do too, the summer people who aren't 'resorty' as Maggie Hardy puts it."

201

Enholm chuckled. "That is an apt definition for those who do not require their view to include golf fairways. The ones you see at the Post Office bought wooded lots here ten to thirty years ago, put in their own wells and gravel drives. Continue."

"You know how Maggie sees High Haven—as a little sanctuary of peace and natural beauty, to be protected as such. And that's what I came for. But now I'm wondering."

"We are getting to the quandary."

David sat back in the rocker and stared into the cool dark night. "If Kingston is reneging on his promise not to develop or if he isn't—regardless—something's going to give here for one reason or another. This ridge will be become a private pricey club, or whatever."

"Change comes gradually, or with suddenness, but yes it comes."

"Before I write this piece, I have to satisfy my own mind on this question: Would opening up this ridge to commercial development have its merits, or be as regrettable as Maggie and Dilly believe? Professor, what about the mountain people themselves? Families who have lived in these parts for generations? What do they want, or should I say, what do they need? At this moment I'm sitting here hating the thought of returning to the usual, and yet I am wondering if High Haven shouldn't open up to the same. You hear that impasse?"

David sank back in his chair. *Okay, I've just exposed myself as a fumbling outsider reporter, and to this native Carolinian who happens to be steeped in sociological research.*

The Professor rocked in silence for a moment. "I appreciate your questions. So many writers from the outside have maligned the Appalachians with their quick appraisals and preconceptions. May I ask what impression of the region and the natives you brought with you?"

"Oh, the notions one garners from the time you're a kid reading about Daniel Boone. Then you grow up hearing about moonshine and corn pone, fiddling, Pentecostal religion and feuds. And sure, you hear about the mountaineers' fierce independence, old fashioned family loyalty, and their stubborn resistance to change. Same time, these are spectacularly beautiful mountains, old as the Andes, I'm told."

"Older," Enholm mused.

"And isolated for a long time."

"For the early part of the century, yes. Until roads came in after World War II. Isolation demanded stubborn survival strengths from the early settlers in these Appalachians. When roads opened up, you had out-migration for jobs and in-migration by urban defectors and corporate interests. In these southern highlands, roads brought vacationers and second home people and others choosing to relocate here. That changes a landscape too."

David looked out on the peaceful dark. "Except places like this." He was quiet a moment, thinking of having to leave and what he was going back to.

"You know, Professor, I'm thirty in September but here's how I feel. I find myself thinking hey, we're all being swept along screaming and kicking like a rock concert crowd trampling each other to get to whatever pied piper's on stage, marketed as the newest hot kick or nirvana."

At the older man's slow smile, David added, "Maybe you can tell I teach teenagers, affluent and hard luck kids, it doesn't make a lot of difference. They think they're originals, acting out nonchalance or pathos, without recognizing they are hypnotized by each other and the hot piper of the moment up there on stage, manipulated into that spotlight by good marketing. A hero is the guy on the screen crashing his car over a cruiser. They don't care if it's a studio stunt driver. They're pulled along by the cruddy foam on the top wave of the culture we create. . ."

David balanced his feet on the bannister and glanced over to the sanguine professor. "I should have a long gray beard, talking like that. But that's why I came up here for a breath of air. And that's why I'd hate to see the demise of High Haven. Lord Byron said, 'High mountains are a feeling, the hum of cities torture' and he hadn't seen what has happened to both coasts of Florida."

He stood up, to sit on the bannister and face Professor En-holm. "I digress. Back to the story I have to write. More than the effect of Kingston's promise, but a look at what should come. Keep it protected or opened to development that would mean money and jobs for the whole area? "

"Have you met people in the valley, the hollow?"

"I've driven around. You don't have to drive far from Kingston territory and Dilly's venerable establishment here to realize incomes must be low."

"What have you seen?"

"Some pastoral valleys that would make a setting for a million dollar estate, but with a sad looking trailer sitting on it. Junked cars in the weeds. I've seen the newer double-wides and old farm homes and new brick ones. They all have TV antennas. The native mountaineer's kids must be plugged into the tube, same as inner-city kids and the rest of us. On my brief forays down to the supermarket, I see old farm couples pushing that basket. I'd think they'd be 'right proud,' to have one closer."

David felt like he was giving his orals and washing out with shallow research. "My observations sound superficial, I'm sure. It's not enough for me either." He dropped back in the chair and rocked with frustration.

"Your question, my friend, has endless ramifications." Enholm sighed. "Do you recall Lyndon Johnson's poverty program? Poor Appalachia was in the national spotlight for a short time. That attention probably served to further establish the image of the fatalistic, backward native. But you are asking about the reality of the present. I offer two suggestions."

"I'm listening."

"First, you should know there are native voices—academics, artists, and other professionals—who care about your question with such passion they make Appalachian issues their cause, their thesis, their career in some cases. They have traveled far afield but have returned home . . . to Kentucky, Tennessee, West Virginia, North Carolina. The Appalachian region encompasses more, but these southern highlands where we rock on a front porch are part of that region."

"This is going to sound like an impatient student's cop-out, Professor, but my time here is running out. I have August left to stay up here and finish the story. My wife returns from Europe the end of August and I have classes waiting in Jacksonville in September." He didn't say time was running out for being with Ariel as well as meeting his deadline. "But go on. Tell me what they say."

"They examine and debate every subject from folk art to the region's long history of economic distress. I doubt the rest of the nation is aware of the rape of strip mining as these voices can tell it. Most all of their writings convey the idea this region is much sinned against by outside interests. They don't agree on everything, David, but they debate with equal zeal and intensity. They are heavy critics of outsiders who write of the area with superficial understanding."

"My time here—"

"Short, yes. I can lend you some of these journals put out by several state universities and presses. The issue in western North Carolina is not coal, but land. And outside ownership, state, federal, corporate and developer."

"Are they saying it's not the mountaineer's fault he's poor?"

"I believe you would prefer to reach your own gut feeling, as you put it. Back to the situation here. Have you talked with the people who would be affected by whatever Kingston does . . . or what happens to him?"

"Maggie, of course. I attempted to talk to Sudie Gurney but that dour woman clammed up. "

"Anyone else?"

David hesitated. "I've had some contact with the McRaes. Two brief encounters with Hoke McRae. Feuding may be over in these parts but that character has a vendetta against the Kingstons."

David paused before adding, "And Ariel McRae. The girl is really bright. I am talking to her about college." *Well that's true.*

205

"She's quite clear on what she wants. And that's to get out of here. She'd be gone now were it not for the deep responsibility she feels toward her mother. There's the family tie thing, I suppose. I've seen Addie McRae briefly. A fragile looking woman in a long cotton thing and straw hat, working in a shed with her herbs. I tried to talk with her but she kept on with her work and said little in her whispery voice. Not much help there."

Restless, David stood up. "I'll read your journals. But did I hear a second suggestion?"

"Tomorrow, I have promised myself to work on my notes. But perhaps the day after, would you care to accompany me on some calls? And yes, I may as well . . . yes, let you listen in on more about the Eve Kingston story than you know at present. I suggest that you wear your jeans as now, smile and keep your mouth and notebook shut."

"Name the time." In the lobby, David waited until Enholm returned from his room with four *Appalachian Journals,* plus several thin volumes.

"When I mentioned voices, I should have included the poets. You will find they chronicle the political and personal as well as the pastoral and nostalgic. I have marked some in particular you should appreciate, given your questions. Miller speaks here in the persona of a native Brier. In Florida, such a voice would be called a Cracker."

Back in his cabin, David made instant coffee and sat down with the Professor's offerings. First, poet James Still's lines about heritage: "*I shall not leave these prisoning hills . . .*" before settling down to *The Mountains Have Come Closer* by Jim Wayne Miller. David turned to the page marked by the Professor.

> *Our people settled in these mountains*
> *and lived pretty much left to themselves.*
> *When we got back in touch we started seeing*
> *we had to catch up with the others.*
> *And people came in telling us,*
> *You've got to run, you've got to catch up.*

Buddy we've run so fast
we've run off and left ourselves.
We've run off and left the best part of ourselves.

And here's something peculiar:
running we met people on the road
coming from where we were headed,
wild-eyed people, running away from something.
We said, What'll you have? and it turned out
they were running from what we were running after.

David closed the book and put his face in his hands, thinking, right, wild-eyed people running away from something. And soon he had to go back.

27

Sudie Gurney didn't mind keeping the big house, doing the laundry and running the kitchen, but taking messages on the phone was nothing but trouble. Miss Persnickety had her private line in the library with its little answering machine but that didn't stop folks from calling the house phone and asking for Miss Kingston. Her own mother, that Marja woman Azzie was married to once, had done that a couple of times, voice trilling on the phone, "Why Sudie old dear, I got you again and I meant to call Baby."

Now here was the kitchen phone ringing with somebody from Colorado for Miss Kingston. Sudie left the supper tray she was fixing, and went out to the terrace where Miss Snippety was talking to the Mason fellow. Tory came in, took the phone, turning her back and talking fast and low to Colorado. Minding her own business with Azzie's tray, Sudie couldn't help but hear, "I thought Dr. Hempton would like to know where she is." When Tory hung up and turned around, of course she had to find fault with the tray. "That's too much food. Far too much cobbler."

Sudie faced her. "Seeing how you've got company and Selena isn't here, I can take it up to Azzie. He can't abide cold food." It had been weeks since she'd been allowed to take up a tray. She had to go up later and collect them when Azzie was sleeping, a big silent body in that bed.

Tory hesitated. "Oh, go ahead. I'm busy. But don't get my father talking. It's bad mood time up there. Food may calm him. But don't stay."

Sudie could have reminded the daughter that ornery man's moods didn't bother her one bit, she'd known Azzie too long. When the girl walked back out to the terrace, Sudie added a quick dab of ice cream on the cobbler before taking the narrow back stairs, and huffing in with his supper. "Come to see you, Azzie."

There he was in the chair by the window, hair so white it gave her a shock. She set the tray on the low table next to the chair. "How you feeling, Azzie?"

"Look who's here . . . Sudie Mae . . . thought I'd lost you."

He was so glad to see her, Sudie wanted to cry. He told her to sit down, the words sounding sleepy but positive like his old self.

"I been here all the time, Azzie. Ever time Lottie and I clean on the second floor, your door's closed. Is Jeb cleaning in here like he's spose to?" She sat on the edge of the chair, looking around at the big room, hands twisting in her lap, happy to see him but pained at the look of him, his eyes sunk deep under those bushy brows, studying her hard. "I been so worried about you," she said. "Lottie too."

"Sudie. Sudie Mae. We've known each other a long time, haven't we? You were there, weren't you? That summer. You were a shy girl from the hollow. I took an extra room at the Inn so you could help look after my son."

Sudie felt her face go hot. "Law, Azzie, that's a long time ago." All these years of taking care of this house, cooking for his company and kin, they had never talked about that summer. Now he seemed to be dreaming out loud about it and asking her questions.

"I came up often . . . to see Eve and the baby. You were there, weren't you . . . rocking him on the porch. I'd ask about your boy friends . . . you'd blush bright pink."

209

Sudie looked away, fingers gripping her apron, embarrassed, remembering how she'd felt watching him drive up in that big car, walk up on that porch, joking with all the guests while he patted little Zack on his little fuzzy head, lying right there in her arms. He'd look around saying, "Where's my little girl? Back there in the garden again?" Some visits he'd put a present in her lap, Whitman's Samplers or a box of chocolates with big roses on them. No local boy had ever done such a fine thing. Sudie had kept those boxes. Back at her own house, they held sewing threads and thimbles to this day. Now he sat here asking her to remember what should stay in the past.

"Sudie, I need to know . . . from someone who can remember the night Eve disappeared. Tell me . . ."

Sudie looked away, across the fine room, remembering against her own will. Eve Kingston put a person in mind of a dark-haired porcelain doll sitting atop a bureau. Or a cape jasmine just bloomed out, the kind that would bruise if touched. Eve didn't sit on the porch with the old couples. She'd go out in the back garden most every afternoon with a book. From her own upstairs room with the baby, Sudie had watched her down there. Sometimes the skinny college boy would be with her, reading poems to her.

Or the red-headed fellow from the kitchen would be there, prancing around, showing off, making Eve laugh. A rascal, that Tice. Once when she was busy in the big pantry, he had sneaked in and pinched her behind. Some girl was always at the kitchen door, begging Tice to come out.

Sudie had to shake those pictures out of her head, and take a new breath before she could say, "That's been too long a time ago to think about now, Azzie."

He went right on as if he hadn't heard. "Tell me Sudie. Tell me what you remember. I have to know."

Sudie stared at her work-rough hands, empty in her lap. Back there she would look at her own plain face in the mirror and then at that lucky girl, so pretty, and already at twenty with so much schooling in her head and a baby son and a fine husband, and wonder, how could Eve cry like that, face muffled in a pillow, the day he came to take her home? But she didn't have the nerve to tell the girl, *You ought to be shamed before the Lord for not being happy with what-all you have, the finest man a girl could want.*

"Azzie, your supper's getting cold. You shouldn't oughta worry your head about the past. What's done is done." *Lord Jesus, help me do what's right for now even if it wasn't right back then.*

"Sudie, bear with me. Don't leave yet." He went on about having a fuzzy head and bum leg and learning to walk again, and having too many days and bad nights to think. ". . . so I must get something settled in my mind. The night she disappeared, you were upstairs, weren't you . . . with the baby, with Zack? What do you remember, Sudie? I was drunk? Did you see us that night?"

"Mercy me." Sudie got up, wanting to run out of there but not to leave him like this. "Azzie, looking back to what's done and gone can make a body sick. Is that what you been doing up here? I reckon that's why ever' body wants to keep strangers out of here wanting to ask you questions. You got to get well and go roaring around again."

"What people? Asking what questions?"

Oh Jesus, forgive me, I've upset the man real bad. "People. I don't know. One's a nice looking young reporter fellow, talked to me at the PO. I'm going now, Azzie. You eat, you hear?" She hurried out of there.

On the back stairs, where nobody could see, Sudie sat down, hugging her arms, shivering. *Keep a secret so long, favor to somebody, keep it buried deep, you don't want nobody stirring it up again, lest of all the one you did it for.*

She hadn't thought of that summer night for a long time and didn't want to now, but it came back: after supper, upstairs, putting the baby down in his crib, then hearing voices in the garden below. Angry voices. Then it was quiet down there. She went on adjusting the baby's bottle. Then she'd heard *his* voice, talking to Eve. Oh, he's mad at her, all right.

Feeling sad about that, she walked to the window and looked down. There they were, just below. Dark, but she could see Eve's pretty white dress blowing in the night wind, and his big shoulders in the fine jacket. Did she see him raise his hand? She hadn't wanted to see him slap that girl. The baby cried about then anyway. She picked him up, patted his back, put him down again, with the bottle, went back to the window. Nobody was there.

Later, she woke up in the small bed by the crib and wondered, had they ever come in to their room next door? Neither one had come in to say goodnight to the baby.

Sitting on the back stairway now, Sudie remembered the painful rest of it. The next evening, after the search, the sheriff had paced the front porch biting his cigar and asking everybody what they knew, what they'd seen. Oh, Lord, how scared she'd been, rocking with baby Zack and not wanting to be asked anything. Didn't the others say Mister Kingston had sat in his Lincoln all night? When faces turned to her, she had to say something. So, she'd mumbled that earlier, maybe she'd heard that kitchen fellow's voice down there in the garden. Well, maybe she had.

Next day one of the Kingston family came and took the baby to Charlotte. Sudie had gone home, back to her own folks' house, with a terrible case of hives. How many Sundays had she sat in church itching and praying for forgiveness for the sin of lying or telling a half-truth. She had terrible dreams about poor Eve falling down from some rocks, lying there dead for no one but bears to know. Not until the kitchen fellow's car was found crushed and burned, skeletons inside, not until the newspaper said *that's what happened,* did the hives go away, either proof she had guessed right, or was forgiven by the Almighty. When Kingston came back and built the big house on the top of the mountain, she had gone to work there, along with her Uncle Hogan.

All these years, with no man of her own, she had been proud to run that kitchen and tend that big house, even when Azzie brought in all kinds of people who liked late suppers and who left ashtrays filled. For awhile there, it meant putting up with his new wife, that woman Marja, and then the child Victoria, with her tantrums. Sudie wasn't a bit surprised that one grew up to be this bossy woman, taking over the house now.

It does nobody any good to think back like that, Sudie promised herself. Hadn't she been a satisfied woman, even without a man of her own? There had been plenty of other Gurney babies to help raise. And Azzie had helped her buy a place of her own, way back there. He was a good man even if he did get so big and important. And talking crazy now.

Sudie pulled herself up and went on down to the kitchen. She'd forgotten to tell him the poached trout was one Jeb caught in his own lake. And the tomatoes and green peas, right out of her own garden. She set to clearing the kitchen but had to stop. Some old sadness settled in so heavy she wanted to sit down and cry.

28

In the library, Tory Kingston poured more brandy. From the first week back at Capstone, she had claimed the room as her operations base, with orders to Lottie and Sudie not to bother dusting or vacuuming in here. Taking over the massive oak desk, she had cleared off the collection of framed poses of assorted people in assorted places, beaming in the company of Alexander Zackary Kingston. Eve still gazed soulfully from her frame, but Jeb had moved the desk so she could avoid looking at the thing.

Sitting here now with brandy, Tory swiveled the chair around away from the sight of Mitch's bills for materials and crew. The mounting invoices were a pain in the ass but she had other, more annoying problems. Selena in particular.

True, to leave herself free, she needed a nurse here to keep A. Z. pacified, and the rest of it. But Selena was one of these conscientious, dedicated types, therefore a Goddamned complication. The woman stayed cloistered in there too many hours with him. And with that cool reserve, had the audacity to question her again about his medications. Was she giving them at the right time? Putting down the right blood pressure reading?

"I can hand out pills as well as you," she had told Selena. "When you're here, the duty is all yours. Sure you're doing it right?"

Selena had walked away from that. Tory told herself now, *What else I'm doing is no big deal, no harm done*. She was merely making sure he stayed sleepy to keep him engrossed in his own physical complaints, and not trying to come downstairs or question what she was doing about the roads.

At the sound of Zack's voice in the hall, Tory took her brandy glass and moved over into one of the winged chairs. She had to get him out before Mitch Mason showed up with his report and his questions.

"Look at you," she said when Zack walked in. For a change, he was wearing a decent shirt and slacks rather than the usual jeans and sweat shirt. "You smell good but look fierce. Did you see the nurse lady as you promised?"

"You're hard to track down." Zack sat on the edge of the facing chair, "You must have something going in Asheville."

"Yes, as a matter of fact." She gave him a smile that suggested private appointments in motel rooms, not bank meetings. Asheville meant both these days and she was pleased with how well both were going. "I'm sure you have no moral objections. Mitch is still blaming you for Lucie's big act off the cliff." *Ahah, that little ringer hit home*. "And how did your visit with Father go this morning?"

"I had to up-date him on the Charlotte business. He nodded, had no complaints. It's hard to believe how little it interested him. And yes, I've talked with Selena. She says we should deal with him calmly and straight forward. No dictatorial or challenging conversations. He needs patience and he doesn't need distractions. Not even TV."

"Dear Selena. What would we do without her?" Tory sipped her brandy.

"I am here to say the same thing, but without the sarcasm. I questioned her just as you wanted me to do. I came away satisfied with Selena Hart. I'm relieved she's here, working with him. Yes, she seems personally involved in the case, but Tory, I'm glad she really cares."

215

"Did she tell you what a good nurse she is? And how father's recovery depends on her full support and autonomy with the patient?"

"Not in that way but it was evident in what she did say. Selena is as concerned as we are about his lack of progress. She would like to have Doc Bradley come up more often, but he has left his clinic with some county nurse for a few weeks who says we should have him checked out again by his Charlotte doctors."

Tory tapped the empty glass, thinking fast before answering. The Charlotte specialist would be busy of course and he'd say bring the man back to the hospital for observation. Oh no. In Charlotte he'd be out of her way but also out of her control. She wanted him here to get that second signature. At the right moment, some night, she would walk into his room with the papers that would put the property up as collateral for the construction loan. He'd be too lethargic or annoyed to demand details.

"Good idea don't you agree?" Zack asked, looking impatient. "The Charlotte man."

"If you want to make him angry, making him think we want to ship him back there when you know he wants to be here." *When you have a problem use it to advantage*, Tory thought grimly. She forced a placating smile, "Zack, I've been tough on Selena, admitted. Let's renew our bargain. You give Mitch Mason no grief when he cuts a road behind the stone cottage—"

"What the hell for, Tory? We don't need any road there."

"But we do. New water lines have to be brought up from Ruby Creek. We need a road around the perimeter for that access. I've spent time working this out." She gave him a confident smile.

"A. Z. know this? Of course not."

"We're talking here about his health, right? Lets not give him more worries. He couldn't be rational about practical matters right now." That much was true.

Zack studied her quizzically. "What's your deal this time? It has to include agreeing to Selena's taking over the medication schedule."

216

"All right. The responsibility can be totally hers. I am terribly busy here and in Asheville." Tory checked her watch. Mitch was due. "She's in there with him now, but you're in a hurry aren't you? Catch her later. Tell Selena for me she can come back for the afternoon meds. I'll give him the last one at night with his milk."

At his silence, Tory gave him her best teasing smile. "Does that ease your mind? And hers? You don't have a thing going with Miss Calm Control do you?" His swift look of consternation surprised her. Something was going on with dear half brother. He was dressed to see a woman this afternoon, though he didn't look happy about it.

He stood up, hands in his pockets, frowning. "I'll tell her that you're off her case, she's in charge. But that also means taking her advice about bringing in the Charlotte man. It makes good sense. If he's so busy and if A. Z. doesn't want to taken back there, I'll fly the man up here for a few hours and fly him back."

Not yet if I can help it. At the moment, she wanted Zack out of there. "I doubt you want to run into Mitch today. He's coming up to talk roads. Maybe later he'll simmer down and forgive you for taking Lucie riding the skies and giving her ideas. Aren't you in a hurry yourself? You don't look like you're ready to lay stone paths somewhere, or find Loren on some trail hike."

"I'm due at the Inn, to meet with someone."

"Don't tell me you've found a Lisa-type female among those old biddies on the front porch? My handsome, virile big brother, whatever are you up to?"

"I don't ask you about Asheville." He started out of the room but turned back. "You didn't mention that other complaint you had about Selena. The business about her using an assumed name."

Tory waved a hand of dismissal. "It was a guess." No need to tell him now what she knew. She gave Zack her sweetest smile. "Don't I deserve thanks for being so agreeable and pliable?"

"That'll be the day. And where is Loren? I should talk to him."

"Maybe he's trail riding in a blue convertible, the one you're worried about. Have you met her?"

"Briefly. Paula Crossing. In fact, I'm on my way to the Inn now to see the lady. Carry on Tory. And remember, you've promised not to interfere with Selena's authority."

"Agreed, brother dear. Go on, have fun. You look like you need it."

When he walked out, Tory poured more brandy, somewhat mollified.

For now, she had to be patient about Selena. Once she had the bank loan, once the project was underway, she could let her father come out of his fog. *Take a look Father dear at what your daughter can do. I am a Kingston you know. I only needed your financial clout.* Once he got past the fury, he would have to accept it. Might even get around to being proud of her. Might even look at her, really look, for a change and admit, *"You're my daughter all right, a gutsy Kingston."* At least that. At least.

He shouldn't care this property was no longer *Eve's* mountain but something called Havencrest. If those mumblings at night meant anything—her father was talking to Eve, for Godsakes— he should be *glad* to be killing her off again.

But if Zack flew the Charlotte doctor up here? And he would. It meant, for the time being, she would ease off the antihistamine in his milk at night and what she called a vitamin in the morning. Over-the-counter stuff, harmless enough, but it increased his sedation just enough. Let this Charlotte doctor see A. Z. at his usual ornery self. That would be a rebuke to Selena's nosy concern.

When she needed it, she had ammunition to discredit Selena and send her packing. Hoke McRae hadn't found anything when she'd sent him looking. But Bo Hilrey had. It had taken some convincing. "I have a right to know something about the person I bring into the house to care for my father," she had told Bo. So he had come up with the name on the license. It had taken several calls before she reached the right Hempton in Denver, Colorado, a doctor's office, a Mrs. Creighton on the other end of the line, obviously an office manager protecting the important boss, a Dr. Drew Hempton.

Tory had asked, "Is Selena Hart applying for private duty work in High Haven, North Carolina the same person as Selena Hempton?" The brittle Mrs. Creighten became instantly curious, also cautious. Tory hung up, satisfied that Selena Hart was indeed a missing person, hiding out, for whatever reasons, and she had only to call Denver newspaper or police to find out those reasons—if the husband didn't come looking for her first.

The phone rang as she heard Sudie on the stairs tell Mitch Mason to go up. Annoyed, Tory grabbed up the phone. Marja, again. Tory told her mother, "I didn't return your calls because there's no need to. I'm busy. I don't understand why you care what's going on here. Yes, yes, he's coming along slowly and yes, I'm looking after my interests. I'm hanging up now."

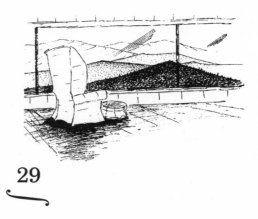

29

"You're the only woman on the planet I'd allow . . . to do this to me . . . being led around by a damn harness," Alexander Kingston grumbled, as Selena released the belt from his waist. He sank gratefully back into his big chair.

She was pleased with their morning workout. Alexander looked good, the mane of silver hair combed back, color flushed from the exertion. The shoulders held their virility, the slacks and long sleeved shirt hid the loss of weight, and his look, following her, had a gleam of determination.

"You're staying for lunch now. Ring the bell for Sudie. I wouldn't mind Zack coming in to have lunch with us," he added brusquely, as she tightened the blood pressure sleeve around his arm.

"Maybe he'll show up." Since Zack had flown Dr. Eston in, and back to Charlotte, she'd seen little of him. Was he off with Paula somewhere? It had to happen. She hadn't seen Paula either. Now she read the pressure gage, knowing he watched her face. She smiled and put the cuff away.

"I like the attention, but not the reason. Sit down and talk to me like a good looking woman and not a nurse."

"That I will. Let me go down and help Sudie bring up the trays."

Selena went down now, thinking, *at last we're making progress.* Dr. Eston had agreed. Why didn't she feel relief?

Since Zack's ultimatum, Tory had conceded to turning over the med responsibility and now stayed absent or in the library most every day. Almost as quickly, Alexander seemed much improved, more like his real self. Tory also agreed with Zack to fly the Charlotte specialist up for a quick visit. After the check-up, patient and doctor had joked together. Zack had been there too, watching and nodding. Tory stood by playing the concerned, relieved daughter.

I'm reacting as distrustful to her as she does to me, Selena knew. As if they were two women competing for the same man. Ridiculous, but in a way, true. Had Tory's jealousy abated that easily? Selena didn't think so. Zack only reported, "The Brat is busy with her road repair and realizes she needs you here."

For a week now, the pall had lifted from the master bedroom upstairs. She could stay to share lunch with Alexander and return in the afternoon after his nap to read to him, or get him talking about his import business, his travel stories. Or make her laugh with some story about Marja, the second wife. No mention of fears. She kept to herself the conversations with Maggie and Professor Enholm.

They had their lunch of chicken salad and tea, his baritone rumbling and pensive. Today, there had been an edge to his intended humor, Selena realized. Going alone to the bathroom, he came back kicking at the walker in front of him, before settling again in the chair, to ask, "Tell me straight, Selena, do I look like an old fossil to you? One with a screwed-up head and a weak leg?"

She sat in front of him. "Alexander, you look like a full color picture from a Sunday School magazine I had once."

"Older than God, huh?"

"No, it was King David in his prime."

"King David. Had his share of women, if I recall. Not that I was there." He reached for her hand and held it though the grip was weak. "What month is this? July isn't it? Almost August?" He leaned back, eyes closed for minutes, holding on to her hand. "Last

August, I was in France three weeks. Had a young woman in my bed those nights. . . . I pleased her. . . . Do you believe that?"

"Of course." She allowed her hand to stay in his. "Any illness seems to turn the world inside out while it's happening. You have accepted that. We are going on from there."

What happened to the progress? The next morning young Jeb raced down the stairs past her, shaking his curly blond head. Selena walked in to find Alexander slumped in his chair, too depressed to talk, or too weak to exercise. Zack was in Charlotte again and Tory away. No one in the big house to hear her concern but Sudie and Lottie in the kitchen.

On this rainy morning, dark as her patient's mood, Selena challenged, "Stop closing me out, Alexander. You handled major challenges in your corporate world. This is more subtle, more personal. Lesser men have made their comeback from more serious strokes."

"Trying to make me angry?"

"Yes. The fighting kind. It's part of your energy. Make it work for you, Alexander, not against you."

He groaned behind closed eyes. "Are you with me?"

"One hundred percent. We have a pact, remember? And that means you must keep talking to me. Honestly. Stop hiding whatever is going on inside. We can handle it."

He looked out to the gray rain that shut out the mountains. "If I sleep, it happens again. Wakes me up. The vibration in my head, a warning, then the pictures start. In a perverse sort of way, I look forward to what they might show me. Haven't yet gotten to the one they mean to show me. Tell me, Selena, give it to me straight. Am I losing my mind?"

Again, she told him this was distorted memory from a traumatic time, something he had not dealt with all those years when he was too busy, too many immediate demands on his mind. Now it was trying to surface and he should allow it do so.

She watched his strong face turn away. "Why, Selena? What good would that do? I know now . . . that people think I killed Eve.

I don't know myself. Stuck with that hellish question. There's nothing I can do."

"You can make your peace with her, and the past, and with yourself." She didn't say, this stress is siphoning your energy, your immune system, therefore your life. She reached over and squeezed his big hand. He gave her a twisted smile.

"Selena, I should have met you five years ago. It wouldn't have been too late for me. I could have hung it up then, we could have traveled. What were you doing five, ten years ago?"

"Blocking the truth from myself, as a matter of fact, trying to believe I was doing what I should be doing." She almost said, *reading for my doctorate, handling a practice and ignoring a difficult pregnancy all at once, husband's orders.* "I have left that marriage."

"He must have deserved it." The heavy brows tightened. "A strong woman can leave a bastard. I sit here facing the fact I might have been the bastard. Can't help it, Selena. I can't get past this mental purgatory. I've tried to remember. . . . I can up to a point, then, nothing. I've asked Sudie. No help there."

She sat back, thinking of her talks with Maggie, with Professor Enholm, thinking of the scrapbook of clippings. What there could help her, help him? "Trust me," she said, holding his hand. "Reluctance to remember becomes a stone wall. You want to go around it to the other side. The truth won't kill you. It's this not knowing that's become the nightmare."

He sat there like stone, eyes closed. "I know I was angry and jealous that night. Angry in the room upstairs. She meant too much to me . . . and she sobbed on the bed, not wanting to leave and go home with me. After supper, I was drinking in the car . . . sitting out there alone. . . . I saw her walk back to the garden."

Selena squeezed his hand. "Go on. Let it come." *Oh God, Alexander I hope I'm not risking your sanity here.* "Did you get out of the car? Go to the back garden?"

"I saw Eve, rocking in the arms of a man. A young fellow who looked at me and backed away. I saw Eve's white face in the dark. Rejecting me. Until that moment, I was a cocky young male who thought he had everything and Eve was the center of it. Now I had nothing. Maybe I struck her. I don't know. She turned away and ran. I tried to grab her back . . . don't remember beyond that . . ."

"Allow yourself to remember. Finish it, Alexander." She waited, watching him rock his shoulders, eyes closed, answering finally in a harsh whisper.

"Her face turning away from me, that's all. Did I follow? Don't know. I woke up in the car in front of the Inn, sick and hungover, then cold sober awake with fear. I went looking for her . . . called . . . no answer. She's trying to answer now, how or why I don't know. But it's hell the nights I wake up in that bed, thinking I hear her voice."

What could she tell him? "Alexander, guilt can block memory or distort it. Believe me, you need to finish this. Unlock whatever happened. Whatever it was I don't believe you meant to hurt her. Alexander—do you hear me?"

He didn't move, his face clenched like his fists. "You weren't there," he said dully. "I need someone who was there . . . to tell me that." He opened his eyes, and told her with finality, "I have to wait it out . . . until she comes and tells me . . . whatever I have to know."

"What do you *want* her to tell you?"

"Forgiveness. I want her forgiveness."

30

After the meeting at the far end of the Ridgeway's front porch with Zack Kingston, Paula Crossing went upstairs, filled the deep claw-foot tub, dumped in bath salts, stepped out of her clothes and sank down in that temporary womb of hot water. Where to go from here? Back to San Diego? Not yet, not unless she meant to live forever in this state of emotional *interruptus*. What now?

She rocked in the hot water, eyes closed, making the deliberate effort to calm down before she reviewed what had happened out there on the porch. Something unfinished for sure. Incomplete decisions caused more stress than making a tough choice as Selena had reminded her during their mutual confessions. So what's the stress scale when you aren't allowed to make a choice? Coming here had brought it all back, hurting like a blunted nerve coming alive again. Memory sharp and sensory again of lying partially zonked out in a sterile clinic, frightened, shamed, a helpless child, knowing that the child in her own body was to be drawn out, pulled out, removed, taken away, no questions allowed. She hadn't told those gory details to Zack out there on the porch. Nor did she tell him about falling in the woods, revisiting the scene of their youthful lovemaking. She had dealt him no sob story. Instead, she had let him know simply as possible why she was here, as if reporting on what happened to someone else.

Reason enough for Zack to look stunned. And after saying it, reason enough for her own voice to close down. One of the Inn guests had pranced over about then, eager to report that some people from a television show had called Dilly. They'd be up here with their cameras first of September. Beaming apologies, the woman asked, oh, was she interrupting something? Both of them had laughed—nervous, looking-away laughs.

Paula kicked at the steaming scented water. Life had its interruptions. That time, for instance, when she must have been fifteen, standing in the wings of the high school auditorium, practicing her lines with fearful anticipation before going out to the spotlight, the chance to prove she wasn't timid Caroline. Hadn't she walked out and opened her mouth, just as the lights went out? Blackout. Power off. The speech aborted forever. *That's how I feel now. Incomplete. So I can't leave.*

She added hot water and sank back again, reviewing how she'd handled it. Zack, I came to see your father because my mother handed him my child and demanded that he be responsible. I didn't know until a few weeks ago that necessary detail. No, Zack, it wasn't his child. But I had to come here to see him to find out what he did with that life put in his hands. And when I saw Loren, I knew.

She had paused then to watch questions churn behind his lean face and intense gaze, a frown hiding under the tousled bronze hair. This wasn't the face of the boy she had dreamed of on endless nights. Back at the San Diego office the women she knew would look at this man and rate the mature Zack a sensitive hunk with an IQ. She couldn't read his grim, rapt silence.

When she paused, he said, "Loren? Your child?"

"I'm sure, yes. Born April 20, seventeen years ago." Because he stared, waiting, she said the rest quickly and without preamble. "I had spent the previous summer with my mother, here at the Inn. I was invited to visit Capstone one day and met this boy and this Collie. I was Caroline Holt at the time."

226

"Caroline, my God . . . of course."

In that awkward moment, afraid the consternation in his face would harden, afraid he would believe she expected something of him, she had rushed on. "When I found out, when I found my mother's papers, I left my future dangling back there in San Diego to come here. I have thought of leaving now as there is no real need to see your father—since I've seen Loren. I can see he has had advantages, an excellent private school. And at seventeen, very independent and resourceful."

She didn't say—but also the loner, robbed of something. Zack must be aware of that void. She looked away, hurting not for herself and this ridiculous awkward moment but for Loren. When Zack spoke again, she heard sardonic self-accusation.

"Advantages, sure. He's had me as a hard-ass big brother."

"You didn't know."

He groaned. "Caroline. You didn't know where. . . .?"

"I'm Paula. Haven't been a Caroline since I left Virginia. My father was kicked out of my life when I was six—his name was Paul. I thought it sounded strong.

"Anyway, when I found those papers after the funeral, I didn't know you would be here, Zack. I came looking for your father. But you had to be told. Unsettling I'm sure, but it's your right. So I've told you."

"Have you told Loren?"

"Oh, God, no. At this point, it's been enough to find him, be with him. Get to know him a little."

"Are you going to tell him?"

"Don't know yet. I don't want to . . . drive him more into himself." She could feel his tension, could guess at his shock, talking about having to drive to Boone tomorrow to pick up Loren, then fly the Bird to Charlotte on business.

He stood there, shaking his head, dealing with the shock, studying her, and promising yes, they'd talk again. She watched him walk off the porch, get into his dusty Rover and drive away, leaving her as suspended as she had left him. They had parted like that, with cautious formality, caught in ambivalence, promising to meet again.

In her hot water womb, Paula allowed herself to ponder this mature Zack. He had been leaning against the banisters, arms folded, curious when she started, his eyes narrowed, frowning. As she rushed on, quietly, he hadn't moved a muscle except the throb of pulse she could see in his neck and the mounting awareness beginning to tighten the lines around his eyes. She'd found herself looking at his hands, the lean fingers that had stroked her again in so many dreams. She moved in the hot water with a moan, telling herself, *you did not come here to fall in love with him again.* She had never wanted anyone who didn't want her. She'd learned that lesson of independence well enough. Clive was different. Her feeling for him had little to do with love. But she couldn't leave this place yet.

The next morning, Paula looked out on a perfect August day, one to be enjoyed. She had to get away from the Inn, had to be busy or scream. Wasn't even ready to talk to Zack again, though he was off for days. But she didn't want to be alone.

Selena? No, not ready to talk yet to Selena who would be busy anyway up there at Capstone. She needed someone who didn't know about her confusion or expect her to talk about it.

Mid-morning, Paula drove up toward Capstone and took the new raw dirt road that cut through the woods around the summit. The convertible bumped along until she saw the stone cottage, very Hansel and Gretel, the way Mitch Mason had described it. The man should be needing some escapism and light company as well, about now. She knocked. Mitch opened the door, blinking at her from his amiable but now haggard face. The poor guy did need company. Hadn't he just returned from his wife's funeral and, no doubt, a bad family scene.

"Hi," she said. "How about riding the Parkway like a tourist? Finding a decent lunch somewhere. You can cuss or cry in my beer if you like. If we can find a beer."

228

He pretended to rock on his heels. "Well, Red Riding Hood, you look well recovered. Staying out of the woods these days? You must have heard I need some rescuing. I've been trying booze and work." He waved a hand at the littered room behind him. "Come in. You'll see I'm not lying on both counts."

He must have cleared away anything mindful of Lucie. Bottles and coffee cups littered the counter. Rolls of architectural drawings covered the couch. More papers on the pine table. "Since you do California malls, you know all about the preliminary hassles of site preparation. Just try working with this topography, all stony mountain under hardwoods and evergreens. But the boss of this project—let's say dreamer—says it's going to happen."

"*This* mountain?" Paula asked. "Who's doing this? *Kingston*?"

"Forget my harangue. This project is not a sure thing yet. As said, the boss person is a dreamer. Stubborn one. She's working on getting the construction loan approved. Down in Asheville. I had to come up with some plans to show them. Forget all that. This hypothetical big project is Tory's little secret at present. Gad, Paula, I am glad to see a friendly face." He scrounged around on the littered bar. "Have some tepid tomato juice. Or vodka?"

"The first. To answer the other question, Red Riding Hood here is keeping her balance for the time being. But I have a great need to goof off today in the great outdoors. Around here, isn't it called lollygagging? I thought you could use the same. What about it?"

Paula drove, Mitch slouched down in the seat beside her, a compact man who had developed those shoulders from real labor, she guessed. His pleasant sun-weathered face could light up with a smile. Pensive smile now, but no wonder. She drove, the convertible top down, the wind blowing her hair against her sunglasses, and deepening his color, as he rambled on with jokes about himself and the local guys doing his roads. Paula decided he was a man who liked people and needed to laugh but hadn't done much of that lately. When he kept waving at every passing driver, he explained, "Around here, you're 'uppity' if you don't *throw up*. Throw up a hand as you pass, that is."

229

Pale summer sky moved above them. Green meadows and rural houses fell past as they drove to Bakersville, a county seat that seemed to have two traffic lights. At "Helen's" they picked up hamburgers and drinks and continued on up into Roan Mountain, each mile offering a different view. At the top, they sat on a bench and dug into their sack of hamburgers and paper cups of sweetened tea.

"Back in the Twenties," he told her, "the Cloudland Hotel sat up here. Imagine the roads they had to travel to get here. Most of those old places have burned. The few left are refurbished like the Balsam Mountain Inn, or redone like the Green Park Inn in Blowing Rock and the big stone Grove Park Inn in Asheville. Our little Ridgeway Inn is the original."

He looked around at open hilltop and rhododendron. "I needed this. Don't worry, you're not going to have to listen to me groan about Lucie."

Nor to my quandary, she thought. But she wanted to know about Zack. "What mountain might you be carving? Is Zack Kingston involved?" She met piercing blue eyes. Knew he was trying to decide how much to say.

"No, Junior is not involved and it's a good thing. I almost kicked his ass after the thing happened. He had been coming around the cottage, seeing Lucie. He took her flying once, you know. Let's don't talk about that."

Paula patted his hand and looked up at the blue sky and white clouds. It would be dead end stupid to care about Zack Kingston. He had a life. But at this calm moment she knew clearly she had to stay here to see more of Loren. Not until then could she decide what was best for him; to leave with, or without telling that young man, look, I'm your mother, but go on with your life. I won't interfere, I'll go on with mine.

Mitch said. "Did I see a shiver? Don't think, just breathe this in. I'm trying to."

She sighed, taking his advise. "So beautiful here. I'm glad you came with me. Lollygagging is necessary at times but better with a friend."

Back in the car, Mitch put the top up, accepted the driver's seat and they wheeled out again. "I didn't answer your question," he said. "But if you understand this information is not yet for public consumption, I'll tell you."

He drove, looking at the curving road, telling her briefly about helping Tory Kingston's project. "Since her father is ill and has to give approval on the construction loan, we've had to move slowly, even on the preliminary roads and the new water lines. The man's accustomed to calling the shots, of course, but she tries to make me believe she can handle him better without yours truly getting in the act." Mitch groaned.

"Hell of a situation for me but I'm strapped. Especially now, I have no where else I can go or want to go."

"She sounds hard to take. And such a cute little thing. I've seen her driving that Porsche."

"Tory is quick and clever and tenacious," he said, wheeling the car around a mountain curve. "But she won't listen to any opinion but her own. She has guts, I give her that, and she's driving ahead on this, keeping it under wraps until the construction loan is in. Why? You don't want to announce a project until you're ready to go ahead. Timing is already against us. Possibly three good months to start, before winter weather. But I need the challenge."

He told her how rural counties like this one still had no zoning restrictions, no land-use plan, a crony old-boy government, one department not knowing what the next was doing. For that reason, getting the necessary water permits had been a slow process rather than easy. Unless they moved patiently, even the county would hold them up.

"Meanwhile, I'm working on infrastructure plans that will accommodate the optimum number of estates, with both distant and pastoral views. That's what it's all about in these mountains for second home buyers."

Paula held her questions and watched him think out loud, alternately grinning or glowering. "Way down the line," he said, "we hire someone like Paula Crossing to handle the marketing. In the Blue Ridge, it goes like this. 'come closer to heaven folks,'

231

translated as 'here's your summer haven, leave all those problems behind in Miami or Cleveland or wherever.'"

She still wondered what Alexander Kingston thought about all this. She had gone to the tiny library at the county seat, an old town farther down the mountain, to read what earlier features she could find about the man. "I thought he was leaving it to the state."

"He must have changed his mind after the stroke. Or after selling his company. Daughter says the man has a big ego, sick or not. He must have decided he can do as well as Hugh Morton over there who owns Grandfather Mountain. Morton held up the Blue Ridge Parkway for years rather than let them finish the last connection by cutting into his mountain. But more recently, one side of Grandfather is getting a first class golf course and upscale homes."

"I've heard some of the developments in these mountains have failed."

"Several big ones went under in the Seventies, but the demand is there. Can't do anything but grow. By the Nineties, a great number of people will have moved in, wanting summer places or year round homes. The older crowd, relocating from the city—any city. Like a lot of special places, Santa Fe for example, you bring money with you. Look around during the summer and you see Florida tags everywhere. It's happening. Why not at High Haven's ridge, now enjoyed, shall we say, by a storyteller's ghost, and old Dilly's summer regulars?"

"Beautiful woods. The view out there. But so remote from highways," Paula said.

"That's a problem. But development money has clout. The state gets around to building roads when development comes in."

Paula said thoughtfully, "To Dilly, construction coming in would be as welcome as Armageddon. And Maggie Hardy! Mitch, does Maggie know about this? She just might shoot the first bulldozer. Or tie herself to a tree."

Mitch winced. "Remember I said all this is premature. In confidence, okay? I'm supposed to be doing road work, period. We

232

won't have bulldozers and loaders and crew roaring around Capstone this summer anyway. The plans I'm working on now are for
the slopes to the west, the one with the lake. But you know those
outcroppings on the high back of Capstone property? Tory wants
that slope blasted down soon as we get moving with big equipment. I asked her, joking, 'Trying to kill off Eve's ghost?' Wow.
Wrong joke."

Mitch's smile turned grim. "Wrong for both of us. Lucie had
the sense of the dramatic, didn't she? Choosing that place to jump,
in front of an audience."

"Mitch—don't let it keep happening in your head."

"Easier said than done. That's why I need this challenge. How
does Havencrest Homes sound to you, market lady?"

"Like a spooky house on the cover of a gothic. You can do better.
Is that her idea?"

"Let's forget the whole damn thing. How long are you staying
here?"

"Not sure," Paula murmured. "By the way, is that character
Hoke McRae giving you any trouble up there? I've heard about
him lurking up there."

"Strangely enough, Tory seems to have stopped that. She
indicated she's confronted the guy and put the fear of whatever
in him. I told you, she's one determined female."

31

Tory Kingston looked across the open knoll, satisfied to see a faint light from the stone cottage. So Mitch was working. Good. She ordered the two Dobermans to stay on the terrace and walked quickly down the dark front drive, wind whipping at her mini skirt and short midriff sweater top. She meant to tease the creep but handle him better this time. She laughed. Moments like this, she marveled at her own audacity, or versatility, in dealing with men. They were all alike once down to their shorts. She thought of Virgil Means last week, a polished face with a beak nose, crisp banker voice as impersonal as the hotel room where they talked land development over martinis. Once Virgil laid out the navy blazer carefully on the second bed, he was a skinny needful son-of-a-bitch.

Beyond the cedars, the pick-up truck was backed off the road, only the nose showing. *The last time I'll come down here,* Tory told herself vehemently. Hoke McRae sat in the truck bed, smoking, his long legs crossed. "Whar's my Doberman buddies?" he drawled.

"Where they belong." Already she was angry but she let him hoist her up to sit next to his animal smell and his pungent sweet smoke. "When a woman shows up at your request, you don't ask for her guard dogs."

She took the joint he poked at her, inhaled a quick drag of the acrid smoke before leaning back against the side panel. She kept her legs extended toward him, to keep him at that distance. In the dark, he was a scarecrow of a man with a mop of hair, broad shoulders rocking as he smoked. But what a stud.

"The reason I agreed to see you," she began and faltered, interrupted by his soft guffaw. He reached for her but she kicked at his lean flanks and he sat up again, with his low, rough laugh. "That's good stuff what you're smoking there."

Tory pulled in another draw, hating the burn but wanting the effect. "That's why I'm here. You can't be using that back slope above the lake anymore. Bo Hilrey says it's been spotted. He knows it's not my marijuana. But get it out of there."

"Hell, no. I got that rigged up. I tie them suckers down so no 'copter can spot 'em. Once the buzzards leave, I let 'em up. Takes time and watching but it's my cash crop, honey. Now if I had me a regular grow house I wouldn't have to go to all that trouble. Your daddy oughta have an old barn somewhere around I could use. After all I done for you. Or all I could do *to* you Kingstons."

"You haven't done anything for me but hand me some crazy talk. I could accuse you of blackmail, McRae. I could swear out a warrant against you."

Hoke sounded peeved. "Aw, after I nosed around that nurse's house for you?" He grabbed her foot and slid his hand, rough but hot and electric, higher on her bare leg. She kicked his arm away. "A lot of good you did me. You didn't find out who she is, but I did. So leave her alone now. I happen to need her around for awhile."

She sat smoking, trembling inside. He moved closer with his heavy tobacco smell. She hissed in his shadowed face. "Stop it. You level with me about your threat or I'll do one that people will believe. I'll charge you with rape, Hoke McRae."

"Rape, hell. I'll tell 'em you're one skinny hot bitch." He sat up again, away from her. "Threaten me like that and I'll cook all your Kingston asses."

Her head spun with the grass, and his threat, and his smell. Damn backwoodsman. Daring to threaten her. "McRae, don't try that pitch about your poor old daddy owning this land. I've looked at the papers. My father bought the High Haven property from a group in Charlotte who had held it for years and never did anything with it. The McRaes may have used it as their own."

He grabbed her shoulders and growled in her face, *"That ain't all I can tell."*

The night spun around her. What was she doing here, with this disgusting man. Oh yes, to call his bluff. She laughed in his face, into his dark gleaming gaze. "I dare you to tell me. I'll show you I don't give a damn."

"Yeah?" His hand pushed her back against the hard truck bed and dusty burlap and he leaned on an elbow, face close, shutting out the trees that rattled and sighed above. He might have been an animal leaning over her, toying with its prey and she, the prey, aware of repulsion and compulsive need to have it happen. She lay still to prove she didn't fear him, or because she didn't want to move. Even as his big hand slid along her bare midriff, his voice lazy. "Let's say I know what happened to Eve Kingston, that's what . . . know she didn't die in no burning car."

"Same old talk . . . old gossip . . . you creep. . . ."

His lips and his hot, stoned breath moved against her ear like a rough caress. "What if I told folks your daddy followed his little girl wife up the mountain and pushed her off the bluff? Then to save his hide, he came back and bought up the mountain, in case they ever found her bones?"

Tory didn't move, couldn't move from under his weight. She wanted only to close her eyes to the night and her ears to his hot words against her face. Wanted to shut out all the threats and let this man turn into the driving thing he could be, taking her into the crazy space of escape her body needed.

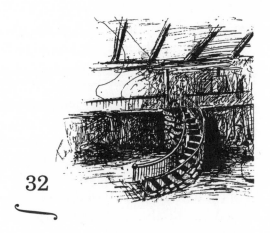

32

In her room at the Ridgeway Inn, listening to ominous rain, Paula Crossing dressed to meet Zack downstairs. Skirt and blouse? No, too ingenue. Jeans? Too casual. She went back to an oatmeal silk knit pants and loose tunic top, good with her hair. In the process, she chided herself. What's the deal? You're only going to lunch with a stranger who happens to be the father of your child.

"Little Switzerland is not far," Zack had said on the phone. "It's another small summer village but not so isolated as High Haven. The Chalet restaurant has tablecloths and a view and they recognize what century we're in, unlike Dilly at the Inn."

He picked her up mid-morning in his Range Rover, joking about the rain, cheerful as a real estate agent determined to show property. Under his polite banter, Paula figured, he had to be wondering what she would want of him. The galling thought made her hyper with the need to assure him she'd done all right in this world. Certainly she had learned a long time ago to look and act the confident, independent woman. As they followed the rain swept road, she asked about his trip to Charlotte, making polite conversation, avoiding even a mention of Loren.

"The Charlotte business is not yet finished. To my great regret, I'll have to go back at least two more times, representing my father. With the Bird, I make the trips short as possible. We'll take the Blue Ridge Parkway, okay?"

"Is Selena still with him?"

"Most of the day. She comes back in the late afternoon."

They rode in silence, past rain grayed woods. What was the protocol for such a meeting, how to start talking about what must be talked about? Now like a polite blind date, he asked about her work in San Diego. She gave perky, confident answers while stealing casual glances at his profile, at his hands on the wheel. This man beside her had inhabited her dreams for so long he had taken on a mythical male quality. The young face never came clear but his touch had heated those dreams.

Out of frustration, she laughed. *To hell with caution.* Here they were sealed inside of a car, enclosed by a rainy world and acting polite as two classmates at a high school reunion. She told him so.

He flashed her an honest grin. "We should talk about Loren, right?"

"Not yet. At lunch. Let's swap tales of these past years, just for the hell of it."

He agreed but already he was into what must have been running in his mind—coming home from prep school that first summer to find his father with a child, and nurse. "God, I never guessed. He must have held back the explanation to keep me on the straight and narrow in school. It had the opposite effect. My righteous indignation gave me the good excuse to dump the L. L. Bean gear, the preppy life, refuse the next haircut and head for California." He shook his head, at the rain or the memory.

"So my own summer of discontent was in time for that great youth movement, repudiation of one's elders' hypocritical, corrupt life. One more mixed-up kid in Golden Gate Park that summer of 1967. And you?"

"I left Virginia behind, on a bus, after—I'd say just before my eighteenth birthday. My mother probably told people I had died of a mysterious disease in some nunnery." She tried to laugh. "I didn't stop running until Texas, one dumb job after another, and a foolish marriage at nineteen that was worse. It took me a few more years before I got to California. I managed to get a work scholarship at Esalen. You know the place on Big Sur? Spent an entire summer eating sprouts and trying not to blow my innocence during intellectual conversations with naked people sitting around in the mineral baths, and oh yes, sitting in Gestalt sessions beating pillows and hating mama and getting rebirthed. It didn't work for me. I wanted to forget."

Paula laughed, remembering. "But the experience there showed me I was pretty confused about my life from day one. You do hit some highs looking for your inner self while gazing out on the Pacific. But back into a rented cubicle of an apartment, you find you need to conform again. Money becomes necessary, then the reality, the mission. You think about dressing for success to get your share. You're sucked up into the cultural rhythm of the moment and then you can't let go." At the moment, the thought of Clive and her own office was not reality but a mirage hanging out there in space.

"And you, Zack? Did you become a full fledged hippie?"

"Never got up there to Big Sur. At some black moment, A. Z. found me out there and asked if I was ready to come home and go to school. The man knows when to persuade by asking and when to demand. Besides, I was homesick for these hills. I came back, a private cynic, and kept a low profile at Duke. I was beginning to enjoy that old campus when I left for a year in the air. Flying copters. Nam."

"Oh." She looked at him, waiting for more.

"My timing was lucky. I came home in one piece and ingrained guilt because of that. Came back into corduroys and gray flannels and a crash course in textiles and country club friends. Being the boss' son, you can guess what the other managers thought of me—an ingrate in for the spoils. A. Z. was a heck of a CEO. He gave those boys a lot of power because it freed him to be the idea man, the ultimate rep, moving around. The man loved his junkets. Had an import business." With a slow grin. "There's a picture

239

around somewhere of A. Z. and some other American types aboard the Onassis yacht."

He kept his gaze on the rain lashed road ahead, so she allowed herself to watch his profile. "You didn't like the business?"

"I let myself get sucked into the company role, at first. Or tried. Even married one of those beauties you meet in a ski lodge in Vail. She was happy with the perks but not with me. All that is past tense. I'm back to bumming. Up here. If I get lonesome for off-the-wall friends I can call on some graying grizzled hippies who live in these hills. Potters. Crazy artists without a bank account. Some were back-to-the-earth people who have settled down to be small plot farmers or artists. How about you?"

"I've been a leasing agent with a mall developer for five years. The kind of job that doesn't leave time to think of much else. They know I came for a funeral. Since, I've told them I needed some time here." She stopped. The question lay unanswered for both of them: how much time would she spend here?

Zack said quickly, "This next exit is Little Switzerland. We can have lunch at the Little Switzerland Cafe or the Chalet, that's the resort."

"You name it." Both silent now, they followed the curving road that showed glimpses of half hidden summer houses. They were heading toward some normal lunch table with a view, where they would have to talk about Loren's future if not their own.

In the Capstone library, Tory shuddered. Nights in this house gave her the creeps, but after five days of fog and rain, and now this stormy night, she was ready to scream. At the desk she poured more brandy, shivering, trying to dismiss Hoke's claim, trying to think rationally about all the other situations complicating her plans. Wind moaned around the house. She hoped the Bird would get itself untied and bashed into the woods. Before Selena left tonight, she had stood in the library doorway, asking for Zack with the quiet persistence and the exasperating cool.

"Who knows when I can expect big brother?" Tory flared. "We don't keep up with one another, haven't you noticed? He's probably shacking up somewhere this rainy night. With Miss Blue Convertible. He left yesterday for lunch and called this morning from Little Switzerland, very vague about his timing."

Tory watched that bit of news make Selena turn and walk out of there without another word. What ho, was Selena's eagerness to see Junior more personal than to make nurse-like reports? *You're not his type,* Tory could have told her. He likes the cuddly ones.

Alone now, Tory paced the library, cursing the thundering rain. Mitch's road behind the cottage was washing out by the minute, postponing the lines going in to handle the larger water system. Excavation on the steep slopes was causing some properties in the hollow to flood. Mitch had to handle those complaints, she wanted no part of dealing with those people. The thought of those grim-faced hillbillies she'd faced down at the lake the other day made her shudder. How dare those men tell her to "git yer daddy down here," grumbling that this lake and land was open for hunting and fishing, always had been, and Mister Kingston had promised it would stay that way. She had driven away and ordered Mitch to have a fence put up. Keep them out.

Tory tossed the empty brandy bottle in the trash and paced again. No word in days from Virgil Means at the bank. Was anyone questioning the signature on the note? That was her real worry. She had taken that desperate risk. Had to, to move along the loan request. Whether sedated or awake enough to curse his lassitude, A. Z. was not about to sign anything these nights when she went in with his warm milk. So she had done the necessary. Easier to copy the Kingston signature than make him wonder at her insistence. She could tell him later he did sign it. Did Virgil have any questions? Was it working?

She paced to the muted sound of drumming rain that was washing away her roads. Right now she needed a soft-lit booth, someone else pouring the brandy. Someone smooth and clever and controllable, the opposite of Hoke.

The feel and smell of him came back with a hot flush of disgust. It did no good to tell herself she was trying to call his bluff, to stop his need to blackmail. She had used him to bruise herself, a self-administered punishment as a distraction. It hadn't stopped the story he growled in her ear. His bizarre story he always began, but didn't finish.

I cannot allow my self to believe it. He was forty something so he couldn't have been much more than five when Eve disappeared from the Inn. Kids hear things. He could have heard the old hill talk, and since dreamed up this yarn to force her to give him some land. He couldn't do anything legally so he was using her for the vendetta against her father. He had to be shown she wasn't afraid of him.

If only the damn rain would stop. And if only Virgil would call and say, *"Approved, I got it through for you."*

In the kitchen later she prepared the glass of hot milk, adding the bourbon and a capsule of antihistamine. With the Charlotte doctor out of the way, she could keep him subdued again.

Rain still thudded against the roof when Tory walked in to her father's room. Her throat tightened at the sight of him, sitting on the side of the bed, haunched over like an old man. She wanted to put her arms around those shoulders. Wanted him to look at her, thank her. She stood in front of him, handing him the milk and waiting for some response, some nod of appreciation.

"Your hair is getting longer," she said, softly. "We need to give you a haircut."

He mumbled, "Don't bother, Selena will do it."

She watched him drink, and set the glass on the bedside table without looking at her. "Nights are hell. Bad dreams."

"I know, I've heard you."

He looked up, frowning, as if to focus her face, someone he didn't recognize. Finally, "What do you hear? And Tory, what are you up to? What's this I hear about roads washing and flooding down in the hollow?"

What did he know? Had Jeb told him when he'd been ordered not to mention anything upsetting? Had Selena?

She began, speaking softly, righteously, about keeping up the place. The look on his face was a kick in her solar plexus.

". . . not only looking after this place," Tory added, vehement now, "but protecting you."

"Protecting me? Good Lord, Tory, you torment me." He sat reeling there on the side of the bed.

"Yes, protecting you—from everyone except your dear nurse who has taken you over."

She saw his angry confusion. Her own anger didn't let her stop. " I suppose she has questioned you on your personal business? Asked you what really happened to dear dead Eve? I come in here late and hear you muttering in your nightmares. Can't you kill Eve off for good? Others think you did."

He continued to rock his body, not looking at her, his words already slurred from his drink. "You never knew Eve. How could you hate her?"

"Don't you *know*?" She wanted to scream at him. "Always, you acted as if she owned this place, owned you. As if the rest of us were accessories in your life? You encouraged that Eve's Mountain yarn. So that stupid ghost tale became fodder for the tourists. And now, this summer, reporters are showing up for the truth. As well as some tabloid TV show who will embellish the truth. All of them intent on talking to Alexander Kingston. Good thing they don't know Eve has been showing up in your nightmares for the same reason." Tory caught her breath. "Maybe Selena has told them."

"Go . . . away, Tory." His hands pushed air.

"Don't you hear me? " She felt drunk with rage at his cruelty, his blindness, his dismissal. "I'm your daughter. I'm the one protecting you, by hanging up the phone, keeping them all out. Me. Tory. Your daughter."

He fell back against the bed, dragged his own legs into position and turned his face away from her.

She walked out, trembling. What had she done? She hadn't meant to tell him all that. Or had she already told him? She groped her way downstairs, threw open the liquor cabinet, looking for anything to douse the rage and dismay roaring in her body.

The hot milk would put him to sleep. Nothing could work for her. Where were her own damn pills? Tomorrow she had to make sure he'd forget tonight. She poured a stiff drink of bourbon. *Control. Had to stay controlled.* Once the loan papers got through the bank . . . once this Goddamned rain stopped, she would be ahead of all of her problems.

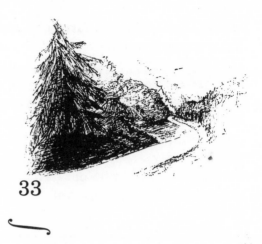

33

Finally, a clear morning. Jumpy after six days of rainy solitude under a reading lamp, with no visit from Ariel, David Tyler drove to the Inn to meet Professor Enholm for their delayed excursion into the local culture. He drove slowly along the rain washed roads looking for some glimpse of Ariel's sassy walk. Still no sign of her. Grimly, he ordered himself: *You've got to stop this.*

Professor was waiting in his Mercedes, looking like any seasoned retiree in his Orvis cap and khakis. David jumped in, with morning greetings. "I've been looking forward to this." As they started off, "I remember you told me to keep my mouth shut and notebook closed so tell me, how do you get the men around here to level with an anthropologist?"

"I'm a North Carolinian, you know. I admit that helps. Enholm is a step-father's name. My grandparents came from near Roan Mountain where I spent my boyhood. So I understand the affinity of the land as you might have read in James Still's writing. My field of study informs and adds to that appreciation."

He maneuvered the Mercedes down to Crest Road, past some walkers, then past the shops. As they followed the winding country road, sunlight flashing as it filtered through August

245

foliage, Enholm's lean face creased into a mellow smile, answering David's questions.

"You ask about relating. An anthropologist's critical research requires both an insider's view and compassionate objectivity. To do a case study of an area, one must be accepted and valued as a friend, not perceived as an interloper. Developing one's authenticity can take time. The inquisitive outsider and the well-meaning do-gooder are met with closed-face politeness." He glanced over at David. "Now for our day, I assume you want to understand the summer resident as well as the native? I offer the option of several stops."

"Lead the way. But don't forget your other offer. About the Eve story."

The Professor's long fingers tapped his steering wheel. "Have you talked with Maggie Hardy lately, or Selena Hart? No?" He was silent a moment. "We shall visit Mrs. Emma Riddle. She's a friendly soul off Old Valley Road. We must arrive after she's done her morning dishes and looked after her cats or the lady will be painfully apologetic. Until then, other stops. Did you read the journals these past rainy days?"

"I did and enjoyed the material, it kept me sane."

If he hadn't known it before, he did now. The Blue Ridge had been an escape place for the wealthy elite for a long time. It was no surprise to read how in recent years western North Carolina had been marketed by brokers selling beauty and serenity as an "escape" to the good life. Major developments had bloomed and bankrupted and risen again. More were undoubtedly coming. David stretched his long legs.

"I appreciated the image of this being a *peripheral* place, geographically, economically and politically. Once you get away from five o'clock traffic, a mountain top is a likely vantage point—very peripheral—to stand and contemplate where you've been and where you might be going.

"As Maggie puts it, a chance to look into infinity. I came to hear myself *think* for a change. Not that my thoughts here have been all that comforting." David hoped the last remark sounded facetious, not the painful confession it was.

Obviously enjoying his subject, the Professor said, "You will want to understand the so-called newcomer here as well as native. Some of the second home people are professional and business people from North Carolina. They own a place in these mountains as part of their heritage, and their escape from the city. Given more days, I could introduce you to the Courtneys, who have built a family compound on a high windy site. Or the George family, prominent in Raleigh, whose mountain place is hidden away on wooded acres, a private but hospitable retreat they share with friends and family and a couple of sleek Weimaraners."

Silent a moment, the Professor's tones turned pensive. "Yes, of course, many are from Florida and other urban areas. I'm thinking of two elegant older women we could visit this morning. Small house, walls framed with good art and university credentials, former professors of music and history, still articulate with their passionate concerns about the state of education. You can detect a quiet bravado in their faces, a quiet denial that one of them is quite ill. Their timeless view has been a true retreat during two busy careers. This summer, their consolation, postponement of inevitability. By fall, they return to retirement centers in Florida as just two more old women."

"You've given me the picture. Any other types?"

"We would be welcomed at another home where a cheery socialite from St. Petersburg turns grandmother to cook for visiting sons and daughters-in-law and children, all of whom will be watching TV. In that living room, the talk would be politics and computers, and football, the view a backdrop, the place an escape from the heat and traffic of Florida."

The Professor listed other possibilities. A retired businessman from Naples who spent his days in front of his computer, his restless wife off shopping in Asheville or wherever. "There you have a couple who would be happier in one of the resorts with a clubhouse. Then, we could call on Joselyn, a widow, quite a pretty woman, bitterness behind the laugh. Husband was a police lieutenant, shot some years ago. Her small chalet, a delightfully chaotic place, bird houses all over the deck. She spends eight months here, alone with her poodle, painting strange canvases."

"That's confirmation enough. Escapes, for all kinds of reasons. Let's get to the people I don't know. And Emma Riddle." They were following a wide creek now.

"There is one stop we shall make first. We're on the other side of Eve's Mountain you know. The slopes to our left are part of Kingston's holdings, also the lake here. We're about to pass a trout fisherman's dream. Big browns and rainbows."

David recognized the soft-voiced respect of a dedicated fly fisherman. The creek gave way to an open lake, flanked by a grassy bank and a chain link fence. The car slowed.

"The fence is new," the Professor murmured. "That's why I want to visit the sawmill." He drove on. "Where we're stopping, there is certain protocol to be observed. You'll be looking at cousins and brothers and in-laws. And the one who comes forward will be boss. If the saw operation stops, our visit is acknowledged. Otherwise, they have ignored us and we dig our toes in the sawdust and leave." He looked at David. "You'll be a stranger, an outsider, to these men. Let me do the talking."

The sawmill was a large shed-like building set back from the road on grounds littered with logs and sawdust. From the open second level came the high-pitched scream of a saw ripping through raw logs. As the Mercedes lumbered in, the grinding shriek of the saw grew deafening. At his guide's nod, David followed behind, taking mental notes.

The shrieking saw ground to a stop. Silence. From the shadowy interior of the open level, faces appeared. Professor Enholm headed up the rickety staircase, David following in his tracks. They came out on the open landing where the huge log-splitting saw sat silent. Nine grimy, sweaty guys moved away from their work stations to light up cigarettes. Some sat down on the floor to open lunch boxes, solemn faced, ignoring the arrivals. A tired looking, wiry fellow stepped out. Between thirty and fifty, David surmised. Crusted jeans and a shirt that once was plaid. The hands that rubbed his scrubby beard looked tough as tree bark. "Morning, Professor," he drawled finally. "You aw' right?"

"Yes. Thank you, Yelton. I'm fine."

Yelton spit over the rail, both hands stuck in his back pockets.

"Sorry to interrupt your work, but I wanted to talk to you," Enholm said.

The sawmill boss kicked wood chips out of the way and studied his shoe before looking up. "It's the fence, ain't it?"

"Yes. And I see a lock on the gate."

Yelton shook his head. "Yeah, we're all real sorry about that. Them fellows should have never said nothing to that girl. She drove in there with her fancy car, saw fellows drinking and fishing and she started giving them hell about using her daddy's property."

Tory Kingston? David wondered. Of course, Tory. He stayed silent as the men bit into their ham stuffed biscuits, but he knew they listened, pretending not to. Yelton looked up at the Professor, "Guess them boys said something that really twisted her tail, cause two days later that fence was put up. I couldn't do nothing to stop it." The mill boss glanced at David, a quick inquisitive lash of jet black eyes.

Enholm murmured, "I was going to show my young friend here a good trout lake."

"Those boys were just a-funning," Yelton said gloomily. "They wouldn't of done her no harm. She didn't have no call to put that fence up."

"Looks like we'll have to fish somewhere else for a while."

"I reckon."

David sensed his leader was ready to go, this visitation over. No, he was asking one of the younger guys in the group, "Harley, how's that baby?" "Doing better," came the mumbled reply.

They plodded back toward the Mercedes under the oak. Waiting there, was a sun-browned fellow, bare-chested in a leather vest, big as a wrestler with a Santa beard. Before they reached him, the professor murmured a quick explanation. "Not local. A marine vet by way of New York who is a local character now, a fisherman and I suspect a tough fellow. Morning Mike," he called out as they approached.

Mike's bloodshot blue gaze raked them both. The accent was Irish, ignoring David and addressing the older man. "See the Goddamned fence? That lake's been open since Je-hova threw up these mountains. Some of those fellows will go home, kick the dog and cuss their old lady and find somewhere else to fish. But we got some bad boys too. They don't like being fenced out of what ought to be open. If you know the old man up there in his castle, better warn him they're mad."

Back in the car, David said, "Were you showing me a closed society back there?"

"Call it a look at family loyalty and something else. Land is a matrix to these people. They believe in free access from a good neighbor, for hunting and fishing when that's been promised. Kingston promised long ago but you know the story."

"In your journals, I read that some of these guys have sold the family farm to outside developers. And local sons go into real estate business."

"True. You remind me. We'll stop at Loafer's Glory."

"A state of mind or a place?" David asked but leaned back glad to be working on his story and not waiting for Ariel.

They ate barbecue at "Pig Out with JP's," crossed old railroad tracks, passed a sign that said "Loafers Glory" and pulled up in front of a small roadside store. "A genuine country store?" David asked. The old wood place seemed to be. The friendly woman behind the counter answered, "It usta be. We bought it a few years back and put in fabrics. When this was a general store, the men would farm all day and come sit around in here the night, jawing and all. Story goes, a wife came in fussing and looking for her husband. Told him 'you're nothing but a loafer and when you're sitting down here you're in your glory.' That's supposed to be how this place got its name."

"And now?" David asked.

"Folks don't sit around a store anymore. Ever' body's got television, you know? They stay at home and watch that. Unless they've moved away."

"Do they still farm here?" David asked, encouraged by Professor's nod.

"Not the farming that usta be. Oh, they still grow some tobacco around here but not the beans and corn crops like before. When the old folks die, the younger ones sell the old place and move on somewheres else."

"What happens to the old home places?" David asked.

"Outsiders. City folks. They come in and buy those old places and fix them up. They come and go for a spell. But most say they'll be coming back here to live."

Back on the road, Enholm mused, "You've had a look at what's happening in places like Pigeon Roost and Relief and School House Hollow and Buckeye Grove. A farmer will tell you he has to sell out to pay bills. Or that son wasn't interested in farming."

"Where do they go, the natives who sell?" He wasn't surprised at the answer. They move in with daughter. Or move closer to the K-Mart.

"Have our travels today helped you? Will you advocate development of this ridge or not?"

"The impressions are cooking but I'm still ambivalent about the answer. Right now I am more interested in hearing that piece of the Eve puzzle you promised."

Emma Riddle's house was like the woman's face, worn by time into a lined sheen, and clean as the faded cotton apron, smelling of cinnamon now. David sank in a stuffed chair, decorated with crocheted doilies. Emma Riddle bustled back from the kitchen with two plates of hot apple pie and sat down herself, pleased at their compliments. Did this woman really know a piece of the Eve puzzle? She was an eager talker for sure. All about family.

"Well there was going to be this pie supper at the school house when I first laid eyes on Lester. Ever' body for miles around coming with food and musical instruments and Grandma always brought apple pie just like this. She was a good one to fry ham meat tender. Those were better years but when I was a little old thing in the Depression, everyone had a hard time getting something to eat. You planted and growed about everything even to coffee beans. A man got fifty cents a day when there was any work to do. Women had to make their own lye soap."

She beamed a smile toward David. "This fellow here likes to hear about old times. My folks might have knowed his daddy's folks up around Roan."

Professor nodded. "Strong people. Through good times and bad." He glanced at David, a silent reminder to sit back and listen.

"Well, when they had to cut Papa open and he was real bad and died, we had to move up to Granny's and live in the smokehouse when the hog meat wasn't in there. Well, Mama married again and he drank and was mean. Sometimes when the moon was full, Mama would get one of her spells. But I had a fine Grandpa and Grandma, they took care of us girls."

"Could we see your sister's picture again? A pretty girl."

Emma Riddle brought back a small framed snapshot, a girl about seventeen with a determined wistful face. "This is Lil Mae," she told David. "Hit still hurts to look at her. I loved that little sister like she was my own baby, even after I had four of my own. I can show you their pictures too. I got one son who drives a tourist bus. And three girls who went off to school. Two are teachers now and one has more kids than I had." She sighed.

"Lil Mae was like a little fiest dog looking for some buried bone, only for Lil Mae it was something she wanted we didn't have. She found herself that red-headed boy, Tice, I'm sorry to say. Went to stay with him in a cabin near the Ridgeway Inn. He had this job in the kitchen. A red-headed devil, I called him, cause he had a devilish eye, just what Lil Mae liked. You could tell he'd never make no husband like my Lester. Hit can still make me cry, thinking about it. I went up there to that cabin begging Lil Mae to come home, she could live with Lester and me.

"But no, she had a strong streak in her. She said Tice was going to take her far away. I told her *you'll want to come back* and she would have, too, but the last time ever I saw her, she was all fired to go."

Emma Riddle's soft mouth tightened up, holding back old tears before she went on. "Lil May expected him to take her away that next night. She went up to the Ridgeway searching for Tice and never came back. I went looking for her same time the sheriff was looking for that city girl."

David glanced at the silently nodding Professor.

"My little sister rode away with that fellow, sure as I'm sitting here. She's the one who got burned up in his car. I reckon that's her bones buried right now up there on what they call Eve's Mountain. Any ghost showing up there is my own baby sister."

David asked, "Then what happened to Eve Kingston?"

"Buried under the county road for all I know," Emma Riddle offered. "They blasted for that road a few years after she got lost. Some boys hunting ginseng found a piece of a locket, the newspaper said, with that Kingston girl's picture in it, holding a baby. If she got lost up there, her bones got buried when they made that road."

On their drive back to the Ridgeway Inn, David asked, "Do you believe what she said? That Eve Kingston wasn't lured away by the kitchen fellow?"

"I do, and I shall tell you why. I have told both Maggie and Selena this, in confidence. Since your search for truth in your story is sincere, I shall also tell you."

The older man drove slowly as he told about Tice and the girl who had to be Lil Mae, David listened with surprise then compassion, realizing he was hearing a brief summary of the man's secret passion and long time guilt. So Edwin Enholm, as a nineteen year old college sophomore, was in love with the young Mrs. Kingston, and he believed he had deserted her to whatever fate that happened. Poor guy. Carrying that burden all his life. "So you came back this summer. . . ."

"I believe Eve died on that mountain above the garden—by Kingston's intention or accident, I can't say. She might have run from him in her distress, and he might have followed. Whatever the answer, I wanted to know if he had lived with that knowledge. I needed to measure his guilt so I would know the extent of mine."

David was silent a moment. "What do you think about the TV company coming in to do the ghost story?" David asked. "Will that shake up anything here?"

Professor Enholm nodded. "One way or another, it will."

34

Selena left her patient in bed, face turned away, his dinner tray untouched. She ran down the narrow back stairs to the kitchen, avoiding Zack and Tory arguing in the library, and hurried off in the VW. This August night she had a mission to do for David Tyler and an intention for herself—to assuage some of her built-up tension by sitting with quiet and peaceful Addie McRae.

That morning on her way to Capstone, she had spotted David loping along Crest Road, head down, hands in his pockets. He waved her down and leaned in the car window, looking distressed. "Have you seen Ariel around? No one has. I have some college information to show her. No," he told Selena, "I haven't been down to the house. The mother doesn't talk to me, so—" He shrugged and gave her a pleading look.

So, she'd guessed right. David Tyler and Ariel. He looked miserable and it served him right, but her worry was for Ariel. "I'll go down tonight," she promised. He nodded, straightened up, and patted the top of the green car. "Tell Ariel I want to show her the Appalachian State campus in Boone, okay?"

Now in the breezy dark, stars bright overhead, she drove toward the hollow. Two other visits to the creek house had been strangely comforting. The inscrutable little woman had begun to accept her occasional appearances as a non intrusive visitor.

Addie talked in whispers when she talked at all. And though Selena had never asked this local mountain woman what she might know about what happened here thirty eight years ago, in time Addie might be willing to tell.

The house sat back on the creek bank under old oaks, more intriguing than the grand and polished Capstone. Sun could flood the kitchen that faced the front porch, yet the narrow hall with its woody gloom lead back to small rooms that seemed to depend on yellowed old lamps.

Once she'd found Addie in the side shed, in a straw hat, the hair tight in a bun, bent to her pots of herbs, willing to name their properties. At another time, she had been an intent figure at her loom, making Selena think of some character doll seen in tourist shops. Quiet as those visits were, being there was restful, much like being still and attentive to some woods creature so as not to frighten it away.

"I am pleasured in seeing the threads become pattern," Addie might offer, then work on in silence.

When Selena remarked on the stacks of paperbacks that Ariel brought in from flea markets, she had murmured, "They're like voices. Some speak to me like friends. Some are foolish. I sent those back." Selena noticed the tattered ones that lay close showed names like Whitman. Emerson, Millay, as well as an old geography and other worn school books.

Before driving into the front yard, Selena made sure Hoke McRae's blue four-wheeler was not in sight. On an earlier visit, Hoke had startled her, sitting in the dark on the front porch swing. The light from the kitchen had shown a disconcerting and mocking smile. Thankfully tonight, no Hoke, but Ariel's red pick-up sat there.

Lilting Scotch-Irish folks melodies from a radio drifted out to the narrow porch as she knocked. "Ariel? It's Selena. Are you here?" From behind the screen, the girl appeared, long hair scrambled around a pale face and barefoot in her short T-shirt. Ariel pushed open the door. "Come on in."

In the yellow-lit kitchen, a pot of soup simmered on the stove with good smells. Green corn and ripe tomatoes filled a basket on the wooden counter. At Ariel's nod, Selena sat down, waiting. Ariel sat too, hugging the tabby cat that jumped into her lap.

"We haven't seen you since all that rain," Selena began. "Maggie Hardy was expecting you to bring in some of your mother's weavings. And David Tyler wants to take you to Boone to look at the state university there."

Ariel cradled the cat in her arms, stubbornly silent.

"Doc Bradley would want me to ask if you have been taking the birth control pills this summer. Ariel?"

"Not doing nothing to need them!" The green eyes flashed. Then, contrite and looking miserable, "I took some of Mama's herb tea I fixed for her and it made me sick. But I'll be aw'right."

Indignant protest or desperation? Selena couldn't tell. "If you need to talk to anyone about *anything,* I'm here." No answer. Maybe something else had kept the girl home? From the radio down the narrow hall came the poignant melody. "I like that sound," Selena said. "Do you sing any of those Scotch-Irish ballads?"

"Sure. Mama likes to hear them." The cat bounced off, leaving Ariel to study her slim bare feet. "Mama fell and hurt her back. I been worried about her."

Once started, Ariel spilled the story in an agitated whisper. Her mother had gone down to the creek pump to see what was wrong with their water. Zack Kingston and the red-headed road man tromped up same time, cussing at each other about the new road washing out and flooding everybody's yard along the creek, ruining gardens. Hurrying back to the house, Addie had fallen. "Dragged herself in here. Been lying in her bed hurting for days, not sleeping."

The girl looked up, the clear green eyes troubled. "Maybe you ought to go in and look at her. She likes you."

So that was the girl's problem. For a moment Selena was relieved. "I'd like to see her, yes." She left Ariel in the kitchen.

From the doorway, Selena looked at the woman on the narrow bed, a slight figure lost in the long cotton gown, head turned to the window view of dark foliage. *The sleeping beauty,* she thought, *forgotten too long in the tower, the small features blurred by age, the long hair turned silver, spread now out on the pillow.*

"Hello Addie. May I sit with you?"

The face turned, pale green eyes blinking to focus on her visitor. "Selena." In yellow lamp light, the faint scar showed, a line from the mouth down to the throat. This woman had suffered once. From a man, likely. Perhaps the Roy McRae, the brother-in-law she shot? The scar caused the smile to pull slightly. The twisted foot showed from under the gown. Addie smiled without stirring. "Sit a while."

She pulled a chair close, asked questions about the back pain and nodded at brief answers. "I can walk," Addie murmured. "So I'm not broken. With rest I always heal. Remind Ariel. She's been so worried."

"May I ask the clinic nurse to come visit? I'm afraid Doc Bradley can't. He's at his daughter's, recovering from his gall bladder operation. I had hoped Zack Kingston would fly him up to see his father, but—"

"No!" An adamant whisper, the small body tensing under the gown.

Selena leaned over to stroke the woman's thin arm. How old, she wondered, between fifty and sixty? Couldn't tell. She must have had Ariel as late as forty. "All right, no doctor, Addie. Rest. Do you have anything for pain? I could bring you—"

"The body heals itself given time. If the spirit is well. And you, Selena? Have you found your peace in these old hills?"

"How did you know that's what I came for?"

"People do."

Selena kept her own voice low, matching that of the woman on the bed. "You know so much more than you say."

"And you. Still young, but you're wise. I see that."

"I once thought so, before things happened to me." Things I couldn't control, with Drew.

"We learn," Addie whispered. "From the things that happen."

"Even when you feel helpless to change them?"

"No. Not helpless."

"So you fought back?"

"I have done that too," Addie turned her head to the dark window by the bed. "It doesn't free you." Sadness in that admission.

"How then? You seem to know a kind of peace, Addie, something more than submission to fate? Free of resentments. And so alone here, except for Ariel."

"Being alone . . . is a trial for most, isn't it? Alone you can, if you will, discover the quiet place that abides within yourself. Like an altar. A safe place. From there . . . you watch what unfolds."

"'But as a victim?" Selena had to wait for an answer.

"When you're young . . . it is easy to believe you are a victim. I learned . . . long ago . . . to sit and watch the creek out there, rushing with spring thaw . . . or running low in summer . . . but always running over the old stones. The flow never moves them, only polishes them. I am an old stone now."

"You didn't learn that when you were in school and that must have been when, as a child?"

Addie looked away again. "A dreaming child. I see her as a faded photograph. Before the pain. But Selena, there has been . . . happiness too. You question that? Will McRae was a kind man. He loved me. How can I remember only the regrets?" Silence again from the bed. "Forgive me, I'm tired."

Selena sat back. How wrong, she thought, how blind we can be, to label people totally according to their appearance and their setting. "I wish you would let me do something for you before I go."

Addie sighed. "Read Edna to me? A page?"

From the doorway, Ariel said, "She means that little book on the table. I bought her some glasses from the drug store. But when she has headaches, she can't read."

Selena opened the small volume of Edna St. Vincent Millay. Loose pages. in the front. Loved pages evidently. She read aloud:

"Ah, could I lay me down in this long grass,
and close my eyes, and let the quiet wind
blow over me, I am so tired, so tired . . ."

"Don't stop," Addie whispered, "read the last."

"Have I looked back at loveliness and sighed
Over my shoulder have I looked at peace;
and now I fain would lie in this long grass
and close my eyes."

Selena closed the book. "Addie? I'm going now."

No answer from the slight figure on the bed. But the breathing was regular, pain washed from her face. Ariel tugged at Selena's shoulder, drew her out of the room.

"Mama heals herself by being quiet. You just helped her quieten down so I thank you. I've made some of her powerful soup for when she wakes up. That might be late tonight. So you tell anybody asking about me—" Ariel paused looking at her bare feet. "You tell that teacher I'll light out of here when my mama mends."

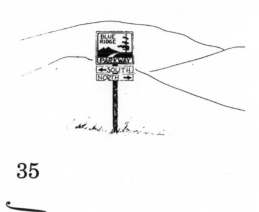

35

Ariel McRae walked into David Tyler's cabin on a sunny morning as if she just happened to be lollygagging around, now that her mother was doing better. Relieved to see her, David shut down the computer. "Come with me today. Let me show you a good college near here."

"Where?" she asked, pacing the room, avoiding the bed. "Don't want to be gone long." She didn't look at him. Obviously, she had decided to shut him out. But kid like, came back around because she was restless and wanted to be moving. It figured. The bottom-less green pool was no longer accessible. He would have to come up from the depths on his own. Okay, he wouldn't touch her, just try to help her. He told himself, *so suffer, Tyler, it serves you right.*

"Boone," he told her. "I want to show you the campus there, to see how close you could be to your mother." He had another reason to go and he was running out of time. He wanted to see what the brochures called "the High Country" as if they were the only highlands around western North Carolina. Yet the Boone area was studded with resort communities in contrast to this rural Mica County.

The next day David would tell the Professor, "You can do my kind of research at a soda fountain if you're lucky."

The way to Boone led through a rolling landscape, dotted with Christmas tree farms, hillsides marked with perfect Frazier firs. David talked college, glancing now and then at Ariel, curled up away from him, in her blue T-shirt and jeans. She watched the passing landscape, looking dreamy and virginal. David hoped she was listening. To please her, he mentioned a letter was coming from his friend who still had ties to Nashville. Ariel brightened and started humming to herself. *I've lost her,* he agonized. *She'll be glad when I leave. But that's good.*

In the town of Blowing Rock, they drove along a main street of shops where country charm had been preserved, in the upscaled, flower-decked version, attesting to the presence of also-upscale summer estates. Ariel watched with narrowed eyes. Blowing Rock's pleasant twisting drives gave way to the highway leading into Boone. Once past the Tweetsie Railroad attraction, the highway took them down a commercial main drag lined with restaurants and service stations and shopping centers. Could have been the fringe of any big city, regardless of the mountains that still shaped the horizons—if you had time to look up from the traffic.

When Ariel murmured interest in stopping at the mall, David shook his head and drove on, feeling like a high school chaperone. "Things to see where we're going."

Both cheered up as they rolled down Boone's original main street, adjacent to the sprawling campus of modern buildings. Here, flyers posted on old store fronts promised coming events and sidewalks looked lively with students.

Ariel bounced up with interest and squealed at a tie-dye skirt spotted in a boutique window. They parked on the busy street, David to wait in the drug store while Ariel looked around.

At the soda fountain of Boone Drugs, David claimed a stool, ordered a Coke and settled in to read the artful folder on the High Country's newest resort development. Was this what Tory Kingston hoped to do with Kingston land? The brochure for Elk River, down the road in Banner Elk, read like a siren's song to the urban weary, with words about panoramic beauty and single entrance privacy. He read the elegantly low key, but potent prose.

"... *within the landscape of earth's oldest mountain range is a beautiful resort community encompassing more than twelve-hundred acres. Available only to its inhabitants, the foliage, waters and wildlife within its bounds encourage discovery and wonder ...*"

He read on about "magnificent residences" and the member-owned private club with its recreational and social amenities.

Someone settled onto the seat beside him, chuckling at his reading matter. David looked over. A woman in her fifties, graying hair tied back from a sun-lined face, moved her package of art brushes out of his way. "You a tourist?" she asked. "Bring money if you're looking to getaway in one of those places."

"I'm looking for opinions," David told her. "Do you live here? An artist, I take it?"

"Oils and mixed media. This drug store is Cheap Joe's, best prices on supplies anywhere around. Hey Margie, coffee with cream."

"What's it like, living here? I'm from Florida," David offered. "You're not a native. Do I hear Minnesota?"

"Good guess. That among other places I choose to forget. I settled in here three years ago. Rent a farm ten miles out of town, rather it used to be a farm. Goats help keep the brush down. The old house is creaky, but we have a heater, electric blanket, a freezer, five cats and Dammit, the dog." She added, "My house partner is a weaver, when she can get away from her job in Virginia. I can't tell you about living on a manicured mountain. That what you're looking for?"

"I'm interested in why people are drawn to these mountains. I have my reasons. Willing to share yours?" At her careful scrutiny, David explained he was a writer, looking for opinions from people who have relocated here, not only retirees but, well, artists like herself and others.

"Others like aging hippies? I hate that tag. I loathe labels, dated or otherwise. Some old farm boys are still suspicious of artists who won't get a local haircut, or come in here willing to take an old house that their own kids don't want. From the real old timers, you feel a definite caution at first. It helps if you show up at the Free Will Baptist Church now, not the one the Floridians take over in the summer. At any rate, don't mention meditating. That's bypassing God, they think. I happen to believe it's the direct route."

At his encouraging nod, she went on. "Around these hills, old timers are afraid outsiders who come in talking about 'community' might be weirdoes planning a commune. Can't blame them in a way. I did the commune scene at the idealistic dumb age of eighteen. Screwed me up for awhile. I went back to school—computers, what else?—married one, I mean it, dull as a dial tone."

She shrugged. "All past. I even have a new name. Sage. I like it here. My old house has a fine view. Worth it all. You don't explain that to an old native anymore than you would expound on brook water to a trout."

"So you've found your right place?"

"Any place this side of heaven has its problems. But it's not phony here, not plastic—not yet, if you know what I mean. You're looking for gut level reactions, right? Here's one. You know the mountain people I appreciate the most? The ancestors of these local folks. Wintertime I look out from my back door to howling wilderness and wonder how settlers way back then wrestled a life out of these mountains. Some old geezer owns that woodland in back of us. Someday his family will sell and my rustic digs will be history, too." She sighed. "Have I talked your face off? But you asked. Well, back now to my seclusion by choice. So long."

The woman left. David turned again to his brochures, to peruse the promises of a saddle club "with its thousand views and home sites of one to five acres." A little fellow who had been watching, big grin on his face, pulled his pie and coffee closer to David, offering with conspiratorial warmth, "Want to know about this place? Well I can tell you. Boone is a nice town. Traffic's a mess. College is growing. You want to know anything else, son, just ask old Warren here."

A retired salesman, David surmised, who needed to talk. Or given the man's size and Yankee accent, an ex-jockey with Saratoga track stories to tell. Apparently Warren was living the advertised good life here, judging from the cashmere cardigan, the gold watch on the wiry wrist and golfing cap on the back of his bald noggin that said, "Elk River Club."

David gave up reading, and asked this loquacious fellow, "You live there?"

Warren tapped his cap. "Sure do. Almost a million dollars worth of house. We're way up there, at four thousand feet, out in the open where they used to graze cows, they tell me. Not bad for a street kid from Newark, right? And I'm not bragging when I say that. It's her house you see, but I buy the groceries, for the parties too, don't think that's not a hefty tab for liquor and imported cheese and shrimp."

They had met on a cruise, the little fellow explained. Patty sitting on the sidelines, all jeweled up and no way to dance, because her husband had bad knees. "You want to hear a small world story? Listen to this, he turned out to be a fellow named Sturges I knew back in the Pacific. We were both in the Seabees back then. Built some landing fields, same outfit. There was old Sturges in a tuxedo, rich as Onassis now, with a pretty wife and his bad knees. And yours truly was there to dance."

David motioned for a refill on his Coke. Warren, a happy fellow now with a rapt listener, leaned closer. "I was a widower, see, getting a free cruise, round trip, to dance with all the single ladies. Now, son, don't think up any jokes about that. It's an honorable pastime for a retired man who has dancing feet and decent table manners and knows how to be companionable." Under the counter, his feet tapped a quick rhythm, while telling David, "I tell you there's a dire need on cruise ships for men who can whirl a lady on those little dance floors, take it from Warren Johnson."

David stayed patient until Warren got past Sturges dying and his widow Patty calling Warren up and then their getting married. Last year they had come up from the town house in Chicago to Banner Elk to finish the big house Sturges had started at Elk

River. "You can drive down that pretty road past Lees-McRae College and never guess what we've got up there." Warren's expressive eyebrows went up and down.

"It sounds ultra special in this brochure," David conceded. "But I have been reading how some developments in the Blue Ridge have cut into fragile mountains, causing flooding of farm lands below. And how some farmers who had sold off land ended up regretting it. Do you hear anything about that?"

Warren pursed his lips. "It's happened, sure has. You're just beginning to hear folks talk about land control. I'm a talker, guess you've noticed, and I know a lot of folks, local fellows, as well as the ones who come in here, about to retire you know, looking for some dream house by their own mountain stream, that sort of thing."

Warren pushed aside his empty pie plate. "Few years back some big outfits came in, bought up a mountain, stuck up a few houses, then went bankrupt because they expected to sell off and get out fast like they do in Florida. But these boys who did Elk River, they're local. They know what they're doing. I'd say they've done it right—for folks like Patty who can afford it. Houses up there all cedar shake, stone and glass, mountain contemporary it's called, grand scale. Did I tell you? Ours looks down on a stable and private airfield that used to be a corn field. Power's all underground, everything's taken care of for you. Has its own water system."

"All that wealth—does it mean local jobs?"

"Well, builders use local labor. And they hire people to keep those grounds and run that club and dining room and haul away the trash. It is super pretty up there, super deluxe."

"But you're down here in Boone Drug Store with pie and coffee."

Warren grinned. "I have to get back to reality now and then. I like this old place. And these streets. I like to see the young people."

"Warren, tell me, do you think there are any mountaineers left around here?"

"Well, I don't know. You see all kind of people being folk artists at festivals. And down in Valle Crucis they made a big thing out of an original country store, so it's got an annex across the street here. And Patty loves to walk through the antique malls looking at old stuff her mama might have used. She's got china cabinets full of the stuff."

To David, he mused, "Mountain folks change like the rest of us. You have to when your town changes around you. You think I'd go around door to door in Newark selling stuff today the way I used to do? Back then, know what I really wanted to do? Be a vaudeville hoofer. Just as well I didn't. Vaudeville gave out before my feet did."

Warren's feet tapped a slow rhythm under the counter. "And here I am sitting in a de-luxe house on top of a landscaped mountain." He gave David a sober smile. "You collecting opinions as to why people come here, I guess. I'd say they come looking for something they've kind of lost, or looking for something different from where they were. I'm not sure if the lookers outnumber the natives yet but if they do I guess it would be sort of a shame."

267

36

After leaving Maggie Hardy's place, the three of them—David Tyler, Professor Enholm and Paula Crossing—stood outside in the shadowy August night taking in low tones. Selena Hart had been there earlier, had made her own impassioned statement, and left quickly.

"I'm in Maggie's court, personally," David said, "but this TV show isn't the problem. Just an advance warning. We all know this ridge will change, regardless, one way or another. One year or the next. Why didn't we speak up and tell her that?"

Professor Enholm's voice was a soft rumble in the night. "I believe Maggie knows that change is inevitable. She is apprehensive about the place being opened to ill-considered exploitation and spoil."

Paula mused, "A nationally syndicated gossip show implying your landlord runs a feudal state and may be a murderer will hurry things up."

Maggie had asked them to meet at her place, had sat them down on her quilt-covered couches, passed around coffee and spice cake and asked their advice. "I may sound like a soft-hearted fool who can't handle change. You may even figure I'm only looking after my own comfort, protecting this place that's my home, but it's this way. Some things are worth protecting."

"We know how you feel, Maggie," David said. "What's this idea of yours?"

"I've been lying awake nights trying to figure out how to outsmart the smart TV folks. Far as we know, they're due next week at the Inn. Perloin Productions."

"It's only a tabloid show, Maggie," Paula said. "They'll give your ghost tale a tongue-in-cheek coverage."

"Of course they don't *believe* that ghost story. It's their *excuse* to come in here and take their pictures and have people recalling that old gossip in front of their cameras—causing it to boil up again, making the whole world wonder if that girl wasn't murdered by you know who. And they'll make Bo's daddy look like a sold-out sheriff when he was a good man. Bo too. And that boy works on his own with some troublesome boys. Professor, tell them what's going to happen here."

"I was observing," Professor Enholm intoned, "that, given time, a personal tragedy—on a national scale or within a community—can become a public legend. Legends serve a purpose, much as a memorial does, planted in a public garden. Dig under the memorial for the original truth buried there, and you may find, and disturb, a grenade."

"And there goes the garden," Paula mused. "Hurting anyone standing near."

Selena had walked in at that moment, windblown and anxious. "I can't stay, but Maggie told me what this was about. I wanted to thank all of you for not insisting on seeing my patient. And do what you can to keep any TV people away from the house. His depression is worse. He couldn't defend himself."

All three of them watched Maggie and Selena in the doorway, quick whispers between the two, and Selena's intense hug, like a grateful thank you. Maggie came back to them, shaking her head. "Gossip tabloids or gossip TV shows, I'm against them. They're bound to cause somebody heartaches."

Maggie sat back down, letting her big gray cat leap into her lap. "Here's what I've been thinking. How to save High Haven from being made a fool of on national TV. Those people will be wanting folks to talk to their cameras, they're expecting old mountain gossip to suit their purpose. So what if I get the right ones to do the talking? Old man Hogan could go on about bear hunting given the chance. And some of the summer people who love it here, they like to talk too, and they don't care one way or another about any ghost story. And there's Ethel who can talk your ears off."

Professor smiled. "I thought you were worried about Ethel Pickett getting in front of a camera?"

"I was. But she'll be there, no getting around that. She's having her hair done like Lucy Arnez. Get Ethel started on a subject like how fine a man her granddaddy was, or how she always wanted to be an FBI agent, or have a job like Betty Furness, and she'll take over. They'll be asking Bo Hilrey about Sheriff Will Hilrey, but I've already told Bo, do like the politicians do. Answer what you want, tell them about saving the folks that year the creek flooded."

Maggie turned her hostess smile on Professor Enholm. "You *could* go on about the history of these mountains, if you would."

Amused, he promised, "If it helps, Maggie, I shall offer authentic details of mountain lore for as many minutes as they allow."

"Oh Maggie, this kind of show would cut him off with that," Paula said. "No aspersions meant, Professor."

David spoke up. "I have an idea. They claim they are coming for a ghost story. They could be steered toward a romantic angle, rather than an unsolved murder."

"They choose their own story line," Paula reminded him.

"Sure, but this would be local color and suit the story line. I'm talking about a ballad, about Eve. I can write one, offer it. About a young woman from the city loving these mountains. Ariel McRae could sing it. Hey, what about that?" He warmed at the idea. He'd be giving Ariel a chance to sing if only for a moment before a camera.

Outside now in cool August dark, Enholm offered to drive them both down to the Inn. David looked at Paula. "Walk down with me? I have a favor to ask and a letter I want you to read. Professor here has seen it."

"Sure," Paula said.

They started down the drive, behind the blinking brake lights of the Mercedes. "A ballad, I'll do a Scotch-Irish kind of ballad," David said, enthusiasm growing. "It would be good theater. If you're here, Paula, you could offer it as soon as they show up. You'd know how to talk their language."

They crunched on down the drive toward the Inn, David saying, "I'm not prying, but I've seen you with both Mitch Mason and Zack Kingston. So you must know what's going on up there at Capstone. Level with me. Is Tory and her brother planning to develop this mountain? Is Senior in on this? Something should have jelled up there by now. I haven't tried to reach Tory Kingston again. Mitch Mason has evaded the question. I have to leave here no later than September one."

Paula was silent for a few steps. "You put me on the spot. To be truthful, I don't know anything definite myself. Zack is not into it. Mitch is hanging in the balance. He doesn't know yet just how far the plans go. Let's say the situation is in flux. I've been rather distracted by my own indecisions. What's this you want to show me?"

"You don't care what happens to this place, I suppose. You'll be leaving."

"I do care what happens here. Very much," Paula said. "These two and a half months have been . . . a learning experience shall we say. I still don't know where it should lead. I realize how much you have come to care about the place. It's personal, isn't it, not just for your story."

David crunched along the path aware of the breezy night around him and the pretty woman walking with him, who was in love with someone else. As he was. In love or mesmerized, engrossed, involved with the girl as well as this place.

"You're right about that," David said. "I realize a person can come here from his particular fast track believing that once in these hills he enjoys a certain anonymity that goes with a getaway. A sneaking sense of superiority goes with that notion. You come expecting the mountains to do something for you. Then, when you stay long enough to look around, and if you're not just a taker, you begin to want to save what you've found. But by *then,* you realize you're in somebody else's back yard and whatever you do should be in tune with the folks who have been here a hundred years before you."

They stood now in the palely lit grounds in front of the Inn where David had left his car.

"I know the feeling," Paula said. "I never dreamed I'd be here this long, even entertain the idea of living in a place like this. Makes you realize how hard you've been driving, with such single minded tenacity toward things you only thought you wanted. I've been driving up to Roan Mountain to sit there and try to sort things out. Where to go from here." She looked at David. "Hey, that was a run-on confession. And I still don't have an answer. What were you going to show me?"

"A letter. I want you to pass it on to Zack Kingston. I understand he's always off to Charlotte on business. I want him to see this and meet me if he will before I have to leave. Since I've never gotten to Senior, it's only fair to let Zack know where I'm coming from in the story I'm turning in, since it involves the Kingston name and property."

David pulled the letter from his sweater pocket, took her warm hand and pressed the letter in it. "What's the mystery?" she asked, but in good humor.

"I've been doing my reporter's homework, Paula. The Professor has helped a great deal. And so has this letter. Jay O'Ryan was an environmental reporter back in Florida when I was a kid interviewing for the school paper. I remembered Jay came back home to these mountains oh, twenty years ago. Did PR for a resort, then went with the Blue Ridge Parkway. I wrote asking his opinion because I knew it would be seasoned and informed. Take it. Read it. And see that Zack Kingston gets it. Tell him I'm available until the end of this month. I have to leave, much as I hate the thought."

In her upstairs room, Paula sat down by the old fashioned floor lamp and read David's letter. Written from Peak Knob, North Carolina. Typed on an old typewriter apparently, but written with spirit, she could tell.

Dear David Tyler,

You remember correctly. This old mountain boy did his stint as a Florida newsman back when you were a high school kid. You've ask for my opinion and though it opens a vein, here it is. It's personal, but from a native who has seen a lot, including the view from behind a government desk.

Back in Florida, I wrote about the protection of natural resources as it affects the quality of human life. The things I wrote, and the hundreds of articles that others have written since, have had very little effect. From my vantage point today, it seems the only significant changes have been in the magnitude of the problems. It's like punching a 500-pound marshmallow: you hit it as hard as you can on one side, your arm plunging in shoulder-deep, but the opposite side doesn't even quiver in reaction.

I take it from your questions you've learned to love the mountains. People do. You wonder what should be the most desirable fate of High Haven and the tract known as Eve's Mountain owned by Alexander Z. Kingston. I've heard of him. As a writer, you want to suggest the best use of the land and not be speaking as an opinionated outsider, a romantic nor with a bias. You ask should Kingston leave his prime acreage to the state, or put second homes and clubhouses over it?

You know what over-developing has done to Florida. The mountains we love are facing a similar situation, the major difference being timing and magnitude. One irony is that many of the changes here are being wrought by those who have fouled their nests in Florida, Georgia, South Carolina and elsewhere. They don't seem to have learned a damned thing.

Here, developers aren't confined by any land-use regulations or strict building codes. You probably have heard who stands in the way of better controls. Native attitudes. Hard-headed mountain politicians. Most mountain people are protective of their right to do as they please with their land. Call it a 'frontier hangover' from the time when there was an abundance of resources and no need to worry about tomorrow.

You ask if second-home development is a boost for the local economies. Construction trades and suppliers benefit early on, but in the long run, I doubt if property taxes paid by residents of most developments are adequate to pay for the increased services——police, fire, water, sewer.

That's not to say western North Carolina isn't getting some well-built homes and well-planned developments. Some are being done by local families. But it's also true some developers have raped land unhampered by land use controls. You say until now Kingston hasn't restricted his land from use for fishing and hunting, to ease local opinion. Whatever his reasons, that's what his neighbors expect. In the mountains, private owners of large tracts often permit hunting, fishing, camping and hiking on their land as long as the uses aren't abusive. Some owners lease parcels for crops such as Christmas trees. It's custom. It's being a good neighbor. If the owner makes a gift of the land to the state, or even more complicated, to a Federal bureau such as the National Park Service or U.S. Forest Service, those prior uses can be altered or prohibited. You can't generalize what's going to happen to a certain tract in government hands but I am saying the public might have a better chance to use a trout stream or grazing field if it's privately owned.

You ask would it help the area if Kingston sold out to developers. I can tell you really care what happens to that ridge.

So what's the answer? I would hope the Kingston family can come up with a better use than cutting up a mountain to make a quick buck. Not that you can make a buck quick in the mountains, as they've done in the past in Florida. I can only tell you what I would do if I already had it made like Kingston, with such land and with more money than time to spend it. I'd do what the Blumenthal family did. Set up a foundation. Make the place a retreat, that's minimal land use but put to fine use. Go take a look at Wildacres near Little Switzerland to see what I mean.

You realize these opinions are from a sixty-year-old fellow who gets nostalgic remembering mountain people and life as it used to be. It wasn't an easy life. It was a time when castor oil and iodine were expected to cure everything. Winter heat came from a wood burning Warm Morning stove in the living room. A time when your big extended family gathered around with a fiddle or guitar to sing Christmas carols. A time when they put up fences to keep livestock in, not people out. To borrow a phrase, 'a kinder, gentler time.' I would love for my grand kids to see just a remnant of what I saw in abundance when I was a child. But it won't happen.

You say you have observed first hand the need to leave a highway behind and breathe mountain air. So yes, people will keep coming, looking for some panacea, at the least a temporary escape from the fast track. Change is inevitable. The concern of a lot of us is: how to grow. I am realistic enough to know that what "once was" will never be again,

Cheers . . . Jay O'Ryan.

275

37

Sometime in the night, Selena woke, heart pounding with apprehension. Had there been a sound? No. The house was still. Beyond the glass doors on the level below, pale moonlight glinted on the open, silent deck. The foreboding sense came from within herself, left from a dream. She held on to its images, seeking its meaning. Yes, she'd been in Alexander's room. He had called, needing her. She was reaching for his medications, the Coumadin and Procardia and Xanax lined up on the mahogany dresser across the room. The bottles kept spilling from her fingers, the carefully kept record distorted, illegible. Tory was standing by his bed. Someone or something else was in the room. Back in deeper shadows. A presence. *Eve?*

This wasn't a new dream. It was a recurring one. *Alexander. I am sharing your nightmares.*

Throwing a sweater around her shoulders, Selena went down to the living room level and padded out to the deck. Moonlight silvered the woods that quilted the slopes above the hollow. A breeze stirred her gown and touched her body like a chilling caress, bringing back the sense of the dream with the presence hovering in the shadows of Alexander's room. *Eve?* But not a young Eve, seeking vengeance.

No, the felt presence could have been an Eve grown old on whatever plane she existed, trying to tell her something.

Hot coffee and bright morning sun again made the night's dreams fade.

Only a residue of apprehension remained as Selena drove to Capstone early. Before the VW pulled to a stop in back, Sudie burst from the house, wringing her hands in distress. "Se'lene, thank Jesus you're here. Jeb ran down here a minute ago saying something's wrong with Azzie. I sent him back up, I was ready to call you up to hurry."

"Zack isn't here? Or Tory?" Apparently not. With Sudie following, she raced up the stairs, dread thudding in her chest.

Jeb stood at the bedside, looking helpless. Alexander sprawled on the bed, still in his pajamas, possibly unconscious. Selena grasped his hand, found it cold and clammy, checked his pulse as Jeb croaked his explanation. "He got to mumbling and weaving around until he fell against the cabinet. I like to never got him back in here. Maybe that's how he's got that bloody nose."

Oh no. Blood could mean internal hemorrhage from too much blood thinner.

She hid her alarm and told them how to help. Ease the pillow from under his head. Build more pillows under his body, from the hips down. "Sudie, cover him with more blankets. Jeb, bring over the blood pressure machine. *Alexander?*"

No response. She shook his shoulders buried against the pillow, called his name again. Still no response. She pressed a knuckle into the solid chest at the breast bone. His face registered complaint and his eyes opened. The knot of fear subsided. "Good morning, Alexander. Let's warm those hands. And do the old blood pressure business."

She spoke gently close to his ear as she took his pressure. "It's dropped too low, that's why you're cold and that's why you were dizzy. I want you to breathe in as deeply as you can, and remember you're okay." *Oh God, I hope you are.* "No dreams now. It's morning. A beautiful morning out there. Hear me? We work together remember, one hundred percent, both sides." She felt his pulse, stroked his face and knew quiet elation when he murmured, "Had a fade out." He could talk. It wasn't a stroke. But a warning. Thank God, he had only hit his nose. The blood wasn't internal hemorrhage.

After the pressure rose slightly and he drowsed under the covers, Selena looked for Sudie. She found her outside in the hall, shivering, face contorted with worry. "Now it's your time, Sudie. Get some of your beef broth or chicken soup, something hot and simple, and a small pot of coffee. And Sudie, isn't Zack back from Charlotte? I must talk with him. And Tory."

Sudie explained Tory had left early that morning and Zack was already driving to Virginia. Loren was up there with a broken leg and smashed motorcycle.

"Do you know how to reach Zack?"

No, Sudie bemoaned, she didn't know exactly the place. "But maybe that red headed lady at the Inn, Paula, she might know. Zack called her soon's he heard about Loren and before he took off. Law, law, if this hain't been the awfulest summer ever for this house."

Zack. Paula. Loren. Of course. She should be happy for them. Instead Selena felt angry; frustrated they left her with no backup here. And yes, lonely. But loneliness was the price you paid for privacy, wasn't it?

Back in the room, she pulled her chair close to the bed. Alexander lay on his side, looking at her from sunken eyes. He reached for her hand. She answered his slight grasp with both hands. His hoarse whisper—*"Still trying to save me Sel?"*—made her throat tighten. "I'm counting on you not giving up. What happened this morning was drug reaction. Too much blood thinner. Try to think Alexander, have you taken any aspirin? I saw some on your bathroom shelves."

His tousled head seemed to sink deeper in the pillow, his eyes closed in a grimace.

"Is she still in your dreams?"

"When I'm deep under with those blasted pills . . . she waits . . . out there. . . . I tell you she wants to kill me. I loved her and she wants to kill me. . . ."

"No, that's your nightmare."

"Something is killing me."

She believed him and couldn't tell him again it was demons of his own making. Remembering her own dreams, she wondered if her own logic was fully functioning.

"It was Eve. I know. She called me Alex."

"Alexander, please, if you believe she is there wanting to speak to you, try allowing her to come into your mind. You've been holding her back. Let her stand there in front of you. Ask her forgiveness however you wish. That is all you want, isn't it? Forgiveness. Then the nightmares will go away. You'll be free of this. Your strength will come back. You'll be able to fight again and pull out of this."

She waited. His big hand lay limp in hers, his forehead creased, eyes tightly shut. Sudie walked in with her tray. "Azzie, I've got you some fine chicken broth."

No moonlight for comfort this night. Unable to sleep, Selena took the old scrapbook of clippings downstairs and curled on a couch with a cup of tea. Again she studied the stories and newspaper photos. Here was young husband Alexander Kingston, muscular shoulders shaping the tuxedo, a thick mane of hair framing the strong face, his expression satisfied and exulting as if unaware the young bride at his side looked tense. Even in the old newsprint, the girl was a beauty, dark hair piled high above a hauntingly lovely face, delicately carved as a museum piece of white marble. The look from the eyes stirred vague questions.

A car crunched to a stop on the drive above. Selena turned on the light at the kitchen stoop and listened to footsteps on the gravel. Then opened the door to a weary-faced Zack in rumpled khakis. He marched inside with a nod, and muttered apologies for the late hour. Selena sat back down to watch Zack pace beyond the pool of lamp light, telling her, "I left Loren in Virginia. He's okay, leg in a cast but preferred to stay with friends, the boy's father is a doctor. I'll have to drive back to get him."

He stopped, looked out into the dark night, then back to her. "Tory called me there about A. Z. having some kind of an attack. What's going on, Selena? He was asleep when I got in tonight. I'm beat but I had to hear from you what happened yesterday. I've heard her version."

"Tory wasn't there until it was over." She answered his accusing tone with her own indignance. So, she was losing Zack's confidence as surely as she was losing her patient. Didn't he realize her own anguish with this situation? Or did he only want to hear impersonal, professional explanations? So be it. She'd keep her caring to herself and stay the Nurse Selena, the way he said it. "Yes, we had an emergency yesterday morning. Fortunately I got there early. Sudie and Jeb helped." She told him about the pressure being too low, and the danger of internal bleeding. "It could have been serious if he had really fallen. He was stable when I left."

"Tory points out you handle his medication most of the time. Maybe—"

"I'm doing something wrong? The hell I am, Zack Kingston." She sprang up, gripping her arms to contain the shiver. "But I search for what *is* wrong here. Something is causing him more dizziness and lethargy than should be happening. It could be an extra medication he is getting without my knowledge. It could be as simple and as dangerous as aspirin. I've told you, too much blood thinner can cause internal hemorrhage. For chemical reasons, he can be weakened and that leaves him in no condition to deal with a growing obsession."

"The guilt problem," Zack muttered.

Hurt on his weary face silenced her angry frustration. "Zack, don't do that to yourself and to your father. Remember, the initial hallucinations began with medication after the stroke. At first he was intrigued by those images, until they focused on Eve. I have come to know your father—"

"To know is to love, eh? Yes, nurse Selena, I've noticed that." He paused in the pacing and looked at her.

"Sorry. I appreciate what you're trying to do. I love the old man too, in spite of—" He shook his head. "Continue. What are you trying to tell me?"

She explained psychosis again, how memories can become guilt. And the guilt obsessive. "Psychotic behavior can happen—"

"Psychotic, huh?" A flip reply, yet agony showed in his look. He rubbed his unshaven chin. "Go on."

"Delusions are fixed beliefs that can be totally false. So what is keeping him vulnerable to delusions and believing them? Drugs or alcohol or over medication can cause chemical toxicity and depression and that leaves him open to this. And in this state, outside suggestions can be lethal."

"You are handling the drugs, Selena."

"Tory brings him hot milk at night. And when I'm not around, vitamins he tells me."

"My God, Selena, are you accusing Tory of deliberately trying to drug him? Leave him helpless to his demons?"

"She may intend only to keep him quiet without realizing the danger of drug interaction. Possibly she wants to keep him too lethargic to realize what she is doing with the property."

"And what is Tory doing?"

"Zack, don't you *know?* Are you so busy running away from your own discomfort in that house you have refused to look at what your sister is up to? What she's doing beyond roads and new water lines for Eve's Mountain? Those plans she works on with such feverish concentration? The plans that take her so often to Asheville. And the reason she brought Mitch Mason here in the first place. I didn't learn this from Tory of course. I've stayed out of Tory's way, as you have, Zack. Don't tell me you don't know about her plans for the mountain beyond the hollow? Maybe Eve's Mountain, too, for all I know. I haven't told your father. He certainly couldn't handle that right now."

"The roads . . . the water lines . . . I know about that, I thought it was keeping her out of my hair and yours. She can't do a damn thing with the property without Dad's agreement. He's in no condition to agree to anything. He wouldn't change his stubborn mind, even—psychotic." He bit out the word.

"Sedated and confused, he could have signed papers, power of attorney, whatever. She is in with him at some time every night."

Zack muttered to himself behind clenched eyes. "The Charlotte runs were necessary, but I've stayed away from the house for a number of good reasons."

Paula is one, no doubt, but how can I blame you for that?

"So I've screwed up around here. But anytime I look in, you and patient seem absorbed. I feel like a third unnecessary party. Did I mention, you're in love with the man?"

"Oh Zack! We both see you don't want to stay. So we don't hold you."

At his silence she went on patiently, "I spend the afternoon with him, reading, while he sleeps. I listen to his mumbles as well as his confidences. I know what's on his mind more than he realizes. I know Tory is disturbing him at night." She met his gaze, saw the confusion flickering there. *All right, so you don't like what I'm saying but you have to know the truth.*

"You really do believe Tory is screwing around with A. Z.'s life?"

"Something is, Zack."

"The ghost?" His laugh was bitter. "Or his guilty conscience getting through to him."

"If he is not guilty, do you want his belief in guilt to kill him?"

"That hurt, nurse. He must have reasons to believe it, chemically screwed up or not. What in the hell do you know?"

"I told you. I listen to him in his sedated sleep, and to his memories and I have found out every thing possible from two people who were there—when your mother disappeared from the Inn—does that surprise you? Maggie and Professor Enholm. I have read the news clippings from the past in the scrapbook your aunt kept. It's right here. Even one of a young Sudie looking wide-eyed over your bald head, you at three or four months."

"Spare me." He stood up to leave but rocked there with fatigue and distress.

"Go home and sleep." She put her hand on his arm in an impulse to comfort him. When his muscle tensed under her touch, she withdrew quickly. Again he was calling her Nurse Selena in those testy tones, so hired nurse she would be.

He turned to go. She followed him out to the stoop, waiting there outside the screen door because he had stopped on the gravel path to look back up to her. "So what do we do? He needs the medication and yet it's screwing him up."

"I believe it's over medication. Simple over-the-counter things can increase drug reaction. Tory could be doing that."

He kept looking up at her, shaking his head. "What do you want me to do? Accuse her? Have a showdown with little sister in Dad's room before I have to go back up for Loren? Let A. Z. know about her project? Accuse her of doping him up to keep him busy with his guilt?"

No! None of that. You can't shock him like that then leave. And if you accuse Tory, she'll throw me off the case, keep me out, and that would be the last thing we want. Oh no. If there's extra sedative involved, I'll have to find it and prevent it." She watched him stride up the path and roar off into the night.

Inside, she grabbed a sweater and went out to the deck, shivering in the dark chill. His departure felt like a slap. An owl's mournful call echoed in the dark. Moonlight and shadows shaped the mountains. What had Maggie Hardy said? Be still and listen and the mountains look back at you like wise old beings who know the answers. Listening, as in tuning in to some power beyond your own, beyond understanding. *All right—what have I missed? What should I know?*

An answer came, yet the same one that always surfaced and she always put aside. It wasn't a medication she could offer, or one taken away, or advice she could give him. Alexander needed Eve's forgiveness more than he needed blood thinner and tranquilizers or a reprieve from whatever Tory might be doing. Selena looked out to the windy August night. From what Maggie told her, this was the kind of night Eve disappeared. *Are you out there,*

Eve? I've read your story. Seen your face in yellowed newspaper pictures. Was his kind of love a trap for you back there when he was so possessive and you were so young?

She stood there on the deck sending a message to this Eve. *I know the man. I think you turned away from a jealous husband that night, meaning to be alone on that mountain path. Didn't you go too far in your wish to be alone? Too far up that high mountain path? Couldn't you forgive him now for whatever happened? Eve, I believe the man deserves saving.*

Back inside, Selena sat down again with the scrapbook. The delicate face was beginning to look familiar, perhaps because she had studied it so carefully. She closed the book and went up to the loft bed. She meant to get to Capstone early tomorrow. The TV crew was arriving in High Haven.

38

"You'd think we were expecting a parade," Maggie Hardy told Professor Enholm, who was standing with her in the shop, watching the morning's action. "I see right now no matter how people fuss about what's on TV, a live camera is going to bring them out every time. Must be why a crowd shows up for a visiting politician. They want to get their face in the picture."

Across the road, summer people from Windycrest and Blackberry Ridge stood around the post office, talking and waiting. Picnic tables in front of the shops had more coffee drinkers than usual. Inside Country Sundries, Ethel Pickett stayed busy handing it out, but as Maggie told the Professor, "all dolled up and ready to get her face on camera."

Perloin Productions was late, ten days later than the initial date, but due any minute now. "For awhile there, I'd hoped they had changed their mind, or we'd have fog, the kind they'd have to grope around in. But look at this."

The September morning had dawned clear and sunny, trees rain-washed and glistening, a crisp tinge of fall in the breeze. "I guess my idea for controlling who talks and who says what has as much chance as ordering the weather."

Enholm nodded. "Did you see David before he left for Florida?"

"He stopped by a minute. Had the longest face I'd seen on that boy all summer. I don't know if he got together with Ariel McRae on his idea for a ballad. Or if he gave it to Paula Crossing. That was a well-meaning notion though."

Thirty minutes passed as they watched from the shop's open door. Cars began leaving. "Our parade watchers are tired of waiting," Enholm mused. "But they'll be back tomorrow to witness the filming."

The road was almost quiet when Perloin Productions arrived, the sheriff leading the way, blue lights whirling. Following Bo Hilrey's cruiser was a white van, no identification on the sides. When the two cars pulled up in front of Old Timey Things, Maggie stood up, feeling fidgety. "If they're like restless tourists, they'll think quiet means boring and not anything for their show." She stood in the doorway, watching.

Bo got out, walking proud in his pressed khakis. Jumping out of the van now was a young woman, the peppy type in jeans with skinny blond hair, like one of those college girls who rode through here, stuck on the back of a motorcycle. Two men followed, a thin fellow, early bald, and a good looking six-footer she recognized. "That's the fellow who stopped in my yard early this spring, asking about Kingston owning the mountain. He'd heard some story teller in Asheville."

Bo led them into the shop as Maggie had asked him to. Russ Bern was the tall handsome one. Blair Vesley, the balding fellow. The peppy girl didn't wait to be introduced.

"Hi, I'm Jodie. Field producer on this shoot. You're Maggie Hardy, right? Sheriff Hilrey here told me you know everything about High Haven and Eve's Mountain. Maggie, meet my crew." Russ was cameraman and Blair the audio-record person. Jodie skittered around the shop, talking non-stop in her quick, husky voice.

"Look guys, props. Pure Thirties, Forties, Fifties. Stacks of it. What a background shot. Look at *this* . . ."

The men went outside to look around. Standing there as if they were observing another planet, Maggie thought. Bo stood with them, thumbs in his belt. Jodie kept prowling and asking questions. "All this *stuff* . . . I love it! I thought you'd be selling sample moonshine in pint bottles and doing a business in ghost pictures. I did a shoot with a Virgin Mary sighting and those folks were selling boards off the fence where the crowd stood. Where did you *get* all this?"

"From local folks and summer people." Maggie could have told her some good stories about that, but Jodie was too busy asking more questions. "Your sheriff says you know the people to talk to. That man! Got to get him in this piece. Bo could play a young Gleason in *Smoky and the Bandit*. His father was sheriff when this Eve Kingston disappeared, right? He says you know some others who'll talk?"

"That I do. I can help a lot." *And may the Lord forgive me for bending the truth.*

Jodie leaned against a counter, still looking around. "You know, Maggie, I've been wanting a chance at this story since Russ brought it to the news desk. We work out of Atlanta, but our bureau has to have the go-ahead from the coast. They almost passed on this one. Thought I'd lost it. Finally the exec director out there decided to go with it. So here I am. Lady ghost with a mountain named after her. I don't mind the romantic angle to a murder story. That's the *juice* in the story." She lifted the Victrola top, let it down and kept talking.

"I did some research but you could tell me how the local scam goes. Was she dumped off the mountain? Left to the bears? Or did the lady run off with the kitchen boy and end up down the ravine? That doesn't pump me as much as the pushed-off-the-mountain version. Right where blasting was done later for a county road. Russ and I have psyched this story out. I pretty much know what I want, but we'll write the script after shooting some interviews."

Ethel walked into the shop, fluttering in her green dress with the flouncy ruffle, red curls in place, inviting them over to Country Sundries. Jodie blinked and said sure, she'd take a look. When Ethel swished out, Jodie asked, "Who was *that*?" but went on talking where she'd left off. Russ motioned from the front door. "Ready?"

"We're checking into your Ridgeway Inn. Can't wait. It's a piece out of the past, right? The same Inn where the girl was staying when she disappeared, right? We'll set up something there and add some ghost images. Oh sure, easy. Don't worry. Maybe a Forties looking female in a white dress. Don't worry Maggie, we'll shoot a few minutes in your Old Timey Things. Jesus, what a collection. Of course we need to shoot on Eve's Mountain, at the tombstone. Show the Kingston estate. Don't look so worried. We're going to shoot around the shops here too."

Maggie pulled in a breath. "That's private property and the man up there is sick."

"So they told me. The ghost's husband, right? We've hit static in trying to set up some time with him. But Russ has checked him out. How? That man has had lots of press. If necessary, we can work around him. Run his picture from the files. Not to worry. Last week, finally, I got through to a member of the family. She'll let us on the property. And show us the grave."

"Tory Kingston?" Maggie looked around for Professor but he had left. "You sure? She's letting you come up?"

"The daughter, right. I get the idea she hates the story and thinks she can put it to rest. That makes for good drama."

"That's just old time talk you're digging up. Nobody knows what happened and its been years ago."

"That's the concept for *Secrets Unveiled*—to dig up old corpses and hoaxes. It's the age of discovery Maggie. Do you know who found out who and what were causing the Virgin Mary sightings, on that Iowa barn window? We did. Spent a week on that story. Those ratings saved our asses for the season. We beat out *Inside Edition*. That week anyway. Gotta go. Blair is a New Yorker with a curiosity for the hinterlands. He's expecting corn pone for supper."

When the van took off up the drive toward the Ridgeway, Bo came in, solemn faced and deflated. "I don't think they want to hear about bear hunting or my teen program or road slides or nothing like that. They're going to ask me on camera if anybody thought the lady's ghost had figured in my daddy's drowning. I asked her if television could give out accusations like that from hearsay, when a sheriff department had to have reliable proof. She just went on talking about having to ask questions anyway."

Maggie felt as miserable as Bo looked. "Paula says when you're looking at a microphone and get a question, you can just nod and go right on to say what you wanted to say in the first place. That's the way it's done. But listen to this. Jodie says Tory Kingston has invited those people up on her daddy's land tomorrow. I couldn't believe my ears."

"Something's going on up there. Aunt Sudie keeps telling me that and now I believe her. The man's getting sicker and Tory Kingston is always blaming his nurse. I've got something else to tell you, Maggie. I know you think a lot about that Selena Hart. Aunt Sudie does too. But I had to look at that woman's driver's license weeks ago. It didn't say Hart. It said Doctor somebody from Denver, Colorado."

"I know all about that, Bo. She just needed to get away." Maggie didn't tell him any more. She'd found that tabloid with Selena's picture on it. Ethel had used it to wrap some onions she'd brought over in the spring. Maggie had put the paper between some old iron skillets, to keep them from rusting. When she found it, and read it, she'd felt nothing but sad for Selena, before she tore the paper up and let Selena know. "Don't you worry about Selena," she said now. "I know her real well."

Bo shook his head. "Might as well tell you this too. Yesterday some detective called from Denver, Colorado, asking where to find High Haven and did I know Selena Hart. He must be coming here to look for her."

M aggie went up to the Inn for supper that night to see what was happening with the Perloin people. She had warned Dilly to wait until their cameras were on next day before trying to tell them about the Ridgeway but there he was, looking like an old dandy in his best plaid vest, standing behind their chairs, talking about the Dilworth family.

The three were more interested in the food. Blair hadn't found any hog jowl and corn pone on Dilly's table and wouldn't if he stayed the summer. Tonight the Ridgeway kitchen, same as every Friday, sent out platters of baked trout fillet, fresh from a trout farm, bowls of crisp slaw, and hush puppies. Up and down the table, women kept asking if they knew Archie Bunker's wife or Ed McMann, disappointed to find the crew was from Atlanta, not Hollywood.

"We're in Atlanta, we talk to LA," Jodie told them in her perky way. "The chief honcho is out there." After supper, the three took a fast look at the grand player piano chiming away in the parlor, then drove off in their van looking, they said, for country music. Peeved, Dilly whispered to Maggie, "Maybe they'll get lost."

Maggie figured Paula Crossing would know what was going on. Paula had talked to Jodie during dinner. In the parlor, they settled onto a couch as Paula explained, "They will pick out settings, shoot the next day and be gone. The film goes back to California to be edited and scheduled. You're right, Maggie, it won't run unless they bring back something good."

"That's why I wanted to bore them."

"Something else. Jodie says LA almost killed the story, and would have. Only someone on the staff out there took a special interest when he found out it was about Alexander Kingston. The executive producer, in fact. Jodie mentioned this by way of saying she might have lost this shoot but is happy she didn't. She's eager to do it."

"What do you suppose that means?"

"The rich and powerful accrue enemies on their way up, you know. It must mean someone's out to get your King of the Mountain for reasons other than to report on a ghost story. And I'm sorry, I really am."

"Then why in the world is Tory Kingston letting them come on the place?"

290

"She must have a reason. I'd guess she expects their cameras to be showing off that spectacular property. Maggie, you may have more to worry about from your landlord's daughter than the story the crew could take back. I must tell you—Tory plans to own that mountain. And develop it. She'd own the property along the road too, your shops, all of it. If she does, that area would turn into a real estate office and landscaped entrance to whatever she envisions to go up on those slopes."

"Lordy." Maggie sat there feeling like a sad lump, looking around at Dilly's parlor, at the old green carpet, the chintz couches, the fireplace. The room looked back like a sweet old thing doomed to die. She patted Paula's hand. "I appreciate you warning me. Do me a favor? Remind Jodie I'll have some people to talk in front of her camera."

Maggie walked back to her house at sunset. Selena waited there, next to her little car. Maggie reported everything but the fact some Colorado detective would come looking for her. She figured Selena had enough on her mind right now. "Zack ought to be here protecting his daddy."

Selena shook her head. "He went back up to Virginia to check on Loren. Tory sent him. She made it sound like an emergency, to get him out of the way."

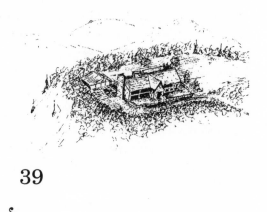

39

From Kingston's suite, young Jeb Gurney rushed down the stairs, his expression letting Selena know he had been run out. A warning about what she'd find up there as the boy and patient had gotten along so well all summer with the morning routine. She found Alexander standing at the expanse of window wall, unsteady as a distraught drunk, dressed but barefoot, needing a shave, again the breakfast tray untouched.

"What's going on down there?" he rasped, dropping into his chair, his face radiating anger and accusation. "You're keeping something from me, like the rest of them. Jeb tells me people are down there. With cameras. Where's Zack?"

"Not here. Calm down and I'll explain." She was seeing a man capable of searing anger, weakened as he was. And as a young man? She stopped the image and the question. "A camera crew has checked into the Inn. They will be shooting the shops and the Ridgeway—"

"You aren't telling me the truth." He muttered what he knew. Tory had told him last night those people were coming. Told him how she'd been hanging up on them since June. A television company as well as a reporter who had hung around all summer. "You had to know. You kept it from me too."

She shook her head but knew to wait, let him say what he did know though the anger was sapping his strength.

"Tory says she was trying to protect me. She believes I need protection. I don't know any more Selena . . . too damn tired to think. Thought I could trust you. I thought we . . . thought you . . ."

"I *am* your friend. You know that. Sit down, Alexander. Hold my hand. Look at me. I'll tell you exactly what is happening. Out there today is a small TV crew doing the Eve story. They claim they're interested in mountain legends." She didn't say, *debunking* the legend. "You must know that High Haven and your dedication of the mountain have become a story told often at folk festivals. This summer several people have wanted to talk to you. Zack and I agreed you shouldn't be disturbed. And yes, Tory, too. Don't worry. Those people down there this morning do not need to speak with you. They know you're ill."

"And in hiding?" He grimaced. "I've been brazen and arrogant in my time . . . in dealing . . . but up front with it, never was a deceitful faker. Never hid from the fall-out. What do I get? A cold, manipulative daughter . . . a son whose attention is a sham. And this personal hell."

"Zack cares for you, Alexander. I know it. Tory believes she's been neglected by you." She didn't dare tell him more, or that Tory had allowed the television crew on the property.

She asked gently, "Do you know anyone connected with the television industry on the west coast?" At his silence, she added, "You were in business and that's show business, I know."

Her question brought a flicker of a weary smile. "Acting is an ego business . . . saw some of that married to Marja." He shook his head, dismissing the subject. "Getting dizzy again. Help me to bed, then go on down, run them away, tell them I don't give a good Goddamned what they want and what they think."

It was only mid-morning but she walked him back to the four-poster bed and helped him collapse there, adjusted his legs and covered him as he mumbled, "I want one thing. To face Eve. Get it over. That's all I want." He looked up briefly. "I loved her . . . but a man can kill the thing he loves."

"A man's insensitivity can kill a woman's love. And accidents can happen during anger." Selena brushed back the shock of white hair. *Am I deluding myself?* Yet her belief in him came back, as a simple fact, beyond rationalization. "Alexander, don't shut me out. I am your friend as well as a nurse. I'll tell you again—chemical depression has contributed to your emotional depression. The truth is something else."

He mumbled, as if he hadn't heard. ". . . so much trouble for you, made you unhappy, Sorry, Selena . . . you tried . . . but you can't follow me to hell." He spoke from the hollow depths of surrender. "She'll come. I deserve what she has to show me."

"And if she came, and told you your hell was unnecessary?"

No answer. The man was beyond reasoning. The obsession entrenched now like a death wish. Seeing that, but hiding her alarm, Selena said, "So sleep. I'll see you later." She hurried downstairs.

In the kitchen, Sudie stood looking out a window. "They're out there now, near the grave marker. The TV folks. She just went out to meet them."

Selena looked. Tory was hurrying toward the three people waiting with equipment at the wooded edge of the knoll, above the front drive.

"Tell me, Sudie, you knew Tory's mother Marja, didn't you? Are they in touch, do you know?"

"I reckon so. You can't miss that woman's voice. She calls here. They fuss on the phone, I know that much. You going out to watch?"

"In a minute. First, may I look around in your cabinets, Sudie? Or maybe you've seen where Tory keeps her supply of vitamins and whatever?"

Without questioning the reason, Sudie went to a cabinet and pulled out several bottles, next to a bottle of bourbon. Selena studied each. Antihistamine capsules, sleeping pills, plus a vitamin bottle containing similar over the counter drugs. "Trust me, Sudie. Put these in a bag and hide them out of sight, in the pantry. Don't worry, I'll take the responsibility."

Selena walked out of the back terrace toward the group. Tory, a neat figure in silk blouse and suede pants, faced the animated young woman in jeans running the operation. The two men were setting up cameras and boom mike and what looked like sound equipment.

Before reaching them, Selena stopped short. From the front drive, Ariel McRae was running toward the crew, holding in her arms a white dress, running like a bride late for the ceremony. No, like an ingenue late for a tryout.

Tory stared at the approaching girl, then screamed with fury, "What in the hell is this?"

Ariel stopped, rooted, clutching her white dress.

Tory's voice shrilled with rage. "Get that girl out of here. Did you think for one instant I agreed to set up some phony ghost scene? I was allowing you here to show this mountain as it is *now*! To put an *end* to the stupid story. The woman has been dead forty years."

Selena turned back toward the terrace. She had seen enough. At last, too late, she understood Tory Kingston. Knew what drove her. Not merely the desire to steal this property from her father to prove to him her cleverness. The real need ran deeper and was far more irrational. Tory was still trying passionately to kill off a dead woman she'd hated since childhood, whose influence persisted and haunted her even now.

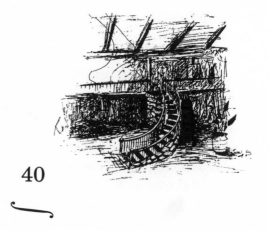

40

"The camera people have gone, Alexander. Do you hear me?"

Selena stood by his bed, willing him to open his eyes, or nod against the pillow. She had told him at noon and again, at sunset. Still no response. She took his blood pressure, and from his silent compliance, knew he could hear her. The reading told her to withhold the blood thinner. He struggled up now, still silent, refusing to look at her, to wheel drunkenly toward the bathroom, slamming the door behind him. He returned, stumbled back toward his bed. With her help, he sank into it like a man giving up to his own grave.

Sudie brought up a tray of hot broth and muffins, took one look at the man on the bed and ran out again, sniffling.

Selena stood at the window wall, looking out at darkening slopes. *She's out there somewhere,* Alexander had muttered more than once. An image became an idea, illogical but persistent enough to make her skin prickle. She went back to the bed, looked down on his still body, the deep set eyes held tight, living his nightmare. "Alexander, hear me. Tory is in the library. Let yourself sleep now. I'll see you in the morning."

She found the library dark except for the brass lamp on the desk where Tory sat, a glass in her hand. "I'm leaving now. He needs to sleep. Don't wake him for anything. No hot milk—anything."

"You don't give me orders—Selena Hempton."

Her arms chilled. What a dangerous little woman. It was time to give a real order. "Tory, you are doing two things that could kill your father. One has been to feed his fears . . ."

"*What?* The failed nurse is accusing *me?*" Tory stood unsteadily, the words slurred but heavy with venom.

"Also, whatever you are giving your father may seem harmless to you, but it amounts to dangerous over-medication. And I know you are doing it to keep him disoriented."

Wild-eyed, Tory weaved toward her, empty glass clutched in her hand.

"Stop where you are and listen to me." At the girl's shocked silence, Selena rushed on. "In a drugged state, Tory, he may not be aware of what you're doing to his mountain but his obsession is a greater danger. He is defenseless against any suggestion of guilt that you may have made. You see, I am aware of your own obsession, Tory. You hate Eve. You think she had the love your father has never shown you. That's regrettable and it's the past. But what you're doing now could kill him."

"Why—you cool bitch! *You're fired.* Get out of this house. They're coming after you anyway, I can tell you that."

Selena turned away and headed down the stairs, braced for anything. Tory clung to the railing, screaming down, "You think I don't know who you are? I made sure to find out. And I can tell them you must have a habit, miss big-hearted-nurse, of needing to kill what you can't cure. Even your kid. I made it my business to find out about you, Selena Hart Hempton of Colorado."

Once outside, Selena breathed again. She drove away, shivering with anger, dismay settling in heavy as the fog. So, Colorado was coming here. She didn't have time to think of Drew, or any Denver authority. *It would come when it had to, so deal with it then.*

Selena drove slowly in the increasing fog. What to do? She had left her patient with a drunken daughter but he couldn't be aroused now to take anything, even if Tory did find the bottles Sudie would have hidden. Tory was almost out of it, too.

Tomorrow she had to get back in that house, fired or not. *Zack, get back here.* He was still in Virginia with Loren but her unleashed anger included him now. Some of the anger was for herself, for wanting him here with her, for needing his trust and help.

The VW's lights hit the gray mist as if it were a wall. She was past the dark shops now, somewhere on Crest Road. She put her head out to find the road edge. Finally, pulled off the road. She had passed her own turn off for the chalet. She sat there, lost in the fog, pulse loud in her ears. She had left Alexander back there lost in his mental anguish, almost catatonic. Waiting on no one, expecting no one, but Eve.

Are you out there? Are you coming to him? Selena whispered.

How easy to say that, encapsulated in this little car. Easy to say, *I have a real sense of you. And not as something fearful. I believe you would help me help this man, if you could. If only you could really speak to him. Show me how to help him.*

Open spaces showed in the drifting fog. She pulled back on the road, knowing it led toward the hollow. It felt right. She didn't question. Looked for a light that would be the McRae house.

As she pulled into the dirt drive, a battered blue truck was pulling out but stopped alongside her. Beyond the open window, Hoke McRae's shadowed face studied her like a dark hunter, observing his prey. She waited, foot on the brake, returning his gaze.

"Well, if it ain't the nurse lady," Hoke drawled. "I reckon you must have some cause to be hanging around old Addie. Princess Bitch didn't tell you nothing, did she?"

Did he mean Ariel? No. Foot tensed on the brake, Selena studied the man in the truck. What did he mean? She said coolly, "Maybe. Why does that concern you?"

"Because it's between that little hellcat and me and it's none of your business."

Did he mean Tory? What was going on between that unlikely pair?

"If you're trying to do business with Tory Kingston, Hoke, good luck. I know how she works."

A gravel laugh from the dark cab. "I know where her nanny's tied. She can't and you can't scare me off'n them Kingstons. I don't care what happens to the old man. That little bitch has got her name on that land now and she knows she's got to give me my right share."

"You think so, Hoke? I'd say you've been taken in. You can't force her."

He growled, "I said it's between her and me. Not Addie."

Addie? She had to keep him talking. "You're looking at a friend of Addie and Ariel's you know. We talk."

He considered that solemnly. "Ariel don't know nothing. And you can't get nothing out of Addie." He leaned out again, banging a fist against the side of the truck, then wheeled out of the yard into the foggy night.

For a shivering moment, Selena didn't move. So Tory and Hoke had some kind of relationship, adversarial surely, but he did know the woman. Threatening Tory with what? Not with any legal claim on the land, surely. So it must be the other thing. Fear of Eve. What kind of tale had Hoke taken to Tory to make her listen, even promise him land?

She rolled closer to the house, turned off the ignition and got out. In the foggy dark, the creek gurgled a melancholy rhythm. Leaves crunched under foot, a reminder: she was running out of time here. She should be worrying about her own future. But later, not tonight. She knocked on the door. "Ariel, Addie, it's Selena, may I visit?"

The door opened. In the dark doorway, the kitchen light behind her, the petite dark-haired girl in the white dress might have been Eve. The Eve Kingston of the yellowed newspaper pictures.

"You wanna come in or you gonna stand out there?"

"Ariel, yes. You looked so—so lovely there, you gave me a start." Selena's skin crawled with inspiration free of logic. If only that vision of Eve could stand by Alexander's bed. No, the man was near psychotic but he wouldn't be fooled, would he, by that young girl?

She followed Ariel into the kitchen. An old Singer sewing machine held piles of the white muslin and pattern scraps. Ariel whipped the dress over her head and stood there, holding the soft whiteness against her flat bra and panties.

"Pretty, ain't it?" A thin chain crinkled around her slim neck, dropping a intricate gold heart between her small breasts. It looked to be a good one. Poor miserable David must have given it to her before he left. Quickly, Ariel dumped the dress on the table and yanked on a shapeless T-shirt.

"You looked beautiful. Ethereal. Did you get to wear it yesterday for the cameras?"

"Yeah. Not up there at the grave, though. Jodie took me down to the Inn. I sat on the porch steps and sang." She smiled. "I sang David's song. Jodie said the whole spot could have been MTV. That's what she wants to produce. But they've gone now." She sighed and looked at the dress. "I had to put it on one more time before I packed it away."

"I'm glad you got to sing. Did you make the dress yourself?"

"Mama helped. First she said she wouldn't have no part in it. Then I sang David's song, it's like an Irish ballad, about Eve loving these mountains and all. She cried and I cried. Then David stopped to say goodby. He told Mama I ought to have a chance to sing. He said the television people were here to do a show and they could make everybody look dumb for letting Alexander Kingston be their landlord and they could make him look like a murderer besides, unless we could give them some singing and nice words about this ridge. Then he left." Ariel buried her face in the dress.

"May I see her?"

Down the dark hall, Selena found Addie seated in yellow lamp light, brushing the long strands of pale silver hair. Instinctively, Addie let the hair fall down against the scarred side of her face.

300

Selena pulled the low rocker closer. "May I sit with you? I'm really troubled tonight. I think my car found it's own way here."

Addie smiled and kept brushing. Selena rocked, studying the woman's face as the brush continued its slow rhythm. "I'm so glad you let Ariel sing. That was wise. And kind." She got a nod for an answer. *Oh, Addie, don't go quiet on me again.* "I'm glad to see you are so much better. You really do know about healing, don't you? Learned from Will McRae's mother?"

"From Nonnie, yes." The whisper again.

"Addie, what about healing the wounded spirit? The spirit that gives us the will to live?"

"Yes . . . it's a choice that has to be made. Not once, but many times."

"What if someone needs help to make that choice? If they're so lost in their sense of guilt, they can't see beyond it?"

"You, Selena?"

"I'm troubled, yes, but not for myself. For the man who is my patient, at Capstone." She didn't take her eyes from the face that still had beauty, even with the ragged scar. "He needs help, Addie. He needs a woman with your gentle voice and wisdom and kindness to sit by his bed, even for five minutes, and just say to him, *It's all right, all right, to forgive yourself.*"

At Addie's shudder, Selena reached out and stroked her thin arm. "That's not hate is it? I don't see you hating the way Hoke hates the Kingstons. You said Will McRae was a gentle man. Did he hate the Kingstons?"

Addie lifted her head. Pale blue eyes flickered with feeling. "Why do you ask me this?"

"Because—this man Alexander Kingston is in his own hell, since his retirement and stroke. He has come to believe he caused his first wife's death. She would have been about your age now. Then she was a girl of twenty."

Watching Addie's face, Selena went on quietly, "A girl who loved poetry, who must not have been ready to be so controlled and absorbed by the man—though he loved her. Loved her, I

301

believe, throughout his busy life. Addie? You know the story. I see you do."

"Why tell me this?"

"Because I desperately need your help. The man is going to die waiting for some evil specter of Eve to stand at his bedside and send him into hell. He believes that, has created that image in his mind. As aggressive as he has been in his life, I can't believe this man would physically hurt someone he loved as he must have loved that young wife. I don't believe that today Eve would be vengeful. If she were here, she would be wiser for her years too. She would want to give him that dispensation, wouldn't want him to suffer the hell he's in."

Addie's whispered, "The past can't be undone."

"But the present can be changed."

"You know I see no one. I couldn't go to that house. Never."

"But if it saved a man's sanity? He needs five minutes of forgiveness as a drowning person needs air. Addie, your soft voice, your size, your kindness could give him that."

Is this making her tremble? But I can't stop now. "Addie, I'll make it easy. I'll work out a way to get you there and back in thirty minutes at the most."

Addie hid her face in her hands.

"I'm leaving now," Selena said, hiding elation and wild doubts. "But, don't close your heart. Help me save this man's sanity and his life. I'm going to arrange everything. I'll be back tomorrow. Right after dark. Addie?"

Selena made herself walk out, past Ariel in the kitchen, and back out into the night. Fog was clearing now. The September night seemed full of promise as well as danger.

After she fired Selena Hart, Tory remained at the top of the stairs, gripping the newel post until she heard the car leaving. Back in the library, she cursed the empty brandy bottle, went downstairs and poured herself a real drink, then made it to the cook's bathroom off the kitchen to be disgustingly ill. Light-headed, she splashed water on her face. This was no time to be out of control. Outside in the foggy night, she pulled the hidden keys from the Porsche's mat and careened away, driving with fear and abandon through waves of fog and black night.

She found Hoke McRae's truck as she expected, at Benny's Bar. Tory parked away from the lights, walked over to the pick-up, reached into the open window and blew the horn, again and again, before stumbling back to the Porsche. Hoke stalked out, looking around. He took his time ambling over to her car, his grin showing in the dim red light of the parking lot.

He leaned in, with the smirky smile. She pushed back his face. "You're welching on your end of the bargain, McRae."

"Maybe I've been putting you on, to see you worry."

She stared. Was he lying about what he told her? Or lying now? She cursed at him, gripping the steering wheel, feeling ill.

"Aw, what you care about that old lady, long as she stays in that house and I don't tell anybody else what we know?"

The possible truth of it surged back, like nausea and fear combined. "She killed your daddy, didn't she? Roy McRae was your father. I've found out a few things about the McRaes. She can throw you out of that house anytime. You'll have nothing."

"I reckon." He looked away, solemn-faced. "Never saw the likes of you, Little Bitch. I'm not hankering to see the inside of that county jail again. It's a rat hole. And you haven't give me what you promised, my own land and a grow house."

Control. Not this panic. She bit out her demand. "If you don't cooperate with me first, do what I asked, you won't get any land. And she'll take what you have. And you can grow old in that rat hole, Hoke McRae. I will see to that." She wheeled off, leaving him there.

41

The morning the Perloin Productions crew rolled away from High Haven, Professor Enholm walked into Old Timey Things. "I didn't fail to cooperate with your plan, Maggie. I did try. As expected, they wanted very little edification on the value of this place from me. So I departed the confusion and drove to visit with an old friend in Banner Elk. So tell me, what kind of a story did they do?"

"You'd never know, watching the way they do it." Maggie set down his cup of hot tea, she gave him the English Rose pattern now, and took the other rocker, thankful for a peaceful morning for a change. "We'll have to wait around antsy to see what they've done to us. Jodie told me they have to edit. Then she said, the coast people have to look at it before your ghost gets scheduled on *Secrets Unveiled.*"

"So it will be the ghost story. But yes, that can include murder. What did you observe?"

"Couldn't watch it all. They took their pictures with a lot of commotion before and after. For about ten minutes here, we had hot lights and wires right in the shop, with Jodie asking questions in her professional voice, off camera. I have to admit, I wanted to show so many things, besides trying to keep her questions off you know what. I brought out my German Berry bowl from the

Thirties, and a child's tin globe, and the brass-faced iron clock, made in 1882 in Anson, New York, and some of the prettiest English tea cups I have."

Maggie rocked and sipped her hot tea. "If they don't end up on the show, that's fine with me. I looked right into the camera and said I don't try too hard to sell those things. People love to come in here and just moon over pieces of the past. I sell enough quilts."

Professor smiled. "And Ethel?"

"Behind the marble counter so nervous I couldn't stand to watch, so I left."

"And our worried sheriff?"

"They had Bo Hilrey standing by his cruiser out on the road so I don't know what he got to say. They went on up to the Ridgeway Inn next. I went up to watch but so many people were standing around I gave up and came back. I did see Jodie hopping around helping the other two set up their equipment. And they told people they'd want to show the porch empty for another scene. Ariel was waiting around in old fashioned white dress. She looked so pretty the girl gave me a start. Then I thought, oh Lordy, they're going to show Ariel in that white dress then have her disappear."

At the professor's interested nod, "I came on back to the shop. The crew came down later and put cameras in first one face then another. For all the worrying I'd done, I couldn't change anything now. I wanted Happy Dowdell from Blackberry Ridge to tell them what he tells tourists. So I just left it to the Lord, what got to be said. Old man Hogan was around with his banjo. And lots of summer people who wanted to talk."

"And the crucial question—did they film up at Capstone?"

"I haven't seen Selena but Paula Crossing said yes, they did. Paula got to be friends with Jodie before they left. Paula didn't see what happened but she said Jodie looked satisfied when they pulled out."

Maggie rocked silently for a minute. "I wonder if they'll show what a fine September day it was, so clear you could see fifty miles, the mountains blue and lilac. Or did they just show our faces mouthing off. I'll remember that the next time I watch the news, when street faces are fussing into a camera and waving protest banners. It can't be the whole truth of a place. So, Professor, I don't know what Jodie and her crew took back with them. We'll have to wait and see."

"Maggie, do you worry that in protecting the place, we may have shielded a man who might be guilty?"

Maggie looked around at the quiet shop. "I won't say I haven't wondered that in the middle of the night. It's not right to ignore somebody else's sins to keep your own comfort. Yet it's not right to judge other people's lives when you don't know the truth, and you're on the outside looking in. Self-righteous people can do a lot of harm when they don't know what they're talking about."

"The television show isn't so conscientious," he murmured. "When does the story run?"

"Paula has to keep in touch with Jodie and find out. Looks like Paula is in no hurry to leave, though here it is September. I think she's already lost that good job she had in California. And Selena! I don't know what she'll do with fall coming on. I haven't seen her for days."

The Professor was at the door when he turned back to ask, "What is it the fellow from Blackberry Ridge tells tourists that you wanted repeated on camera?"

"When they find out he's a summer person, not a native, and they ask 'Where do you live *normally?* Happy tells them, "I live here *normally*. Wintertime, I live *ab-normally* in Miami."

42

In a chill dawn, Selena drove to Sudie Gurney's house in the valley. Sudie came to the door in her bathrobe. Sudie took one look and said, "You come right in."

At the kitchen table, Selena drank black coffee gratefully, pushed the mug aside and leaned toward the woman's sympathetic face. "You're going to think I'm a little crazy but please listen. First, before you go to Capstone this morning, you need to know what's happened."

She told Sudie how, yesterday, she had to admit to Alexander that reporters with cameras were on the grounds. Left him in bed in deep depression. Last night Tory had fired her. "I won't try to go back this morning. Jeb will be there as usual, right? And you'll be there all day. No matter what Tory says, you must find opportunities to go upstairs and look in on him. The minute Zack comes in, call me at the chalet. I'll be waiting. Tell Zack we have an emergency. A real emergency."

Sudie moaned, "Lord Jesus, have mercy on Azzie."

"Sudie, I have a plan. I've thought it out but it can't work without help from you and Jeb."

Sudie listened, pale eyes blinking behind her glasses, moaning, *law, law*. When Selena finished, Sudie was shaking her head. "Don't know if Zack will go along with such as that. Once when he was a boy, down at the creek panning for rubies, he looked up to see her staring at him, quiet as a deer, then running away like a scared rabbit. He came in saying, Sudie, I finally saw that little old crazy woman from the creek house."

Selena admitted. "It will take some explaining. And there's not time to explain. When do you expect him back with Loren?"

"Don't know, Se'lene. *She* told him not to hurry."

"That means at least, we won't have to explain to Zack tonight. We won't have to deal with him."

"How you going to get *her* out of the house?" Sudie asked.

"I'll call Mitch Mason, ask him to get Tory to the cottage. We won't have a great space of time to do this, and it has to be dark when we try. I don't even know, until I go back there, if Addie will agree to come with us. But I had to be sure first that you and Jeb will help."

A t one o'clock that afternoon, Sudie phoned Selena from the Capstone kitchen, saying Tory was outside pacing around so it was safe to call. "Azzie is just lying there, won't eat or nothing. I took up some hot beef soup but he took no notice. Didn't answer me. I couldn't talk to him because *she* was sitting in there, in his big wing chair staring out the window and drinking her brandy. Then this morning, when I was dusting the hall, I heard her on the phone with her mama, that Marja, carrying on, accusing her mama for getting her into something that didn't work. When I walked in, she hung up, bossy as usual."

Yes, she'd asked Tory about Zack. "She told me Loren's leg was getting put in a cast. I bet she never told Zack a thing about Azzie being so down."

Hanging up the phone, Selena stared out at her mountain view without seeing it. She tried to reach Doc Bradley at his daughter's in Morganton. A recorded greeting. She left a message. "Doc, it's Selena. Please get to Capstone quickly as possible. Emergency."

The afternoon crawled by. She thought about sitting in the hot Jacuzzi. No, too keyed up to leave the phone. *Zack, I wish you were here but tonight will be easier if you aren't.* How could she expect Zack to understand? He didn't know what she knew . . . or suspected . . . or hoped. She was willing to risk Zack's wrath if it meant giving Alexander what he needed. *Forgiveness.*

The main danger was Tory. It had to be done quickly, while Tory was out of the house.

On the deck, she watched the light fade over the mountains and more fog come in. Finally, heart pounding, she dialed Mitch Mason's number, to tell him Tory was highly nervous, a problem for both herself and her father, and to please call her to come up to the cottage, to keep her there talking.

To Selena's surprise, Paula Crossing answered Mitch's phone. "He went to some county meeting tonight. I was here helping him. What's up?"

Selena began her message but Paula interrupted. "Level with me. What's happening?"

"Paula, the truth. Tory was drunk last night and fired me. Alone with her, in his condition—in her condition—he's in danger. I must get back in there tonight. I need you to get Tory out of there before eight o'clock and keep her up there with you as long as you can manage. Turn on the outside lights if she starts back to the house. Trust me, all of this is necessary."

She hung up, grateful for Paula's quick promise to do her best and not ask any more questions. It occurred to her Paula could have been in Virginia with Loren and Zack.

As the mountains darkened, she paced. Finally, seven o'clock. It took twenty minutes to get to the McRae house. How long to convince Addie to walk out of that house, go where she'd never gone before? Jeb was to be there, waiting outside in his new truck. Sudie would be at Capstone, in the dark yard, to let them know if Tory had crossed the knoll to the stone cottage. Endless traps between those steps, but the major one depended on convincing Addie to go with them.

Driving to the McRae house, Selena realized with panic she had no explanation for Hoke, even Ariel, if they were there.

309

Mercifully, the yard was empty of either Ariel's red pick-up or Hoke's battered blue one.

The porch door to the kitchen was open as usual. She called, "Addie? It's Selena. I've come for your help." She walked down the dark hall toward the dim light from the back room. Addie sat there, the long silver hair tied loosely at her neck, the straight cotton dress reached to the twisted ankle. Selena's heart pounded, thinking, *the sleeping beauty forced to wake to the present.*

"Addie? Yes!" Selena looked into the pale green eyes with a shiver. *This will work if she will come. This is not an insane notion.*

"Alexander is very low, Addie. He could be dying. He needs your voice there saying—whatever in your kindness and wisdom you might say. We can take you there in Jeb's truck and bring you back. You would be gone only thirty minutes."

A motor hummed outside. Thank God, it was the purr of Jeff new truck not Hoke's noisy one. "Forgiveness is the greatest gift to give another, and it is healing too, for ourselves. Addie?" Selena waited for her answer. Her hope rose when she realized the faint scent of wisteria came from Addie. And she wore Ariel's gold heart at the neck of the pale cotton dress.

Without answering, Addie stood, reached for her walking stick then set it back. Selena held out her hand. Addie nodded, then walked ahead with measured steps through the kitchen and out to the porch. At the sight of Jeb's shiny truck, humming out there, she shrank back. "No, only with you, Selena."

The VW's headlights caught the drifting fog as it followed Jeb's truck. Addie sat in silence, *silent as a ghost,* Selena thought. Her own voice seemed muted, saying, "Jeb is a good boy and strong. He'll carry you upstairs and down again." Now, if Sudie would only be out there to let them know Tory was away from the house. Yes, thank God, Sudie was there, waving them to come on in. She had left the back of the house dark, only a small light in the kitchen.

Selena parked in the darkest shadows. Sudie was to stay on the terrace, waiting to warn them if any outside lights came on across the knoll. Jeb knew to move the VW out of sight but close as possible. As Jeb helped Addie out of the small car, Sudie stared and wrung her hands. Finding her voice, Sudie said, "Jeb's gonna carry you real gentle up the back steps unless you want to go through the house and down the hall."

"No, not the house," Addie whispered. Eyes closed, she allowed Jeb to scoop her up in his strong arms. "You just a lil' bit of a lady," he said and led the way up the back stairs and down the hall toward Kingston's suite. Selena followed.

The hall was shadowed from a single table lamp. Jeb set Addie down just inside Kingston's room. Selena held her trembling shoulders close a moment, whispering, "Say anything you find in your heart to say about forgiveness. We don't have long. Just be with him."

The room was dark. Only a yellow night light glowed on the table beside the four-poster. With a shiver of private exhilaration, Selena led Addie to the chair, pulled close to the bed. They both looked down. Alexander lay on his back, like a sodden weight in rumpled silk pajamas, silver hair splayed on the pillow.

Selena eased Addie into the chair and backed away into the dark, to watch silently, alert to any sound outside the door. In the amber light, Addie's slight figure and silvery hair seemed an apparition, leaning closer now to the man on the bed.

The whispery voice made him stir. Yes, he was listening. Frowning, but listening. *God, let this work,* Selena prayed, watching from the dark. Watching Addie nod then bend again to speak to the man. Calling him *Alex?* Addie reaching up now, taking something from around her neck—the chain and heart?—holding it up to him. His big hand raising to take it, then pressing it to his face.

His voice now, rumbling, as faint as a man talking in his sleep. Questions? Addie nodding. Selena moved closer, her own pulse loud in her ears. She only heard Addie's *"Never . . ."* the rest lost to whispers.

Alexander's head rocked against the pillow. His hand lifted to cover his face. *Is he crying? What have I done?* He reached out now, touching the silvered hair, Addie bending close to allow it. His hand fell back. Addie reached out, her own hand tracing his cheek. Wiping away tears?

Jeb appeared in the hall doorway, giving a frantic signal. Trouble. Selena moved quickly toward Addie's chair, put a gentle touch on her shoulder, nodded at her white upturned face. Before moving away from the bed, they both looked down on Alexander. His eyes were closed. *Maybe I've killed him. The shock could have killed him.* But he stirred.

Her arm around Addie's thin frame, Selena guided her toward the door and into the hall where Jeb waited, his harsh whisper warning, "Gotta hurry, Ma'am." Jeb swept Addie into his arms and headed toward the back stairs.

Selena waited, listening to Jeb's fading steps, before returning to the room, turning up the bed lamp to look at the man on the bed, to quickly test his pulse. A bit fast but strong, steady. He looked up at her, trying to focus, wanting to talk. "Selena. You were right . . . she came . . . Now I can sleep."

She squeezed his big hand, turned the light dim again and hurried out. They had to get Addie out of there, back home. At the bottom of the stairs, Tory appeared, staring up, seeing Selena and screaming in rage. *"You're trying to kill my father!"*

Selena looked down on her small gesturing figure and used the first thing that came to mind. "Why is Hoke McRae looking for you, Tory? Is he still downstairs?"

Tory's face registered shock before she backed away, toward the dark foyer. Selena ran down the back stairs, out to the two cars on the grass, in the dark. Jeb waited at the VW guarding Addie inside. Sudie's pale face looked out from the front seat of the truck. "Follow me Jeb." Selena slid behind the wheel of the VW and drove off quickly toward the front drive and out of Capstone grounds. Beside her, Addie leaned back, eyes closed, hands clasped, as if unaware of the bouncing car. Selena reached out and squeezed the thin boned hands, murmured her thanks and drove in the silence she knew Addie needed.

43

A single light showed from the McRae house. Selena pulled up in front and helped the silent Addie out of the car. As they moved toward the porch, Hoke's pick-up rattled into the yard. He leaped out and stalked toward them, assessing some meaning that turned his look menacing, his question a low growl. "Where did she take you, woman?"

Selena held on to Addie's arm, thankful Jeb's red pick-up was bouncing now into the rough yard. Hoke wheeled around, staring at the shiny truck and the muscular boy jumping out.

"Addie, go on inside," Selena said, more calm than she felt. "We'll handle Hoke."

"Doncha worry." Ariel stood in the doorway in a nightgown. "Mama get in here." She shouted out to Hoke. "You stay away from here till you get your head on straight or I'll shoot lower than your gut. Go stay with your girl friend."

At her shrieked demands, Hoke stood transfixed, like an animal caught in headlights before he continued drunkenly toward Selena and Addie, on the porch now. Jeb spun the man around, swung a fist that sent Hoke sprawling on the porch steps. Breathing hard, as if surprised and pleased with himself, Jeb stepped away from the older man. "That's the best thing you can do, McRae. Get away from here until you sober up. We'll stay here till you do."

A sullen Hoke got to his feet, spat at the muscled kid and without a glance at Addie and Selena at the door, stalked to his truck, gunned the motor and whipped out, scraping the edge of Jeb's new truck. Jeb shrieked.

"Mama, whatever you been doing?" Ariel demanded.

"My room," Addie whispered. "Don't want to talk."

Selena waited until Ariel came back to the porch, and promised to lock the door. She drove away, holding back assessment and questions, driving the narrow mountain roads, focused only on the path ahead. Jeb, with Sudie, followed to see her safely home inside the chalet, the door locked.

Alone, Selena walked out onto the dark deck, aware of her furious heart beat and inner trembling, reaction flooding in. She had gambled with the lives of two vulnerable people. She had followed some intuitive drive, like a path opening without road signs, but one she had to take. Even now she hesitated to embrace the incredulous scene she had witnessesd. Had Addie called him *Alex?*

The night breeze found her face wet. Tears of gratitude. She had not been a fool to want that meeting to happen. If only both Alexander and Addie could handle the experience. Finally she went up to the loft bed to lay awake until dawn, reliving the night and wondering at its outcome. Tomorrow, she knew, would be a day of waiting.

A t ten that morning, the phone rang in the chalet, Doc Bradley's voice on the other end. "I have your message, Selena. And one from Tory Kingston. She sounded highly upset. Made some strong accusations against you. Says you sneaked in the house last night. What's going on Selena?"

"I need to tell you. But not on the phone. I want you here more than Tory does. Have you talked with Zack?"

"She couldn't tell me how to reach him. How is Kingston?"

"In deep depression. Today, I don't know. I have reason to believe he is in danger, serious danger, left in her care. She fired me, you know. May have locked the doors. She is clever as well as emotionally a danger to herself and anyone in her way. But Doc, I must get back in—"

At his silence, she added, "I can imagine what she's told you. The girl is possibly manic depressive. But it's Alexander we have to worry about right now. If you can travel at all, please get here as soon as possible."

"She intends to keep you out. I'll be in touch with you when I get there." He rang off.

With Loren in the back seat, his leg cast extended, Zack sped down the Virginia highway, heading south for Capstone, glad for the opportunity to get this confession done with Loren. So far, tough duty. He should be seeing Loren's face to continue the conversation but it was easier this way, facing the traffic, talking to the back seat.

"When you're older . . ." He stopped at Loren's derisive protest. "Okay, put it this way. You're young, but you're no sheltered kid. So I'm asking you to understand, and not close up on me."

"You've always shut me out. Am I supposed to call you Daddy now? Because you just found out you screwed up some girl?" Loren's answer was cold with scorn. A tremor of feeling escaped as he added, "I like that woman. Paula. Or I did."

"Then you should be glad to know it wasn't like that, Loren. What you're saying happens, it's true. Horny young guys have their brains in their pants most of the time. But it wasn't . . . like that . . . that summer I knew Caroline . . . Paula, that is."

No answer from the back seat. Zack gripped the wheel and raced past a lumbering truck. He had given Loren the facts before they started. It had taken longer than he'd expected. Had delayed their departure. On the phone, Tory had sounded impatient, but told him not to hurry. This time alone with Loren couldn't be hurried. Now was the best time to deal with the boy's reaction. Son's reaction. *Why didn't I know,* Zack asked himself for the umpteenth time. *Why hadn't I guessed?* He thought about Paula. She would be ready to deal with her end of it once they got back to High Haven. She'd likely do better than he was doing now.

"I'm making a couple of confessions here," Zack said, still focusing on the road ahead. "I was lonely that summer. Angry at my father's hanger-on friends and restless to get into college, not the intended prep school." How could he make Loren understand? He couldn't tell him the real reason he was torn between love for the big guy and gnawing suspicion since childhood that his own father was guilty of the ultimate hypocrisy. That was his own burden, not Loren's.

"Let's just say for a while there, that summer in question, I found comfort, not casual sex, in the woods. Something very complete in itself can happen to a vulnerable person and never again the same way. You go on and find another relationship if you're lucky, if you've learned anything about yourself. Maybe the young ego is too needy and what happens then might not be the pairing you'll want later in your life. But at the time . . . What am I saying? It will happen to you. Only reason it won't, if you're too closed up in yourself. That's no good."

I'm making a mess of this, Zack thought. He needed more time. Months of time maybe. Years. At Loren's silence, he went on. "Believe me. That relationship, brief as it was, has affected my life and how I've dealt with women." He shut up. That was one of his own problems.

No answer from Loren.

"When I came back the next summer and found you in a crib set up with a nursemaid, no explanations, I was one angry self-righteous kid. The way you feel right now, Bud. I took off for California, very unoriginal reaction at the time, but it provided a fine excuse for showing my contempt for dear old dad. So, things come around, don't they? If you're feeling that for me now, because you didn't know the truth—"

"You haven't even been friends with me," Loren muttered.

"Because of what I've just told you. I was the hard-ass brother because I did see myself in you. The loner. I've opened some valves here, Loren. I'm trying to be honest with you and myself. We don't have to perpetuate this distrust, son to father." As between himself and A. Z.

316

"You've been honest. I give you that," Loren said. After a moment, "My leg hurts. Do we have to drive all night to get there? I need to stretch. I'd like to hobble toward a steak."

The *we* sounded beautiful. "Let me give Tory a call and see how they're doing."

When he got back into the car, Zack told Loren. "Phone's busy. I'll try down the road. And sure, maybe we'll find a decent restaurant next stop." He was on the highway again before he realized, this late I could have tried to reach Selena at her place to find out how A. Z. is doing.

Selena awoke with a start, pulse thudding with instant impatience. The clear sky and green slopes beyond the deck were of no help. This would be the second day Tory was alone with her father, and responsible for handing out the right meds. And here in the chalet, a day of waiting on fate set in motion. Had Tory seen their two-car getaway last night after her screaming entrance? What was Alexander's condition today? Surely Sudie would call but not when Tory could listen. Why hadn't Zack called from Virginia? Doc Bradley had promised to be here by this evening, hours from now. What had Tory told him? Regardless, he would have to call her back up to the house. But when?

By mid-day, no calls. Selena heated soup but couldn't eat. Stood on the deck, looking toward Capstone's summit. *Alexander, do you think I've abandoned you?* What kind of mental state was he in today? Finally, she rang the house, began to speak, but the phone was slammed down. She called Sudie's house and reached a niece who said, "Auntie didn't go to work today. She felt nervous and had Jeb take her down the mountain to the Food Lion."

Should she call Maggie Hardy or Paula Crossing? No, what could she possibly ask of them? In the afternoon, Selena grabbed up the phone, overjoyed to hear Zack's voice. His hurried message chilled her elation. He had spoken to Tory earlier.

"Selena, we're still on the road but on our way finally. Loren's with me, leg cast and all. After Tory said A. Z. was okay, we checked in for the night and got up today with carburetor trouble.

317

Tory put him on the phone. Actually the man sounded happy. Talked crazy but like a happy drunk, saying the time had come for us to have that talk." He paused, still hurried, hesitant. "Tory says she fired you with cause and she'll explain later. I'm sorry. We'll talk when I get there."

"Zack, wait." She began to tell him no one was monitoring the medications for two days and that his father had an emotional experience and Tory and his father shouldn't be alone together. It sounded ridiculous she knew, and too quickly he interrupted, "I tell you A. Z. sounded really good and Tory said not to hurry. Selena, we're waiting at this excuse of a service station. We should be there tonight by ten, if Loren doesn't need more stops. I'm handling a problem here with Loren but the trip is helping. That's why I stopped last night. Got to go now."

She hung up with leaden despair.

An hour passed. Dusk came, gray with no colors. Selena looked toward Capstone. *I should be there. I'm needed.* The sense of it grew like a rapid heart beat. She went back in and called. This time Tory answered, voice slurred. "Tory, I should stop by and check your father's pressure. Just to see how he's doing." The line hummed.

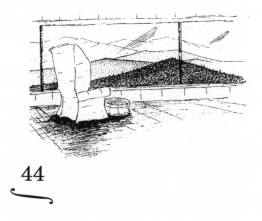

44

Tory sat drinking her brandy in the dark of her father's room.
Hours, now, she had waited, watching him there on the floor,
telling herself he wasn't dead, it was just a stupid fall while
they were arguing. Now and then he moaned.

Darkness beyond the window wall crept into the room, and
into her head, making everything strange like a weird nightmare
becoming real.

She felt sick as hell again, too sick to stand up. Had she called
Doc Bradley? She'd hung up on Selena for sure.

Control. She had to get her mind clear again, back in control
so she could tell Bradley what happened. Had to begin at the first
of this miserable day. Had to tell Zack too, he'd be roaring in here
any time and she would tell him, how everything had gone wrong
since morning. Jeb came, yes. But not Sudie. Jeb had finished
upstairs, and had driven away before she could drag herself out
of bed. She had meant to have it out with him, demand why he'd
been here last night. He and Selena were up to something. Yes,
Selena had been here. The nerve of that woman!

Something else had happened she needed to remember,
couldn't remember. Too damn sick. Too much booze last night.
Couldn't find the sleeping pills or her lithium. She'd kill Sudie for
moving them.

Reeling around in her room, she had heard her father calling. With that woman out of the house, *he was needing her now! Calling to her!* She dressed somehow dizzy and ill.

She was shocked to walk in and find him moving around with the walker. Zeb had him bathed and dressed and he looked haggard as hell, but he was on his feet, looking happy, talking nonsense and demanding breakfast. Then Zack on the phone. She had to keep Zack away until she had things under control. So she handed the phone to A. Z. long enough to let him talk one minute, then she took the phone back and told Zack not to hurry. She needed time to get her head clear. Those Goddamned washed out roads! Where was Mitch? No, where was Hoke? Hoke and his lies. An ugly impossible lie she refused to believe. Yet what he told her was like a grave opening and something pale and white coming out, murmuring, *He loves me, your father still loves me and never wanted you to be born. . .*

Zack mustn't know about Hoke. But he had to know about this miserable day. How she had to go down to the kitchen, no Sudie around, and make his breakfast. He wanted oatmeal. The smell of hot stuff made her ill.

She took the revolting bowl back up to him, sat it down on the table beside his chair and waited for thanks. Oh no. He was stalking around again, talking to himself, for Godsakes, crying one minute, smiling the next. So this was the way he was coming out of the nice haze she'd kept him in.

Watching him, she knew she'd forgotten something. Maybe the damn meds. Had she skipped yesterday? So she'd double up the Coumadin today in case Selena got back in here, to count pills with Doc Bradley.

He had taken them without protest, had sat down to his cereal, with only a nod to her. She stood there waiting, sick and seething.

And what did he say? *Thanks Tory. You're drunk at 10 in the morning you know. Go get some sleep.* He began eating the disgusting oatmeal, with his flushed face and labored breathing.

She run to his bathroom to be sick. Then to the library to find her brandy. The desk top looked back at her with its stack of bills, mocking her. All those washed out new roads, and pipe line hassles. The brandy hit her throat and stomach like fire. Welcomed fire. Now she remembered. When Hoke called late last night, from Benny's Bar, it hadn't been just another threat. He sounded anxious. "Your nurse lady knows about Addie." She had felt hot, then cold, but she told him what he'd better do. She had poured another drink from the downstairs bar. And another. She mustn't tell Zack that.

She would tell him how she went back to her father's room. Found him walking the room again, staggering around without the walker. He had braced himself by the balcony door, to look at her—*finally, looking at her*—but only to ask for Zack. He wanted to tell Zack his old man was not guilty. And she, Tory, had to get it straight too. What had he said?

"You came in here nights and fed me that crap about what people thought. That I had killed Eve. Well you were wrong, whatever you or anyone else believed. Selena was right."

"Right about what?" she'd asked, fear crawling her body. *They were all conspiring against her with their false stories.*

"Eve," he said.

"You're crazy," she said but he wasn't listening.

"Eve was here. She doesn't hate me. She ran from me that time . . . she ran up the mountain path . . . she knew the path, no one guessed that . . . but up there is where she fell. I had turned away, angry. I failed to go after her . . . Where is Selena? Why isn't she here? I have to tell her."

"I fired her. Two days ago. You've been out of it. You still are."

"What?"

"I threw her out. She's the reason you're talking crazy."

She wouldn't tell Zack that part either. She'd just tell him they had been talking and his big face had tightened with anger. He had headed toward the phone. She reached it first and threw it on the floor.

"Call her, Tory." He stood, weaving, the deep voice breathless. "Get her here! I need her. I have to tell her."

"No!" The wail came out of her depths. "Look at me, Goddamn you! Look at your daughter!"

He swayed there, in the middle of the room, a sad old man, his sadness an accusation. "I see you Tory. I see you're drunk."

Didn't he understand, even yet? She had to make him *see her*. Listen to her. That's when, yes, she had told him her plan, her project, proof of her cleverness. It wasn't the way she had intended for him to learn about Havencrest. She had meant to show completed scale plans, announce that roads and water system were in, have half of the loan spent before she allowed him out of his medicated fog to see what she could do . . . had done. If he ranted she had stolen his land, she could say he'd signed papers and his precious mountain would belong to the bank unless the project went forward.

She would tell Zack, *I wanted to force him to be proud of me.* Grudgingly but proud of his daughter, a Kingston.

So yes, she told him what she had been doing and watched the words whip across his face. Saw his brows tighten, his dark pupils flash anger and pain. But no love. No pride. For all her trouble, he had told her with deadly quiet. "You, Tory, are a conniving female, more unforgiving and vindictive than your mother."

Ah, she had more to tell him, now he was listening. "You don't know how unforgiving Marja can be. Didn't you ever realize my mother felt just as cheated as the rest of us with your dedication to dear little Eve? Do you know who Marja's current lover is? Some big honcho in the television industry. He's the one who sent down that crew to make a fool or a murderer out of you with the Eve saga. Marja pushed the idea. They did it, too."

That got to him, sent him rocking there on his feet, moving like a blind man. "Why did you do this to me Tory, why make people hate you?"

Behind her clenched eyes, she knew, *I hate myself because my father hates me.* She heard him stumble. Over the dumb phone? She opened her eyes to watch him stagger, entangled in the cord, then fall with a heavy thud onto the green carpet. She screamed for Jeb. No one came. She bent down beside him, her big powerful father, lying on his side. Pushed him over to his back, put a pillow under his head. Covered him with a blanket from the bed. Knelt at his side, wiped blood from his mouth with her hand. He still didn't move.

How long ago had that been? Hours now. Lost count. She didn't feel drunk anymore. Embalmed maybe, but still hurting. When did she eat last? Couldn't remember.

"Water," he whispered now. She brought a glass, put a hand under his neck and tried to raise his head. The water spilled. With a wet tissue she brushed his lips, softly, like a good daughter. Stroked the frowning forehead, the closed eyes, the tousled white hair as he mumbled, "Help me." On her knees, she bent close. "I'm trying." He didn't look up but murmured, "Something's going wrong, Selena."

Tory pulled away.

"Selena."

She stood up, replaced the phone and walked away from his covered bulk. She found the bottle of brandy and fell into the wing chair, letting its size and firmness embrace her, as he might have done, as he never had. Darkness took over the room. When the phone buzzed, she let it ring until she remembered it could be Doc Bradley. Or Zack. It was Selena's voice. Tory slammed down the receiver.

She knelt down beside him again. His forehead felt clammy. She dared not test his pulse. Had she called Doc for help? But he'd already left. Maybe she should call the county emergency or the sheriff. She did that and went back to the window with her brandy to wait again like a good daughter.

The sound of a car downstairs roused Tory. She looked toward the four-poster. No, he still lay motionless on the floor. She leaned against the window and saw Selena's VW in front of the house. Saw headlights of another car down below. Heard the front chimes. She stumbled across the room, turned on a lamp, trying to think, the room spinning around her. A phone was ringing. She made her way downstairs slowly, and threw open the heavy front door. Selena.

"Let me come in, Tory. You look ill. Let's check on him together."

Selena was coming in. Couldn't stop her. Too Goddamned sick. Had to get control here. When people were against you, you used the hindrance to advantage. "Look who's here. Nurse Selena. Been neglecting your patient. You go on up."

Selena hurried past her and up the dark stairs. Tory wheeled into the dark main room, looking for the bar, fighting down nausea and a strange wild sadness. *Control*, she warned herself. The damn phone kept ringing. She groped around both ends of a large couch to stop the thing. Found it, heard Hoke on the line, warning her, like a hissing snake, she'd better deliver on her deal and in a hurry. She shut her mind to what he was saying but it slithered in, incredible, incomprehensible. She told him, "Sonofabitch, you're the one to get moving."

Car lights flashed on the front drive. Tory threw open the door, shaking with relief at the sight of old Bradley's Buick. Was she crying? Didn't believe in crying. He hurried toward her with his little black satchel.

"Thank God you're here." She clung to his lapels for a moment, trying to focus his face, a concerned doctor face. She backed away, pointing upstairs. "Hurry. I couldn't stop her. I think something terrible has happened. She wouldn't let me see him. Selena, up there with my father." Tory trailed a few steps after him, but stopped at the foot of the stair, crying up to him. "The police are coming after her from Colorado."

45

Before dawn, a faint, high moan echoed in the mountain dark, like the cry of an unearthly woman.

In her log house below Capstone, Maggie Hardy woke, listening without moving under the quilt, thinking in that instant, *Eve Kingston's ghost is out there after all.* She sat up, shivering in the flannel nightgown. Here it came again, now a metallic moan. On the end of the bed, Hemmie sat up, a dark silhouette, ears back, tail whipping, listening to trouble in the night. *Hemmie, it's a siren. Coming up here.*

Throwing back the cover, Maggie went into the dark living room and sat on the window seat, shivering in the September chill, listening to the distant wail coming closer. In these mountains it was a sound that could shiver the spine and sadden the heart. Sirens were expected on city streets. Folks left cities to come to places like this, believing they were getting away from that kind of trouble.

There, again. It took time for a sheriff's cruiser and any emergency vehicle to come up from the county seat. Bo wouldn't be racing up mountain roads in the night to calm some old drunk fool of a husband. He'd call the man's kin, or his neighbor and then send someone up in the morning to check.

No, they were bound for the Kingston place, Maggie knew. In her very bones she knew someone up there in Capstone must be dying . . . someone who shouldn't be dying.

She didn't know who was doing the dying and who was calling for help, or if the trouble was inside or from outside, maybe from Hoke McRae. Kingston was supposed to be doing better if you believed what Tory Kingston told Matt in the PO three days ago. But one week ago, when Zack stopped in the shop, he looked worried, like she'd never seen him. He was thinking he might have to take his dad back to Charlotte. Who knew what was going on up there? Selena was back and forth but hadn't stopped in days.

The siren was closer. Maggie hugged her arms, waiting for the lonely sad wail to reach Crest Road. Suddenly, a car whipped by. In the beginning light she could see it was Doc Gordon Bradley's old Buick heading for Capstone. *Lord, whatever has happened up there, don't let Selena be in the middle of it.* From the first Maggie had believed in that girl. Selena had honest eyes, even if she didn't talk about her personal business. Only after Maggie told her about finding that awful tabloid story, had Selena told her all about her little boy.

Headlights flashed through the woods from the drive below. Maggie pulled in a long breath. Let it out. Took another. Two vehicles whipped past. The sheriff's cruiser and an emergency rescue van. With a sweep of headlights they were gone, red tail lights disappearing as they rounded the curves that snaked up to Capstone.

Now, silence. Only the wind moaned in the chill dawn. Bo and the ambulance boys would be going inside the house now, to find what they had to find.

She told herself, *Maggie Hardy, get hold of yourself, things have to be faced by morning.* She dressed, ears attuned, then went back to the window, to wait again. Here they came. First Bo's cruiser, the whirling blue lights looking so sad. Then the ambulance van. Then Doc Bradley's Buick. Finally, Selena Hart's little green car. So, she had been up there.

The sky was still gray as granite when Maggie dialed the Ridgeway Inn. Dilly's hello sounded like a croak. Poor man. She told him, "Put the coffee urn on in the parlor. Everybody around who heard those sirens will be showing up to find out what happened."

The sun was coming up when she hiked down the drive to the Inn. A few cars were already there. Two more coming in. She recognized summer people, the ones who didn't leave until after the leaves changed. Mitch Mason and Professor Enholm stood at one end of the porch talking. Out came Paula Crossing, wearing jeans and sweater, surprising Maggie with a quick hug before reporting she had just called the county hospital. The emergency van had arrived five minutes ago. Alexander Kingston was the patient. She would have to call in thirty minutes to find out what was happening.

Maggie took her hot coffee back out to a porch rocker. The sun was up now, slanted September sun, putting trees and roads and faces in a different light, a golden light, streaking warmth across her lap and the cup in her hands. She didn't want to answer questions from curious people who didn't realize the tranquillity of this ridge was at stake as well as some lives. But she was glad when Professor Enholm came over and sat down.

Maggie sighed. "When real problems come, the things you fussed about before seem awful foolish."

"The TV show being foolish, you mean."

She nodded again. "Worrying about those folks bringing in trouble when all the time that big house up there was brewing its own trouble."

"I've talked with Mitch Mason, Maggie. Whatever is happening to Kingston right now is not the only danger brewing for High Haven."

"Whatever happens, I won't regret trying to save a place where you can rock on the porch and look out at infinity to soothe your soul."

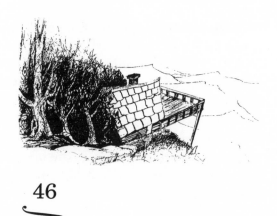

46

In the gray dawn, Selena sat in the VW, waiting, as the other cars moved out of Capstone grounds. The emergency van led the way, sheriff's cruiser and Doc Bradley following. She knew, even with sirens on, it would take thirty minutes to get down the mountain, moving past September tourist traffic, to reach the county hospital. They had not invited her to get in the van with the crew. Doc Bradley had told her to go home.

Selena followed them down, numb with despair at Alexander's condition, and the scene with hysterical Tory. She watched the procession take the road that led down the mountain before she turned up Bear Wallow Lane toward the chalet to wait for word on Alexander's life. His life and her fate.

The chalet was a chilled and silent place, the September morning light as piercing as cold silver. She had no strength to bring in logs, make a fire. She made a cup of instant coffee and walked with it, seeing nothing but Alexander's heavy face against the carpet, unconscious. *Hold on Alexander, breathe, live,* she'd told him then, and said it again now. *I came back to help, but I was too late. Don't give up. You were happy twelve hours ago, free of what was killing you. You laughed on the phone to Zack, you had something to tell him.*

She sank onto the couch near the phone, holding the hot mug to her forehead, her temples, before setting it down.

This must be how it is to wait in the eye of the storm, a vigil in unnatural quiet, listening to the sound of your pulse, knowing the fury will start again, to unleash what had been set in motion. Waiting, she let herself go back over the frantic hours she had just lived through.

She had called Tory again at nine last night. Heard the receiver slam down again. Knew she had to go to Capstone, regardless. Convince Tory to let her inside. Tory was obviously drunk and alone with her father. Alexander needed her, of that Selena was sure. She parked and rang the bell at the front entrance, knowing not to try to walk in the back as usual. The door opened finally. Tory stood there, belligerent and unsteady, her eyes bloodshot and feverish. Deciding what to do, Selena could tell. Then Tory stepped back with her false smile, the cunning manner, and motioned her in. "Nurse Selena. You've been neglecting your patient."

So, there *was* trouble. Selena ran past her and up the stairs, heart pounding with foreboding. Alexander lay on the floor, covered, his breathing shallow, his face ashen and clammy. Blood at the corner of his mouth. Another stroke? If he'd fallen, this time it meant internal hemorrhage. Selena was still on her knees beside him when Doc Bradley walked in, panting, alarmed, asking his terse questions. Both of them worked silently, emergency mode, as the faint wail of sirens echoed, coming closer.

Three young men trooped into the room with their oxygen equipment and stretcher, followed by a hard-breathing, gloomy-faced Sheriff Hilrey. Selena stood back. When the four men placed Alexander on the lowered stretcher, cranked it up, and rolled it out, Selena followed the silent Doc Bradley down the stairs.

In the dim-lit foyer, Tory stepped back from the procession. At that moment she looked small and vulnerable, staring at her father's face before screaming with real terror, "She's killed him . . . she's killed my father."

The men moved on out with their heavy burden. Tory followed them to the door, whimpering, "You'll see. This nurse kills what she can't cure. Ask Colorado. They're coming after her. Doc, do you hear that? They are coming after her."

Watching, Selena wanted to shout, *It won't work, Tory, whatever they believe, it won't undo what's been done.* Nothing came from her throat. How futile to explain now. How could any of these men know what was behind Tory's hysteria, her accusations? That she was flinging from herself something inconceivable—like finding a bloody knife in her own hands—the realization she had done this thing, had possibly killed her father. They couldn't know Tory Kingston's vindictiveness came from a lifetime of smoldering jealousy for any woman important to her father.

Doc Bradley stopped Tory at the door. "They don't need you out there." Still numb and silent, Selena watched him lead Tory to a couch. He opened his satchel, gave her a shot, told her to sleep and walked away, leaving Tory there, still whimpering her accusations. "Go home, Selena. Wait there," Bradley had ordered, his voice brusque. He looked shaken.

Silently, she had followed him out and watched them leave before driving on to the chalet, numb with emotional fatigue, thinking, *Alexander. Hold on, hold on.*

Selena roused herself from the couch and looked at her watch. Seven-thirty. She dialed the county hospital. The patient Alexander Kingston had been moved from the emergency room. He was being flown to Charlotte, at the request of his doctor and son. *So Zack had arrived at Capstone and had gone on to the hospital.* By the time he got to the house, Tory would have been back under control again, cunning and capable of telling her lies convincingly. So be it. Exhausted, Selena sank into nightmarish sleep.

Bright sunlight and the phone woke her.

"Selena?" It was Paula. "As they say around here, *you aw' right?*"

"No, but thanks for asking. Have you found out anything?"

"Kingston is in intensive care in Charlotte. They told me his family is there. No, haven't talked with them yet." Paula hurried past that. "Zack and Loren must have reached the house soon after everyone left. He must have taken off immediately with Tory. They're all at the Charlotte hospital. I have the number here for you."

Paula's voice softened. "Selena, something else. There's a man here at the Inn from Colorado looking for you. It's bad timing, I know, but you are one tough female under that calm exterior, so you can handle it. It would be wise to see him right now. Get it done. You have things to tell him, remember."

Selena threw cold water on her face, brushed her hair back and waited, still in the eye of her storm.

The man arrived. He was young, in a business suit, introducing himself with formal dignity, though murmuring about being lost once this morning on unfamiliar roads. Selena nodded at his offered credentials, invited him in and offered coffee which he declined politely before he sat down.

"So. Here I am." She sat opposite of him "Did my husband— did Drew Hempton send you?"

"The famous Dr. Hempton doesn't run our department." He smiled briefly. "I'm here because I need your testimony. A disgruntled employee of yours came to us, one who had been a caretaker for your son. She was concerned about your absence and has a fine dislike for your husband. We listened to what the woman had to say about the situation in the home with your child. We had not closed the investigation on child neglect or abuse."

Selena sat back, hands folded, ready for whatever. Even curious.

"This woman told us a great deal about the home situation— your care and concern, Dr. Hempton's attitude and actions toward the boy. We had inquired about your whereabouts from a Mrs. Creighton in your husband's office. Our inquiry visibly upset the woman, made her quite indignant and defensive regarding Dr.

Hempton. We learned he was looking for a private investigator to find you."

"I expected that," Selena said and wondered at the man's wry smile.

"So, we sent him one of our own. We were interested in knowing why Dr. Hempton was so worried about finding you but indicated no concern about the child."

She nodded, a total weariness threatening to close in over comprehension. She shook her head and murmured, "I'm sorry . . . ?"

He repeated his last remark. Her husband was now under investigation for child neglect or abuse, resulting in Roby's death. No charges had been made yet, nothing in the papers yet. Recent new questions put to Dr. Hempton had resulted in his unwise legal threats . . . "and outright accusation of you," the man continued. "We are satisfied with our findings but need your testimony in order to pursue this case against your husband."

That, she heard. He was offering her a legitimate avenue for retaliation. *Vengeance* was another word for it. She thought of Tory, how vengeance against Alexander had worked like a hidden pathology.

"What can you tell us? "

She told him quickly and simply of Drew's threat and warnings "something would happen" if Roby wasn't put into custodial care. She told about the weeks before, and the night and morning it happened. She told him about finding the toy bear thrown on the floor. "While I slept, Drew must have picked Roby up from his room and left him free in the house. And left the terrace doors open. I don't believe he meant . . . for tragedy to happen."

"We can't press even a case of criminal negligence unless you return to make the statement."

"No."

"Without your testimony—"

"I know. If I have a choice, it is simply not to look at Drew. Or that house. Ever. I have my own personal regrets to deal with but ruining Drew's career won't change that. It will be punishment enough for him if he knows I know the truth and you know the truth. All I want is a peaceful divorce. That I do want."

Was she sure? Positive. Her visitor stood. "Your husband should be quite relieved to agree to that, and at your own terms." His formal manner gave way to a conspiratorial smile. "If I were standing here as a personal friend, Selena Hart, I would suggest you make sure your attorney lets his attorney in on the full story of your willingness not to accuse him of criminal neglect."

When she was alone again, Selena filled the Jacuzzi on the porch and sank into its hot depths. She rested there, free of the past, trying not to think beyond the moment. Yellow leaves scudded across the deck, a reminder the summer was over, winter a deadline. In the meantime, Tory Kingston was accusing her of killing what she couldn't cure.

Hours crawled by. Daylight faded. Why didn't Zack call from the hospital? Again she called. "Are you a member of the family?" The voice came back, cautious and monotone. "Alexander Kingston died thirty minutes ago."

On the deck, she forced breath into her tight chest. She couldn't cry. She reached out to the man from her own soul. *Alexander, you had so much life in you, you almost made it out of that morass. But you went free of your guilt, didn't you?*

The moonless night carried the smell of smoke. She stood at the edge of the deck. Yellow light flickered from below the steep slope. From inside she grabbed the binoculars and came back out to focus on the intermittent light and curl of white smoke. Something was burning down there on the creek in the hollow, where the McRae house would be. She ran for the car and crunched down the drive toward the hollow.

Along the flat country road, a stream of neighbors were running toward the fire. Selena pulled into the open McRae yard as two men ran toward the smoking house with a small hose, trying to train water into the kitchen window behind the porch, glowing now with orange light. She jumped from the car and ran toward the house, screaming "Addie . . . Ariel!"

333

They appeared at that moment from the side of the house, the thick underbrush catching their long nightgowns, Ariel leading her mother to the yard clearing.

Selena ran forward and drew them further away from the house into the cold dark where they stood, huddled together, staring back as a crimson tongue of flame leaped from the kitchen window.

A pick-up truck roared into the yard, scattering the cluster of gawking neighbors. Hoke jumped out and ran toward the house, ignoring shouts from the men. He leaped on the porch, silhouetted by fire, calling out for Ariel, for Addie.

"Hoke! They're out here," Selena screamed. He turned, dazed, as a gust of fire broke through from the kitchen wall. His tall frame recoiled, stumbled back, as the flaming wall burst free, collapsing on the man and the porch.

Moans rose from the watchers. Three men ran forward, and now a girl stumbled out of Hoke's truck, to run toward the flaming porch.

All three fell back from the heat. Only the girl, a chubby blonde in a Benny's Bar T-shirt, stayed there, screaming, until men pulled her back.

Selena ran to the hysterical girl, who sobbed in her arms. "He didn't want to do it. She made him do it. That Kingston woman. I told him she'd never give him nothing and when he finally believed me, he went plum crazy, drove back here like a madman and tried to stop what he'd started."

An older woman came over to claim the girl. Selena went back to Ariel and Addie. "That was Pat," Ariel said. Selena put her arms around Addie's trembling shoulders, as they watched flames consume the creek house.

47

The September morning Maggie Hardy learned Alexander Kingston had died in Charlotte, she opened the shop and went straight out to the back to sit on her tree stump. When she needed to simmer down and ask for answers from the Almighty, this was a private ritual she preferred to a Sunday visit at the Free Will Baptist Church. Many a summer morning, the view of valley and surrounding mountains could be hazy as a surreal watercolor, mountain tops floating out there in drifting clouds. No matter how ethereal or transient it looked, she knew those old ranges were rooted in the earth, and enduring—a reminder that the truth of a situation was not always the way it appears at the moment.

This morning, as High Haven's landlord was being buried in Charlotte, Maggie sat on her tree stump sighing out some positive requests. One, for this ridge to be spared a ruinous fate and two, for Selena Hart to somehow get out of her terrible trouble.

She knew this much from Sudie. The morning Alexander Kingston was taken off to the hospital, Sudie and Jeb rolled up to the house just as Zack and Loren drove in. "We waited down stairs," Sudie had said, "until Zack ran upstairs, then you never heard such shouting from *her*. When they both came down, Zack was holding on to that sister of his like he had a little wildcat. He

335

told me Azzie had been taken to the hospital and that's where they were going. But Maggie, oh Jesus, that girl was still crying and shouting back to us that Selena killed her daddy. We stood there, Jeb and me, not knowing what to do, until Loren called back to say Zack wanted us to lock up the house and go home until we heard from him."

Now, four days later, Maggie still didn't know what would happen to Selena or High Haven. At the Ridgeway Inn, poor Dilly wouldn't talk about it, like a man waiting for undeserved fate. When Professor Enholm came in for his regular morning visit, Maggie said, "No word from Zack yet, Professor, what do you think?"

He polished his glasses and set them back on his nose. "For a man like Kingston, the funeral and some immediate legalities could require his son's presence for some time. However, this community needs to know what can happen now. Have you seen Selena?"

"All I know she took in Addie and Ariel after the fire. That means she's not alone up there, waiting to hear if the Kingston family believes those awful accusations." Maggie looked out on the sunny September road. Already the trees in front of the post office were turning. "Selena didn't say much about the fire except about taking those people home with her. I hate to think of Hoke McRae getting burned up in front of everybody, even if his middle name was trouble."

"How did Selena look to you? The daughter has made serious accusations."

"She seemed distracted and breathy, like a person running ahead and not looking back at what's following at her heels."

Maggie waited until three women made their way into the back aisles. "She did tell me that, before Alexander died, she had found out the truth about what had happened to Eve Kingston. Told me with a clear-eyed look, *Maggie, I believed in an innocent man. And you protected an innocent man.* She said don't ask how she knew, just be glad the man didn't have to die with that guilt on his conscience."

The Professor nodded.

"But she's in trouble. I didn't make Selena feel bad by asking if she'd heard from Zack in Charlotte. I didn't even remind her that the chalet will be too cold to stand soon as November winds blow. And to think, she came here looking for peace."

He stood, looking up toward the Inn. "We seekers always find answers but not always the ones anticipated."

"You mean David Tyler, too. He left so depressed. And you, Professor?"

"I have concluded my field study. I shall write it this winter in Chapel Hill." He was silent a moment. "My personal mission is alleviated somewhat by Selena's findings. I have one regret. I wish I could have spoken to Kingston. We both had to come to terms with the past. One can remain stuck in painful realizations or one can go on, the wiser for that witnessing. I regret he didn't have that opportunity. So I must value my own. At any age, one must know the past but live accordingly in the present."

Maggie waved goodby to the trio of browsing women as they left the shop. "This place is my present and I thought my future. What's going to happen to Old Timey Things?"

"Dear Maggie, I wish I had those answers for you, and Dilly, and myself. I'd like to return next summer and find this place here. By the way, Paula Crossing has talked with Perloin Productions. The show airs in two weeks, the first of October. Paula was on her way somewhere, but she hasn't checked out of the Inn." He smiled. "I'm getting to be a dispenser of local gossip like our friend Ethel Pickett."

The shop phone rang. It was Selena, calling from her chalet. Maggie hung up smiling. "You must be right about staying in the present. Selena sounds almost happy, still running ahead of her storm. She's set up a little bedroom for Addie and wants to know if she could have back some of Addie's weavings for the bed, to make her feel more at home. I've got a stack of them."

The professor beamed. "I would be pleased to take them over. I never managed to meet Addie McRae."

"Why sure. Let me put together some things they can use. Now remember Addie is not one to talk, but that little woman is no crazy like some people say. I call on her once a year at her house to pay her commission. She has a bad foot and a little scar by her mouth but she'll remind you of an old Victorian doll that might break. I say old. You can't tell really."

He took the basket and drove off in the old Mercedes.

48

In the chalet's loft bedroom, on Selena's bed, Ariel finally stopped sobbing to lie still as a spent child. "It's all ruined. I'm ruined. Never will get to do nothing. Even if Jodie gets me that audition she promised."

"Does Addie know?" Selena sat on the edge of the bed. With a cool cloth she wiped the girl's pale face. Wet black lashes hid the remarkable green eyes.

"Don't know. Mama has been funny, even before the fire. Sent me off on some excuse that night she left the house with you. Said she went to help somebody. I know who. What good did it do? He died anyway."

"I like to think it did a great deal of good. I believe your mother saw that it did." She brushed back the girl's damp hair. "This isn't the end of the world, Ariel. It's the beginning of all that will happen to you, for you, that's still ahead. I'll talk with your mother."

Selena stood, looking down on the chalet's main room. "She's coming out of the room now." A tiny alcove bedroom, but it offered the privacy Addie needed.

"Don't mind her not talking," Ariel murmured, with another hiccup of a sob. "She's been in there getting over the fire and I reckon, praying for Hoke's soul. You go on down. She might talk."

Selena had waited for this opportunity, just as she still waited for Zack's call.

Sunset was reaching into the room when they sat down together, Selena curled at one end of the couch, Addie sitting upright, hands clasped, saying finally, "You have been so kind, bringing us here. But you must know this is strange for me. My house is gone."

"I know. That creek house was your shelter for so long." She knew to be patient, waiting for the story locked in this woman's heart and mind for more than thirty years. The fragile looking woman sitting here was still Addie McRae, thin body lost in the full cotton robe, silver hair to her shoulders, the profile still finely etched, yet drained of youth. Gently, Selena said, "You weren't always there. Before the creek house, what came before?"

"All of that is in the past. Buried there."

"But still in the heart and mind. If you did look back, what would you see?"

"Pain. Black and red pain. It screamed in my bones. And darkness, consuming darkness."

Darkness, unconsciousness. From what, Addie? "When did you come out of that, where were you? . . . You did come out."

"Slowly. Flecks of light showed through that darkness. It was a tunnel I kept crawling through, trying to get out of the pain."

"You must remember coming out—and who helped you?"

"One day I woke to a shaft of sunlight and a face, creased like an Indian's, a old woman's face, the high cheekbones, the sunken mouth. The eyes might have been the light, calling me out. That was Nonnie. She kept bringing me out of the darkness, day by day."

"Will McRae's mother, you mean. The one who taught you about herbs and potions. Old secrets about healing." *You're smiling Addie, you do remember.* "Tell me about her."

"Her body was old, brittle as winter branches, but she had her own wisdom. I learned about endurance from Nonnie. She cooked and cared and endured the men around her . . . with the kind of strength only a woman knows. But you know this,

340

Selena. I've seen it in you. The strength of will. It was her will that sustained Nonnie. It pumped in a sorrowful heart under her flat breasts."

"The men in the house—"

"Roy and Will, brothers. Roy's wife had died, left him with a child. Hoke. The boy loved Nonnie and he hated me. He blamed me for the killing."

"He was a child when it happened?"

Addie nodded. "You've heard the stories. Hoke has his truth. Ariel hers. The men in these hills have chosen theirs. Why ask me this, Selena?"

"The past isn't really buried until you look at it and choose to leave it behind. It may be a burden you can put down now." *Am I doing this for Alexander? Too late? Or for Zack? And yes, for Eve.* "You weren't always there in the creek house. Did you wake up from the pain in that house?"

Addie leaned back, eyelids tight, quivering. "It was Nonnie's house in the Tennessee mountains. In time, we were in the creek house with Roy and Will and the child Hoke. I have vague memory of a journey. It was left in the past with all the other I dreamed about."

"Before the pain of broken bones, what came before? You had a life before. Did it seem like a dream?" At Addie's silence, Selena asked more softly, "Tell me about the child you dreamed about."

"She knew fine rooms, servants, uncaring adults. Later, the faces and rooms seemed to be all white. But the same domination. Helplessness with that."

"A convent? "

Addie nodded. "Then she was thrust into other rooms, other scenes, expected to be a woman. For awhile she seized on love, welcomed it, but then—" Silence again. "She was still a child having a child and ill."

"And not ready to be wife of a man whose professed love meant more domination? Did she run away from him?" *Where did you run? What happened to you?*

341

"She ran as an angry child runs from a hurtful scene."

"From a dark garden? Ran where?" Selena watched Addie nod, eyes closed.

"Ran without thought, up a small rough path into the mountain, a secret path she loved, discovered on other summer days. It was no path for an angry child to take on a dark night, blinded by tears. It seems to have happened to this other self, but I felt the shame, Selena."

"Not shame. Truth. Release. You ran and somewhere up there—you fell?"

Addie's voice sank back to the whisper. "Fell forever, into hard punishing darkness. Then the dark tunnel of pain. It was a long time before Nonnie brought me out of it."

"Will McRae found you, didn't he?" Selena asked, with quiet elation. *We have broken through.* "And he took you to Nonnie, in Tennessee, then brought you and Nonnie back to the creek house. And you stayed. Did you love Will?"

Addie leaned back against the couch, her voice stronger, her eyes open, but looking into the past. "In time I did. He tried to protect me from Roy. He and Nonnie both tried. Roy had driven cars for bootleggers as a boy, then he was a stock car racer often gone from the house. Until his crash. He came home a wild man, angry, a drinker. This was not a dream. It was too real."

What held you there? "What happened?"

"Roy was like the oil from his stock cars, poured into our own peaceful pool. He was the stronger, with this strange control over Will. It took great courage for Will to stand between Roy and my bed. Sometimes, Roy would find me alone. I couldn't escape him. I still had no strength to escape anything."

Selena thought, *Roy is Ariel's father*, but she said nothing,

"That night, Roy stumbled into the house and came to my bed. Will tried to drag him out. They fought on the floor in the hall. Roy on top, his big hands around Will's throat, choking the life out of him. I remember an explosion. Roy reared off Will and crumpled. Nonnie stood in the door, in her long gown, trembling, holding the rifle."

Selena reached over to squeeze Addie's clenched hands. "Go on."

"Will dragged Roy out to the yard, and stayed there with him, sobbing. Nonnie didn't move. Didn't speak. I thought she was dead, standing on her feet. I walked her back to her bed, covered her. I scrubbed the blood from that wood floor, or tried. When the men came, I met them in my bloody gown. Told them I had to do it or he would have killed Will."

"And Nonnie?"

"Never spoke again. She lasted until spring, for her own reason, to take care of me and help deliver Ariel. When she put that pink child in my arms, she smiled and spoke for the first time. I think she said, *life goes on*. She had loved Roy as much as she loved Will. Ariel was three months old when Nonnie died in bed."

"And you stayed with Will."

"Nothing else was real. Or possible." Addie glanced at Selena. "Don't you see? Will loved Ariel. He loved me, the kind of love that comes only from a man who is gentle with what he cherishes. He had been made to believe that gentleness for a man was weakness. He loved Roy too. Sadness ate away in him, became a dark hole that sucked away his life. Ariel was still a little thing."

"And you had to put up with Hoke in the house?"

"When he was there, yes. I have held a gun to him. For Ariel's sake."

Selena took in a new breath and dared ask, "Why didn't you let anyone know—who you were? Why didn't you go back?"

Silence. Again the old whisper. "There was no going back. To think of the past was to think of someone else, a dream mixed with the pain. The falling. My mind and my mirror reminded me I was Addie, with a broken body. And I had my child and the creek house."

"All these years, living on the creek, below Eve's Mountain, did you ever see Zack Kingston?" Selena said the name softly.

"There were times I watched a young boy play along the creek. I watched as a woman might, wanting another's child she had no

343

right to. Later, I would see the young man down there with his fly rod. I watched from a distance. I kept Ariel away."

So you didn't hate the Kingstons. You were keeping Ariel away from Zack. "All this time, haven't you been lonely? In that house hidden away for years until the road came in, and trailer homes that followed?"

"For a long time during the pain, and after, I was empty of self. But when you are forced to surrender the false self—that is when you discover your real core. Emptied of false needs. And no loneliness when you feel you are a part of the earth around you. I had the creek, the woods and the books Ariel brought me, like voices, teachers or friends. The creek is alive with meaning too. It can be turbulent, peaceful, frozen or breaking free."

Selena took a breath of courage to ask, "When did you remember who you were?"

Addie's smile was wistful. She touched the scar on her cheek. "It came . . . gradually. One day after Nonnie died, Will gave me the chain and heart, said he'd found it. The initials on the back had meaning to me. I said nothing. Don't you see? I was Addie McRae then."

"Ariel doesn't know."

"My spirited child. She is of the present. Ariel has so many expectations. I try not to be fearful for her. From the first, she has had the strong will. I'm glad, though she has much to learn. I know not to hold her when she needs to go. From Will and Nonnie I learned about giving love without demanding return."

"I'm glad." Time enough, Selena thought, for Addie to learn Ariel was pregnant. Or perhaps she had guessed. A vital question had yet to be asked but Addie was getting up, saying goodnight. At the door of the alcove bedroom, Selena put her arms around the slight figure. "About our bedside visit . . . to Capstone . . . I hope you are glad you spoke to Alexander the way you did. I hope you realize you made him happy, before he died."

Addie nodded. "You asked a great deal of me. But I went. It was not as difficult as I feared . . . seeing him. I was afraid for my own guilt. A very old guilt of that girl I chose to remember as

344

someone else. She was a dreamer, a child. But until you told me, I did not know of Alex's belief. Yes, I wanted to assure him he had never harmed me. Never."

"How did you make him believe you?"

"I brought him the chain and heart. Put it in Alex's hand. Left it in his fist. He thought he spoke to a vision, but it was enough that he accepted absolution."

"Eve is a lovely name."

"The name of an innocent, from the past. I have left her back there. Selena, I am Addie. I must rest now. Is Ariel still in your loft bed? Where are you sleeping?"

"The big couch is fine. Goodnight Addie. Yes?"

"Our visitor this afternoon, who came with the basket from Maggie? I found myself talking to him, about the ridge, the hollow, the Inn. Even he seemed to be part of some dream . . . or memory. He asked to come again and sit with me."

Selena smiled. "He's a professor, who likes to read poetry."

49

Selena returned at dusk from the highway stores and parked in front of the shops to deliver Maggie's order. "Oh, a Godsend, thanks," Maggie said when Selena walked in. "There's somebody waiting for you back there by the old bottles."

Zack? Not likely. Twice he had called the chalet when she was out, Ariel taking the brief, urgent message. He was tied up with lawyers in Charlotte but Selena must stay, not leave, he had to talk with her. If she had answered herself, she would have told him, *I'm not leaving no matter what you have to tell me, I have my own plans*. For four days now, she had held those plans close; they gave the comfort of purpose.

Selena found David Tyler leaning against shelves of dusty bottles, a study in dejection. He brightened and wrapped his long arms around her for a moment. "Selena, I had to see you first. Is Ariel still with you?"

"Ariel and Addie. I called because I knew you would want to know."

"Would have come back anyway. To do what, I'm not sure. I've given notice at my school. Sarah is moving to Palm Beach with her mother. Her own choice by the way. She doesn't even know about . . . anything. Will Ariel see me? How is she?"

"Let's go. Maggie is closing up." Outside, in chilled October air, and blowing leaves, they stood talking. Before taking off in their separate cars, a subdued David handed her a folded newspaper. Alexander's face looked out of the page, triggering a wave of sadness.

At the chalet, David grabbed her grocery bags and followed down the path. At the door, Selena told him again, "No matter what she says, Ariel needs to talk with you. She's usually on the deck with the radio. Addie stays in her room most of the time."

At the round table with her newspaper, Selena watched the meeting on the deck. First, Ariel's startled response. Then David's outstretched imploring hands. Finally, they came in. "We're going for a ride," Ariel said, looking pouty. She marched out, David following.

The folded paper was turned to a lengthy obituary. "Southern Industrialist Alexander Zackary Kingston, Sr., 68." The photo was obviously cropped from some social business occasion, the big craggy face exuding confident charm, yet the smile free of arrogance. She scanned the extensive coverage then began reading from the first again, slowly, until distracted. Someone banged at the side door.

A hyper Zack Kingston strode in, in a business suit, shirt open, his face working with emotions she couldn't read. "I couldn't get here until now." He stood there, studying her. The same dark brown eyes as Alexander's, the same heavy brows, his lean face registering distress she couldn't read. "I've been stuck in the necessary up to my neck and without the Bird. I walked out of a meeting this morning and drove here. Selena, we have to talk."

"I know." Thankfully, Addie's door was closed. "I'm here. I'm not going anywhere."

She searched for the indignation to defend her professional integrity, but it wasn't there. She wanted to grieve with him. He had watched his father die. She got up from the table and let him follow her to the couch. "First, tell me about him, Zack. Did he regain consciousness? How was he, at the end?"

347

"Conscious off and on." He sat on the edge of the recliner chair, frowning at the memory. "Stroke and internal hemorrhage from his fall, they said. He surfaced long enough to talk to me. He was one tough bird, actually." Zack shot her a searching look. "The man had something he wanted to get across to me. Another reason I was in a sweat to get back here and talk to you. But after the funeral, the legal mess had to be dealt with, or lose the whole mountain." He rubbed a hand over his face. "Still not settled. Then there was Tory."

"Of course. But tell me first about Alexander."

He moved over to the couch to face her. "All the time, sitting beside his bed, I was cussing myself for not being with him, really with him, this past month when he was getting worse. I should never have left it all up to you."

"So you believe Tory?"

He flashed a look of surprise. "You've been thinking that? God, no. I had Tory in the psycho ward upstairs while he was dying. They didn't let her attend the funeral."

"I didn't know." The relief had a numbed quality. Who had told him how things really were in that house? Paula? Had Paula been in Charlotte with Zack?

And Loren, of course. That would have been natural. She should be glad for both of them, rather than sitting here hurting and feeling utterly alone. No, *I have plans too, remember.* Calmly, "I want to know what your father told you."

"Some crazy thing about you bringing Eve to him. I didn't question him because he was happy, believing that. The man had an enormous burden off his chest. He wanted me to know that if I harbored any idea my old man had caused my mother's death back there, I could forget it. I've been swallowing down that gall all my life. Don't know how you managed it but you freed him from that obsession. Did I believe it? I did. A man doesn't lie on his death bed."

"I'm glad. I'm so very glad." She took a deep breath. "What about Tory?"

"Little Victoria is screwed up. It goes way back, we should have known, but you try not to see that kind of thing. Some of it

348

could be our fault. The family, I mean. She was always the Brat and we treated her like one. And her mother. Did you know Marja has been behind the TV appearance here? That tabloid show? Don't ask me how. Tory went bonkers, hysterical, once Doc Bradley and I questioned her. The hell of it is, she really loved A. Z., in her own way."

"I know. Obsessively. On some level she must have realized what she'd done so she had to accuse me. But how did you know?"

"I got to the house just after they took him away. Got there late because I had no idea what the hell was going on in that house. We kept stopping, the cast giving Loren fits and I needed to spend that time with him. Enough about that."

"And when you got there?"

"Tory was up in A. Z.'s room. She had found something under his pillow that had made her *wild*." He shook his head at the memory. "I may not be making sense. Haven't slept lately. And I have so much to tell you. Ask you. I drove non-stop here first chance. The legal morass isn't finished. It's a mess."

"What did Tory find?"

"A little thing, a chain and heart under his pillow. Don't know how it got there. Well, she went berserk just as I walked in. Bad scene. Loren and I managed to get her into the car, to the county hospital. Doc gave her a sedative. We had A. Z. flown to Charlotte. A friend flew Doc Bradley and Tory and myself. We had her sedated by then. Doc got Tory into the psycho ward upstairs. The rest of us stayed with him, Harpy, that's his old office manager, Doc and Loren. Toward the end—."

Selena didn't move when his hand reached out to her arm like a silent question. "Tell me."

"I was alone with him when he talked about my mother. He wanted you to know."

"I'm glad. Thank you. What's happening now with Tory?" And Paula Crossing? Moving away from the electric warmth of his touch, she walked over to the open view of russet and gold mountains. He was there as quickly, leading her back to the couch.

"Tory is out. Released under conditions. She's to stay on her medication and see a psychiatrist. That'll be in California. She wants to see her mother. So let her give Marja some trouble for a change. She's already in self-denial. Is that one way to stay sane?"

"One alternative, but not a permanent solution."

"I agreed to sign her release, if she'd level with me on how far she'd gone on the property deal. It worked. She's big on making deals. My conditions included she is never to set foot in Capstone or on those grounds again. She will get her share of the rest of the estate but no part of the mountain. Selena, the woman didn't mean to kill her father to get that property, but it worked out that way. God, it's been a nightmare I should have prevented. I had reasons for staying away. Wrong thinking, but I did. Not any more."

His whole face changed. The old gleam back. "Take a look at a former procrastinator. Junior here is ready to be a fully functioning fellow. With plans."

She nodded. So Zack was still her friend. Ready to impart his news about Paula. Abruptly he bounced up to pace in front of her.

"Where to start? Not in the order of importance, but the situation with the bank is one hell of a mess. They have two A. Z. Kingston signatures that look real. If we don't make the right moves, the bank has the mountain property, all of it."

She watched a Zack charged with eagerness, not the laid-back man who used nonchalance as cover-up and not the impatient, worried son. She wondered if Addie McRae was hearing this conversation from beyond the closed door.

"I have a plan for Capstone's acreage, if we can hold on to it. It's a project and a direction I must have looked for all of my life. Nothing like Tory's so-called Havencrest homes. That debacle didn't get beyond Mitch Mason's layout, though a great deal of loan money has gone into the roads and water system." He still paced in front of the couch.

"You may be surprised but I went to Tommy Hill, he's my lawyer, about this just before dad died because I already knew enough to know we'd be in a mess at the bank. Weeks ago, when I was going back and forth to Charlotte on the damn clean-up business, I talked with David Tyler. Interesting. Remember the writer who was around here all summer?"

"David is here. Came in today. He's out with Ariel."

"Oh? With that kid?"

"She's almost eighteen now. What did you and David talk about?"

"Made me wake up to responsibilities I have been ignoring. A. Z. had ignored them, too, for that matter. That is—what should be done with a thousand plus acres here. Ready for this?" He sat down, his eager face demanding her attention.

"Cut that mountain up for home sites the way Tory planned and you ruin it. Elevation is too steep, roads would continue to flood the hollow below. Sites would never sell anyway until a highway comes closer. But that wooded land is ideal for low-impact use, in the way that's been done over at Little Switzerland with the Wildacres Retreat."

He told her about the Blumenthal family foundation using the hilltop acreage of their private mountain for a self-sustaining retreat, with accommodations and meeting rooms on the summit, the place used from May through October by non-profit groups. "Anything from environmental planning, health care studies, as well as art, music camps, writers." He would ask Paula to help promote the place. And allow Mitch Mason to build it. Why not? He could make use of what was started.

"Zack, that sounds perfect for this mountain."

He sat down beside her, grasping her hands again, making her face him. "It's the kind of project I've always needed but had never found. One with purpose. Do you agree? Will you help me do it? I need you to be with me on this, Selena. *God, I need you.*"

"You said Paula would be doing that." She took back her hands.

"As promotion, yes, that's her specialty. Oh—I get it. You know about Loren of course. That's another thing I had to tell you." He leaned back and ran a hand over his unruly hair.

"Appreciate my honesty, okay? Some time back, Paula and I went off to talk this thing over. About Loren. And to deal with what that past summer had done to both of us. For me, it left a residue of male guilt, translated into the idea I should be the big rescuer of vulnerable females. As it happened, they usually turned out to be more resilient than yours truly. Talking things over with Paula helped cure that notion. From an unhappy start, she has done well. Really. I'm glad, no, relieved is the word. Paula is also tired of wasting time on the past, as well as hanging on to what she doesn't want which seems to have been something out there in San Diego. That's why we had our good laugh."

"So, what happened?" She felt extremely light now, able to laugh, able to wait and hear all of it.

"This was weeks ago. We drove to Little Switzerland in the rain. Then fog set in, total. We checked into the Big Lynn Lodge like a couple of tourists. Here's the truth. We spent the night in bed giving up on youthful romance and talking instead. Good middle-of-the-night confessions. By dawn we were laughing."

"And you found out . . . ?"

"That you can't go back to being in love the way you were the first time, when you were that young. You can't be that person again, not when you've lived longer and hopefully wised up to what you really want." His face went serious again. "I couldn't say this before, or on the phone. I had to be here to tell you in person. But sometime this summer, I began to realize what I *did* want. Yet every time I saw you, and tried to talk to Selena, I'd get Lady Nurse. You and A. Z. seemed to be shutting me out, both of you."

"We needed you. I stayed angry and disappointed you weren't there. Maybe you didn't know, Zack, I am very good, too good, at hiding my feelings."

"I saw you being warm with my father. Thought you were in love with him."

"I learned to know him," she said thoughtfully. She didn't say, *Just as I learned to know you.* "That can be the start of loving. Even watching him ill, I could see what he had been, and why

352

women would respond to him. The aggressive male, yet tempered by a capacity for really caring for a woman's feelings. That's why I believed in him. He must have learned he had been too possessive as a young man."

"I watched you more than you realized," Zack said, leaning back, looking at her. "So I decided to get lost until A. Z. improved and you could listen. Then Paula's news. A real shocker. I had to get to Virginia and talk with Loren. Tough. Thank God, it's working out. We're okay now. He stuck with me during this ordeal. Kids aren't as independent as they try to pretend. I needed him for the first time and that's what *he* needed." He stopped and searched her face.

"Selena, I'm trying to tell you that I want you and need you." He pretended to groan. "You're smiling. Nurse, that's bad for my heart."

"I'm thinking of our ride down to the highway stores, that first time I saw your father. You let me know I wasn't your kind of woman. Except as nurse and friend."

He did a comic recoil. "What a jerk. That was the old hang-up. Keep confident women at arm's length, the good friend distance. Until I realized I was in love with a friend, who stayed starchy Nurse Selena to me, and, I thought, in love with her patient."

"Zack, he was my cause when I needed one desperately. I don't know what Tory told you about that . . . you're nodding . . . but Colorado has been settled. Or will be. I'm divorcing it." She felt suspended in uncharted territory. "I thought you and Paula—"

"She and Mitch are together, didn't you know? They called after the funeral. Paula had been helping him get over Lucie. That did it for both of them. Selena, do you hear what I'm saying? I'm having a terrible time telling you I love you because I've never meant the words this way. I want you with me, all the way. I'm a man with a mission and you're central to the whole plan. Nurse, take my pulse and you'll see. All that pumping is about you. And us."

353

She let him draw her up from the couch, hold her just close enough to search her face. "Your pulse is over working here too," she told him, touching his temple with her finger, stalling, to deal with her own tumult. Could she allow herself to trust, to feel, to love again? Foolish question. Allowed or not, caring for this man had begun from the first and grown like a secret inside of herself.

"You have four frown lines here," she told him. "Sometimes just three. So you see, I've watched."

He pulled her closer against the vibrating heat of his body. She wanted to stay there but stepped back. So much life danced in the Kingston brown eyes, so much life and need hidden back in her own. "Your project sounds wonderful, Zack, truly."

"It is and it needs you. You're the heart of the whole plan."

"Wait. I have plans too. No, not to leave. I made a commitment this week, one I can't go back on. I don't know how my plans would fit with yours." She knew her voice sounded cool, as if she weren't trembling inside.

At his puzzled, "Try me," she explained. "I've promised to look after some lives. One of them has not yet arrived. Ariel is pregnant. She also has an offer to make an audition tape in Atlanta. David will be going with her, I'm sure. But she'll come back here and be with me until the baby comes. Then, if the opportunity develops and Ariel has her chance, and it looks like she will, she'll take it. Leave the baby with me."

"I'm listening."

"Oh I know! Both David and I will be expendable in time. Sooner or later, I will have to give up what I've learned to love. That's an inevitability. You don't know this about me, you don't know about the child I lost but I want to be a mother again, even for awhile, because I know I can now. That fact is very important to me, Zack, just as your plan is to you. Your wonderful project."

He shook his head in smiling relief. "Selena, that house is big enough for all of us. Besides, Loren is in the picture too. I have started being a father, belatedly. It will work for all of us."

He pulled her close again. "We can start off being a full-fledged family, how about that? Nothing I'd like better. I'm ready for that. Lord, am I ready."

She allowed her head to rest in the warmth of his neck for a moment before moving away again to see his face. "There's more. Addie is part of my commitment, Zack. She has to stay with me. Besides Addie will help me care for the baby."

He frowned then smiled. "That house is big enough for all of us. Sudie and Lottie will be in hog heaven having a big family sit down to their cooking. It'll work out."

Her pulse raced. She felt as if she stood on a fragile bridge with all she wanted waiting on the other side. "It will work only if you can accept Addie for who she is, not just because I've promised to give her a place to stay. She is the one I took to your father's room." She saw puzzlement she expected.

He dug into his pocket and brought out the delicate chain and heart. "Tory found this in my father's bed. That's what sent Tory into her hysterics. It's engraved, Alex to Eve. I didn't know what to make of it. I knew you could tell me. I'm lost here. What am I supposed to know?"

"Addie is here. You need to speak to her yourself, alone, before we talk about anything else. Don't look so alarmed. She's a shy little lady. Wait here."

The room was almost dark. She turned on a lamp by the couches, and before tapping on Addie's door, looked back at him. Zack was pacing. *I don't mean to test you Zack, but this has to happen and we have to know now.*

In the small bedroom, Selena found Addie propped up against pillows, in the yellow cotton robe, a closed book on her chest, her eyes closed, the silver hair spilling against the pillow. But not asleep. "You are a strong spirit in a light body, Addie, and you can do what has to be done. Come out and meet Zack Kingston. He is suggesting we all live at Capstone. You can say whatever you want to say. But this meeting has to be. It should be now. No one else is here."

Addie looked up. For minutes she didn't move. Then she slipped her small white feet from bed, sat up, accepted her slippers, and without a word, allowed Selena to walk with her into the room.

"Addie, this is Zack Kingston, Jr. I shall leave you two alone." Quickly Selena went up to the loft bedroom, and fell across the narrow bed, heart pounding. *Let it work out for both of them.* She had to stand up and look down. Had to know what happened, not to intrude but to watch and hope.

They stood in the shadowed room, Zack towering over the slight figure in the long robe. Light touched the silver hair. Selena thought, *the ghost of young Eve.* Finally, Zack took Addie's arm as a man might with a fragile stranger. He led her to the table, saw her seated and sat down facing her.

Their voices were too low to hear. Minutes passed. And more. Watching, Selena feared her own sighs would be heard. No, they were talking down there between the silences. Zack stood now, reached into his pocket. brought out something he laid on the table. The chain? Minutes passed. He got up, and stood at Addie's chair. He was putting the chain around her neck. Then with his hands touching her shoulders, and stroking her hair.

Now he helped Addie up. Together they walked slowly across the room. Zack opened the bedroom door for her, waited, closed it behind her and stood unmoving for minutes before walking over to the glass doors, to face the darkening mountains.

Selena came down to stand at his side, silently watching him rock there as disbelief became belief. She ached for him, felt a rush of love for him, released now, undenied. He turned with a wry smile. "I just had another free fall but I hit down into reality. I'm shook up, Lady Nurse."

"Should I go to her?" Selena asked.

"Not right now. I think she's all right. I'm the one who needs help." When he opened his arms she went into them, to be rocked there.

"How did you *know*?" he asked, lips brushing her face. "No, tell me all of it later, from the beginning. All I want to know now—Selena are you with me? Can you love me back, Selena?"

She could not tell him how ready she was. If only she could unlock the passion known once but denied since. "I'm out of practice. See?" She put both hands on his face and met his lips, softly.

"Lordy, lady. Don't stop." He pulled her close, gently, then tight against the full length of his body. The contact opened her own locked channels. *Yes, this is how it feels to trust yourself . . . to love someone.*

50

The *Secrets Unveiled* show ran on an early October night, as a full moon silvered the Ridgeway Inn. For the expected crowd, innkeeper Dilly rolled the alcove TV into the front parlor. Some of the older guests remarked it was probably the second time he'd done such a thing since the moon walk, July, 1969.

The gathering included people from nearby ridges staying through leaf season as well as those whose lives had become involved in High Haven during the summer.

Overnight tourists were there too, amused and entertained by all this expectation. Crest Road had been lively for weeks as September ended and color crept across the Blue Ridge Mountains, leaving golds, russets and reds shimmering under October blue skies. Leaf watchers, with cameras dangling from their necks, had browsed "Old Timey Things," sharing their exuberance, Maggie Hardy assuring them, "A good October in these old mountains is a sight to satisfy the soul." When they asked about the local ghost, she had told them, "Well, if you turn on a TV Thursday night for *Secrets Unveiled* you'll see somebody's version. We don't know what that is until we see it ourselves."

Paula Crossing, who had stayed in touch with Jodie of Perloin Productions, did tell Maggie and Selena certain insider things about the show. The executive director out in California had almost canceled the story after Kingston died, but Jodie had saved her film work by selling the director on going with a new idea. "I have an idea what she means but we'll have to wait and see what that is," Paula had said.

By seven-thirty, every seat was filled in the big parlor, plus chairs brought in from the dining room. The place hummed with talk, lively as a family reunion expecting to see some favorite son get a handshake in the Oval Room. Those who had been around in August were waiting to see their faces on TV. Old Tom Hogan, handyman, banjo and fiddle player, had shown up, grinning in anticipation. Sudie and Lottie Gurney were home watching, he announced, "but I wouldn't miss being right here for a barrel of monkeys." Professor Enholm sat with the bookstore people. Paula Crossing and Mitch Mason sat together.

Maggie wasn't surprised that most everyone who knew anything at all about High Haven had their eyes on Zack Kingston, the new landlord, sitting on the chintz couch with Selena Hart. He had to keep bouncing up to accept condolences for senior Kingston's passing and to answer questions about the cultural retreat he planned for Capstone grounds. Each time he sat down, his arm stole back around Selena's shoulders.

"Doesn't Selena looks like a peach rose in bloom?" Maggie whispered to Ethel Pickett who was all dressed up for the occasion and swinging her high-heeled shoe with impatience.

Ethel shrugged. "Well, I was right about Tory Kingston."

Doc Bradley had let it be known—saying so at the post office one morning so everyone heard it then or later—that Tory Kingston was a "sick girl." She had become disoriented with her father's death. "Selena Hart did the best a nurse could do, under the circumstances," he said, sounding melancholy, it was reported.

Maggie leaned over Ethel to ask sober-faced Ray Pickett, "You don't mind them adding a little office and a cafe down past Caleb Potts do you? Going to have a stone front like the rest of us. People will still want your soup. We could use something besides Dilly's big suppers." Maggie saw Professor Enholm smiling at that. She would just have to admit to the man that some changes weren't unwelcomed.

At five minutes to eight, as the waiting audience fidgeted through more commercials, Selena jumped up and came back from the lobby with Ariel McRae. The girl looked like a leggy young bird in her short loose T-shirt. She came in biting her lower lip, plopping down on the low stool Zack placed for her in front of the TV.

" Do you see what I see?" Ethel hissed in Maggie's ear.

"I have eyes." Maggie looked around and sure enough, David Tyler stood back in the archway from the lobby, watching from there.

The crowded room hushed as the *Secrets Unveiled* logo flashed on. First came scenes of old English manors and South Carolina houses. Maggie recognized Jodie's professional voice in the background talking about apparitions in old houses and asking if *"spirits hover where tragedy once happened."* Then answering, *"Some say perhaps they do in places kept natural"*. . . Asking next, *"Can this still happen today?. . . . Some claim it may, in places like the Blue Ridge Mountains of the ancient Appalachians."*

Then came the faded High Haven sign along the road and Jodie's voice in the background, saying, *Ghosts are still part of mountain lore, but what's behind those tales?* Rapt watchers leaned forward as if to find out.

On the screen now, there was Tory Kingston, standing on the open knoll, waving her hand toward the wooded view as Jodie's smooth voice said, "Natives and visitors to this ridge retell the tragic tale of a city girl who was lost in these mountains she loved. Some say her presence seems to persist. Not all agree." Tory's snappish voice was saying it was a stupid story.

Tory was gone in a flash and there was Ethel's face, her lipstick looking fierce, earrings dangling, declaring, "I've heard that story a long time . . . now when my daddy was alive . . ." Ethel's mouth kept moving but again it was Jodie's husky voice going on. Maggie's face flashed on, leaning on her stack of quilts, saying, "If we have any ghosts around, they have to be the peaceful kind,"

Maggie whispered, "Good Lord, I never knew I sounded so southern." Ethel looked like she could cry. Ray Pickett swallowed a sneaky smile.

Next they were seeing Sheriff Bo Hilrey out by his cruiser, sounding gruff and flustered, then some people standing in front of the post office talking about the story with dramatic gusto and stealing glances at the cameras. Their voices faded as Jodie asked, *"Perhaps something did happen here in this village that lives on . . . "*

The camera seemed to float up the drive toward the Ridgeway Inn, to a girl in a white dress sitting on the front steps. It zoomed in on Ariel's dreaming face, framed by the cloud of her dark hair. Maggie thought, *Oh my lord, Eve.*

The sad sweet melody went along with the double exposure of a ghostlike Ariel against the mountains.

"That's my banjo you're hearing," Hogan spoke up.

The ghostly Ariel was singing, the voice pure and clear as a mountain stream, singing the ballad David Tyler had written for her. About a city girl who didn't want to leave the mountains. The crowded parlor stayed quiet as a caught breath.

> *Don't take me away from this high place.*
> *Don't ask me why I stay,*
> *Here in wind and forest, by creeks*
> *that sigh and moan,*
> *My heart belonged to the mountains,*
> *My spirit has found its home."*

With another chorus the picture faded out like a sigh. The camera backed off, showing the Ridgeway Inn, the steps empty.

A noisy commercial flashed on. And that was it. For a moment, the room was silent, as if disappointed not to have seen more, or stunned at how beautiful Ariel looked and sounded. Paula clapped, Mitch Mason joining. Then Selena and Zack. The whole room applauded. Ariel buried her face in her hands for an instant, stood up, looked around startled, then walked out, chin-up and face glowing. David Tyler followed her out the front.

Paula came over to Maggie as everyone began moving about. "Timing makes fate. The show had been receiving flack from the press for too many reenacted murders. Jodie sold them on mythic and mellow. It may be the only time, but they did it."

Dilly rolled the TV out of his parlor, a flustered host disappointed his dining room was never shown. He turned on the grand player piano.

It was there Maggie found a pensive Professor Enholm watching the jumping yellow keys as if the ghost of Chopin himself sat there in a frock coat, bent to the keyboard. Maggie sighed before he looked up. "To think I worried and fussed all summer about what they would do to us. And it turns out to be Ariel's show. It gave me a start there for a minute, seeing her in that white dress."

"And for me, Maggie."

"Someday that girl will be on TV with her own name. I bet poor David Tyler will be waiting in the wings."

"And in time, watching somewhere else, in front of a set," Professor Enholm agreed. "David probably knows that too. Here comes Selena. After I greet the lady, I shall leave you two alone."

Selena surprised Maggie by hugging her like a daughter. "We're moving to Capstone tomorrow. Ariel and Addie want to stay in the stone cottage but we'll be together up there. By Thanksgiving, when Loren comes back from school, we're having a family dinner. Sudie and I agreed you are like family."

Selena hesitated for a moment, the blue-gray eyes bright with meaning. "Maggie, as soon as you finish closing the shop, why don't you come on up and meet Addie? Get to know her. Really know her. I think she's ready for that."

The End

ABOUT THE AUTHOR

Marian Coe is a former staffer with the *St. Petersburg (FL) Times*, a poet, and author of two inspirational books, *On Waking Up* and *Women in Transition*, and the mystery novel, *Legacy*. She and artist husband Paul Zipperlin are at home in Largo, Florida, also Mitchell County, North Carolina, where she is one of the "summer people" of which she writes in this novel.